BY CHUCK WENDIG

Zer0es
Invasive
Wanderers
The Book of Accidents
Dust & Grim
Wayward
Black River Orchard
The Staircase in the Woods
Monster Movie

THE HEARTLAND TRILOGY

Under the Empyrean Sky
Blightborn
The Harvest

MIRIAM BLACK

Blackbirds
Mockingbird
The Cormorant
Thunderbird
The Raptor & the Wren
Vultures

ATLANTA BURNS

Atlanta Burns
Atlanta Burns: The Hunt

NONFICTION

The Kick-Ass Writer
Damn Fine Story
Gentle Writing Advice

STAR WARS

Star Wars: Aftermath
Star Wars: Aftermath: Life Debt
Star Wars: Aftermath: Empire's End

THE STAIRCASE IN THE WOODS

THE STAIRCASE IN THE WOODS

CHUCK WENDIG

DEL REY

DEL REY

UK | USA | Canada | Ireland | Australia
India | New Zealand | South Africa

Del Rey is part of the Penguin Random House group of companies whose addresses can be found at global.penguinrandomhouse.com

Penguin Random House UK,
One Embassy Gardens, 8 Viaduct Gardens, London SW11 7BW

penguin.co.uk

Penguin Random House UK

First published in the US by Del Rey, an imprint of Random House,
a division of Penguin Random House LLC, New York 2025
First published in the UK by Del Rey 2025
001

Copyright © Terribleminds LLC, 2025

The moral right of the author has been asserted

Penguin Random House values and supports copyright. Copyright fuels creativity, encourages diverse voices, promotes freedom of expression and supports a vibrant culture. Thank you for purchasing an authorised edition of this book and for respecting intellectual property laws by not reproducing, scanning or distributing any part of it by any means without permission. You are supporting authors and enabling Penguin Random House to continue to publish books for everyone. No part of this book may be used or reproduced in any manner for the purpose of training artificial intelligence technologies or systems. In accordance with Article 4(3) of the DSM Directive 2019/790, Penguin Random House expressly reserves this work from the text and data mining exception.

Book design by Fritz Metsch

Printed and bound in Great Britain by Clays Ltd, Elcograf S.p.A.

The authorised representative in the EEA is Penguin Random House Ireland,
Morrison Chambers, 32 Nassau Street, Dublin D02 YH68

A CIP catalogue record for this book is available from the British Library

ISBN: 978–1–529–10104–1 (hardback)
ISBN: 978–1–529–10105–8 (trade paperback)

Penguin Random House is committed to a sustainable future for our business, our readers and our planet. This book is made from Forest Stewardship Council® certified paper.

MIX
Paper | Supporting
responsible forestry
FSC® C018179

*To the friends I've made,
the friends I've lost,
the friends I've yet to meet.*

THE STAIRCASE IN THE WOODS

On Friday, June 5th, 1998, five teenagers went into the woods surrounding Highchair Rocks in Bucks County, Pennsylvania.

Only four of them came out.

0

The Heart of It

"Friendship is like a house," she said to him, his head cradled in her lap. "You move into this place together. You find your own room there, and they find theirs, but there's all this common space, all these shared places. And you each put into it all the things you love, all the things you are. Your air becomes their air. You put your hearts on the coffee table, next to the remote control, vulnerable and beautiful and bloody. And this friendship, this house, it's a place of laughter and fun and togetherness too. But there's frustration sometimes. Agitation. Sometimes that gets big, too big, all the awful feelings, all that resentment, building up like carbon monoxide. Friendship, like a house, can go bad, too. That air you share? Goes sour. Dry rot here, black mold there, and if you don't remediate, it just grows and grows. Gets bad enough, one or all of you have to move out. And then the place just fucking sits there, abandoned. Empty and gutted. Another ruin left to that force in the world that wants everything to fall apart. You can move back into a place like that, sometimes. But only if you tear it all down and start again."

1

Owen

MAY 30
PITTSBURGH, PA

Owen slept in the midst of mess and wreckage, as he did most nights.

Sometimes it was the tangle of a forever unmade bed, other times pages torn from notebooks out of frustration, pages scrawled with erratic, mutant half-formed almost-ideas. But last night, as with many, it was computer parts—parts old and new: a vintage Sound Blaster sound card rescued from a first-gen Pentium; a baggie of RAM chips like loose teeth; a snarl of cables; a PowerColor Red Dragon AMD Radeon RX 6800 XT GPU that he'd managed to buy off Craigslist, of all places, since the guy who'd had it didn't know what he had, meaning Owen got it for a song.

His body slept, bent into shape around the chaos, careful even in the night not to kick anything off the bed. He didn't writhe. He slept like the dead. Even when the dreams came—the same dreams that were just another kind of mess and wreckage, dreams of a set of stairs, sometimes in the middle of the street, sometimes descending down into the forest floor, sometimes in the middle of his high school gym, sometimes floating there in the big black nothing. Stairs that in the dream he never walked up or down, even though he knew he was supposed to. Stairs he was too scared to touch with even the front of his foot. Stairs that shuddered and whispered words he couldn't understand, in a voice he recognized, a voice of a friend long gone, a friend abandoned.

Then—

Bvvt, bvvt. Bvvt, bvvt.

The sound from an older-model iPhone as it vibrated. It slowly scurried its way across a crowded nightstand, its suicide blocked by the obstacle of mess on the floor: to-be-read books, a coffee mug, a blister pack of melatonin, a half-empty bottle of trazodone.

The sound dragged Owen out of the depths of that dark dream. The sour feeling of it remained, stuck to him like tree sap. He pawed at the nightstand, extracting himself from the chaos of computer parts and tangled sheets. Wincing in the harsh platinum light of late morning, he looked at the phone, then sat up.

The caller:

Lore.

Panic laced through his chest, tightening it. Not just panic. Anger, too.

He cleared his throat, went to answer, then paused. Should he? Could he?

Owen denied the call, kept the phone face down against his chest. He looked around his apartment—a spare, bland, chaotic space, because he did little to organize it, little to decorate it, little of anything. It was just the bleak place in which he existed, the place he slept in and showered in and ate gussied-up instant ramen in.

. . . because you don't deserve anything better. The thought circled his brain again and again like an EDM loop.

He thought about burying his head under the pillow again, but he checked the phone for a voicemail—

But instead, it rang again. Lore.

Shit.

If she's calling, it's important.

Biting his teeth, he answered it.

"Lore," he said, his throat still full of morning gravel.

"Can you believe it?" she asked.

"What?"

"What what?"

"Okay, let's start over. Oh, hello, Lore," Owen said, more smartassedly than he meant it to be. "It's nice to talk to you. It's been a long time. May I ask what this is in reference to—"

"Jesus, you didn't check your email."

"What? No." He rubbed his eyes with the heels of his hands before popping her onto speaker. "It's still . . . early."

"It's ten A.M."

"Like I said, early."

He flicked to his email.

Nothing new had come in.

"There's no—" he started to say.

"It's to us. To the—to all of us." There was a beat before she said: "The Covenant."

The Covenant. As if that was even a thing anymore. That, a bone long broken, left unhealed. Hell, when was the last time he had heard from her? Three years now? Four? Right. He'd last heard from Lore right at the start of COVID—she thought maybe it would be the thing that got them all talking again. They did one Zoom call, all of them, and that was the end of it.

He was about to say, *Nope, no email,* but then, *ding:* one appeared.

"It's from Nick," he said, as if she didn't already know.

Blinking more sleep crust from his eyes, Owen squinted at the email, scanning it—

It didn't take long to see.

Hell, Nick put it in the first line.

"Holy shit," Owen said.

"Yeah."

"Fuck."

His heart, which had been racing, now felt like—well, like it had stopped. As if it had died in his chest. Maybe it wasn't even there anymore, had fallen down some elevator shaft deep within him, gone forever, never to be seen again, beyond rescue.

Just like Matty—

No.

Don't do that.

Don't go there.
"I need a minute," Owen said.
"Sure. Yeah. Cool. But not too long."

He thought he'd call her back in five minutes.
Maybe ten.
But he sat there on the bed for an hour.
He read and reread the email. It felt unreal. It felt impossible. Owen kept reading it, thinking that the text would change suddenly, that it would delete itself or dissolve like the residue of a lost dream.
But the email remained.
And with it, the news.

2

The Email

From: Nick Lobell
To: Owen Zuikas; Lauren Banks; Hamish Moore; Matty Shiffman
Subject: You are cordially invited to my funeral

So, I'm dying from pancreatic cancer! It's not too bad yet, but they say it's going to get real bad, real fast, and that this fucker is going to kill me quick as shit. As such, I'd like to see you jerks one more time before I waltz my way off this mortal coil. So consider this a formal invitation to my funeral, or pre-funeral, or still-making-memories-memorial-service, or whatever. I'd rather give you a chance to pretend I'm a good guy and you still like me while we're all still alive than when the cremation furnace turns me to human kitty litter. It'll be fun! I'm up in New Hampshire now. I bought you all plane tickets, which I attached as PDFs. Nonrefundable, in case you need that additional dose of guilt. It's a long drive from Logan, so I'll get a driver for you. I hope I get to see you all one last time. If not, I understand. Actually, fuck that—if I'm dying, I might as well go out honest: If you don't come, fuck you. In fact?

I'm invoking the Covenant.

Be here or get fucked. Love you lots.

P.S. Hey, Nailbiter, I know you're not going to want to get on a plane, but you gotta get on that plane, I don't care if you chew your fingers to stumps.

P.P.S. Lauren, I'm not calling you "Lore," and you can't make me.

P.P.P.S. Hamish, you dick, bring weed. NH hasn't legalized yet.

P.P.P.P.S Matty, miss you, brother.

—nick

3

Invocation

Finally, Lore must've lost her patience. His phone vibrated. He didn't want to answer it. Didn't want to talk to her. Every part of him itched with anxiety just seeing her name there on his phone.

But he knew Lore too well. She would call and call and call. The woman would fly here herself and rappel in through the window like SWAT. Lore was a Hunter-Killer drone on a kill streak. It was why she was successful at, well, everything.

"What the shit," she said when he answered. "You planning on calling me back or what?"

"Yeah. I dunno. Sorry." He didn't want to get into why he didn't want to talk to her. So instead he said, "I just keep reading it. I can't stop reading it."

"Owen gonna Owen. Always tonguing that broken tooth."

"Don't."

A pause. "Sorry." Another pause. "Hey, so we're doing this, right?"

"Going? To his . . ." *Funeral,* he tried to say but couldn't.

"Yeah. To fucking New Hampshire, of all the places."

"I dunno, Lore. I dunno."

Silence on the other end. "You do know. You gotta go. We all do. Nick is sick. We owe him this. Don't we?"

Owen tried to imagine Nick being sick. Nick was like a human cigarette. All tar and nicotine. Was it possible for cancer to get cancer? But then his mind put Nick in a bed. Frail and crooked—the man-sized cigarette cooked down to the filter, the rest of him ash.

Same way Owen's own father went out. The way most people seemed to go out. In a hospital bed, like a wilting plant in a pot of dry, dead dirt. Owen tried to shake the image. He chewed a thumbnail.

It was clear Lore couldn't abide the silence. So she filled it with:

"The Covenant, Owen. Nick invoked the Covenant."

"So what? The Covenant's been broken since . . ." He couldn't finish that sentence. They'd all broken it in their own ways.

Her especially, he thought, but dared not say.

"Maybe this is how we fix it. Even a little. We gave it a name, not to make it real, but because it *was* real. Once upon a time."

"Lore—"

"Shut up. You're going. We're all going."

Dog with a bone.

He sighed. "Yeah. Okay. Yeah."

A pause.

"You think Hamish will come?" she asked.

"I have no idea." And he didn't. He'd last seen Hamish on that Zoom call, and nothing since. Those bridges had burned long ago, leaving only the chasm. "I dunno if you check his socials, but Hamish is different these days."

"Seems like."

Seems like. Sounded like Lore hadn't been talking to him either. Which made him grotesquely, uncomfortably happy. Owen would've been jealous to learn they'd been talking still. That somehow *he* had been the one left out. Of course thinking that just made him feel extra shitty. But what didn't?

"Flight's tomorrow," she said, filling the void of silence Owen had accidentally left wide open.

"Wait, what? Tomorrow? Shit."

"Oh, what? Got something big going on?"

You know I don't, he thought bitterly, but didn't say that. Instead he deflected: "I have a shift at the bookstore. But I figured you'd be the one who was busy. All the stuff you've got going on—I mean, it's impressive. It's great. I'm happy for you." Saying those things felt like acid on his tongue. He felt weak, like he was capitulating. Like he was just a shadow cast by her light. "Seriously, I mean it," he added, wincing. *Really gilding that lily, Nailbiter.*

"Hey, thanks. It's been good. But I can make the time for this."

"Good to be the boss."

"Sure." But the way she said it sounded like she didn't mean it. Or she didn't like him saying that. Owen couldn't tell, and he wasn't comfortable enough to probe for the truth. "You saw he cc'd Matty, right?" she asked.

"He, ah, he does that sometimes."

A pause. She didn't know that Nick did that sometimes. Which meant—what, Nick wasn't emailing her? Just him? Huh.

She finally said, "I can't tell if it's sad or sweet or just fucked up."

"I think it's all of the above."

"Yeah. Well." A sound like her sucking air between her teeth. "I guess I'll see you tomorrow, Owen."

"See you tomorrow, Lore."

When the call ended, he bit down and ripped off a half-moon of thumbnail in one go. It bled.

Owen looked around his apartment, which he could do from the edge of his bed. It was essentially one room, not more than five hundred square feet. Place was a mess. Not a hoarder's mess, not a filth pit, either. Just clutter at the edges because he was trying to live an adult life in a place that was too small for it, and no amount of Marie Kondo was going to fit his existence into an apartment this miserably cramped. Didn't help that his computer—a gaming rig, mostly, a Frankenstein monster of bartered or refurbished parts—took up a good chunk of the desk. (Next to it: a little cairn of bitten fingernail slivers.)

He stood up and went to the corner of the room next to his shitty IKEA dresser. There, under a pile of old *Omni* magazines, was a file box. He hooked it with a foot and pulled it out. The magazines slid to the floor in a pile, and he didn't bother to pick them up. Owen knelt and lifted the lid of that box with some trepidation, as if it were the Ark of the Covenant and opening it would release the souls of the damned, eager to melt the face off his skull.

But the dead souls that awaited inside were just stacks of old notebooks from high school and from college. They were not his notebooks, not entirely—and they were not Lore's notebooks, either. They were *theirs*, shared property, or so he'd always believed them to be. All throughout school, the two of them used these books for an unholy host of purposes: to write shared stories, to design adventures and characters for D&D, to draw stupid shit and share stupider jokes, and of course to design games. Pen-and-paper games, board games, but mostly video games. Inside were maps, lines from text adventures they programmed in fucking BASIC, bits of dialogue, little sketches of everything from Pokémon rip-offs to riffs on *Fallout*-style power armor. Half of it was derivative shit, they both knew it. But there was good stuff in there, too. Original stuff. *Real* stuff.

And it was supposed to be theirs.

Not his, not hers.

Theirs.

Of course, Lore went off and did it all, didn't she? Conquered the world. Hunter-Killer, hungry for that streak. And all he'd conquered was a shitty apartment and an endless series of dead-end jobs. *She left me behind*, he thought with no small bitterness. *She's living our dream. Without me.*

Though, of course, it was way worse than that, wasn't it?

He needed to pack, but instead he stood there, paralyzed.

Looking out the window in his apartment meant looking at algae-stained brick. He sometimes searched for patterns in the brickwork: faces, animals, landscapes, anything to help him not doomscroll on his phone and get lost in an endless loop of bad news. He stared now, trying to find something to take his mind off tomorrow, but the only pattern that emerged from the smears of seasick green and the lines of rust-red brick was a staircase in the middle of nowhere, leading to nothing, calling his name.

4

Lore

MAY 30
SEATTLE, WA

The cursor, aptly named, for it cursed her. A blinking line in the empty white void, mocking Lore from the laptop screen sitting on the kitchen nook table. At the top of the document, a name: *hitchhikers_guide_thru_hell_DESIGNDOCv1usethisone*. A placeholder name, obviously, even though it was (or rather, would become) a game about *literally* hitchhiking your way through *literal* Hell. Lore didn't know what it would end up being called. *Glitchhikers* was already a game. She liked *Bitchhikers*, but that didn't really mean anything except sounding edgy for the sake of edgy, and besides, ByteDog wasn't going to publish it with that name. They wanted to call it *Hellhiker*, which she hated. *What if I make the player protagonist a witch, and we call it* Witchhiker? she'd asked. They'd all made a face, the same face, a sour, just-tongue-kissed-a-dead-fish face. So, not that, then.

Cursor, cursing her. Blank document, a hole in the universe.

The document always started off blank, she knew. Day one, every document was blank. Problem was, this wasn't day one.

The document had been blank for six months.

In her hand, a single capsule, the color of sawdust. Lore got water from the fridge dispenser, popped the capsule, drank it back. Something to open her up. Keep the ants in her brain moving, keep them lined up and productive.

She needed it. They'd paid her a lot of money for this game.

And so far, she had nothing to show for it.

It's fine, she told herself. *You're just fucked up about Nick.* And fucked up about having to travel today. And fucked up about having talked to Owen. And seeing Hamish soon. And then Matty...

You're just fucked up is the answer, she knew.

Still. She'd never had this before. Never had real writer's block or coder's block or art block or any kind of block. Sure, maybe for an hour. Maybe, *maybe* a day. But more than that? Nah, never. There was always a way through. Shoulder to the door, fist through a window, hard head slamming forward into drywall, whatever it took. Lore knew she was fucked in a lot of ways, but this was never one of them. And these little microdose motherfuckers, they were one way to clear her mental pathways.

They hadn't worked this time.

But they could. They would.

She'd do work on the plane. A change of perspective, in her head and out, would help. And maybe, in a weird way, seeing the others would fix some shit, too.

Still, that capsule she just took? It was her last.

Time to cook, she thought in her best Walter White voice.

I need a big kitchen, Lore had said when she was on a hunt for a house. *A chef's kitchen,* she added, emphasis on *chef's,* even though she was no such thing. This house, a Craftsman-style home in the Queen Anne neighborhood of Seattle, fit the bill with its broad-shouldered kitchen, which was good because Lore loved to cook, even if she didn't love to eat. Cooking was sensual, tactile, beautiful; eating was crude, sticky, texturally upsetting. The feel of it in her mouth made her shudder as if she were sucking down spider eggs and broken glass. She liked meal replacement shakes and breakfast cereal. Everything else could go. But cooking—an act of arrangement and creation—brought her, well, not *joy,* exactly, but something resembling satisfaction. She didn't eat her food. She didn't play the games she made. Didn't read her own writing or ever look through her sketchbook. What she made was for others.

True for most things, but not all things.

Like, for example, what sat out in front of her now:

A little bag of brown powder; a small digital kitchen scale; a small electric coffee grinder (cheap, not a burr grinder); a pill bottle of niacin, aka vitamin B_3; a screw-top jar of empty vegan gel capsules. What she would make of these things would be for her and her alone.

She had all of these spaced out in front of her on a lava stone countertop glazed the brightest robin's-egg blue.

Missing one thing, though, wasn't it?

Back to the bedroom she went. Up the bending staircase, an assault of colors along the way, because everything in this world was trending toward that *gray-brown greige* awfulness and she fucking hated it. Houses bled of life by the vampires of capitalism, a trend made into a trend by people who would make you pay top price for something that cost them less to make because they didn't have to paint it or glaze it or stain it. Lore couldn't stand that shit. So she put as much color into her house as possible. A fucking *riot* of color: kitchen the color of sun and sky, bathroom like a mermaid's tail, bedroom painted in blood. Art everywhere, too. Book covers, game covers, weird-ass modernist abstract pop art, too. None of it her own because, JFC, she wasn't a narcissist.

Now: the bedroom.

Again, red. Red as a Ruby Slipper apple, so red it was almost black.

She paused for a moment to look to her bed, with its black silk sheets, under which slept two of her recent lovers: the first, Cedar, lying face down, tall, thin, and lissome like a sylph, the light catching in the long trench of their spine; the second, Shar, face up, tits out, splayed out like a starfish, long black hair swallowing the pillows beneath and behind her. Cedar was timid and gentle, while Shar was eager and hungry, though both deferred to Lore's chaotic neutral energy. All around them were the tools and devices of another night spent well: two kinds of lube, ten feet of rainbow jute shibari rope, a vibrating cock ring, a cold metal butt plug, a glittery green dildo made to look like a dragon's cock.

A good night. Though one whose memory was already fading, like the taste of dessert lost to a sip of water. *That's how it goes. Nothing lasts,* Lore thought.

Into the walk-in she went, confronted with a tall mirror she used to get ready when she had to do events, be they in-person or virtual. In that mirror she could also see the bed at the far end of the bedroom behind her. Gently, Cedar stirred. They didn't sleep deeply, though Shar you had to wake up by practically waterboarding her with a wet washcloth. Lore took a moment to watch Cedar gently uncoiling, still not all the way awake yet. Mumbling. Murmuring.

Lore reached up to the top shelf, finding the little ornately carved wooden box—an old box, one that she'd had since she was a teenager. The carvings on it were vaguely Celtic-ish, with all its whorls knotted together. Once she kept tarot cards in here, alongside a little thin sachet of purifying herbs—supposed to magically keep the cards free and clear of negative energy, which was probably nonsense. Eventually she ditched the cards and kept weed in there. These days, no more weed—weed made her weird, made her paranoid, made her *slow*, and Lore needed to keep sharp, sharp as a thumbtack in your eye. As such, in the box was where she kept a baggie of dried mushrooms that looked not entirely unlike shiitake but were, in fact, a fifty-fifty split of *Psilocybe cubensis* and *Psilocybe cyanescens*.

She held the box in her hand. The wood felt warm. The whiff of the ghost of that herb sachet tickled her nose: patchouli and cloves and lavender.

It was in that moment the sense memory brought another memory along for the ride, one she'd forgotten:

Owen had bought her this box, hadn't he? That day down in New Hope, at the little hippie occult head shop. She didn't have money and he had a little, so he bought it for her. Gods, she'd forgotten. So much from that time was foggy now. Hard to access. For good reason, probably. *Owen,* she thought. Her middle was suddenly a bundle of snakes, twisting around one another. Gods, she missed him sometimes. But she wasn't good for him. That's what she told herself, that's what she always defaulted to. *He's better off on his own, better off not needing me, not using me like a crutch,* because he ended up resenting her, and then she ended up resenting him, and it was just a sucking and slurping resentment sixty-nine.

Two thoughts at the same time:

Fuck you, Owen.

I miss you, Owen.

She stepped back from the shelf, the box in her hand, and then she caught a glimpse of the mirror reflecting the bedroom behind her—she saw the bed and its occupants, Cedar, Shar, but also—

A third person.

A young man. Shirtless. Chestnut hair mussed up, and he did that thing where he tossed his head back to flip the lock of hair from his forehead. His arms were spread out, one across Cedar's back, the other toying with Shar's hair.

Matty, she thought, strangling a cry.

Matty winked.

She spun around in the closet and stormed out of the room and, freeing her voice from the strangle, yelled at him:

"*Hey!*" And she wanted to yell at him to *get out* but then also *no, no, don't go,* but any other words she wanted to say lay trapped in the meat of her throat.

Cedar cried out in alarm, rolling over and sitting upright fast, nearly falling off the bed. Shar stayed asleep, breathing loudly. Cedar blinked past their own golden locks, looking left, looking right.

"What's wrong?" they asked, mouth tacky with sleep.

"I—"

Matty was gone.

Of course he was.

Because Matty was *gone.*

It was the shrooms, she knew. It was them. It was seeing the box Owen had given her. It was reading Nick's email. All that mud that had long settled to the bottom of her had been stirred up now, and thoughts about Matty were surely swimming around those turbid waters.

"Nothing. Sorry. I—" Lore looked at the box in her hands. "I'll order dinner. Wake Shar up. Then I have to leave. Flight to catch. Red-eye."

"Oh. Yeah. Sure." Cedar rubbed their eyes with the back of a hand. "What time is it?"

But Lore didn't answer them. She was already walking back downstairs to the kitchen where she'd grind up the mushrooms and make her weekly microdose capsules. Capsules that, when it came time to catch her flight, she left there on the counter, because if she was already hallucinating, what was the fucking point?

5

Nailbiter

MAY 31

Pete the Greek was from Philly, used to run a bar until it got shot up by, in his words, "this drunken Irish fuck." Pete took three bullets himself, two in the back, one through the left biceps—all scars he liked to show off to whoever came into his place. Thing was, his place wasn't a bar in Philly, not anymore—it was a used bookstore in Pittsburgh. ("I'm a youse guy in yins territory," he was wont to say.) The store, Squirrel Hill Books, was owned by Pete's sister, who lived in Florida, and figured that Pete needed to relax in his later years, and that a used bookstore would be just the pace he needed.

Pete didn't read anything but the newspaper. He was proud to have never read a book in his life. His mobile phone was an ancient flip phone—one step above a pager.

So, there he sat behind the counter. Surrounded by books he'd never read, never would.

He looked up over the lip of his paper at Owen, who waited at the counter.

"You're not in till tomorrow," Pete said.

"I can't come in tomorrow," Owen said. He nibbled at a fingernail. "Or the next day either. And not sure about the following—"

"Then you're fired."

"What?"

"I don't have anybody else. Means I have to cover for you, and I don't want to, but Sissy"—that was Pete's sister—"says the place has to be open, and you're my guy. My only guy. So if you're not gonna be my guy, you're fired."

"It's only a few days. A friend—" *Is dying*, but it came out different. "Is dead. He died. Going to his funeral."

From Pete, a grunt. "Sorry to hear that."

"Yeah. Well."

"How long you worked here, Owen?"

"Six months."

Pete looked him up and down. Evaluating him, and not in a good way. "Look at you. Always wearing black. Always looking like your dog got run over. And you got those—" Pete pulled at his own ears. "Those big holes in your ears. That loopty-loop in your eyebrow. Who knows what you got elsewhere. Nobody else is gonna hire you, that's for damn sure. I dunno, Owen. You just go through job after job after job and for what?" He shrugged. Then sighed. "Fine. Back in three days, not four, and you keep the job. If you care."

I don't, not really, Owen thought, but he forced a smile and said thanks.

Pete grunted. Conversation over, it seemed. On the way out, Pete yelled at him, "And quit biting your nails. I keep finding the little nail bits all around, it's fuckin' disgusting, you hear me?"

He did not want to fly. He hated flying. He hated everything about it. The discomfort. The waiting. The disassociation. And of course, the persistent chance of death, given how the mere act of being in a plane felt like grave hubris.

He stood there in the Pittsburgh airport. He'd made it through security. Owen found the gate with an hour to spare, and it was in this spot he stood rooted, as slowly the crowds gathered, as they started to call boarding groups, as they called *his* boarding group, and still he remained where he stood.

They're going to close the door.

That thought danced a sideways eight around his head again and again, looping back on itself so many times it started to sound like gibberish.

They're going to close the door, Owen.

They're going to close the door.

His mouth was bone dry. His hands and armpits were swamps.

"Last call," the gate attendant said, "for Flight 1213 to Boston's Logan Airport. We are boarding all groups. Last call."

P.S. Hey, Nailbiter, I know you're not going to want to get on a plane, but you gotta get on that plane, I don't care if you chew your fingers to stumps.

Fuck.

Owen got on the plane.

You can handle this. It's no big deal. Hour and a half. You can handle this. A mantra he repeated as his heart tried to kick its way out of his chest, as his jaw tightened so hard he could feel the tension in his pinky fingers, as his mind built up every mental wall it could to block off the catastrophizing images of people screaming while the plane plunged like a gull diving toward the sea.

"You're bleeding," his seatmate said. Lumpy guy, smelled like hoagie oil.

Owen looked down. Sure enough, he'd picked away a half-moon of thumbnail and tugged it to the side, and a bubble of blood had ballooned up. Now both hands had thumbnails bitten down deep. He'd been trying to control it.

The blood was red as a clown's balloon.

"It's no big deal," Owen said, realizing it was a weird thing to say. (Just another thing he could worry about later. *Hey, remember when you said a weird thing to the guy sitting next to you on the plane? It's three* A.M., *a great time to think about this, isn't it?*) To clarify, he said, "I'm okay."

"I didn't used to like flying either."

"All right."

"You know how I fixed it?"

"Make little fists with your toes?"

The guy grinned. "*Die Hard*. Ah. Yeah. But no. Marijuana."

"Weed. Oh. I just—I just assumed you had a trick."

"That's my trick. Weed. I mean. Medical marijuana."

That's not going to help me now, Hoagie Guy, Owen thought, but kept his mouth shut. He offered a cursory thanks, then went back to staring at the seat back in front of him, fighting off the feeling of a heart attack.

His therapist—when he could afford her, anyway—had diagnosed him with OCD. He'd always figured OCD to be that thing where you had to have your books arranged alphabetically, or where you had to flip a light switch a specific number of times for the universe to feel okay. But she said his thing was obsessive thinking. Intrusive thoughts. Catastrophe lived inside his skull, sharks circling in that dark water. It was that and the nail-biting, and the cuticle picking, and the hangnails, and the occasional hair plucking, and all the other repetitive "self-grooming" habits that Kirsten, the therapist, said embodied the BFRB (body-focused repetitive behavior) part of OCD. "It's not unusual for people who have experienced trauma," she explained. (Implicit in that: *people like you, Owen.*) She said also, "You live in your amygdala." The fear center of his brain. Said he was like a lizard caught in the shadow of a bird circling overhead. Sometimes he froze, other times he ran.

Story of my life, he told her.

He would've told her more, but that had been their last session. Three years ago now. Because COVID really fucked everything up. After that, he lost (yet another) job, lost health insurance, had too little money.

Without the job, without the insurance . . . no more therapist for him.

So he never really did find out how to get out of the place of fear.

He built a house in that part of his mind and rarely left its cold comfort.

The plane did not crash. It could have at any moment, he knew. It sometimes hit a puff of cloud and the plane would buck and bounce like a spooked horse, keenly reminding him there was nothing underneath. Nothing but the void. He thought he'd read somewhere, too, that planes were rarely serviced nowadays. Pilots had less training now, too. Climate change had made turbulence so much worse. His mind conjured everything short of gremlins on the wing of the plane. For most of the flight, he wanted to crawl out of the seat and find stable ground, but there was no stable ground up here. So instead he just sat in his seat, rawdogging the flight, white-knuckling the fuck out of the armrests, feigning being fine even though he was sweating and shaking like a detoxing addict. And whenever he forced his mind out of that place, it went instead to thinking about Lore, Hamish, Nick, Matty—and the terror of seeing them again. How they'd see him. How they'd judge him, and how little he'd done over the years. It was more terrifying than flying, thinking about that. More terrifying than crashing.

And then, it was over.

The plane landed.

They didn't crash.

But a little part of him wished they had.

6

What They Each Wanted

What Lore wanted was this:

She just wanted it to be *cool* again. To be *fun*. For this to not be a celebration of Nick's life and some proactive memorial just before he died, but instead just to be like any other time they had hung out years ago. She wanted to tell stupid stories and dumb jokes. She wanted to get high with Hamish, to drink beer with Nick—and she wanted Owen to just be *normal,* for god's sake. Just regular Owen, sweet Owen, don't-rock-the-boat Owen, stop-looking-at-me-like-that Owen. And she wanted Matty to be here. Matty would just show up, walking out of the airport like it was nothing at all, like he'd just taken a trip and they'd missed him for a while. But none of that would happen. Nick was still dying. Hamish looked like a douchebag now. Owen was gonna be weird because Owen was Owen. And Matty wasn't ever coming back. So, realistically, beyond the fantasy, what Lore wanted was simply this:

She wanted to survive this experience, to make it through to the other side, and to get back home and get back to work.

What Owen wanted was this:

He wanted it to feel like they had never been away from one another. That the time that had passed since they had actually *seen* one another in person—what, eleven years now?—would be no gap at all, just a crack in the sidewalk easily stepped over. They would come together and it would be like magnets snapping together, *click*.

They'd fall into patterns. They'd have their inside jokes. They'd tell one another about their lives, but they'd remember the times they had together, too. He'd get a famous Hamish hug. Lore would say sorry to him, and together they'd rebuild the bridges they burned. Nick would be funny Nick, not shitty Nick. And they'd all raise a glass to Matty, Matty who was the best of them, Matty who'd left them. They'd crash together, and maybe it would be weird and maybe it would be messy, but they'd sort through it all, the good and the bad. But that wasn't possible. Because the bad was so bad, it made the good seem impossible, as if it had never been present in the first place. The good was a guttering candle against the cold wind of a deep dark moonless winter night.

It never had a chance.

7

You Are Three, You Come with Me

They met just outside baggage claim at Logan Airport.

Lore and Hamish were already there, talking—a little thorn of jealousy hooked into the meat of Owen's heart at that, stupid and silly but it scratched him just the same. Lore looked like Lore, but like a reduced sauce of who Lore was and always had been: hair dyed of smoke and lavender over an undercut carved with geometric lines, wearing an outfit that Owen would best describe as *apocalypse prepper* Blade Runner *chic*. Pair of custom headphones around her neck, the cups ringed with pink lights. Doc Martens lacquered with stickers. Thin soft hoodie with a cross-body bag. Pockets everywhere. Even her carry-on was badass: some kind of frosted metal with pink wheels, pink edges, pink handles. Every inch of her, cool as fuck. *Like she's trying too hard,* Owen thought suddenly, a poisonous plant grown up out of jealous earth. An invasive thought he had to kill quick.

As for Hamish—

He'd seen him online, obviously—Facebook and Instagram and even Twitter back when Twitter was a thing. And so Owen figured he was prepared to see what Hamish looked like now, but—

It still knocked the wind out of him.

Hamish looked the opposite of himself.

He had always been big, always tall. But most of his bulk was gone, winnowed down to an athlete's form. And now he was clean-cut, well-kept. V-neck T-shirt under a light blazer. Copper-top hair close cropped. A beard shorn so close to the face it barely qualified as a beard and looked more like it had been painted on. This was a guy who owned a Peloton. Who ran marathons. Who not only had a robust 401(k), but had *opinions* about them. *That's not Hamish,* Owen decided. Another bad, mean idea. Another invasive he had to stomp out. *People are allowed to change,* he thought, less like a belief he agreed with and more like an argument he was desperately trying to make to the jury of himself.

The sounds they were making indicated small talk: that gentle murmur of inconsequential chatter, like the noise of a small creek cutting through a soft forest.

"—yeah, yeah," Hamish was saying, chuckling as he talked, "three kids, Taylor, Emma, and Chad, and of course each of them do their own sport, you know. Emma does field hockey, Taylor, she's our soccer fiend, and Chad runs cross-country, so dude, I'm pretty sure we're just an Uber for our kids at this point." It was weird for Owen to hear it, because it was Hamish's cadence—he used to get high and talk all the time, just an endless stream of consciousness yammer, but always about wild shit like *Star Wars* or Bigfoot or some new live bootleg cut of some jam band he loved. But while the cadence was there, now it was strictly middle-aged Dad vibes instead, like an artificial intelligence online had stolen his voice but not his personality, deepfaked for this airport meeting.

Lore said, "Cool, man, that's great," and to Owen's ear it was very clearly her meaning the absolute opposite of that, or at the very least Lore transmitting the signal that she gave absolutely zero shits at all about this conversation. She started to say, "You know, I think kids are way overscheduled these days—"

"You have kids?" Hamish asked, surprised.

"Oh, hah, fuck no—" But then she turned and saw Owen, and her face did this thing where it went through a series of expressions, a roulette wheel spinning until it finally landed on something resembling happiness and surprise, or at least the artifice of it. She said his name, and in it, he heard the doubt give way.

She didn't think I'd show up.

"Owen, hey," she said after a few perfectly awkward seconds. Lore went in for a hug.

He returned it—it was weird, ill-fitting, like a sweater that was too big, too roomy, to really feel comfortable. As if she didn't know how close they were, or weren't, still. Which was fair, he thought. Owen had the same question, though bitterly, he suspected he already had that answer.

Hamish, on the other hand, said, "Hey, buddy!" and went in for a big hug. Felt genuine. Robust. Like one of his old hugs—the difference being there was so much less of him to hug now—a body hewn of rock, not soft happy marshmallow. It turned what was supposed to be a Hamish hug into something sharper, less comforting.

"Hi, guys," Owen said, forcing a smile. He was still shaky from the flight—the ghost of adrenaline still haunted his body's hallways. "Good flights?"

"Yup," Hamish said, nodding along.

"Long," Lore said. "Red-eye. Plus, after parking on the runway for too long, it was like almost seven hours in that sky chair. How about you?" But even before he could answer, she grinned. "You still hate flying, don't you? You're not white as a sheet, exactly, but—"

"More gray," Hamish offered.

"Yeah. Gray."

"I like the flying, it's the constant fear of crashing I'm not into."

"I have some stuff for that," Lore said. "For anxiety. Stuff that'll open you up, clean you out."

Hamish snorted. "I don't think ex-lax is gonna help him, Lore."

"No, I mean—open up and clean out his *mind*, not his ass."

They all laughed. It was a good moment. A small respite. Stupid banter felt right. Like maybe they *could* snap back into place, like LEGO bricks clicking together.

Owen said, "I take some stuff, but um—I probably should keep on my regimen, or whatever."

They all nodded at one another.

And then—the moment was over. They stood there, sharing air, the frequency between them feeling increasingly dead. Nobody knew what to say.

All around them, the chaos and bustle of the airport exit filled the void.

"Nick is picking us up, right?" Owen said, trying to chip away at the wall of ice that had suddenly sprung up between them.

"Yeah, yeah, I think so," Lore answered.

"Fucking Nick," Hamish said, his gaze cast to the middle distance. "Fucking cancer. I can't even believe it."

"Fucking cancer," Owen echoed.

"*Fuck* cancer," Lore said. And they all nodded at that, as if cancer itself could hear them and see them agree that it could get fucked. If they'd had drinks, they would've clinked them, Owen decided. But they had none, so mostly they just shifted around awkwardly.

Hamish sighed. "He's young, too. I mean, we're not *young* young, but for cancer? We're young. I mean, did you think—" But the words died in his mouth before they could come to life. "I dunno. I dunno! I just know a lot of times it's all the awful shit we put into our bodies—the foods we eat, the sodas we drink—"

"You know, no, it's also the shit they pump into the air," Lore said, by way of correction. Owen could feel Lore getting spun up—like one of the turbines from the flight whirring to life. "Not to mention the shit they spew into the water. And the ground. It's in the plants now. Poison, all of it."

"Yeah, well," Owen said, interrupting whatever Hamish was about to say, "I just hope he's going to be as okay as he can be through all of it. Whatever he needs this weekend, he gets. Right?"

They all seemed to agree to that.

(Though they didn't really have any idea what that would come to mean.)

And then a beat-up-looking black Escalade pulled up next to them, giving a few short goose honks. *Wonk-wonk-wonk.* They shared quizzical looks as an old man, maybe in his seventies, got out. The old guy, with thinning hair and a well-oiled mustache and goatee, stiff-legged over to them and said in what sounded like a thick Russian accent, "You are three, you come with me."

Again, they shared looks.

"We're waiting for our friend," Lore said, confident.

"I am Roman, your driver. Nick. Nick is your friend."

"Oh."

"That's us," Owen said. "I guess."

"Cool," Hamish said. "Good to meet you, Roman. Let's ride."

8

Vehicular Combat

Owen sat in the front, the other two in the back. The Escalade was roomy but worn-out. A soft decay had taken hold of it—scuffs on the leather seats, dings on the dashboard. It smelled strongly of old man cologne and air freshener, and Owen detected the ancient scent of cigarette smoke clinging to the car like a ghost refusing to leave this mortal coil. It made him want one; he hadn't had a cigarette in ten years. For some people, outside the nicotine buzz, what they loved was the oral fixation. Owen had cherished having something to do with his hands—something that prevented him from fidgeting, biting his nails, clenching and unclenching his fists. (The trazodone helped, but imperfectly.)

It was noon on a Friday. Traffic getting out of Boston was ugly—a lot of stop-and-go, a chorus of honking.

"Normally, hour drive," Roman said to them. "But 'cause of accident, ehm, two hours. Maybe little less."

"Cool," Hamish said.

The ride was quiet for a while, though the silence among them was loud.

Then Lore leaned toward Hamish and said, "So you said you have kids? How's that going for you?"

Owen's ears perked up. Lore, to his knowledge, gave literally zero shits about other people's children. And hadn't Hamish already told her about them?

"Ah, yeah, man, it's good. It's weird, it's hard, but it's like they say, it's really rewarding. It changes your life, totally, totally."

"So, how did you tell them that you were voting for Creel?" she asked, the question like a wrecking ball aimed right for Hamish.

Owen blanched, and turned around to rubberneck this conversational collision. Hamish looked like a raccoon caught in a trap. Lore on the other hand looked predatory—she'd twisted her torso around and was pinning Hamish to the seat with a hawkish, talons-out stare. It was a familiar look. Long as he knew Lore, she could get like this—zeroing in on a topic and launching herself at it like a human piranha swarm. She *loved* debate class in high school and could debate you about anything—from why *Star Wars* was more politically relevant than *Star Trek* to how hatred of MSG in food was a white supremacist tool. She got off on getting her opponents to tap out. And even when they did, sometimes she kept going.

"We don't have to—" Owen started to say, but Hamish was already answering her question.

"Man, you're coming in hot, Lore. Nice to see you, too. Shit. Uh. Yeah, I fuckin'—I voted for Creel. First time, not second or third. How'd you—"

"C'mon, you posted it to Facebook and shit. You had the red hat selfies and went to one of his Nazi rallies and everything."

"Maybe it was just a Phillies cap."

"It wasn't—no, it was *so* not a Phillies cap, I know what a Phillies cap looks like, we all know what a Phillies cap looks like. Don't bullshit me."

Owen said, "That guy ruined Phillies hats. Every time I see one..."

But they didn't even seem to hear him. Lore continued on:

"You were proud of it, and you know it."

"Then," Hamish corrected. "*Then* I was proud of it. Not so much now."

"Why not now?"

"Well, look at him. I mean—you know. I dunno."

"C'mon, please." Lore shook her head. "He always was what he was, and he told us from the beginning. When someone tells you who they are, believe them. Isn't that the saying? You knew who he was and who you were voting for. You probably voted for him the other times, too, you just won't say it out loud. You took the hat off, oooh, but I bet you still own it. If I squint, I can still see it on your head." She rolled her eyes. "Half of America put the hat on and took the mask off and that was that, and that's where we're at now."

At that, Hamish struggled uncomfortably in his seatbelt. "Fine, you've made up your mind, can we talk about something else?"

"You still a Republican?" she asked.

"Y—no? Libertarian, kinda. Technically independent—"

"What happened to you?" she asked.

"Lore," Owen said, "c'mon."

"No, no, you hate this, too," she said to Owen, accusing him, pointing a finger. "Don't deny it. You don't get it, either. *That* isn't Hamish. It's like a—a clone of him, a Thing-version of our old friend."

Hamish shot Owen a desperate look, as if to say, *Save me, bro,* but Owen gave a soft shrug and refused to throw a life preserver when he said, "Yeah, no, I—I really don't get it."

"Dude," Hamish said, half pleading. Owen felt cowardly. But sometimes you just wanted to stay out of Lore's way.

"Just say it," Lore challenged Hamish.

"Say what?"

"Say you don't think people like me should exist."

"Whoa!" Hamish said, laughing a big laugh that was more a defense mechanism than anything else. He held up both hands. "What the fuck, Lore. I surrender. Okay? I don't know what you are talking about, so I give up."

"You don't just *get* to give up. You can't back out of this. You think people like me shouldn't exist. We shouldn't have books to read where we see ourselves, we shouldn't be able to get married or have kids or, fuck, own fucking property; no, you think we should be legislated out of existence."

"People like you?"

"Yes! A queer woman—"

"Queer? I thought that was a slur..."

"*A queer woman,*" she said again, louder, "who is pansexual—"

"The hell is that?" Hamish asked. "You bang pots and pans?"

"Hamish, Christ," Owen protested.

"I'm genderfluid, pansexual, aromantic, AuDHD—"

Hamish's eyes went wide. "I seriously don't know what any of that shit means, Lore. They don't hand out manuals for this stuff—"

Lore held up her fingers and began to count them off, loudly explaining each item on the list, each at higher volume than the last: "Genderfluid, meaning I currently go by *she*—or sometimes *they*—as pronouns. Pansexual, meaning I'll fuck anyone regardless of what their gender presentation is."

"I thought aromantic meant you didn't have... sexual partners," Owen interjected.

"No," Lore answered, sounding freshly irritated. "That's asexual. I'm aromantic. It just means I don't form romantic bonds or have those kind of *lovey ooh-la-la* feelings for people."

"See?" Hamish said. "Even he doesn't have the, the, the fuckin' glossary, and he's a lefty like you—"

"Sorry," Owen mouthed to her, quietly.

Lore ignored him, kept on. "*Finally,* AuDHD means I meet the diagnostic criteria for the overlapping conditions of both autism and ADHD."

"You're kidding," Hamish said, looking bewildered. "You're not really autistic, right? There was an autistic kid in Emma's grade this year and, I mean, that kid wasn't okay. Sweet kid but, uhh. You're not like *that.*"

"Autism is a spectrum."

"Like gender," Owen said, and he realized suddenly it sounded like he was trying to earn, what, brownie points from Lore for having the correct answer? It made him feel suddenly selfish and a little stupid. *You should just shut up.*

"What, is everything a spectrum?" Hamish asked, but it wasn't a serious question. He didn't roll his eyes, but he might as well have.

"Yeah, actually," Lore said. "Everything pretty much is a spectrum."

"Everything but politics, I guess."

Lore was about to lay into him further, her cheeks blooming with something beyond just indignation. She was angry now. Spitting mad. This wasn't just Lore's usual heat-seeking missile. She was pissed. Wanted blood. Hamish saw it, too, and quickly stammered out an apology: "Hey, hey, sorry! Sorry. Okay? I'm sorry I voted for Creel. I regret it. It was stupid. I'm an asshole, I get it, but like, relax, I'm not some frothy QAnon fuckin' Creel-mouth who's out there burning books and telling people vaccines are poison, okay? It's fine. We're fine."

Owen watched Lore settle back into her seat—but while the hot anger dissipated, something cold lingered. Her mouth formed a stiff line when she said, "No, you're not a true believer. In a lot of ways, you're worse. You're one of those *just asking questions* guys. Some devil's advocate dickhead dumbass who passes along someone else's disinformation and bigotry with a shrug and a wink, and maybe you *say* you're done with Creel but you'll vote for one of his Diet Fascist lackeys. You'll say, *Oh, I don't care about trans people,* but what you mean is, you don't care *for* trans people. Even if one of your kids is trans, or gay, or autistic." There, Hamish seemed to flinch. "You won't ever vote to help them, and you'll probably think, *But kids shouldn't be trans or see trans people or have a gay teacher,* or *Why do my white kids have to have shame over slavery*—hey, it's not like we personally enslaved Black people, and *If homeless people don't want to be homeless, maybe they should just get a job,* and, you know, whatever helps you sleep at night, Ham. I vote the other way, and frankly I don't know that shit's getting much better anyway—the homeless are still homeless and the Middle East is still a fuckshow and Russia is still ruling the roost and the earth is really starting to boil now, so fuck it, what does it matter anyway, right?" She threw up her hands. "Fuck it all to hell."

At that, she slumped back in her seat, arms crossed. She wrangled her headphones off her neck and popped the cups back over her ears. Music began leaking out from around the edges—a dull throb of something electronic. Her eyes closed as if she was shutting them, and the broken world, out.

Owen and Hamish looked at each other, and each made that awkward eyebrow-raise half-smile combo.

"Yeah," Owen said.

"Yeah," Hamish said.

"So, ahh. What do you do for a living now?"

"Mortgage broker. You?"

"Oh. Used bookstore. Clerk. Part-time."

"Sorry." He winced. "I mean, cool."

"Yeah."

"Yeah."

Another awkward smile.

Then Hamish looked out the window and Owen turned around and the car drove on, in silence. The only other thing anyone said during the whole drive was five minutes later, when Roman said, mostly to himself, "I think people are all big mess and the sooner we realize that, the better. *Psh*."

9

This Is Not the Hotel

Lore knew how to sleep angry. Some people did not. Cedar certainly didn't—you had a fight with Cedar, or gods, even a mild disagreement, they could not go to sleep until it was resolved. Lore was no such animal. The world was fucked up, everything was fundamentally broken, and she was upset *all of the time.* As such, it was easy for her to simply disassociate—she disentangled herself from the world, freeing herself from its foul roots and grasping claws before falling into dreamless sleep like a vampire when the sun rose.

Being creative was the same way for her. She knew way too many artists and writers and game designers who couldn't do shit if they were feeling anxious, so when the world or simply their small lives got them down, they were stuck in that place. Unable to do shit. Unable to *make* shit. Not Lore. For her, creativity was a door. She could simply walk right through it, close it behind her, and be in a different room, a room where her only impetus was to make, design, create, iterate, reiterate.

Point was, after her fight with Hamish—which she told herself was not a fight so much as it was just her challenging him, shaking him up, trying to find the Hamish That Once Was—she put on music (*Love's Secret Domain* by Coil) and fell right the fuck to sleep.

She awoke when she felt the car slow. Idly, she reached up, eyes still closed, and turned off her headphones. The music and the hiss of the noise canceling ended, and the sounds of the world rushed back in—

Immediately, she heard a voice. Owen. "What is this? Where are we?"

At that, she drew a deep breath and sat up.

The Escalade had pulled off into a small gravel lot off what looked to be a local two-lane highway. Beyond it, a forest—dark evergreens and the brighter green of spring leaves popping. Not many cars going past.

"This is not the hotel," she muttered.

"We are here," was all Roman said, killing the Cadillac's engine.

"It's Nick!" Hamish said, happy as a Labrador retriever—and just as eager, since his next move was to pop open the door and bolt out.

Sure enough, out the open door, Lore saw him.

Nick Lobell.

Still rangy and lean, not tall exactly, but long like a fox. Older now, though. As they all were, she supposed. Still the fox, but one that had gone through too many rough fencerows, that had survived too many scrapes but had lost some fur along the way. But he still had that same chaotic spark—as if he was still the same kid who stole his neighbor's lawn mower and drove it nine miles to the mall, then left it there and took a bus home. Everything for shits and giggles.

Lore shrugged at Owen, who shrugged back.

"I guess we get out?" he said.

"Are we picking him up?" she asked.

But there was no answer forthcoming for either of them. *Guess we're doing this,* she thought, not wanting to get out—in part because that meant seeing Nick, and seeing Nick meant acknowledging what was *happening* to Nick. But the ride was the ride and they were buckled into it.

She got out of the car.

Owen followed.

"The Covenant!" Nick shouted at them from over Hamish's shoulder, because he was already in a Hamish bear hug, lifted high, his legs dangling, his chin resting on the other man's chest. He cackled and *oof*ed as Hamish set him down, then slinked his way over to the other two, smirking.

"Hey, Nick," Owen said. "It's good to see you." They hugged, too. But Nick and Owen, they hadn't always had the tightest relationship, Lore knew. Every friendship group like theirs had little dyads and triads and shifting alliances—but those two, they had never been close. Nick scared Owen, she'd always thought.

"Nailbiter," Nick said—his nickname for Owen, given Owen's predilection for chewing his fingers down to the bloody quick. "I knew I could guilt your ass into coming."

Then Nick turned his attention to Lore.

"Holy fuck," he said. "Look at you. I think you're the coolest person I know, *Lauren*." She was about to protest but he cut her off, laughing. "Sorry, sorry. *Lore*. I was just fucking with you in the email, man, I'll call you whatever you wanna be called. I'm just glad you could get away from your *wildly successful life* to come hang out with us plebes and proles."

Next to her, Owen seemed to... bristle a little. Didn't he? Did she imagine that? Maybe not bristle. But *twitch*, at least.

"Hey, you know—the Covenant," she said, though it felt false on her tongue—not quite a lie, but closer to a sales pitch.

"Of course we'd show up," Owen said. "We all knew we had to. For you." At that, it was Lore's turn to bristle at what felt like competitiveness from Owen. *Nick wasn't talking to you, Zuikas.*

She was about to say something—say what, she honestly didn't even know, something about his cancer, maybe, about how sad she was, about how *fucked up* it was—when she heard the sounds of bags hitting gravel behind them. Roman was getting out their luggage. Here. In the middle of Assfuck, New Hampshire?

Jesus, were they even *in* New Hampshire?

"Hey!" she barked to Roman, who did not seem to acknowledge her yelling. She turned back to Nick. "Hey, uhh? What's the deal here?"

But Nick was Nick. He just grinned like the same guy he always was, the kind of guy who would sneak acid into your iced tea. (Which he had done.) (More than once.) "Jeez, I dunno, Lore," he said, but it was an act, just him being a cheeky dick.

"The fuck?" she said, then hurried over to Roman as he pulled out the last bag—hers, the backpack. She caught it before it hit the ground and tried to put it back into the SUV, but he was already closing it up. "Fuck, what, no. What. Hey—hey, driver guy, I don't want to stay here."

Roman shrugged. "This is destination."

Then he headed back to the driver's side.

Lore felt someone next to her. Owen, who seemed to be catching up to the situation and realizing what was up. "Lore, hey—wait. Are those our bags?"

"Uh, *yeah,* Zuikas. Yeah."

"Why are they on the ground?"

She mimicked Roman's Russian accent: "*This is destination.*" Then she dropped the backpack on the ground with a thud before fetching her phone out of her pocket. Hamish and Nick were walking up at this point.

Owen asked, "Nick, what is going on? This isn't a hotel—"

"It's cool," Nick said. A very Nick answer. He loved knowing more than everyone. Loved holding all the cards. Lore, meanwhile, was pulling up the Lyft app with her phone. Aaaaaand, no signal. They were in a dead zone. She lifted her phone up in the air and waved it around as if she could somehow access a cloud of 5G just out of reach.

Roman drove off in the Escalade. Gravel kicked up behind his tires, and the SUV hit the highway and then was gone.

Lore watched it go as irritation flooded her veins.

"What the bedazzled fuck, Nick," she said.

"I'm sure it's fine," Hamish said. Just cool with it. That, too, was very Hamish—the old Hamish, anyway. Small favor, that.

"This is the woods," Owen said. Like, *duh,* but he was right. Ahead of them was just trees. Trees here, trees there, a ribbon of cracked asphalt between them. "Where are we supposed to go?"

"I can't even get a signal," Lore complained, holding up her phone as if to demonstrate, *Look, no signal, nada, nothing.*

Nick just laughed it all off. "Jesus, you people. This isn't fucking *Deliverance*. It's New Hampshire. Okay, fine, New Hampshire gets a little weird out here, but whatever. I'm just saying *trust me*, okay?"

"Famous last words," Lore said. "Remember when he said we were going to see Luscious Jackson at the Troc?"

Hamish filled in the rest: "And instead, we helped him buy weed from some freak show in Glenside?"

Nick shrugged. "Whatever. I needed you guys for backup, and it was a dicey situation. It was fun! The weed was good."

"It was cut with something," Hamish muttered.

"Like I said, it was good. Anyway, whatever. Relax. We're going camping, you dicks."

"The fuck we are," Lore said.

She expected Owen to jump in and agree. Even in college, he was a sensitive sleeper—needed the room dark, a noise machine, all that crap. But instead he said, "Hey, guys, if Nick said we're camping..."

Coward, she thought.

"We didn't sign up for this," Lore said.

Nick rolled his eyes. "Listen to you. You show up here not ready for an adventure? Come on. We used to camp all the time. It was our *thing.*"

"Not because we *liked* camping!" Lore said, protesting. "We camped because we needed a place to go and drink beer, smoke up, and trip balls, and we had no money but we all had camping gear and, and—" *And you remember what happened the last time we went camping,* she wanted to say, but she undertook the considerable effort necessary to hold her tongue and choke those words back down into her roiling belly. "We're adults now. We don't have to camp. Owen. Jesus. Come on. Back me up."

"I mean, I wouldn't hate a hotel," Owen said, shrugging.

Hamish erupted.

"You fucking assholes, Nick has cancer!"

And then, quiet.

No cars on the road, no wind, no birds, nothing but the distant roar of a plane somewhere. The air was still and filled with the tragedy of reality.

"I mean, fuck," Hamish said, now more quiet. "Nick asked us here, and we're here. It's not going to kill us to hang out with him on his terms. Besides, he's right. We used to camp out all the time. It could be pretty great."

Now, Nick looked a little *reduced*. Like something had been taken out of him. Again, the image of the older fox, scratched and scraped and scarred. Humbled by the hardships of simply existing, and surely weighed down by—

Don't even think about it.

Don't think about that day.

Don't put his name in your mind.

(Matty.)

Nick shrugged, said, "Don't do it for pity." He smirked. "You can do it for the guilt, though. Listen. I set up a campsite. Nice tents. Little grill. There's food. It's not a far walk. Oh, hey, I got beer—good beer, too, not like the piss-in-a-can we used to drink, not Natty Light or, fuck, what else did we used to drink—"

"Coors Light, Keystone, Yuengling if we had money," Hamish said.

"Worst was Hamm's," Owen said. "I hated that stuff. PBR—"

"Fuck that, I *still* drink PBR," Nick said.

"I don't know what you all are talking about," Lore said. "I didn't drink any of that swill. It was all Boone's Farm for me. Kiwi Strawberry. Makes for the tastiest hangover chunks to blow the next morning, if I may say." She did a chef's kiss gesture.

At that, they laughed, and then laughed even harder when Nick said, "Don't worry, I remember, and that's why I fuckin' bought a bottle for you."

"You did not!"

"I did. I swear to Christ, they still make that shit."

And Lore laughed, and they all were suddenly having a good time, but through it came the cutting realization that she would be spending a night in the woods, and the last time that happened, they lost a friend, and she did not want to be reminded of that, not now, certainly not all night long. But she, as noted, was a master of compartmentalization. She would go through that door and slam it shut behind her, letting no ghosts—

(Matty)

—follow her through.

"So we're all in?" Nick said, finally.

Lore nodded and Hamish whooped a *yawp* of assent, and Owen smiled but didn't say anything. They all got their bags as Nick was pointing to a trail that broke off from this little gravel lot, winding its way through the trees. Lore started to go with them but noticed Owen was hanging back, staring out at something. She paused by his side and asked, "What're you looking at?"

But all she had to do was follow his gaze with her own in order to find the pair of ink-black crows picking bits of mashed squirrel off the road. Red threads like wet yarn plucked by plundering beak. A beat-up minivan blasted past, and the crows took flight into the trees, carping and nagging as they went.

A wind kicked up. Colder than expected. It shook the trees.

"Guess we're doing this," Owen said, and sighed. He looked sad. And she understood that. If only he could close it off, the way she did.

Owen turned to follow after the other two, and Lore asked him to wait up.

Into the woods they went.

10

A Walk in the Woods, Part Two

Owen had for himself an unspoken rule, one so unspoken he hadn't even put it into words for himself until now: *Don't go into the woods.*

And he had not. Not since—

(*Matty*)

—high school.

You go into the woods? You might not come out of them.

It was stupid, he knew. The logic didn't even hold. It wasn't the fault of the forest that day. Still, now, walking through *these* woods—struggling with his fucking carry-on bag because caster wheels did not work on the forest floor—he felt this cold, dark feeling settle onto his shoulders. A free-floating oppression, like the air was heavy and wanted to push him down into the scrub, into the dead leaves, until the underbrush grew over him and swallowed him up. The trees seemed too tall. The shadows too long, too dark. The light seemed to go sideways. It felt otherworldly, like one step behind an oak or onto a patch of ivy and you could be gone, forever, and wouldn't even know it until it was too late.

(*Matty...*)

But he'd agreed to go on this adventure. To follow Nick, foolish as that was, because his old friend had ended up with terminal cancer.

Owen switched to carrying his bag instead, which worked, but he kept crashing it into the tangle of understory, and at one point the suitcase's wheel caught in the fork of a branch of some viny plant, and he nearly fell when it jerked him backward.

"Here," Lore said, "lemme help. It's got two side straps—I'll grab one, you grab the other. We can't go side by side, but I'll lead, you follow, the bag between us." Owen nodded, and her plan worked. It was still annoying—but doable.

"Great," Owen said, as they made their way down the trail.

"Problem-solving is a huge part of game design. Game playing too, obviously, and writing fiction—but it really shines during game design because everything is connected to everything else, and sometimes stuff breaks. And you have to have some real come-to-Jesus conversations with yourself when you try to figure out how changing one bit of innocuous code fucked up the rest of it."

"Thanks for explaining that to me," he said, unable to bottle up the bitter sarcasm. "Since I'm a total rube, apparently."

"Sorry, sorry."

"You really have done it all."

"Not by half. Still more to do."

"Well, I'm proud of you." Those words were hard to say. They weren't a lie. Not exactly. He *was* proud of her. But that pride came duct-taped to a whole lot of other baggage, didn't it?

"You're not," Lore said.

"What?"

"You're not proud. You're jealous."

Said with the certainty of a hammerblow to the back of the head.

"I am. You know I am. Proud, I mean."

"Fine. Maybe you are. A *little*. But you're jealous, too. What I've achieved, where I'm at. This was supposed to be you. Or you always thought it would be you. And I think that fucks with you."

He scoffed. And he was about to say more but then bit his tongue. "No, you know what? We don't have to do this. Let's just—let's change the subject."

"Too much history between us for weak-ass small talk, Zuikas. Say your piece, speak your mind. Do it."

He suddenly let go of his end of the bag. It dropped to the ground and Lore jerked backward, overcompensating for the change.

"Fine," he said. "Let's talk about—what's the studio calling it? *Hellhiker*?"

Lore froze. She eased her end of the suitcase into the brush and turned around. The forest seemed to darken. The trees, tightening.

"What about it?" she asked, ice in her voice.

"You know what," he seethed. "That was *our* game, Lore. We thought that shit up back in college. We had a whole notebook full of it. And you just—you just *took* it—"

"Well, not like *you* were doing anything with it."

Another hammerblow. To her mind, probably, a mercy kill. But the hit left him reeling. She must've seen it on his face, how hard she'd hit him just then.

"Owen..."

"No, you know, yeah, you're right. It's probably smart, just leaving me behind." That's what she'd done, after all. Moved on without him. And it probably was the smart move, wasn't it? He was dead weight. Dragging behind her, slowing her down, her having to wade through his mental emotional bullshit all the time. But then again, that's what friends were supposed to do, wasn't it? *It was all her fault* became *it was all my fault,* and round and round that carousel went. It wasn't a new conversation Owen had with himself. He'd been having it for decades now. Since the end of college. Since ... whatever this life of his had become in Lore's considerable shadow. And at the end of the day, maybe none of it mattered, because she had accomplished what she accomplished.

No matter who she had to climb over to get there.

"Jesus, Owen, come on."

"You know what?" he said, a little too aggro, maybe, but too late now. "I got this. I can carry my bag just fine. You go on ahead. I'll see you at the campsite."

"Fine. Yeah. Okay."

Lore forged on ahead, leaving him behind. Like always.

Lore and Owen had been friends for a long, long time, and now they weren't. None of them were. She knew why. There were a lot of reasons, but those reasons had one origin point, like the hydra—many heads, one body, one heart. They knew it, too, but they all needed to say it out loud. They needed to get it out, to purge what was in them.

For her fantasy bartender management game—basically, Tom Cruise's *Cocktail* meets *D&D's Forgotten Realms*—she did a lot of research into medieval stuff, including the medicine of the Middle Ages, because, you know, of all the potions and draughts and tinctures and shit. One of the things they believed was that you had all these humors—blood, bile, all your bodily fluids. And when you were in good health, that all circulated fine and kept you going. But when you were sick, it meant something had entered you. An ill spirit, a demon, an infection, whatever—and the only way to get it out was:

Bloodletting.

They had a variety of tools for it—lancets and fleams and cups and, of course, leeches. (The practice had a cool name, too: *venesection*. And you bet your ass she used that in the game. Your character could join the College of Venesection and make a variety of fascinating *blood cocktails* to feed to the most monstrous patrons of your made-up bar. And you can bet your ass she put a 'u' in 'humours' to make it sound more fantastical.) Did venesection work? No. No fucking way. It was primitive, brutal business, and was as likely to result in further infection or even death—but it was still one of their primary ways of dealing with disease for centuries.

Thing is, though it was a terrible practice for physicians, it served Lore as a very good metaphor for the problems among people. *These people, in particular.*

They had a lot of bad blood between them.

And it was building up inside them. The only way to get it out was to cut it out. And that meant Lore showing up with her knives out.

Sure, she *could* compartmentalize. But here? She didn't want to.

Not anymore.

They'd compartmentalized all of this for far, far too long.

It was time to open up and let the blood flow.

Owen was about ten, fifteen feet behind her. Trudging awkwardly through the brush. Struggling with his bag. She wanted to help him, but he didn't want her help.

Ahead of her, Nick and Hamish walked together, side by side, talking. Nick was shaking his head, agitated. Hamish threw up his hands, frustrated or fed up, and then let Nick walk on ahead as he fell back.

"Hey, man," Lore said to him. "You good?"

"Not now," he snapped at her. *Well, that's not very Hamish of you*, she thought, and then he headed toward Owen instead.

"Well, fuck you, too," she said under her breath, and put some pep in her step to catch up to Nick.

A voice then whispered in her ear, crisp as someone snapping a twig—

"*All alone again, Lauren?*"

She gasped and whirled around.

Hamish and Owen were giving her a confused look.

"Did you hear that?" she asked them.

"Hear what?"

"I—" *A voice. I heard a voice. I heard his voice. Matty.*

"Lore?"

"I thought I heard a—an animal. Like a bear." She shook her head. "It's stupid. Never mind." And again she hurried forward, now chased by the feeling of being watched, being judged, and—

Though she didn't understand it, not yet—

Being *summoned*.

The voice, that question, it lingered in her ear like an endless echo. A dead voice, bouncing back and forth, back and forth, till it became a meaningless hiss.

11

Sour Times

As they walked deeper into the woods, the trees seemed to grow taller, the understory thicker. The air was cold and damp now—humid, like in a rainforest. There came with it an almost narcotic effect. Lulling. Hypnotizing. No longer pushing Owen down, it seemed instead to be drawing him deeper.

He couldn't chew his fingernails, given how he was dragging his bag now with both hands. So instead he gnawed his lower lip. Nibbled a piece of skin off it. Tasted a hint of fresh blood and winced.

Next to him, Hamish hauled his own suitcase through the brush, branches and twigs crashing. He looked over at Owen and asked, "You pissed at me too, dude?"

"No," Owen said. "We're good, why?"

"Lore's mad at me, obviously, and Nick is salty, too."

"About what?"

"I dunno. That I guess I never really responded to any of his emails." Hamish paused, looking around the woods. "You?"

"Respond to his emails? Sure, sometimes." Nick sent emails around any time he had some new theory about Matty or about the staircase. He always wanted them to get together, even if just on a Zoom call or whatever, but Owen always told him no, he was busy. *Even though I wasn't busy*, Owen thought.

"I should've, I guess. Fuck." Hamish sighed. "You know, it's just like, I guess I thought that chapter was closed. It happened. It was fucked. But we can't go back and change things like that. But I figured

I could change myself, right? I improved myself, I worked hard on myself, and—and Nick is still Nick, still stuck back then, still living in the past . . . and god, now he's dying. But I'm healthy now, you know? Real healthy. A good mindset. And I think we just need to move forward instead of always looking back—"

At that, a cold wind crawled through the trees. Even in the heat, it sent chills up Owen's arms, his neck. Like ticks crawling.

Hamish kept on rambling. That familiar Hamish cadence, but now more anxious, more irritatingly self-assuring, as if he was trying to talk himself out of something—out of feeling bad, out of being Lore's punching bag, out of being here at all. He used to be all *Cool, man, whatever,* but now he was dragging around more than that one carry-on, wasn't he?

Still, Owen tuned it out. Mumbled an *uh-huh* or a *mmm* here and there, nodding along, but all the while pushing on through the woods, his legs burning, his shoulder aching, wanting to chew his fingers down to the first knuckle.

Onward they went. The four of them trudged through the woods. A half hour, then forty-five minutes, then an hour. They were all mostly quiet now—Owen thought, *We're already tired of one another's company,* though he wasn't sure that was it, not exactly. Owen was swatting away mosquitoes. He already had a couple good-sized bites on his neck. He was sweating. Sticky with spider web. An elbow, etched with thorn, a streak of blood smeared there when he wiped at it. But it was more than that, too—in the space between his heart and his stomach was a roiling, tightening bundle, like a knot of starving tapeworms looking for egress.

Close to that hour mark, Nick must've felt their agitation, and he called out: "We're almost there, me hearties! Just imagine the cold beer!"

He kept on. Hamish just after.

Everything in him screamed to turn around. *Go home, Owen.* Even though for him, home was an alien concept. His apartment was a box, a cube, a place for function and not for comfort. And growing up, home was . . .

Well, it was no home at all. It was a place to escape from. That was all.

Sweat ran down his back, cold as ice. The hairs on his neck and arms all rose to standing like the living dead. His gorge rose as his guts flopped inside him like a dying fish. At first he thought, *I'm getting sick*, and that just sent a new ripple of panic through him—getting sick out here? In the woods? An hour from the highway? And if he was really, *really* sick, like norovirus or, fucking hell, COVID, how would he even get back? *I could die out here*, he thought, almost absurdly.

But then it hit him—he'd felt this feeling before, and *not* when he was sick with something. No, this was different. This was special.

And it was way, way worse.

He hadn't felt this in over twenty years.

"Something's wrong," he said, his lips dry as Bible pages.

"I don't feel good," Hamish said quietly.

Owen's hand let his bag go—a reflexive action, one he didn't even think about—as he hurried to catch up to the others. "Lore," he said, in a loud, hissed whisper. "Lore! Lore, I think—"

"Fuck," Lore said. And he heard the urgency in her voice.

Ahead, she and Nick stared into a wider, more open space—what looked to be a clearing. Lit with bright, cold light.

He and Hamish headed toward them—

But even from here, Owen could see what Lore was seeing: the top of it, poking out of the trees, just a glimpse of an old railing, the final right angle of the last step, the dark wood, the crooked balusters—

Lore staggered forward, eyes fixed on a distant point.

Owen went with, his guts churning. Next to Nick now, the four of them stood in a line, gazing into a clearing where the sunlight seemed to be a spotlight, a great garish beam illuminating a single, horrible, impossible thing:

A staircase in the woods.

12

The Second Staircase

I see you, Lore thought. Horrified and entranced. Fearful, yes—

But something else, too. Hope. Mad, alien, deranged hope.

The staircase had no house around it: It stood alone, a beast of thirteen steps. Dark wood was its material; it stood tall and crooked. The baluster and handrail looked freshly oiled. The steps themselves were ragged at the edges and uneven, forming not right angles but rather off-angles, as if the stairs did not entirely fit together. Trees sometimes bent toward the sun, but here they seemed to be bending away from the staircase, as if in fear, trying not to be caught in its trap. Other greenery, too, refused to get near it—nothing grew at its margins, and though all around the forest was alive with ivy and bittersweet and honeysuckle, none of it dared to climb the staircase. The staircase ascended up, up, up, its steps leading to nothing but open air. But Lore knew that wasn't really true, was it?

A wind swept through, swirling dead leaves and a shimmer of pollen up those steps. Or was it drawn there, by the staircase itself?

Lore felt herself drawn closer, even as she rooted her feet to the ground.

She looked to Owen, who stood horror-struck. His mouth formed words but made no utterances.

Lore said the words out loud:

"There's no campsite, is there?"

Nick shook his head. "Nope."

"Fuck," Hamish said quietly, but then yelled it out again so loud that birds stirred in the trees above and took flight: "*Fuck!*" He dropped to a crouch and buried his face in his hands, growling into his palms before taking one hand and punching the ground once, twice, three times.

Owen bent over and vomited.

Nick, for his part, walked out in front of them, his arms wide like a carnival barker or a used car salesman.

"It's time to repair an error," he said, and the tone in his voice reminded Lore of something else, and now their old friend's posture made even more sense. Because it called to mind an old-timey preacher. A pastor or pardoner making you an offer. A one-way ticket to confession, restoration, and salvation. "I brought you here because we fucked up. We broke the Covenant. And now we have the chance to fix it."

13

Where Is Matty Shiffman?

JUNE 13, 1998

"Mister Zuikas—Owen—I'm not going to be tricky with you," the detective said flat out. The fluorescent light above them cast long, strange shadows down her face. It made her look tired—not just regular "didn't get enough sleep" tired, but tired in the weary way, weary to the bones, to the marrow. *Soul-tired* was how Owen thought of it, and though it was perhaps a poor moment for it, he mentally checked that term, *soul-tired,* as one to remember, because it might be good in a story or a poem someday.

The detective continued:

"I'm not looking to trip any of you up, Owen. I'm not looking to play games. Your story matches the story of the other three with minimal variation. Which is okay. Because, you know, memory is a funny thing." She offered a half shrug, then tossed a casual glance at the open file folder in front of her. With a long, knot-knuckled finger, she poked at a paper and slid it around a little on the desk in front of her before sighing. "Where is Matty Shiffman, Owen?"

"I don't understand. You said our stories all match—we told you, we told you where he was. Where he went."

"I know. I know. You all went up to Highchair on Friday. Saturday morning, he was gone—he left the campsite, bailed, and that's that. You spent a little time looking for him but assumed he went home. The end. Right?"

Owen nodded. He tucked the flats of his hands under his armpits. His nerves felt like sparking wires. He deeply wanted to fidget. But he tried to keep still.

"Then you came back out of the woods, found out he hadn't come home."

Another nod. Hesitant.

"Middle of the day, you all touched base with one another, and nobody had heard from him—his parents hadn't heard from him, either. They called Nick Lobell's house first to see if he was there—"

Owen had almost missed it. A little slip of the gears, there. She had changed the story. Just slightly. Just a tweak. On purpose? Or an accident?

"Lauren," Owen said, stammering a correction. "They, ahh, they called Lauren's house first. I think."

Then he saw the teeny tiny smirk tugging at the edge of Detective Doore's mouth. It *was* on purpose, the slipup. *You are playing tricks,* he thought, wary.

She knew something.

She's not tired, he thought. *She's just pretending.*

She knew they were lying—or at least damn sure suspected it.

Shit shit shit shit.

"Right, they called Lauren's house first. Sorry, my eyes are getting old, Owen. You need anything, by the way? Water? Coke? Coffee? I know kids aren't supposed to drink coffee, all that stunting-your-growth thing, but my grandmother—Depression-era woman, my grammy—fed me coffee and buttered bread every morning starting when I was five. And I topped out at six foot."

He shook his head stiffly. Owen just wanted this over with. This was the fourth time now he'd had to sit down with Detective Doore. Another detective, Chuck Lundy, stood by the door, flipping through an *US* magazine with Jennifer Aniston on the cover.

"You're chewing your fingernails," she said. "Nervous?"

He hadn't even realized he was doing it. *Shit shit shit.* He tucked them back under his armpits. "No."

"Okay." Doore kept looking over her files. "So. You all . . . had a powwow, then realized Matty had not come home like you thought, and then you—"

"We called the police. Right then and there. We called you. We did what we were s'posed to do. We, we—we did the right thing."

He heard the defensiveness in his voice. It made him cringe inside. *She's going to smell your weakness, like a wolf sniffing out sickness in the herd.* Owen knew that if any of them were weak, it was him. He was scared out of his mind. Even Nick had said it—*If any one of us is going to break, it's Owen.*

A real vote of confidence there.

But Nick wasn't wrong, was he?

Owen told himself, *I won't break, I won't break, I won't break.*

He just had to hold the line.

He just had to tell their story. The story they'd rehearsed again and again and again. The one they'd agreed was the best one to tell.

Matty left the campsite Friday night after we went to bed.

Matty took his stuff.

Matty was gone when we woke up.

The end.

"We found his stuff," Doore said matter-of-factly.

Owen's heart did a small lift in his chest. The cops were *supposed* to find his stuff. It was a part of it—part of the whole plan. Owen had to concentrate real hard not to say anything here that would spoil the fact he knew where they'd found it.

"Oh?" he asked, doing his very best acting. He was never on stage during any of his school's theatrical productions, but rather on the tech crew with all the other geeks and goths and all-purpose weirdos. But he put on his very best cocky and confident Matty Shiffman impression—Matty, who was in every production, usually in a big role. "Where was it? His, uh, his stuff, I mean."

Doore sucked air between her teeth. "Bottom of one of the biggest cliffs up at Highchair Rocks—north side, far end of the Oswald Lambert Loop trail, toward the Vista Point there. His backpack and tent were down there, amongst some pretty sharp rocks, let me tell you."

"Oh, god," Owen said, feigning horror. Not sure if he was underselling it or overselling it or just sounding super fakey. "He—he must've wandered out at night, and I guess he—I guess he fell."

"You'd think. But there was no body to be found, Owen."

"Maybe—maybe he was able to crawl somewhere, or even walk—"

"Odd, though, that there'd be no blood, no hair, no torn clothing, nothing. Certainly no footprints, either."

"I don't understand—so he just threw his bag and tent over a cliff?"

Doore shrugged. "It *is* something that someone on drugs might do."

Owen flinched at that.

She continued her line of thinking:

"You're teens. Just kids in a boring-ass nowhere town, nowhere state, nowhere part of the country. And I know, I know, you all said there was no drug use up there, but—come on, Owen. We asked around, it's what we do, you know, as police officers, and it seems your group had at least a bit of a reputation for being drug users—and it didn't take much to pressure a local dealer, Eddie Vidich—the one who lives in the trailer park off Stump Road?—into giving up the fact you bunch seem to have procured a variety of illicit substances from him before going into the woods that Friday night." She pulled up the piece of paper and gave it a long look. "Marijuana and LSD."

"I—I don't do drugs, just drink sometimes—"

Shit. His middle cinched up. He just did it. He just broke. Not completely, not utterly, no, but—

"So you *were* drinking up there."

"I—"

"Who bought, and brought, the alcohol and the drugs?"

"I—we didn't—"

"Was Matty on drugs? Who got him those drugs?"

"Please—"

She paused. "You sure you don't need something? I bet a Coke would be good right now. Your mouth is probably dry. It is kind of hot in here, the AC is on the fritz, and—well. You want anything?"

"Do I need a lawyer?"

Detective Doore leaned in. Another smirk teased at the edges of her thin-lipped mouth. Her face no longer looked weary—it looked alive, awake, eyes bright, the lines of her long face deepening with interest.

"Do *you* think you need a lawyer, Mister Zuikas? Lawyers are for guilty people. Are you guilty of something, Owen?"

"No. N-no! You just seem—"

"I seem aggressive. I'm sorry, I am, I'm just trying to get to the bottom of things, okay? The drug thing, I mean, someone could be held responsible for that. One of you buys drugs, you supply them to Matthew Shiffman, he gets a bad batch and loses his mind in the woods, dies out there somewhere of exposure—that's, well, I don't know for sure, the DA handles that. But probably manslaughter."

"We don't know that he's dead!" He was sweating. He wanted to cry. He wanted to die. *This is your fault,* he screamed at himself inside his head. *You stupid baby. You could've gone after him. But you didn't. This is your fault, you weak, scared, stupid piece of shit.* "We *don't* know that he's dead," he said again, in a smaller voice.

She leaned back with a sigh. "It's been three days, and after forty-eight hours, you have to start making some assumptions, Owen. Past tense is what we're thinking for poor Matthew Shiffman."

"Jesus." His voice almost broke. He tried very hard to hold back tears.

"Matthew—Matty—Shiffman was a good kid, by all reports. Gosh, not just a good kid, but wow, a kid with a *future*. A go-getter, one of those kinds who does everything. Everything. Star pitcher for the Colonials in the spring, record-setting sprinter in the fall for track and field. The lead in the school musical. On student council. Part of the honor society. Gifted class. And roundly, routinely liked. So for him to just, *poof,* go missing, that's a big deal. His parents won't let this go, nor should they. Somebody's going to get put on a hook for this, and I don't want it to be you, Owen.

"You seem like a nice kid. But you're weird. You dress in all black. The Satanic Panic may be over, but—hey, all that Marilyn Manson, Nine Inch Nails, White Zombie stuff, that's going to have people suspicious, you know? I don't know what happened up there. I really don't. Maybe it's just like you all said. Maybe he was sober as a judge and went out into the woods to go home and—and somehow got lost or got dead. Maybe something worse happened, though. Maybe you all killed him. Jealousy over how good he was. Or as some ritual sacrifice. Or just for kicks—thrill-kill fuckups just trying to feel something." She smiled stiffly and raised her eyebrows. "So I'm going to ask you again, Mister Zuikas. Where is Matty Shiffman?"

Owen pushed the heels of his hands into his eyes so hard, the darkness behind his lids turned nuclear white. Tears pushed their way out. He felt his sinuses thickening with grief and fear.

And then he told Detective Doore one piece of absolute truth:

"I have no idea where he is or where he went," Owen said. "None of us do."

14

Home Is the Place You Escape

JUNE 5, 1998

Owen was nervous. Good nervous, mostly. Seeing friends, going camping—escaping home for the weekend—it was a lot for him. Because anything that was anything was a lot to Owen. Going anywhere, doing anything, seeing anyone? A test, a trip, a meal, too much homework, not enough sleep: It all felt like the crushing depth of being underwater, an emotional case of the bends.

And it tended to put his brain in these loops, right? *Did you do this, did you bring that, did you say something stupid once that people will remember, do people even want to see you at all, are you late, are you early, what the fuck is wrong with you?* Sometimes the loop was one thought, one question, whirling around itself, a tree choking itself with its own growth.

So that was him today. The day he needed to escape home to go camping. Problem was, the loops in his brain rattled him enough that he often—unconsciously—started biting his nails. Sometimes until they bled (and on rare occasion got infected). He wasn't going to do that today. He didn't want anyone to see. To judge him. Not Lauren, of course, but also Nick. Nick had a way of finding that thing you didn't want him to see and just *digging in*, like a drill bit.

But Owen had other ways of expressing nerves. Little ways of destroying himself to ease the anxiety. Biting the inside of his cheek. Chewing his lip. Digging his nails into his palms, should he have nails that weren't yet bitten down below the tips of his fingers. Plucking hairs from places when people weren't looking, like an eyebrow, or the top of his arm, even from inside his nose. Picking scabs, if he had any. Picking skin. Scraping the cap off a blackhead. Chewing the sides of his tongue. Peeling calluses. The body was an endless expanse of opportunities to *pick* and *pluck* and *bite* and *peel*. It made him feel better. It made him feel worse. He did it anyway because he couldn't help it.

He looked down at his nails. They looked good today.

He chewed the inside of his cheek. Not to bleeding. There were vents there—skin flaps—from the frequent chewing. He thrust his tongue into them, as if they were gills he could tickle.

Deep breath. Saw himself in the mirror. He looked as good as he was going to.

Let's go, he thought, and forced himself to smile at himself.

Camping was supposed to be an easy escape. The way forward should've been clear. It was Friday afternoon. Mom was at the store. Dad was still at work. Plenty enough time to throw clothes and snacks into a backpack, hop into Matty's car, and speed off to a weekend in the woods with his friends. He could get drunk with Hamish. Play Magic with Matty. Get his balls busted by Nick, probably. And maybe he and Lauren would finally get some face time to talk about . . . well, everything. College, their game, and their future. But when he stepped out of his room, he found his father there in the living room. Sitting forward in the dusty old recliner. A beer in his hand.

"You're home," Owen said, trying to keep the shock and disappointment out of his voice. He put a thumb in his mouth, biting at the nail.

His father, a bent stick of a man, sniffed. "Where you going?"

"Out."

"Out where?"

And it was here Owen knew: His father wasn't going to let him go anywhere. His plans, crumbling. The dreams of a weekend with friends, fucked.

"With the crew," he said, in a small voice.

"*Nngh*," his father grunted. "Go on, then."

Owen's heart lifted—the fog cleared, the path was lit. *Almost free.* "Thanks. I'll—I'll be back on Sunday morning, I think—"

"I don't care, Owen." The man leaned farther forward, the can on his knee, and he stared out at his son with dark, hateful eyes. "I don't care if you go, don't care if you come back. I'm done giving a shit about you. Never seems to pay off, does it? My friends at the jobsite, they all got kids they're so proud of, and they ask me about you, and what can I tell them? What do I got to show for it? Mopey, soft kid, soft like his mother, scared of his own shadow, can't dig a ditch or hammer a nail, probably a drug addict for all I know. So I don't say anything."

Owen felt tears hot at the edges of his eyes.

"Dad—"

"Go on, get out," he said. Not loud. But firm. Angry. Acid.

Owen hurried past his father, out the door. Trying not to think about how there was something worse than a father who hated you— one who didn't care about you at all.

Still. An escape was an escape. And it was easy, this time, at least. If not precisely uncomplicated.

Lauren was thinking about Matty again.

She stood there primping in the mirror, which was a thing she did not do. Not ever. Not for some stupid boy. And Matty was just a stupid boy, she told herself, even though she knew he damn well was not. And then there was Owen. Owen liked her. She knew it. How could she not? And it wasn't that she didn't like him—they'd made out a few times, and it was good, even great. But like, they were friends. Best friends. Making out was fine, but anything more than that felt fucked up, like incest or something. Besides, they wanted to go to college together, they wanted to *work* together and write stories and make games and—

She didn't need him to be more than that to her.

Matty, on the other hand...

Matty was fun. Hot. Smart.

A friend, too, obviously—long a part of the crew, their Golden Boy. *God, I want to climb him like the rope in gym class.*

But it was more than that—he was *driven*. He got shit done. Matty had ambitions—he wanted to be a doctor, he said, or maybe a lawyer, and to meet someone who could even think of *being* those things was amazing. Like it proved something to her, that you were allowed to *have* ambitions. That you could be more than what you were now. A future You, better than shitty current You.

I want to be ambitious, too, she thought whenever she was with Matty.

Nick saw her and Matty Frenching outside of school a month ago, and he told her, "You need to pick a lane, Laur. Owen's fragile." And she told him, "I didn't even think you liked Owen that much," and he said to her:

"The Covenant."

That phrase. The Covenant. The promise that bound them all. The thing that made them more than just friends—that made them a real, true crew. Bonafide. Nick wasn't using it cavalierly. He was trying to drive something home.

And it did. It drove into her gut like a fist.

Okay, fine, Nick, I'm picking a lane.

So she was picking Matty.

And meanwhile, she'd get out of this empty house. Her mother was away again—this time, a trip to the Poconos to one of those trash-ass resorts with the big tubs that looked like cocktail glasses. Off with, who was it this time? Brett? Brad? Some B-name d-bag. Boyfriend Number Thirty-Seven. Mom was never home, which meant Lauren came home from school every day to an empty house, had to make her own microwaved dinners half the time, had to clean up, feed the cat, empty the litter box, take out the trash. All this stupid adult shit. Always doing it alone. Alone, alone, alone.

Well, not this weekend. This weekend, it was the woods, it was the good drugs, it was getting away from this home and going to her real home, which was wherever the crew was hanging out. *That* was home to her.

Time to not be alone, she thought. *Time to go home.*

15

A Walk in the Woods, Part One

It was a climb to Highchair Rocks. Not literally a climb—the journey was not vertical and required no rappelling. But the trail, starting at the west gate of Remington Dover State Park just north of Harrow, gradually grew steeper and steeper until the incline made your legs burn and your Achilles tendons feel like guitar strings about to snap. Most hikers had to reach out along the path to grab at trees and rocks along the way to help haul themselves forward. (Just don't grab for the thick fuzzy ropes of vine hanging down—those who made that mistake walked away with a nightmare case of poison ivy, the kind that got between your fingers and blistered on your palms, rendering your grip both useless and itchy. So itchy, in fact, you'd probably rip the meat of your hands open just to satisfy the constant needling urge to *scratch*.)

Those who braved the trail—and who could manage such an unpleasant ascent—were rewarded with a rocky pocket of forest rimmed at the south edge by a handful of glorious vistas. One could look out and see the tops of an old pine and spruce forest running the length of Black Creek, or in the other direction, you might see the old mill and the raw red planks of the covered bridge beyond. On a clear day, you *might* even see all the way to Haydock Mountain (not a mountain, really, just a *very impressive hill*), and even spy the cobbling of the boulder field of Ramble Rocks Quarry near it. Extra bonus: A person could see one helluva sunset *and* sunrise here, given the way this southern edge jutted out, offering access to both the east and the west. Sun went up, sun went down, and Highchair Rocks was gilded by the growing light of day's advent, and the fading glow of day's demise.

Which meant it was a pretty excellent place to get high.

Or drunk. You know, whatever.

So that is why five teenagers—each sixteen or seventeen years old, all of them soon to be seniors at Central Bucks North High School—headed into the woods that Friday. They wanted to be high up. They wanted to *get* high, high up. They wanted to laugh and feel shit and tell scary stories and bust one another's balls. Really, they wanted to be with one another in a world that did not seem to care very much about them. School was out. Fuck yeah.

They did not know what they would find up there.

Or what they would lose when they found it.

Here, then, was how a crew, *this* crew, came together.

It was survival, at first. A way to survive at school, yes, but also a way to not be at *home*.

Lore was always alone at her house, a latchkey kid for years now. Owen knew the people at his house didn't want him there, not really—his father hated him, his mother kept quiet. Hamish's parents fought like you wouldn't believe, always yelling and throwing things. His father was fire, his mother was gasoline, and Hamish just wanted to be away from it. Nick loved his father, they all assumed, but his mother had left long ago, and Nick needed people other than his dad to hang out with, even though everyone loved his dad. Matty was the only one who didn't really hate home, or so he said. His parents loved him, but everyone knew that their love for him was conditional. They pushed him—too hard, sometimes. *Get good grades. Join this club. That team. Try out for the play.* Matty couldn't slip, or they'd freeze him out. He never said as much. But everyone saw it. No way not to see the pressure they put on him, the cracks it formed.

They found one another through the years, not all at once. Lore and Owen in elementary school. Then Hamish. Nick and Matty in junior high. They were each the other's respite. A safe space, a found family, a *real* home, existing wherever they each were at any time—they could always shelter in place with one another.

They were more than just a clique, more than just fellow wanderers. They were the crew, bound by their Covenant.

Owen in 1998: just a slip of a kid, really, nearly insubstantial, like he was painted upon the world, a streak of dark ink, human eye shadow. Wore jeans, never wore shorts, and everyone was glad for that, too, because Nick always said, "Your legs are so pale, Zuikas, looking at you is like looking at a solar eclipse, all dark but somehow still bright enough to burn the eyes out of your head." Shirt was a Black Flag tee, which was maybe weird because Owen didn't really listen to Black Flag. They were too, what, aggressive for him, maybe? NIN was aggro, too, but in a softer, more vulnerable way. Less pure rage and more . . . spasms of animosity and injury. Didn't matter, really—Owen's NIN shirt was in the wash. The clothes hid scars others couldn't see. The pockets hid the chewed pens and pencils. Even if they didn't hide the hangnails or chapped and bitten lips.

He wasn't exactly an outdoors kind of guy—he would've much rather been inside, designing Angelfire websites for the burgeoning internet, or listening to music so loud that his ears felt like they were going to squirt blood, or writing stuff in his journal that was weird, sad, funny, or just sorta fucked up. But this was where his friends were. (Where *Lauren* was.) And he wanted to be with them.

Of course, the one person he didn't want to be with was himself.

Owen's greatest fear was the dark, because in the dark, he was alone with *that* person, always. And though the darkness was mighty, the darkness of his own thoughts was all the blacker, and (felt) all the truer.

Which was why he liked having friends.

Having friends meant not being alone with himself.

Because Owen was certainly not his own friend.

But *they* were his friends. They had his back, even when he didn't have his own.

Lauren, who would not become Lore until she and Owen went to Sarah Lawrence, dropped back to the end of the line, where Owen walked. She moved to just behind him as he hauled himself up over a crooked, knobby root.

"*Move your ass, Zuikas,*" she said in a faux gruff tone. Like she was their gym teacher, Coach Hutchings.

"Fuck off," he said, but it was a playful fuck off, not a *fuck off* fuck off.

"You're moving like treacle."

He grunted. His legs felt like hot rags spun up and wrung out. His knees felt like hard rocks wrapped up in those rags, too. "I'm just trying not to break a leg. Or my head. Or touch poison ivy." Still, he gave himself a little push, though. "And I don't know what 'treacle' is, Laur." (Laur, just the short form of her name. For now, at least.)

"It's—I think pudding? It's a Britishism. I read it in a Pratchett book. It's like, molassesy, but I think you mine it out of the ground? I don't fucking know. It just means you're slow."

"I know I'm slow."

"Do you need your inhaler?"

"I don't think so," he said. He had asthma, but a particular kind—*exercise-induced asthma,* they said. He found out he had it when he nearly collapsed, wheezing, during gym class last year when they had to run a mile. He also found out that he had some kind of knobby knees situation—"growing pains," they said, but then they also said it was called Osgood-Schlatter disease? This kind of exercise—hiking up a steep, steep trail—was fine for his asthma, but shitty on his knees. They throbbed with their own horrible heartbeats.

"Just making sure, dude. Don't want you dying out here, because I need my writing partner. I can't do it alone."

"Thanks, Laur."

"Oh, hey, dude. *Dude.* Listen. I thought of a new game idea."

Owen stuck out his lower lip and used it to blow the beads of sweat gathering on his upper lip. "Oh yeah?"

"So, like, get this—it's *Pokémon,* but instead of catching cute little Japanese critters, you're out there trying to catch Lovecraftian nightmares and pit them against one another—"

Owen laughed. "Right, so you throw your ball—"

"Or your *obsidian prism trap* or your *void sphere* or whatever—"

"And you catch a frolicking Nyarlathotep—"

"*Nyarlathotep, I choose you!*" she chirped.

More laughter. "Oh my god, *totally*. And it doesn't just have to be Lovecraftian stuff. Imagine it with cryptids. Skunk ape, Mothman, *a wild chupacabra goat-sucker appears,* and then you could—"

Ahead and above them, Matty Shiffman called.

"Laur! Hey! *Laur!* C'mere! You wanna see this!"

"Shit," she said to Owen. "Hold that thought."

Then Lauren pushed past him, hurrying back up the hill to meet Matty up there. Leaving him all by himself. *Again,* he thought, somewhat bitterly.

Owen kept going. Slowly, now. Not in a hurry because—

Well. Just not in a hurry.

But only ten feet ahead, he found Hamish there, bracing himself against a paper birch, sweat dripping from the long oily coils of his hair.

"Fuck, man," Hamish said, breathing heavily. "This fucking sucks."

"No kidding."

Owen reached behind his own backpack and pulled a glass bottle out of one of the side pockets. It was a mango Snapple. Half drunk, but not yet piss warm. With a bit of a flourish, he handed it to Hamish.

"I present to you—*nectar of the gods,*" Owen said.

"Fucking fuck, thank you." Hamish uncapped it and took a huge swig. "*Wahhh,*" he said, a guttural gasp of refreshed satisfaction after having gulped more than half the bottle. "So, you bummed?"

"Bummed? About what?"

"Laur being at Matty's beck and call."

Owen stumbled over his denial as it tumbled out of him. "What? Wha? That's—that's not a thing, man. She's not—it's not like that. The fuck, Ham."

Hamish shrugged, handed back the Snapple. "We all know you have a thing for her."

"I do not have a 'thing' for her. We're friends."

"Friends."

"Just friends."

"Uh-huh. Sure. That's why you two were making out last Christmas—"

"Drinks. There were drinks. We were drunk. People do stupid shit when they're drunk." Owen frowned over the Snapple bottle as he finished it off. It was true. They had gotten drunk at Nick's house and wandered out past their shitty aboveground pool and into the maze of overgrown roses Nick's mom had once preened over year after year before she ran out on the family. That's when Laur smashed her mouth against Owen's and pushed her tongue in his mouth, and it was both his first kiss and the best moment in his life, so far. And yet, he also told himself, it was a fluke. Just a weird stupid moment in time.

A weird stupid *amazing* moment in time.

"People do the stupid shit *they have always wanted to do* when they're drunk, man, c'mon."

"You headbutted a tree last time you were drunk."

Ham laughed. "Oh, haha, yeah, I did. Hey! That tree had it coming. Trees have had it *too good* for *too long*, man."

That got a laugh out of Owen, too. Hamish really *had* headbutted a tree. One night he'd gotten hammered on some unholy combination of Goldschläger and Jäger. Usually Hamish was nothing but love and laughs when he was lit, but that night he got surly—less the usual Phish vibe and suddenly, inexplicably, more Rage Against the Machine. Hamish took out his rage not on a machine but on an old oak tree in Nick's backyard. Needless to say, the oak was untroubled by Ham's head, but the tree gave Ham's head a pretty good dent. His face ended up a streaky mask of blood. Later, Hamish blew it off, made it seem like he was trying to be funny, but Lauren said it meant Hamish had "a core of anger somewhere deep down."

The ghost of that injury could still be seen on Hamish's forehead—faint but yellow, like an old piss stain on pants.

"We're *just* friends," Owen said again, when they were done cackling.

"Just friends," Hamish reiterated, as if to add, *Yeah, sure.*

"Yeah. Yeah."

"So you don't care if she fucks Matty."

"She's not going—I mean, she's free to if she wants. Matty's my friend, she's my friend, I don't really see them having a real relationship, and it's not like they're *compatible* in any real way, but okay, sure, whatever."

Hamish shook his head, scratching at the patchy scrub of muttonchops that had inspired Nick to call him Hobo Wolverine. "Okay, if you say so, I'm not gonna harsh your b—"

Up above, a voice rang out. Lauren's voice. To Owen's ear, it contained both wonder and alarm.

"Guys!" she yelled down from the top of the trail. "You need to come and see what we found up here!"

16

The First Staircase

After the trail reached its peak and leveled out, it turned to the east, but dead ahead sat the staircase. The stairs and risers were pale and faded, like old bones. The paint, cracked and chipping. The wood, not soft, not rotten, but worn. The balusters—though Owen would not have had that name for them, not then—were twisted into spirals. The railing, too, screwed into a spiral at the end, like water going down a drain. The structure rose up out of nothing, and went to nothing. A staircase to nowhere.

Tall trees on either side of it cast mottled shadows on the pale staircase. The wind stirred debris on those stairs, an invisible broom sweeping them clean. It howled through the balusters, like someone whistling through stiff grass.

Owen shivered looking upon it. It felt wrong. Like it didn't belong.

Matty came up to Owen, gave him a gentle elbow to the ribs. "You see this? This is nuts, right?"

"Yeah," Owen said. He had to admit it felt good to be noticed by Matty. Like you were in his light, made brighter by it, less scared, less stupid. Matty never really belonged with the rest of them: They were kinda freaks and he was, well, not. Sure, they all pretended they were equals to him, but in the deepest parts of themselves they all had to know, right? That Matty was better? That he was above them, or at least that he was the first among them? The one, Owen thought, who mattered the most? *Dear leader,* he thought.

"You like weird shit," Matty said. "Right? Horror stories and stuff. Urban legends and all that. You ever hear of this sort of thing?"

"No. I—I don't think so."

Then Lauren was next to them. Out of nowhere, popping up next to Matty on the other side. "I like that kind of stuff, too, you know," she said. It sounded to Owen like a kind of pleading—a bid for attention. *It's pathetic,* he thought, and then hated himself for thinking that. No, she wasn't pathetic. He was the pathetic one. *Just let her have this, you asshole.* Then he heard Hamish's voice in his head, chiding him. *Just friends. Yeah, right.*

"Let's fuckin' climb it," Hamish said, his words mumbled as he spoke around the Camel cigarette he'd just twisted between his lips. He fumbled for a Bic lighter as Nick snatched the cancer stick out of his mouth and popped it in his own. Hamish went after him, but Nick was fast and nimble, ducking and feinting before snaking around the trunks of trees—Hamish was like an orangutan chasing a ferret, pawing clumsily for the thief that was his friend. Those two were always fucking with each other. Well, Nick was usually the one fucking with Hamish, because that was Nick, and that was Hamish.

The fucker and the fucked-with.

"Don't climb it," Matty cautioned. "You'll get hurt and mess up the whole weekend."

"Who knows how long it's been here?" Lauren said.

As Nick was dodging Hamish's every attempt to reclaim his cigarette, he was saying, "I've been up this trail a dozen times. Fuck, I was just fuckin' here like, a month ago. And this staircase? It wasn't here. It wasn't here! I swear to it!"

"Bullshit," Matty said.

"It's true! Not lying."

Hamish finally gave up the chase, and Nick leered at him, finally pulling out his own lighter—his lucky Zippo, chrome with the Jack Kenny whiskey logo on it. He flicked it open with Andrew Dice Clay panache and lit the cigarette.

Owen shrugged. "Maybe you came up a different trail. There're a lot of paths up here. And it's not like there's . . . much to differentiate them, right? Trees and rocks and whatever."

"That's what it is," Hamish said before trying one last time to snatch the now-lit cigarette out of Nick's mouth, but Nick did a juke and got away clean again. "Dude. Gimme that back. That's the last in the pack. It's the lucky one."

"No, bitch, I got the lucky lighter, it's mine." He blew a cloud of smoke at Hamish and chuckled. To the others, Nick said, "Whatever. This is the same trail I always come up. I'm telling you. It's fucking marked at the bottom, you dickheads. It's the start of the Lambert Loop trail. These stairs were *not* here before."

Lauren waved him off. "Come on, the trail loops around this area and goes back down the other side. You probably came up that way every other time and you were too high or drunk to know the difference."

Everyone laughed at that, except Owen. Owen couldn't take his gaze away from the staircase. If it *had* been here before, wouldn't vines be climbing it? Poison ivy, honeysuckle, stuff like that? Wouldn't there be dead leaves glued to the stairs by time and rot? How would it even be here? There should be a house. If time took the house, how did it not take the stairs? For a moment, as Owen beheld the stairway, it seemed to lengthen—stretching out in front of him, adding stairs upon stairs, as if it were climbing itself. As if it were going somewhere, punching a hole in the distance, in reality, in the universe. It made him dizzy.

The staircase didn't belong here. It didn't belong in a way that went far deeper than just *a staircase shouldn't be out in the woods*. This felt like something weirder, something worse. Like this staircase did not belong here in the world at all.

It's not from here, he thought—an absurd notion. And yet.

"All right, let's set up camp," Matty was saying, "enough with the stupid staircase," and of course everyone listened, because Matty told them to, and they knew to listen to Matty. Out of the corner of his eye, Owen saw Nick start to grab one of the tents, and Hamish nabbed the other. Lauren lingered, waiting for Matty to follow—

But Owen was transfixed on the staircase, and Matty was transfixed on Owen. "Hey, man, you okay?" Matty asked him.

"What? Oh. Um. Yeah."

Matty said in a low voice, "It really *is* strange, right? The staircase. There's no . . . house here. I don't see the frame of a foundation or anything. No other ruins or the remains of any other structure."

"Yeah." Owen shook himself from the reverie. "I'm sure there's a normal explanation, though. A . . . prank or something. I wouldn't put it past Nick to mess with us."

"Totally." Here, Matty blocked Owen from following the others, though—not really in an aggressive way, per se. Just easing in front of him. "Hey, I wanted to ask—we cool?"

"What?"

"I mean like, we haven't hung out as much lately."

"Oh, shit, yeah. It's just been—" *It's just been that you and Lauren have been up each other's asses, and also you have sports, and you have the play, and, and, and.* "It's been a lot going on. Next year's our last, and I guess we're all just trying to get through it."

"Yeah, man. I hear that. But!" Matty clapped Owen hard on the arm—*whap*. Matty was big and tall, and he'd always been a bit rough-and-tumble. A bro who was a nerd, a nerd who was a bro. "Fuck it, that's why we're doing this campout. Hang out, drink some drinks, tell some scary stories—and I brought my Magic deck, man. I'm gonna finally kick your ass tonight—it's a red-green-artifact *steamroller* and you do *not* stand a chance."

"We'll see," Owen said, a gleam in his eye. It was rare to kick Matty's ass at anything, but Magic: The Gathering was one place where Owen could do just that. (That and maybe *Doom* deathmatch.)

"All right, come on, let's catch up with the others." But Lauren wasn't far—she was waiting for them both a little farther down the trail. *Not for us,* Owen thought. *For him.* That was fine. It was what it was. He didn't really have feelings for her anyway, he told himself.

He looked once more over his shoulder at the staircase.

And for a moment, he thought he saw it shudder—not like in a hard wind or as if the ground shook. But shuddering like a wolf waking up—a stretch and a flex, as if ready for the hunt. *It's just your imagination,* he told himself. And he turned his back on the stairs, even though he really, really didn't want to.

17

Teen Shit

Tents up. Fire going. Hot dogs on sticks, marshmallows on sticks, hot dogs and marshmallows together on the *same* sticks—that one came to life once Nick and Hamish started smoking weed out of Nick's glass pipe, the one he called the Purple People Eater. Snacks were open, drinks were out—cheap beer and a bottle of Jameson stolen from Nick's dad ("stolen" because Nick's dad knew they were taking it and didn't give a shit). Owen started with the beer—Coors Light, which made him sad to drink because Coors Light *was* sadness in a can.

He asked Matty, "Ready for me to kick your ass at Magic *again*?"

Matty said, "Yeah, yeah, sure thing, yeah," but Owen could see by the look on his face that it wasn't happening. "I'm just gonna run off with Laur here for a minute and go look at the uhh, the vista—" And Lauren gave Owen a look. She hung that look on him like a heavy coat, and he didn't know what it was or what to do with it. Was it guilt? Shame? Sadness? Condescension? Was it a silent apology? Was she judging him or judging herself? Or maybe the beer was already making him fuzzy and she was looking right through him, seeing through time to whatever was to come with her and Matty.

And then those two were off, and Nick was at one side of him and Hamish the other. "We'll fuckin' play Magic with you, man," Nick said.

They played a few games. Nick had a play style that he called Chaos Monkey Mode, where he did random shit every turn, totally unpredictable—*ook*ing like a mad chimp whenever he did something truly bizarre, like giving one of his opponents the gift of a good enchantment for no discernible reason other than to fuck with the game. He didn't play to win, he just played to amuse himself. Hamish played to win, on the other hand, but never really had a strong grasp of the game's mechanics—mostly he was just a "spawn tons of creatures and march them into battle again and again" kind of player. Not much strategy. Though they weren't playing, Matty was pretty good at the game once in a while, but couldn't hold a candle to Lauren, who mostly said she hated the game ("So boring and pedestrian," she always said with a vigorous eye roll, even as she shuffled her deck and readied for war), and yet she always had a keen stratagem every single match. In truth, she was Owen's only real competitor. But she wasn't here. She was off with Matty. In the woods.

Playing her own game. A new stratagem.

Just don't think about it, Owen told himself.

It's fine.

You don't care.

They're just looking at the vista.

First game ended, and Owen won—but barely, if only because Nick *high* played better than Nick *sober* for some fucked-up reason. Hamish, not so much, who mostly just sat there giggling at his cards and saying their names in increasingly goofy voices. "*Merfolk Looter. Goblin Lackey. Balduvian Horde!*" Eventually he just made up his own card names. "Yawgmoth's Yum-Yums! Crovax the Fuckin' Uncrustable! Phrexian Butthole!" He and Nick were laughing so hard, they were crying at this point. The fire nearby snapped and popped, coughing up embers that rose on spirals of smoke, dying in the air.

Owen put down his beer and switched to the whiskey. It tasted like the campfire. He hated it. He loved that he hated it. So he drank more.

"I bet they *fuckin',*" Nick said finally, when their laughs had subsided.

Hamish snorted. "Yawgmoth and Crovax?"

"No, dickhead, Lauren and Matty. I bet he's got her up against a tree right now. Going to town. Poundtown, population: those two."

Owen made a face and drank more whiskey. It hurt. Good. Fine. Yes.

Hamish gave Owen a sad, protective look, then chastised Nick, saying, "C'mon, Nick, don't be gross. They're our friends."

"Gross is who I am, Hamish. Tiger can't change its spots."

"Nick—"

"Oh, shit, you think maybe he's putting it in her ass?" At that, both Owen and Hamish shot him a warning look. Nick held up his hands in faux surrender. He laughed, cruelly. "I mean, maybe *she's* putting it in *his* ass, no judgment, it's almost the year 2000, if people want to get freaky-deaky, I very much support it. Whatever makes their grapefruits squirt, yanno."

"*Nick.*"

"They might not be doing anything," Owen said, erupting.

"Don't be retarded," Nick said. "They *fuckin'*."

"You can't say that," Hamish said.

"They fuckin'?"

"No. The, the, the other word, the r-word."

"Retarded? I just said it, retard. If I can't say it, then how did I say it?"

"It's not cool to say it. You're not supposed to—"

"I can say anything and everything, that's the amazing thing about words. They're just words. They don't mean anything. Monkey grunts and insect clicks. Just because you're offended by one doesn't change my ability to say them, you fucking retarded-ass—"

"*Nick,*" Hamish said, and the way Hamish said it, it meant that he really, really fucking *meant* it. Like he was serious. Hamish didn't get deeply serious all that often, but when he did, you knew it was real. Like, headbutt-a-tree real. "I'm calling Covenant."

"Covenant. Okay! *Okay.* Fine, whatever. It's not like I mean it in the bad way. I don't say *retarded* and mean actually *retarded* people—"

"Yeah, you fucking do. You say it meaning someone or something who's stupid. You mean it like mentally challenged, handicapped and shit. You can't—it's not cool. You know, Mikey Hart's sister has Down syndrome, and she knows what the word means and it hurts her when she hears it—"

"Ugh, god, you are seriously the worst right now, Ham. You're absolutely crushing my high. Bringing me down, man."

"It's fine, you're fine, we're all fine," Hamish said, chuckling. It was his way of smoothing it all over. "Besides, there's more weed where that came from, brother." He clapped a hand on Nick's shoulder, and the two of them got to the act of sorting the sticks and seeds from whatever weed they had brought with them.

Nick said, "Well, whatever they're doing, Matty and Lauren are missing out." Then he perked his head up like a startled meerkat in a nature special. "Wait one fuckin' minute. Zuikas. You don't—nah, it can't be. You're not *into* Lauren, are you?"

"No," Owen said, protesting. He felt like Nick was just messing with him. Nick knew, right? They all knew. "I—no, what, I don't know." He stood up suddenly, the bottle of whiskey still in his hand. It sloshed around. "I have to go take a piss."

They called after him, calling his name, telling him to come back, but he waved them off and hurried away from the firelight. He didn't really have to piss. Instead, he wandered farther into the trees, sipping the whiskey that once burned him like a candlewick but now had just turned him numb and melty. Less the wick, more the wax. He pushed Matty and Lauren out of his thoughts and instead stood there in the darkness, listening to the night bugs *chack*ing and *clack*ing and *buzz*ing. He let the night wash over him. Tried to empty his head entirely—but as it emptied out, something slipped in.

The staircase.

He'd forgotten about it, but now, it stood tall inside his mind—unasked for, unbidden. As if it had risen there, built on the earth inside him. So real he could nearly touch it, even though he couldn't really see it, even though it wasn't even near him. But inside the darkness of his brain, it was there, waiting. The stairs easing forth until they were right in front of his feet. Like a dog nosing your hand to pet him, it was as if those stairs wanted to get under the front of his foot, pushing him up so that he was upon them. Like it was begging him to come to them and climb them. It had no voice. But it was urgent. It demanded to be thought of. To be seen.

To be *used*.

He shook his head. Drank more. Let the whiskey push it out. But then he thought, *Maybe it's the whiskey doing this to me*. Or the contact buzz from the secondhand smoke. Or a bad hot dog. The staircase was the staircase; it was weird, but that's all it was. It didn't have thoughts. It didn't *want* anything. It was just the ruins of an old house in the middle of the woods.

Shut up, Owen. Shut up.

Stupid betrayer brain.

But even as he turned to go back to the campsite, he was almost sure he could see the staircase out there, way out there, in the trees. Rising into the dark. A shadow blacker than night, like a shape cut into the fabric of the world.

18

Lauren and Matty

The woods up here were thick, the understory forbidding, and all the two of them had was a little Maglite flashlight. Matty led the way, because that was Matty—always leading the way. Lauren hated it. And she loved it. She hated that she loved it. She always told herself she wasn't the kind just to swoon and get giggly over some boy, to be captivated by him, to be *in thrall* to some dick-having member of the population, but here she was. Her small, soft hand in his, being drawn deeper into the dark forest, like the foolish girl in a fairy tale.

She wondered aloud if maybe they should turn around. "We're gonna break our necks out here," she said, laughing, because she was already a little drunk on the pink diabetes wine from Boone's Farm. "Or wait, shit, isn't there a cliff?"

"There's a lot of cliffs up here," he said ahead of her. No fear in his voice. "We're on Highchair Rocks, Laur—it's a hundred feet up on all sides."

"That means it's a hundred feet *down*."

He just laughed. In the darkness, his voice seemed to fall behind him, like something he dropped, something for her to pick up. "You're a glass-half-empty type. I love that about you."

Lauren took a fast step forward and with her free hand smacked his ass. "I thought you loved my *sweet sweet boo-tay*," she said, cackling.

"Oh, I love that too," he said, drawing her deeper into the darkness.

It had started a year ago. Almost to the day.

They were drunk at a party. Well, a "party"—Jeff Warnick had this big-ass open expanse of a backyard and his dad was sorta rich and his parents traveled all the time, so most weekends Jeff lit a bonfire, and whoever wanted to come over and hang could come over and hang. Sometimes it was six people, sometimes it was six*teen* people, and that day, a Saturday in June, it was close to sixty—all moths to a flame. It was fireworks and keg stands, it was bong rips and diving boards, it was Jeff's nutso pitbull Murray running around and humping every leg that wasn't actively kicking him away. There was a fight at one point—a sloppy fracas between Earl Coons and Billy Boback, the two of them punching and pawing at each other like a pair of drunk bears, all over some perceived slight, something about Shannon, Earl's girlfriend, and something about Billy being a quote-unquote "little pussy bitch pissant pussy."

Lauren was a little drunk—just fuzzy enough to feel that numb benzocaine tingle in her lips and gums, and she didn't want to be near the fight in case one of those two assholes accidentally fell into the bonfire and barbecued themselves, or got someone else barbecued by jostling into them. So she wandered off to the edge of the property, near the post-and-rail horse fence.

That's where she found Matty. He, too, wanted to get away from the fight. And he was a little drunk, just like her. They made each other laugh for a while and then, next thing they knew...

They kissed. Hard. They made out like *bandits*.

It was the first time, but it would not be the last.

They told each other it wasn't serious. Just a fling, a stupid physical attraction. And so they found each other once every few months—often outside, because it turned out that the wide open nowhere was a very good way to get away from everyone else—and it always went the same way. Got a little drunk, made each other laugh, and then messed around. But then it was late April this past year when she and

Matty got together at the playground outside Minsi Trail Elementary to get busy, but then he said, "You ever notice the pattern?"

Lauren didn't know what he was talking about. "I notice patterns," she said. "I'm good with patterns, okay?"

So he said, "You missed this one," and pointed out that before they got it on, they *always* made each other laugh first. "I have a good time with you, and you have a good time with me," he explained to her. "We actually *like* each other, Laur."

"Yeah, we're friends," she told him, as if to say, *Duh*.

But she wasn't getting it. "*Yeah*, and then some, which is why we should make this . . . a thing. A real thing."

"But we're *friends*," she said, more dour this time, because to her, that was the most important thing. Their friendship. This hooking up thing was just a side business. As the saying went, friends with benefits.

"Laur, I dig you," he said.

"I dig you, too."

"No, I *dig* you." Said like someone drunk, or high, except he wasn't either when he said it. (Matty *did* get drunk but did *not* get high. His parents expected a certain level of performance out of him and demanded a particular future, which he was happy to supply. Failing a drug test, he said, would ruin all that. When she asked him if his parents drug-tested him, he laughed it off. But she wasn't so sure.)

"Matty—"

"I want to do this for real."

"It hasn't been real this whole time?" she asked, smirking, and reaching behind and sliding the flats of her hands into the tight rear pockets of his jeans.

"You know what I mean. I want to do *us* for real. A relationship."

And that word struck fear and excitement through her like she'd never before experienced. A lightning bolt through her heart—enough voltage to both kill her ass dead *and* bring her back to life again, reborn. *A relationship.* Zap.

"I—Matty—we'll go away to college year after next and—"

"I'm not looking to get married. I just want to make it official with us. No more of this running around behind our friends' backs. Boyfriend, girlfriend. Holding hands and going to movies and all that cheesy shit."

"Ugh," she said, still smiling. She squeezed his ass. "I don't like cheese." Lauren tried to be funny and cute because it was easier than thinking about the friends they weren't telling—which, translation, meant Owen. Owen, who was truly her best friend in the whole world—and the one from whom she was keeping this secret. She knew he liked her. It was obvious. It radiated from him like sunlight off a switchblade—it was so bright it nearly blinded her, even if he thought he was playing it cool. But Lauren thought they were too close. Too similar. They could never. They *should* never. But Matty... she was close with him but not *close*-close. Not best friends. Just friends *enough* to fuck it all up.

"So how about it?" he asked.

"I'll... think about it."

"Oh." It was impossible not to hear the disappointment in his voice. It rang like the peal of a sad, long bell. "All right." He mumbled something about having to go home, and she spun him around and pressed herself up against him.

"I said I'll think about it, Pouty Pete," she said, not knowing what that corny shit even meant. Didn't matter. She pressed her mouth against his, and they both breathed in sharply through their nostrils and then it was *on*.

Today, out here in the woods, she was going to tell him yes.

Yes, she'd be his girlfriend. Yes, they could be together and tell the whole fucking world about it. She'd never quite tell him she needed him, because Lauren would tell him and tell everyone that she didn't *need* anybody. Not today, not ever.

But she wanted him, and that would be enough.

Though sometimes she wondered whether or not she wanted

him, or simply didn't want to be alone. Maybe it didn't matter. She promised him she'd think about it, and she thought about it, and she wanted to be with Matty.

End of story, game over, fuck it.

They pressed on deeper and deeper until a break in the darkness of trees gave way to the bright indigo nothing of open sky. A half-moon looked down. A wind stirred, restive. He said, "The cliff's edge is just over here—"

But she didn't want to get that close, and by now, her impatience was burning her up like a bad case of the flu. She planted her feet and pulled him toward her—he *oof*ed and chuckled as she kissed him long and hard. So hard their teeth clacked. So hard she knew they might each have brush burn around their lips afterward, skin reddened like smeared lipstick. So hard that for a half second, she was able to convince herself that they had actually, literally, honest-to-fucking-god become one person. But then she pulled away, gasping as if she'd just resurfaced from beneath the surface of a churning sea.

"Hey, I wanna tell you something," she said, wiping her mouth.

"Okayyyy," he said, expectant.

"First, though—"

She dug a little tin case out of her pocket. An Altoids tin. She held it out for him gently. Not for him to take, but instead, she rested the tin on her palm—an invitation for him to open it. Like a little treasure chest.

"Go on," she said.

"Is this a ring?" he asked, playfully. In a higher register, he asked, "Gosh, am I the luckiest girl in town?"

"Just open it, you goon."

So he did. Inside, two white cubes awaited—the size and shape of six-sided dice, but without the black dots. "What am I looking—" he started to ask.

"Sugar cubes," she answered, by way of interruption.

"Am I a horse? Is this my treat?"

"It's a treat, all right. These were hard to get."

"Okay, now I really don't follow you."

"Sugar cubes, yes, but dosed with acid."

"Acid."

She shrugged and offered a Cheshire cat grin. "LSD, dude."

Matty laughed, but in a hollow, awkward way. "Are you serious?"

"Serious as the star."

"You don't mean—Laur, I can't drop acid."

"Sure you can. It's easy. Just pop the sugar cube in your mouth. Yum."

"No, I mean—I don't do LSD, I can't—"

She rubbed his arm to comfort him, but also, okay, in a condescending way. *You poor sweet fool,* she thought. It was so cute. He had no idea. So she explained it to him: "It's fine. LSD doesn't show up on a normal drug test. I know your parents make you get tested—but this only shows up in the hair, and someone's only going to test *that* if you want, like, some classified job in government. Besides, I want us both . . . to be open for this. Wide open, all the way. Like, a commitment of sorts."

The moon behind him drew a bright line around him. Painting his edges, like he'd become a doorway, a portal, through which he wanted to escape. *Man, you'd think I was already on acid,* she thought.

"It's not just that, Laur. You hear stories, you know? Like that guy who did acid and then believed he was a glass of orange juice and if you moved him, he'd tip and spill himself and die. He ended up in an insane asylum—"

"That's a bullshit story."

"And they say if you take acid X number of times, you can be declared legally insane, even if you don't think you're a glass of OJ."

"Dude. Matty. C'mon. Those are—that's just propaganda. Government propaganda, CIA nonsense, to get people to not take this stuff, to not open their minds, because when they do, it changes them. And that's what I want for us tonight—this stuff is special for me, and I want us to take it together, and then you and I will *be*—"

Together, she was about to say, but Matty pulled back for real this time.

One hard step in reverse.

"I can't," he said.

"Oh."

Now: her turn to be disappointed, it seemed.

He said it again—

"I can't, Laur. You might be okay with this sort of thing, but I have a future to think about. I really—"

This sort of thing, she thought, repeating his words again and again in her head.

"Really what?" she asked, words tinged with bitter root.

He sighed. "Hey! Let's head back to camp. They're probably wondering where we went and, um, we can tell some pretty killer ghost stories, right? C'mon." In his voice, she heard something, though— a sudden distance, like they were two different people now.

No, like I'm someone different now, to him.

He moved toward her—

(Her heart quickened.)

—then past her.

Brushing his hand against her arm, her back, as he went.

Fuck, she thought.

Her disappointment gave way to anger.

You might be okay with this sort of thing—

I have a future to think about—

What, like she didn't? She wanted to scream at him: *I'm ambitious, too. I'm smart and I get what I want. I don't need you, Matty Shiffman.*

I can do this all myself.

She let the anger have its moment, then she hit it over the head and threw it in a deep grave, and from that earth she grew a garden of vigorous indifference.

Can't hurt me if I don't care, asshole.

"Fuck it," she said to herself in a happy-bitter voice. She took both of the acid-drop sugar cubes and popped them in her mouth. She let them melt before crunching the last of the sugar granules between her teeth. Lauren imagined them as tiny bones. *Matty's finger bones,* she thought, and it was a dark, insane, totally fucked thought, and she loved it. She laughed like wind chimes in a hurricane and then followed him through the woods, back toward camp.

19

Tales Told, and a Covenant Invoked

So, with Matty and Lauren back, the five of them sat around and told scary stories, as was the way. Not just ghost stories, either, but local weird folklore shit—the Ratfinger Man of Dark Hollow, the glass house cannibals of Haydock Mountain, the eerie ghost lights of Hansell Road, the haunted quarry at Ramble Rocks, even the 120-year-old orchard cult of Henry Hart Golden. Hamish tried to get Lauren to tell them more about her neighbor's house, which was supposedly haunted—Owen knew a little of it, since her neighbor Scotty (who was older than them by a few years, already off to college) told stories about all his electronics coming on at weird times in the night and how he sometimes heard what he called "angels singing" inside his walls. But she didn't want to tell anything. She just sat there on a fallen log, knees pulled up to her chest, arms wrapped so tight around her shins it was like she was trying to disappear inside of herself. Lauren had found her tie-dye sweatshirt and put it on, too, and she peered out from the darkness of its hood. Sometimes smiling, but not in an okay way—and not at anything they were saying or at anything going on around her. Matty, on the other hand, joined in with the rest of the group, laughing and telling stories. Acting even louder and happier than usual. *Like he's putting on a show of it,* Owen decided.

All that meant something was up between Lauren and Matty.

They had come back out of the woods not too long after they went in—upon return, their energy was different. Matty came out ahead, Lauren a good ten steps behind. He seemed troubled then, and she seemed... almost venomously carefree, arms swinging, chin up, but eyes decidedly *down*. She plonked herself at the fire and snatched the bottle from Owen's hand and drank a good glug of the whiskey before giving him a wink and a sneer.

"You okay?" he had asked her.

Whiskey in one hand, she gave him a thumbs-up with the other.

"Aces and eights," was all she said.

But since then, that energy had shifted. Matty *had* seemed off—but now he was on, on, on, like he was emceeing the whole thing. Lauren, on the other hand, had fallen into her own quiet darkness. Withdrawn into the sweatshirt. The fire danced in her eyes as she stared into its heart.

Owen felt happy because those two weren't getting along.

And then he felt shitty because he felt happy.

He wanted her to be happy—

But then, a smaller, meaner, and all the more selfish voice whispered, *But you want her to be happy with* you, *isn't that it, Owen?*

His happiness, then: a big red balloon, blowing up, up, up, all big and bright and bold, but empty inside, airless and hollow.

Hamish was telling a story at this point. Something about some creepy book called the Voynich manuscript—bound in human skin, five hundred years old. "It's, like, written in code, right? A, a, you know, a whatsitcalled, a cipher. And it has all these photos—hah, no, I mean, shit, *drawings*, it has all these fuckin' drawings of weird plants and animals that don't exist and these naked preggo ladies in, you know—" He used his hands to mime the shape of something oblong. "*Vats*. Or whatever. And—"

"*Jesus*," Nick said. "You tell a story like Phish plays a song."

"Shots fired!" Matty said.

Hamish laughed. "You fucker. I'm just high."

"All right," Matty yawped, clapping his hands as he stood up. "Let's do it."

"Do what?" Nick asked. "Insult shitty jam band Phish some more? I'm down, but we might hurt Hamish's fee-fees."

"No. Let's go back to the staircase."

Owen's blood turned to ants, his veins their tunnels. He shivered as goosebumps prickled his skin. "I dunno. It's dark, and you said it wasn't safe . . ."

"I might be too high to fuck with a staircase," Hamish said.

Nick shrugged. "Yeah, man, I'm comfy here, and there's a fire, and there's beer, and I don't wanna get up. Besides—" He pointed his lit cigarette across the fire toward Lauren. "I don't think she's all that interested."

No response from Lauren except a single middle finger thrust out and up.

"Whatever," he said.

"So you all are little scaredy chickenshits," Matty said, holding up both hands in a kind of faux surrender. "Okay, sorry, I didn't realize you were all a big batch of sad soggy pussies."

"Fuck you," Nick said.

Hamish waved Matty off. "Whatever, dude."

"It's just dark," Owen said again, defensive.

Lauren said nothing, gaze remaining fixed on the fire.

"I'm invoking the Covenant," Matty said with some finality. He shrugged and threw up his hands as if to say, *Well, that's that, what choice do I have?*

Something passed between them all—jaws eased open, brows furrowed, bodies shifted uncomfortably. Like they couldn't believe it, an eerie, ozone electricity buzzing in the air. Matty? Invoking the Covenant? Now, over this?

It was the end of an era. They all felt it. The sea change.

And then came the eruptions of discontent.

Hamish: "That's not—no, you can't—dude, Matty, dude, c'mon—"

Nick: "What the fuck, Matty."

Owen: "Matty, Matty—*Matty.*"

Lauren, loudest of them all, and with more than a little anger dosing her words: "Not how the Covenant works, *bro.*"

She was right.

20

A Brief History of the Covenant (1995–1998)

March 1995, ninth grade.

Hamish has a group of kids who bully him every day—metalheads, mostly, not the cool metalheads who listen to Metallica and Anthrax and Gumdropper, but the shitty heavy *heavy* metalheads who liked Cannibal Corpse and Slayer. There's three of them, all seniors: Bryan Weems, Kenny Melzer, and Tom Szumelak. Weems is the leader, if he can be called that, and the other two are the lackeys who laugh at everything he does, who do everything he says. They target Hamish because he's fat. He's sweet. He's kind of a hippie, even back then, even in ninth grade, and they fuck with him all the time. *All* the time. Mostly simple monkey shit, like calling him names and shoving him into one another, or into lockers. Sometimes they lift his shirt up over his head and tuck it under his chin, then slap his belly hard, leaving red marks that turn into dappled bruises.

It escalates one Monday in March.

Hamish uses a bathroom far away from his classes, and even though it makes him late, it usually means the bullies don't find him. But they figure it out, and Weems—with his saggy old dog eyes and his big gums and his long rancid red hair—comes in flanked by Melzer and Szumelak. Melzer looks like a wad of chewed buttholes in a Pantera shirt, and Szumelak is skinny and gangly like a rain-soaked scarecrow. Hamish is pissing at the urinal, and they come up behind him, whip his pants down, and as he struggles to bend down to pull them back up, they slam his face into the urinal he just pissed in. He chips a tooth. Splits a lip. The blood joins the piss on his face. They laugh and kick his exposed ass with their work boots, and then they're gone. Hamish cries so hard he throws up.

The others aren't there when the attack happens, but they're there for him after, and it's Matty who says, "They say you just gotta ignore a bully, but that's wrong—you can't ignore them or they keep getting worse. I say we take the fight to them." And Nick, already smoking at the age of twelve, is like, "Matty's right, guys—they mess with Ham, we mess with *them*."

They all agree.

And so they seek their revenge. It's a multitiered plan. It starts that Friday. All five of them stay after for play practice because either they're in the cast (Matty, Lauren) or working tech crew (Nick, Hamish, Owen). They find the lockers of Weems, Melzer, and Szumelak. They grate half-rotten apples and lumps of pork roll over their locker vents—easy as slicing cheese. They save the cans of tuna fish for Weems's locker. Then that night, they go to each of their houses and dump gallons of milk on their lawns. Finally, they fuck with Weems's car. He's got a white 1990 IROC-Z Camaro. They let the air out of the tires. They cover the windshield in egg and hairspray. And then finally, the pièce de résistance—Weems leaves the window cracked, so they buy ten thousand crickets from the local Pets Pets Pets Emporium, and shove them all (or at least the ones that don't hop away) through the open space, then duct-tape it shut.

It pays off. It pays fucking *dividends*. Lauren lives five houses down from Szumelak, and she says even from her place, his house stinks—the milk has soaked in, gone rancid, and their front lawn smells like a diseased dairy farm. And at school on Monday, those three lockers are so foul, so besieged by fruit flies and houseflies and cockroaches that the school brings in freelance janitorial staff to help clean it out—*bonus*, the three bullies all get in trouble. Detention for weeks. It's clear they wouldn't have done this to themselves, but the principal doesn't care—she just needs someone to blame, and they make it easy to blame them.

As for the car, well, they never see the result, but they still tell stories about how fucking awesome it had to be when Weems opened the car door that day and got pounced on by ten thousand starving crickets. And they saw the car in the school parking lot—the windshield never really looked clean again, and the smell of cooked egg and hairspray never really went away.

It's a temporary victory.

The three bullies now have not one target, but five, and they go after them without mercy. They kick their asses—all but Lauren, who they just threaten to rape and kill. The attacks intensify, but that's all right, they tell one another, because it means Hamish doesn't have to suffer alone. It's a day in late April when they give a name to it.

It's Owen, actually, who names it. They're watching *Raiders of the Lost Ark* and Matty asks what a "covenant" is, and Owen explains it: "It's like a promise, a rock-solid, die-hard, go-to-the-grave promise. A bond you can't get out of. It's like what we all have." And that's when they start calling it that. The Covenant. It's how they're there for one another. How they'll do anything for one another. Get revenge. Take a beating. Do what needs doing.

The next day, it gives Hamish a little extra juice. When Weems comes at him first thing in the morning, Hamish punches him in the eye. Bursts the blood vessels there. Gives him a helluva shiner. Weems gets dizzy, goes down, the other two just run the fuck away. It's amazing.

After that day, the three fuckos leave the five friends alone.

They chalk it up to Hamish giving Weems what-for right in the fucking eye, though that's not really true. Only Nick knows the truth: That night, knowing full well Weems will want revenge, and the kind that might really, really get Hamish hurt, he leaves an envelope under Weems's windshield to be found the next day before school. In it are two things—one, an index card, on which is written:

Take a good look, because you won't see the next one coming.
P.S. Leave Hamish alone, you fuck.

It is unsigned.

The second thing in the envelope—and the thing that Weems is supposed to take a good look at—is a shiny brassy 7mm Remington Magnum rifle round.

June 1996, the end of tenth grade.

Nick is gonna fail his school year. He's smart, he's always been smart, but also, he's fucking stupid, because he won't ever play the game. Any assignment he doesn't like, he just doesn't do it. A teacher he doesn't like, he won't play by their rules, not once, not ever. He's all sandpaper and tornadoes with anyone he doesn't like, and he's this way, he says, "on principle." But usually, *usually*, he manages to scrape by, right? Not this year.

No, this year, of all the fucking classes to fail, he's going to fail gym.

They have a new gym teacher this year, Mrs. Garsh, and Garsh—whom Nick calls "Garsha," for no discernible reason other than it makes him laugh—runs her gym class from her golf cart. They run the mile, they play flag football, they do Frisbee golf, there she is, on her golf cart, chugging alongside. And Nick, again on what he considers "principle," says, "That fat-ass has the nerve to ride alongside us and tell *us* to run faster when *she's* the one who needs a hard dose of physical education." But Hamish points out she's got a goofy knee, like it kinda bends weird? "Not her fault she's got a bum knee," Hamish says, but Nick doesn't care, and then just takes to calling her "Gimpy Garsha" instead. And he still won't go to class, so end of the year comes and now he's failing.

He has one chance to pass gym and make it to eleventh grade:

He has to write a paper on the history of physical education in America.

And he has less than a week to do it.

One page for every day missed, so—nineteen pages.

Nick is, um, not the king of focus. If this were the present day, he'd be called ADHD and maybe given an IEP to help—but in 1996, sure, they call him ADD, but it's mostly an insult, and there's no help to go along with it. And the paper they're asking him to write, it's not exactly a *scintillating* topic.

So, he'll fail. He won't be able to pull it together.

But all it takes is two words, uttered by Hamish:

"The Covenant."

They know what it means. They're a crew. All for one, one for all, united we stand, divided we fall, nobody gets left behind, when you're a Jet you're a Jet all the way, word is bond. Or what's the one from *The Outsiders*?

If we don't have each other, we don't have anything.

They have his back, just like he and the others had Hamish's.

They write his paper for him. All of them. It doesn't have to be great. It doesn't even really have to be *good*. It just has to be *okay enough* for him to fucking graduate. All of them hang at the library all day the weekend before the end of the school year—instead of, you know, going to parties and all that. They do enough research on the history of physical education in America that they cobble together nineteen pages of purely functional mediocrity on the subject.

Sure, they grouse sometimes. They bitch about how *it'd sure be great if Nick had his shit together enough to do this himself*. But he doesn't, and they know that, and it is what it is. So they do the work. They get it done.

And Nick makes it to eleventh grade.

Eleventh grade, 1996–1997.

The Covenant comes up more and more that next year. Owen's father, angry about something that isn't Owen, takes it out on his son by denying him a day at Dorney, the amusement park, and instead makes him stay home and dig up a busted septic pipe in the back yard, one that's been busted for months, but he's decided now, *now* is the time it needs to be fixed, and so Owen does it, and it's brutal miserable work, made all the more miserable by the fact his friends are off having fun at Dorney Park. Except they're not. They show up. They bring their own *shovels*, for fuck's sake. They help him dig, standing around in gray water waste seeping up in the yard. Because: *the Covenant*.

Lauren wants to take a digital art and programming class at the local community college, but her mom isn't ever around, and Laur doesn't have a car, or money, or any of what she needs. But together, her friends do. They pool the cash. They take shifts driving her to class. It's six weeks, three days a week, after school. They get it done. That's the Covenant.

The only one who never invokes it for himself, who never really benefits, is Matty. He says, "I'll use it someday, I'm sure, but for now, I got what I need." And that's enough for them if it's enough for him.

It becomes a shorthand, those two words. Not just *I need you*. But maybe *I need to hear something nice*. Or *I need the truth from you right now*. Or even *Hey, you're pushing too hard, you're actually upsetting me, I need you to dial it down*.

That is, to them, the Covenant.

21

Matty Says the Words

"Not how the Covenant works, *bro*."

That sentence, an indictment, still hanging in the air like something altogether more acrid than the campfire smoke. A bitter, burning tang.

Something had gone wrong between her and Matty. It was plain to see that now. This wasn't just a fight. This was, to Owen, something fundamental. And Matty didn't like it. Didn't like—what, exactly? Owen didn't know. He could tell only that Matty was bothered by something—something had challenged him, had set him off his perfect axis, and now he was spinning wildly. It was strange to see.

Good, he thought.

Followed up by: *Fuck you, Owen, these are your friends.*

No one else said anything. The campfire crackled—the only response.

"Fine," Matty said, laughing it off at first, but then the reiteration of that word came with a harder, sharper edge: "*Fine.* Figures, right? Time comes I want to call on the Covenant, I don't get to? Whatever. I don't need it. I don't need you. You guys don't want to come with me, don't come with me. But no one can stop me. I'm going to go out there. I'm gonna climb those creepy-ass steps. And then I'm going to jump off them, into the dark. If I'm not allowed to invoke the Covenant, then I'll get you the old-fashioned way. I dare you. I fucking *dare* you." He grabbed up a flashlight and gave it a baton twirl. "You coming? Or are you all cowards?"

Matty didn't wait for their answer. He marched off into the woods. Silence spread in his wake.

"He seems fuckin' serious," Hamish said finally, a throaty chuckle in his voice that was half amusement, half worry. "Maybe we should listen. It's Matty, guys. It's *Matty*. If he wants to use the Covenant like that..."

"*Welp*," Nick said, standing up. "I won't be suckered in by his Covenant bullshit, but I am definitely vulnerable to a man telling me I'm a pussy if I don't do a dare, so I'm going with him. Follow the bouncing flashlight, I go."

He started to wend his way around the tents and the campfire.

"No," Lauren said, abruptly. "Matty's right. He never calls upon the Covenant for himself, so if he wants this to be that, let him. It must be important to him, and we *do* things that are important to one another." She said it like it was an obligation—something she had to do, even if she didn't want to.

She got to her feet, joining Nick. But as he and then Hamish went past her, she just stood there, staring again into the fire. Lauren put her hand out in front of her face, as if to feel the warmth of the flames—but it was like she was entranced by her hand. Slowly, she moved it toward the fire. Closer. Closer—

Owen got up and gently caught her wrist.

"You okay?" he asked her.

She seemed startled by the question. Or by his presence entirely.

"Y—yeah. Totally."

He didn't want to ask, but he asked anyway: "Is... Matty okay?"

"How the fuck should I know?"

She yanked her wrist from his grip. And with that, Lauren spun heel to toe and marched off into the woods.

Leaving Owen alone.

He didn't want to go into the dark. But he didn't want to be alone, either. So he did what he always did: He followed after.

22

The Trip

Lauren left the fire behind, a fire in which she saw her future—a bright unfuckwithable blaze forward, an effulgent laser, a bright beam burning everything ahead of it into cinder, where she could be anything and do anything and no one could stop her. Like Matty said: *I don't need you. You guys don't want to come with me, don't come with me.* She'd really done a number on him, hadn't she? She tried to imagine it: Matty, having some vision of what it would be like to be with her, to finally have them as girlfriend-boyfriend. But along she comes and tries to get him to do, *gasp,* drugs, bad drugs, your brain as a fried egg, your mind as a glass of OJ knocked off the kitchen table, and Golden Boy Matty doesn't like that. He's disappointed in her. *But maybe in himself, too,* she thought. Maybe that was just her fantasy interpretation. Still. It felt good. It felt right.

She stepped deeper into the forest, which throbbed around her like a shadow with its own dark heartbeat. The trees bent away from her as she walked. She could see Matty's flashlight dancing ahead, his own mighty light with crystalline spires firing off it like searing arcs from a Fourth of July sparkler scorching lines into the night. And beyond him, she could *feel* it as much as she could see it—

The staircase. Black and made of night's own bones.

Lauren cackled madly, nearly weeping as she picked up the pace. Owen called to her, but she chose not to listen.

Here was the thing about dropping acid, at least with Lauren: It wasn't like they said, and that was why she loved it. All the movies and all the stories had it where you ate the acid and next thing you know, your world was melting and you either took a ride on some fucking rainbow unicorn bullshit *or* you woke up covered in blood and found your family dead because you got so high you thought they were all bowls of Jell-O and that knife in your hand was a spoon. It was all the stupid shit Matty was afraid of—that he'd take it, and it would break him.

It would. Break him, that was to say. Just not the way he thought.

To Lauren, acid was a slow hill to climb—about an hour in, you spent a little while feeling a bit queasy, and then you got really, really awake. Only *then* the actual *acid* part of the acid started, and though she knew they called it "acid" because it was lysergic acid diethylamide, to her the name was apt in a different way. It scoured you. Burned you clean of a lot of bullshit, like scrubbing the barnacles off the boat hull that was your mind. Yeah, sure, okay, you hallucinated—trails of light off your fingertips, a Celtic knot tapestry on your friend's wall turning and twisting like a snake, gnomes hiding in the grass, various lattices and cobwebs overlaid across the world as if you were seeing through some shared illusion and into the programming that built reality. It was what it did to *your* programming, though, that Lauren loved the most when it came to dropping acid—

See, everybody's own personal programming got fucked up all too easily. Other people hacked your software, inserting their own dangerous code. Bad ideas, insults, lies, all of them your brain was in danger of accepting and plugging into its own program. But acid? Acid deleted a lot of that. It went through and rearranged your own brain. Tied emotions together you didn't realize needed to be tied. It shoved aside the intrusive code and brought your own native programming back together—no more bugs or errors. It was like defragging a hard drive. Your brain and all its thoughts and all its feelings were suddenly better organized. More efficient. After dropping acid, Lauren always felt like she'd been... upgraded. Broken down and built back up. Clearer, cleaner, brighter, huzzah.

That was acid, for her.

Usually.

Tonight, though—

Tonight she'd taken two.

She'd never taken two. They were dosed for one—a good dose, an average *normal person* dose. But two of them. This was, in the parlance, a *heroic dose.*

It terrified her.

Excited her, too.

Because who knew what would happen now?

23

Ascent, Descent, and Memory

This is what Lauren would remember about that night:
She was going to do it. She was going to go up the staircase with Matty, and whether this was to join him or spite him, she didn't yet know. No matter what, she was better than him, and like the song sang, *Anything you can do I can do better.*

But then, the staircase loomed large in her vision, and also in her mind, as if it had gone beyond the real and had entered her skull—like a tumor pulsing there in the meat of her mind. It was tall and black and made of shining bones, bones of copper and bronze, bones of polished wood. She didn't know where her friends were. (*They're here*, a small voice told her, a voice she could not trust.) All she could care about was the stairs, and as she watched them, they seemed to grow before her, extending both up and out and toward her like an unfurling tongue slick with eager spit, the air stinking of bad breath and rancid oranges—the stairs went up, not a stairway to Heaven but somehow up and into Hell, as if they were beneath that demonic kingdom, digging their way into its belly like a sharp stone, and here she knew, she *knew* this was just a bad trip, none of this was real, and this was like the first time she'd dropped acid, when she'd been happily watching the fleur-de-lis of old wallpaper bloom like living flowers, meanwhile chewing her thumbnail and the skin around it, and suddenly she realized, *I've gone too far, I've bitten the nail off, the whole tip of the thumb, my thumb is gone, and I am chewing it, eating it, I've become Owen*—but the guy who sold her the acid, he said, *You start* to have a bad trip, all you gotta do is remember one thing: "I'm on drugs." And so she'd written it on an index card then, and looked at it, and that's what it said in big capital letters, "YOU ARE ON DRUGS, DUMBASS," and she looked at her thumb and it was fine, all there, not even a spot of blood. And now, seeing the staircase loom larger and meaner and darker, she repeated that to herself in a small whisper: "You're on drugs, you're on drugs, you're on fucking drugs, you're in drugs, you *are* drugs"—shit, things were *unspooling*, and now something else was here with them. Hell made manifest. Hell as a structure. Hell with corners and walls, Hell with hands, Hell with wallpaper and doorways and shuttered windows, the latticework of that demonic architecture constructing itself piece by piece, like invisible hands making, fuck, what were those old toys, those old fucking toys her mom had in the garage—Tinkertoys, right, right, Lucifer's own Tinkertoys, constructing themselves in front of her. *You're on drugs, drugs, you're on acid, you dropped acid, you dropped, dropped, dropping—*

And then Matty was at the top, and he was happy, and Owen was asking him not to go, not to jump, and Nick and Hamish were just fucking around, barely watching any of it, and she saw the black tunnel open up at the top of the steps, a hole in everything, a hole in the universe, and she tried screaming the words, *Do none of you see this?* but it came out small, the squeaked chatter of a panicked vole, "*do-none-of-you-see-this,*" spit on her lips, orange oil in the air, smoke from somewhere—and she cried out to Matty but it was late, too late, too too late—

This is what Owen would remember:

When he walked up out of the woods, toward the staircase, he followed Lauren. He tried talking to her as they went, but she just laughed like she'd heard a joke from someone who wasn't there, and then she traipsed on ahead. When they got there, to the stairs, Matty was already on the second step. Doing a kind of Gene Kelly *Singin' in the Rain* bit, la-dee-dah, dancing up one step at a time. Asking, "Who's gonna do it? Who's coming with me? Hamish? Nick?" But the two of them were monkeying around, not paying attention. And Lauren—she was suddenly goggling at the staircase, her jaw slackened, and Owen thought, *She's on drugs, shit.* She loved dropping acid when she could get it. It hit him then: Maybe that's what she and Matty were fighting about?

It was then that Matty turned to Owen—

"Owen. Buddy. C'mon. Let's climb the creepy stairs."

Beneath Matty's feet, the floorboards groaned like a child in pain.

Owen's mind raced. *Everyone thinks I'm a coward. I am a coward. I'm always scared about everything. They're just steps. Just a staircase. Creepy, sure, but that's all in my head. I can do this.*

Matty didn't even need to say *I dare you.*

Owen remembered stepping up there onto the first step.

How cold the banister felt under his hand.

How the wooden step seemed to sag at first—and then rebound, as if it was lifting him up, encouraging him to *climb, climb, climb.*

The air around him seemed to go still.

Matty kept climbing.

Owen took a few more steps.

The banister, colder. The stairs, almost with a cradle's rock now, trying to urge him forward and upward.

Lauren, behind him, mumbling something. Babbling.

Hamish and Nick, still on the ground, grabbing each other's necks, sack-tapping each other, howling with laughter and fake outrage.

Matty, up there, reversing his way up the steps, looking backward at Owen, grinning the way only Matty did: a big toothy smile, happy because his life was excellent, happy because he was good at nearly everything he did, happy because his future was presented to him like a delicious buffet of food with all the best cuts of meat and tastiest treats—and as he waved Owen up, as he stepped toward the topmost step of the staircase, Owen thought bitterly, cruelly, *You may be smiling, dude, you may have it all, but I don't think you have Lauren.* Matty must've hurt her, rejected her, that's what Owen told himself.

And for a moment, he felt superior. He felt supreme. It felt right and righteous to be angry toward Matty. *Must be nice to be you, you prick,* he thought coldly.

Even as Matty said to him: "See, I knew you could do it, Owen."

And that's when the world opened up behind Matty.

Owen smelled a sharp exhalation of must and mold, mingled with the tang of citrus oil, like the stuff his mother used to clean their dinner table. And beneath it all, the smell of rot. He was sure he saw something there—a shuddering space, a hallway, a room, something. A contained space. Flickering light like from a lamp with a bad plug. And then Matty turned to jump and—

In that one moment, Owen knew he should tell him not to jump. Matty did not see what was there, but Owen did—and he knew he should scream and shout and try his very hardest to get Matty not to jump—

But he couldn't get the words out.

They stuck in his throat.

(Maybe because he wanted them to.)

And then, Matty jumped—

There was a feeling like a silent thunderclap. Something that reverberated without sound, that made Owen's eyes water and his knees go weak.

Matty went through that strange open space, into the room beyond, the room that could not exist, and then—

He's gone.

Those words came out of Owen then, quiet the first time, louder the next—"He's gone!" And only then did the others start to see. There was laughter and incredulity. It was just a joke, they thought. Something insane. Hamish shook his head wondering how Matty pulled it off, walking around to the other side of the steps to see where Matty had landed, the beam of Hamish's flashlight searching, searching. Lauren and Nick came up behind Owen, urging him to hurry up the stairs, to see where Matty went—yelling at him to go, go, go, move, *move,* where the fuck did Matty go, Owen what happened, Owen *move* for fuck's sake, move—but Owen felt more scared than he'd ever felt in his life.

His feet were rooted to the spot. The staircase was inside his mind suddenly, growing steps, wooden slats appearing out of nowhere and unfolding like a deranged child's toys, like the staircase was more than just this place in the woods—like it was a thought in his head he couldn't pry loose, a terrible thought growing and growing, a cancer. It wanted him. It wanted them all. He didn't want to be swallowed up by the staircase. By the darkness. By the rooms beyond. He started to crumple, started to weep. Knees weak. Melting. Nick tried shoving him. But he wouldn't budge. At the top of the steps, the other room—the hallway, if it was that—was gone now. All that remained was the slashing spear of light from Hamish's flashlight below. Owen finally cried out, turning around and running back down the stairs. He tumbled into the trees. Vomit came up out of him, a hot geyser of acid, the raw ruin of a whiskey burn searing him like fire. And in its wake—in the emptiness that followed swiftly after—he felt something far worse: guilt. The whiskey went out. The shame flooded in. *I could've stopped him.*

I wanted him to jump.

The world shuddered. Matty was gone. And soon, the staircase was gone, too. As if it, and Matty, had never existed in the first place.

24

The Only Way Through Is Out

Now.

This new staircase stood there. Waiting silently. *Patiently.* Nick stood near the first step, but not on it, his arms spread wide, a fire in his eyes. Vigor and regret and righteousness burning off him like embers flung from a campfire.

"The Covenant," he said, with some finality.

Owen wiped vomit from his mouth with the back of his arm.

"No campsite," Hamish said again. "Jesus, Nick. What the fuck."

"No cancer, either, I bet," Owen realized out loud.

Nick just shook his head. No apology in his eyes.

Hamish started pacing. Leaves and sticks snapping under his feet. "Fuck. Fuck. *Fuck.* Nick, you fuck. You can't—you *shouldn't*—"

"I can and I did!" Nick screamed, his voice ragged. Quieter now, he said: "Matty called on us to come with him that night. He said it, he invoked our bond, the Covenant, in calling us to that staircase. And *we didn't go*. We fucked around while our friend went up those steps and disappeared. And in the years after? Did we look for him? Did we stay together, work together, *find him together*? As friends? As family? No. We didn't. We didn't do shit except fall apart and fuck off. But now here's our chance. I found this staircase. And I got us all together, here, today." He paused, looked to each of them, his stare deliberate, as if he was marking them. "The Covenant. The Covenant! *The fucking Covenant.*"

"Fuck," Hamish said, face buried in his hands. "We don't even know if that's how we lost Matty. We don't *know* that. We were young, Nick, we didn't know shit, maybe we, we, we . . . *misremembered* it—"

"And it's not—that's not the same staircase," Owen said. "The staircase from Highchair—that one's gone. This one's different, Nick. Different staircase, different location, how do you even know—"

But it was Lore who answered.

Lore, who hadn't said anything up until this:

"Only one way to find out."

No.

She hard-charged to the steps—

No!

Owen reached for her, but she was fast, too fast. Slipping away from him.

Already at the steps.

"Lore!"

One foot on—

Wham.

The whole staircase shook.

With movement from her? Or because it was eager, because it was hungry?

"*Lore!*"

Second step, third, fourth—

No, no, NO—

Owen called after her, yelling her name again and again.

"Fuck!" Hamish yelled.

Nick clapped and cheered, watching her intently—

She reached the top step—

And was gone.

Owen made a sound—a keening gasp of shock. "No, no, no. What the—no. Lore. Christ, Lore—" He started to walk to the side of the staircase, heading toward the back of it to see where she'd landed, because she fell, right? She jumped off the back and fell, that's what obviously happened, and she might've been hurt. But Nick stopped him. Blocked him. "Nick, *move*—"

Nick grabbed Owen's shoulders, gripping the collarbones so hard it was like he was using them as handlebars. "Clock's ticking. Time's almost up. I'm going. You don't have to care about Matty, but now Lore's gone, too. Can you live with that? I can't. Make your choice, Zuikas. I choose the Covenant."

And then Nick hopped onto the first step—

"*Nick,*" Hamish said, hands into fists, shaking the air like it was a screaming baby. But it was too late—up the steps he went, taking them two at a time. "Nick!"

Nick bellowed it one last time—

"Remember the Covenant!"

And then he jumped—

Off the step—

Into nothing—

And he, too, was gone.

Owen paced. "Jesus. Shit. Jesus. Hamish—"

But Hamish stood quietly at the base of the steps. Looking up, like a kid who'd lost his mother at a grocery store. Shattered. Searching. *Despairing.*

"Hamish, no—"

Hamish, still looking up, said quietly, maybe to Owen, maybe to the others, maybe to the staircase itself:

"We lost more than just Matty that day."

And then he started to walk up the steps.

One step after the other. Slow steps, as if he wasn't sure.

Owen begged him. "C'mon, we can talk about this, Hamish. *Hamish.*" Tears crawled down Owen's cheeks as Hamish ascended the stairs.

Now at the top, Hamish didn't jump so much as he took a deep breath and stepped forward. A big, wide step—a long stride to nowhere. The world swallowed him up. One moment, there was Hamish. And in the next? No one. As though he'd never even existed.

The air at the top of the staircase shimmered, like heat waves leaving a house in winter, the door open, the warmth stolen into the cold.

Make your choice, Zuikas.

Remember the Covenant.

The staircase shuddered. He felt the gentle tremble of the ground.

The top of the staircase pulsated.

I can't do it.

I'm too scared.

They're gone and I'm alone and—

25

See, I Knew You Could Do It

Owen gave up, gave in, and climbed the stairs. One step at a time. It was all he could do. It pulled at him. His friends were gone. The Covenant was gone, too. Unless. Maybe. *Maybe.*

At the top, now.

He felt the world shudder.

The darkness, shimmer.

He stepped off the top step.

And then he was gone, just like the others.

Gone from here, at least.

But not from there.

26

Where's There, Mon Frère?

The crew never understood why Lore hated being at home as a kid. They saw that her mother was always either at work or out with some boyfriend, and they thought, *How excellent that must be.* It must be pure, unmitigated freedom, they thought—no oppressive parents, no stupid rules, no vegetables to eat. Microwave some bagel bites, watch some *Judge Judy*, hell, kick back with something from Mom's never-actually-locked liquor cabinet. Smoke weed, jill off, look through the medicine cabinet and take whatever was in there.

You basically own the place, Nick said. Hamish wanted to get high in every room. Matty said, *Wait, so nobody's breathing down your neck? Nobody's telling you to get your homework done or study for this or practice for that? It's Heaven, Laur!* Even Owen didn't get it, not really. *It's better than my house,* he told her once, with a half-hearted shrug, and she of course took that as a challenge, as competition, because what wasn't?

But what none of them ever understood was the feeling of that house.

Of being alone, when you weren't supposed to be.

The silence always felt loud. The air always felt empty and cold, like you were stranded on another world, with no one coming to get you. It wasn't just that it was lonely—it was that she always felt like the last person alive.

And the memory of that house—of being alone and lonely and crushed by an empty world—was the same thing she felt upon transitioning from *there* to *here*.

Where, then, was here?

Lore stepped off the staircase—

Then the smell of must and dust and mold—

Then a crinkling crackle in the deep of her ear forcing its way through her eustachian tubes, pushing so hard they might just burst—

The wave of emptiness hit her, pressed in on every inch of her, grew inside her like a widening, deepening hole—

And finally, a sharp, involuntary breath in—

Lore held that breath deep.

She stood still. Flexed her fingers, as if to make sure they were still there, and attached. Wiggled her toes, too, in her boots. Then she felt her face, just to make sure—well, she had no idea why it wouldn't be there, or why her fingers and toes would not be attached, but everything was where it was supposed to be. Except, she supposed, her entire body.

Because her body was not in the woods.

Lore stared ahead at a hallway.

At the end, a door. And another door to her left.

Along the right, a long stretch of wall papered with a menagerie pattern in faded greens and blues—she spied peacocks and hares and butterflies, and in other places pairs of eyes staring out from behind dark foliage. The paper peeled in places, curling in strips like leprotic skin. Patches darkened with water stains.

At the top, someone had crudely carved a message in erratic slashes of wallpaper: THIS PLACE HATES YOU.

A chill clawed its way up from her feet, a centipede winding its way toward her scalp.

She tried to remain present, to *focus* on what had happened and where she was, but a question slipped through—

Why did you do it?

Why did you go up those steps?

To find Matty, she told herself.

Half true, she knew. Half a lie, though, too.

Focus! she chided herself. *Where are you, Lore? Look around.*

Okay. The floor beneath her was dusty, creaky wood. Chipped and scratched, as if by the unkempt claws of a big dog. *Or wolf,* she thought.

Above her, a flush-mount light fixture of cracked, dirty glass, held in place by a mount of leaves and vines of brass. Of the three bulbs inside, one was burned out, and one flickered incessantly, ticking and clicking with the sound of a moth tapping against a window. *Tick tick. Flit. Buzz.*

The door straight ahead of her and the door next to her were both made of wood stained dark, like the deck of an old ship soaked with seawater and blood. Simple metal doorknob. Each looked old, older than the knobs that had replaced whatever had been there first.

The door next to her had an additional detail that summoned in her a strange surge of nostalgia—

Three cartoony scratch-n-sniff stickers sat in the center of the door. Roughly the height of a child, eight or nine years old. One a slice of watermelon, one a lawn mower, the third what she thought at first was an inflated pink balloon but then realized, no, was a blown bubble, like from bubble gum. Each had a goofy face, bucktoothed and goggle-eyed. Lore took a thumbnail and scratched it across all three, *kkkt, kkkt, kkkkkt,* and then stooped to sniff—

The smell of rot hit her. A roadkill dead meat smell somehow intermingling with the pickled odor of an old folks' home—*crushed squirrel, stale pissy diapers, the sourness of age.* And as if to make it somehow worse: a whiff of bubble gum just after.

Lore stepped backward, suppressing a gag.

The wave of nostalgia that had gone through her died fast, replaced with the returning sensation of being deeply, cosmically alone.

"Fuck," she said under her breath, cupping her hand over her mouth.

She took a step back, suddenly realizing—

The stairs—

I'm going to fall—

But there were no stairs behind her.

The staircase was gone. All that waited behind her was a small wooden door raised from floor level. Just a dumbwaiter. Like in an old house.

She opened it up. More must, dust, mold smell—and that commingling of rot. Lore quickly closed it. *Where am I? This hallway doesn't make any sense.* It didn't seem to go from anywhere to anywhere. It was a rectangular space in three dimensions with two doors—three, if you counted the dumbwaiter.

Instinctually, she reached for her phone—newest iPhone, a Pro Max model. It had power but no signal. She went to the settings, looking for any Wi-Fi signal or Bluetooth. There was nothing. *"Fuck,"* she said again, then slid the phone into her back pocket. As she did so—

Her skin prickled.

Behind her, she felt someone coming up behind her—that sense of presence, of shape, of weight, plus the shifting of floorboards—the feeling that they were right behind her, about to breathe on the back of her neck—

Lore turned, found no one there. A phantom of stirred air.

"Matty?" she asked, quietly at first, then louder as she called out his name: "Matty!" It felt insane, that somehow he'd be here, in this—what, house? It looked like a house. What the fuck was this? How did she get here? *I teleported. I'm dead. I'm a ghost. I'm hallucinating. I'm dreaming. In a coma. This is VR.* Her brain flipped through the options like fingers flicking through vinyl at the record store.

And then, there it was again:

The feeling, the *certainty*, of someone standing behind her. Now, since she had turned around, from the other side.

Lore spun around—

And this time found that she was not alone.

She cried out in surprise—

At Nick.

Nick, who stood in the middle of the hallway, where she had appeared.

He faced the door, and turned toward her. "Lore?" he asked, his voice uncharacteristically small.

"Nick," she said, the desperation in her voice radiating like a lighthouse beacon. Being here, even for the few moments between then and now, felt crushing, like she was in the cold void of space and couldn't get air. Now someone else here felt like a lifeline. Nick, her improbable savior.

She strode toward him and threw her arms around him.

Awkwardly, he hugged her back, hard.

"Where the fuck are we?" he asked her, his chin digging into her shoulder. "Is this somebody's house?"

Lore didn't know how to answer that question. But she felt it again—a fresh disturbance of the world around them, the feeling of her sinuses swelling as if a storm were brewing somewhere—

Hamish crashed right into them, almost knocking them over.

And he, to her shock, was not the last to come through.

27

The Lowdown

It was Lore who caught Owen as he stepped off the staircase and into the hallway. She was quick to steady him so he didn't fall. Her hands on his shoulders, she told him what was happening calmly, but quickly: "We seem to be in a house. Or a hallway, at least. I have no idea where. The forest is gone. So are the stairs. We're all here. Our phones do not work yet, no signal." A pause. "You okay?"

Owen exhaled and blinked.

"Yeah," he said. And he was. Lore's concision actually helped. Part of him wanted to question why she was being nice to him—maybe she appreciated him following after her. Or maybe these were just extraordinary circumstances.

Hamish leaned against the wall, mumbling to himself. Nick stood at the far end of the hallway, staring at a door. He touched the doorknob, not yet turning it.

"I want to open it," Nick said, agitated. Impatient.

"*No*," Lore said. "Just . . . wait. This place isn't right."

Owen felt it. She was right. The air made him feel ill. Like there was a white noise frequency all around them. His head felt strange, too. That feeling of being watched—someone's gaze boring its way into the back of your skull.

Lore met Owen's gaze one more time, conveying what he felt was the psychic message of *You're okay,* one last time. A curt nod, then she headed toward Nick to ease him away from the door.

Owen, meanwhile, walked to Hamish.

"This is fucked," Owen said. He tried to summon some courage. "You good?"

"Yeah, yeah, yeah," Hamish said, except, no, he was not good.

"We'll be all right."

"We made our choice." Said as if Hamish were trying to convince himself that it was both true and that it was the right thing. "We're here now."

"We are, yeah."

Hamish craned his head to look up at Owen.

"I'm surprised you came."

"Not more surprised than I am."

"You shoulda stayed. I'm sorry."

Owen's gaze drifted upward, to the message slashed into the wallpaper—

THIS PLACE HATES YOU.

"Fucked up, right?" Hamish asked, standing just beneath it.

"Yeah."

His brain whispered that phrase back at him a few more times—

This place hates you . . .

This place hates you . . .

This place hates you . . .

"Hello?" Hamish yelled suddenly, a nervous edge to his voice. "Anybody home?" Quieter now: "Somebody's gotta fucking be here. Right? Shit."

Nick and Lore both shushed him. "Christ, Ham," Nick said.

"Sorry."

The four of them met in the middle of the hallway.

"I guess let's split up—" Nick started to say.

"No," Lore said, firmly. "We do not split up. Not yet. Not until we know what we're dealing with here. This doesn't feel right."

"Jeez, what doesn't feel right?" Hamish asked sarcastically. "It's totally normal to walk up a set of steps in the middle of the woods and appear in some weird fucking hallway with some weird fucking message."

Nick threw up his hands. "We just need to pick a door and go through it. What's the big fucking deal? Let's move."

"Lore's right," Owen said. He felt it, too. Something in the air. Something in the pit of his stomach. Turning over and over again. Restless and sick. For a moment, he thought he heard something: voices, mumbling, murmuring. But then it was gone again. "We should stick together. Horror movie rules."

"Besides," Lore added, "Matty split up and we didn't go with him, and look what happened then. We need to stick tight."

"Pick a door, then," Nick said.

And then, as they all stood around, trying to think their way through a course of action—

A phone rang.

28

Answer Me

The sound of the ringing phone came from the door closest to them. Not the one at the end of the hall—but the one across from the message.

No, Owen thought. *Not a message. A* warning.

He looked at it again, and in the garden menagerie art of the wallpaper, he blinked and out of the corner of his eye was *sure* something moved—something in, or on, the wallpaper. A shifting of shadow, an adjustment of space. Fingers wrapping around the filigree of vine and leaf. Eyes watching. But when he blinked again, nothing moved. All was still.

A shudder danced over his neck, like a hand hovering just above the skin.

"It's coming from in here," Lore said, pointing to and pressing her ear against a door. A door, Owen noted, with three faded cartoon stickers in its center.

The door to a kid's room, Owen thought.

Ring, ring.

Ring, ring.

Two rings at a time. Tinny and sharp.

"Open the door," Nick said, impatient.

Lore reached for the knob, but Hamish caught her hand.

"What if we shouldn't?" he asked them.

"Why?" Nick asked.

"Could be some kinda . . . trap."

"A trap? It's not D&D. It's not a dungeon. It's a room. There's a phone ringing. Someone might be on the other end of it, and we can ask for help. Or we can call someone—Jesus, use your head."

Lore nodded. "We can't just stay out here. We open the door."

So that's what she did. She turned the knob—

And let it drift open. No creepy creak. Just a silent *whoosh*.

With that, they stepped into—

Instant vibe: 1990s teen girl bedroom. Owen knew, and liked, that gender expression didn't necessarily mean this was one thing over the other, but in the nineties, that spectrum was much narrower, and to him, this felt very much like a girl's room—forgotten, wrecked, lost, ruined. Spice Girls and TLC posters, both pocked with dark mold at the corners. Queen-sized bed with fuzzy peach comforter and heart-shaped pillows. A white corner desk held an ancient desktop computer with a chunky CRT monitor on it—the glass of the monster cracked, the desktop tower on the floor having fallen over in a tangle of its wires, like a soldier who'd died in a pile of his own guts. Dolphin lamp, chipped. Christmas lights strung up along the room's edges—on and sparkling, not in a steady pattern but rather in an erratic flicker with no rhyme or reason to it. And there, on the bed:

A plastic clamshell phone, the kind that showed off its neon innards.

He had had a phone like that once. Used to talk to Lore on it for hours. Which his father hated. Of course.

This phone was off its cradle, a coil of phone cord connecting the two.

And yet, even off its cradle—

It still rang.

Ring, ring.

Ring, ring.

"Don't answer it," Hamish said.

"We have to answer it," Lore said.

This place hates you, Owen's brain told him.

Hamish sniffled, blinking back tears. "It makes me sick. Something's wrong here, and I don't think any of us should answer it."

That feeling in Owen's gut deepened, too. Now it was a bundle of worms, a wad of them slithering all over one another, pushing, pushing, crawling through his middle like it was just dirt. Owen nodded and said, "Hamish might be right."

"Jesus," Nick said. "*I'll* answer it—"

But Lore was already stepping forward and reaching for the phone.

She picked it up, still holding the receiver out in front of her—

It stopped ringing.

They all shared disconcerted looks. Owen gave her a slight nod—because at this point, *might as well, right?* She nodded back.

And then brought the phone to her ear.

"Hello?" she said into it.

Owen did not hear what was said on the other end.

But he knew what he saw.

He saw Lore's eyes go wider. Her mouth opened just a little and a small sound came out: an ill-stifled whimper. "What? What are you saying? Talk to me. *I can't hear you.* I can't—" A spike of shrill sound, like a machine screaming, erupted abruptly from the phone's receiver, and Lore flinched away from it and threw the phone to the bed. She held her hand over her ear, wincing.

Owen raced over to her. "You okay?"

Lore backed away from the bed—and by proxy, the phone—and pressed her back against the TLC poster, then slid down the wall till she was sitting on the floor. She stared off at nothing, still holding and rubbing her ear.

Nick loomed over her. "What was it?"

She shook her head.

"*Lore,*" he repeated, snapping his fingers. "Who was on the phone?"

"It was him," she said, finally, in a small voice.

29

Mister Mumbles

The first time Lore and Matty slept together, 1998, eleventh grade, was in her bed, in her house, because nobody was ever home and nobody cared what she did.

She hated bringing anybody to her house. It felt embarrassing, though she didn't know why, not exactly.

But Matty's parents? They didn't like her. Thought she was weird. They didn't dig any of Matty's friends, actually—Matty was an achiever, on the fast track to an excellent life, and to them, they were just the mud he was stuck in.

As such, if they wanted to fuck, it was her house or no house.

It wasn't their first time having sex—just their first time with each other.

It wasn't great.

And it was also *amazing*.

Because two competing things can be true at the same time.

He wasn't good at sex, but he was soft and slow in a way that surprised her for such a go-getter. And she sucked in bed, too, but she was aggressive, eager, nearly feral—and somehow, that combination worked.

And because they had the time and the space to be with each other and to relax afterward, they passed out in a tangle of sweaty limbs. That's when she learned how Matty talked in his sleep. Little mumbles and murmurs, a soft run-on babble-gush sound punctuated by real words—a sound at the time she thought was funny and sweet. Because it humbled him in a way. It made Matty seem like a regular messy human instead of the sports-grades-theater god, the big boisterous monumental straight-A slate of a human being so many people thought he was. It made him smaller. And because of that, more precious.

She had loved that sound once.

Would've given anything to hear it again, or so she thought.

But then she picked up that see-through plastic phone and put it to her ear—

And that is who she heard on the other end.

Matty.

Mumbling. Murmuring.

Soft run-on babble-gush.

His voice was small again. So small he seemed to be lost—a mouse lost in a tangle of pipe.

Humm mm ff Lore nnnuh mmm lmmm where are you wuhh help mm . . .

She panicked, tried telling him she couldn't hear him, couldn't *understand* him, wanted to know where he was—

And then a rusty screwdriver of raw static drove itself into her ear.

An ear that was still ringing, the shrill drill bit of tinnitus spinning in the deep of her skull. Owen was next to her now, rubbing her shoulder, and it felt awful to have him that close, like he was encroaching upon her, smothering her—and Nick, too, standing there, asking her, *Who was it who was it,* snapping his fingers at her like she was a dog. She spasmed away from Owen and then barked at Nick:

"It was him. It was *Matty*. I couldn't totally hear him, but it was him and—" Her words dissolved under the whining threat of tears, so she bit her teeth and buckled down to swallow those feelings. Firmly, she said: "It was him. He sounded lost. Distant. But he's here, somewhere." *And we can find him.*

Nick, eager now, leaning forward like a cat ready to pounce: "Matty? You *heard* him? You heard *Matty*. This is good. This is so fucking good. It's fucking *great*—" He slapped Owen on the shoulder. "Right, Zuikas? Fucking *great*."

"Fucking great," Owen repeated, but to Lore's ear, his heart wasn't in it, not at all, and she wondered: *Did he come here to find Matty?*

Or did he come here to chase me?

But then she saw Owen's gaze drift away from her, past Nick—

To Hamish.

Hamish, who was not with them, but rather at the door where they came in.

"Hamish?" Owen called to him.

"Guys?" Hamish said. "Did anybody close the door behind them when they came in here? Because—" He did his hands in a lazy game show reveal: The door was, in fact, closed. Painted yellow on this side. Actually...

Owen stood.

"It's not the same door," he said.

"What? Fuck you," Nick said, turning to look.

"It's not. See? The door we opened—it was wood, old wood, dark wood. This is—it's different, cheaper—"

Hamish clarified, numbly: "It's a traditional six-panel medium-density fiberboard door, barebones shit, same kinda door you'll find in half the middle-class homes of America." He put his hand on it, then curled his fingers into a fist and knocked softly a few times. Lore flinched, half expecting a knock back. But none came. "So you're right. Literally not the same door."

At that, Hamish reached for the doorknob.

The door opened.

And Hamish cried out—a ragged bleat of shock and panic.

"What is it?" Nick asked.

But from her vantage point on the floor, Lore could already see what it was that summoned that sound from Hamish, drawing it up like rancid well water—

The hallway they came from?

It was gone.

30

The Diary and the Knife

The four of them now stood in this teen girl's room, on one side of the door, staring across the open space to the *other* side of the door, where once upon a time, there waited a hallway. A hallway they'd been in only minutes before.

And it was now gone.

Instead, they stared across the doorway into what looked like a dining room.

The walls were wood paneled. The table, covered in a plasticky tablecloth decorated in yellow flowers, orange birds, green ferns. A tacky not-really-gold chandelier hung above it, the kind with fake candles and glass bulbs shaped like flames. The chandelier gently swung back and forth, the spiderwebs attached to it swaying and stretching, but not quite breaking. The table was set with paper plates and glassware. On each plate was a piece of yellow cake and festive generic birthday icing. Half eaten. Forks askew. A few flies buzzed above.

Owen felt sick.

Beyond the table, on the far side of the room, next to a bookshelf on one side, a kerosene heater on the other, was another doorway closed by a louvered bifold door, the unfinished wooden slats cracked and crooked. A closet door, maybe.

They all stared, silent for a while. Unsure what to say, or do.

It was Hamish who eventually broke the silence: "That could be my grandmother's dining room. I mean, it's not, it's fucking totally not, I just mean—"

Lore jumped in:

"Late seventies, early eighties vibe. Knickknacks on a shelf in the corner, the cheap tablecloth, the—the wood sconces with mulberry red candles. Not just grandma energy. This is just what people's houses looked like in the seventies and eighties, man. People who would become grandmas one day, I guess."

Owen, frustrated, said: "Who cares whose room it is? It's not a hallway, and more to the point, *not* the hallway we used to enter this bedroom. The house, or whatever this place is? It shifted. *It fucking shifted.*"

This place hates you, this place hates you, this place hates you—

He stuck a thumbnail in his mouth, peeling a crescent off of it.

Nick started to walk through the door.

Hamish put a hand on his chest, hard.

"Dude. Wait."

"I'm just checking it out."

"We need to just stop for a second."

Lore nodded. "Yeah. Okay. Yeah. Hamish is right." Owen felt a twist of petty jealousy: *Oh, sure, he's right, but not me for saying hey let's stop talking about interior design eras for a minute.* "If this place really does shift, then what if it does it while one of us is in *there* and the rest of us are over *here*?"

"But we know Matty isn't in *here*," Nick hissed through his teeth. "And he might be that way. So I want to go that way."

"Nick, c'mon, man," Hamish said. "Let's just—fuck, man, let's just calm down, take a minute, sit down in this, uhh, this girl's bedroom and think. Okay? Can we just stop and think?"

It was hard not to hear the panic vibrating at the edges of Hamish's every word. It contrasted hard with Owen's memory of him. As a kid, Hamish had always been a leaf in a stream—just happy to float wherever the water was taking him. He was the easiest going, a wad of human Silly Putty eager to be molded. Life and time had changed him.

It had changed them all, hadn't it? A small voice inside Owen said, *Not really. You're still the same, Zuikas.*

"Fine. Yeah." Nick shrugged and backed into the bedroom, going over and sitting on the edge of the bed. "Whatever."

Owen sat at the desk.

Lore stood.

Hamish paced.

"I'll start," Lore said, talking it out. "We started in a forest. There was a staircase that was not supposed to be there. We walked up it, and as a result, we all *went* somewhere else. Here. In this ... place, this house, this structure. A hallway that led to this room where a phone was ringing and where I heard our lost friend, Matty, on the phone. And then there was another shift. Right? The hallway is now gone. It's been replaced with a dining room. What else? What am I missing?"

"It's fucked," Hamish said. "It's all fucked, man."

"Very helpful, Ham," Nick said.

"And the rooms don't really match," Nick said. "This room is for a girl in the 1990s. That dining room? Like you said, late seventies, early eighties. The hallway and stairs and shit, with all that wood? I'd say, older, maybe much older."

"Not necessarily," Owen said. "Not everyone has an interior designer make one house look consistent. A couple inherits a house, an old house, they make changes where they can. Different generations inhabit the house, decorate it differently. It's only rich people that have really consistent visions for their houses and have the money to implement those visions, right?"

"Right," Lore said.

He felt a twitter of validation. *Senpai noticed me,* he thought foolishly.

"What else?" she asked.

Hamish offered: "These two rooms shouldn't connect. Nobody is putting a girl's bedroom right off a dining room."

"*And* someone's already been here," Nick said. "That table in there has cake on it. Half eaten. Like a family was in there chowing down and got raptured or some shit."

As the others spoke, Owen looked at the computer lying on its side down near his feet. He leaned over and got it back upright before seeing that it was unplugged. He spied an outlet against the wall—cracked white plastic. Then he looked up. Christmas lights, blinking.

"There's power," he said suddenly. "Electricity."

He plugged in the computer and turned it on.

It started to boot.

"What kind of system is it?" Lore asked.

"It's like a—maybe a first-gen Pentium, by the look of it. A Gateway. Remember those?"

Lore laughed a little. "Yeah, the cow boxes and stuff." She stood up and came over to him, stooping over and watching the screen. A Windows 95 logo booted. "Gateway, Pentium, Win95, the TLC poster, the Spice Girls—"

"So this is a teen girl's bedroom from 1995, '96, something like that."

"Yeah, looks like."

Lore put her hand on his shoulder.

It steadied him. Amazing how easily she could keep him steady—or knock him off his axis in one go. *Don't forget what she did to you,* he reminded himself. At that thought, it was as if she could hear it, as if his bad thought was a short sharp electrical shock—she pulled her hand away suddenly.

In its absence, a strange, almost cold pain. Isolation and loneliness.

Lore reached over him and grabbed a pen and a small pink book. The pen had a wispy end, like the hair of one of those little troll dolls. "Feather pen," she said. "And this is some kind of diary. It's locked, but—"

She wrenched it open, and the lock popped off.

"Settle down, Hulk," Owen said.

Lore shrugged. "You know me. Lore stands for *Lorge*." She started flipping through pages as the computer booted all the way up, took them to a garish teal desktop with big chonky icons. As Lore went through the book, Owen grabbed for the two-button mouse, moved the cursor over the icons.

My Computer, Network Neighborhood, Recycle Bin, Solitaire, Control Panel, System, and so on. "She was a Prodigy kid." Lore, he remembered, used CompuServe. The others, AOL. But Owen, too, used Prodigy as a way to get onto some early version of "online." Though both he and Lore also used dial-up clients to access various BBSes—bulletin board systems, hyperlocal online hubs run by users out of their homes. Lore ran one for a while called Bizarroland BBS. On a lark, he tried clicking it, but when he did, the icon turned to a spray of pixels, like graffiti painted on the wall in Pac-Man's world. "Shit." Then he saw another icon, down in the corner of the screen, hidden away from the others:

oldtimer.jpg

An image file.

His heart crawled up into his throat, lodged itself there.

A pulse beat kicking at the sides of his neck.

Owen clicked the file.

It opened, blank.

But then it started to render, pass after pass, an image refining itself pixel by pixel, layer by layer.

Lore, meanwhile, was chatting about the book. "Typical teen girl squad shit, blah blah blah, she likes this boy, his name is Grady, Grady with hearts all around him, Grady written in cursive, in different colors, ugh. Her name is Marsha, by the way, but she seems to go by Marshie. Marshie. That's too cute by a country mile. *Marshie*." Flip, flip. "She hates her parents—girl, who doesn't. She thinks her math teacher is weird. She's sad a lot. Welcome to being a kid in the nineties, I guess. Lots to worry about, and she talks about some of it. Acid rain and ozone layer and will anyone ever love her and she's afraid of sex but wants to have sex and—" Flip, flip, flip. "This is just a page where she writes the lyrics to TLC's 'Waterfalls' over and over again in an increasingly erratic—" Flip. "Oh. Oh shit. Oh no."

But Owen was barely listening.

On the screen, the JPG finished rendering.

It was a photo. Of a pocketknife. The knife lay on its side, the blade half open, at a forty-five-degree angle. Nickel bolsters at the end, brass pins holding it together, and a little metal inlay icon that read OLD TIMER. The brand at the base of the blade read SCHRADE.

The edge of the blade was darkened. Just a little. Wet and red.

"Are you listening to me?" Lore asked him.

"I—" He hadn't been. Not really. Not since that image came up.

"She killed herself."

"What?"

"This girl. Marshie. I think she killed herself." Owen felt dizzy at the thought of that. The knife in the photo. He knew that knife. He had one growing up. Used it for... well. Had she used one just like it? He understood her, suddenly. The worries, the anxieties. The unreturned love. That *feeling* deep down in you that you're not good enough, not anything, that you're just a hole to throw things into, a hole that sucks the light out of the room, out of the world. That knife, how it could open you up, let it all out...

He shook his head. *Don't think about it.* That was one of those thoughts that would bore its way into him, termites chewing him to pieces.

Lore kept on:

"Marshie told Grady she liked him, and—and he made fun of her. Jesus. Said she was ugly. Had a butterface. Fucking prick. She said she's gonna kill herself and even talked about how she's gonna do it, she's gonna end it all, and then—these brown spots, I think they're blood—wait, what the fuck?"

Then, two things happened simultaneously—

First, the image of the knife, oldtimer.jpg, glitched hard. The image broke into RGB pixels, distorting it so deeply that barely any of the original photo could still be seen.

Second, Hamish screamed.

31

Here's Marshie

Lore knew what it was like to be called ugly. When she hit it big on the game scene, they were already judging her—she wasn't hot enough, she was too much the cyberpunk tomboy, too much the uppity half-a-dyke, her tits were too big, her face was too "severe"—her only value to those shit-heel online mutants was how fuckable she was to them, but aye, there was the rub, because if she was too fuckable, or even fuckable at all, that'd be a whole different problem. Hell, they called her a slut already, as if she'd fucked and sucked her way into the industry. Truth was, they didn't want her in this space at all, not as anything other than some bouncy booth babe. A model, a *toy*, a poseable sex doll. Anything else just meant she was intruding.

Anything else meant she was *stealing* opportunities from *lesser men*.

It was in this way she understood—and hated—the girl, Marshie.

Marshie, you stupid thing. Putting all of yourself in some stupid boy's hands so that he could either lift you up or break you down.

That's what was going through her head as she read the girl's diary. She started to tell Owen what she was reading, even though he looked shell-shocked enough that she wasn't even sure he was paying attention. Staring as he was at the computer screen. And Hamish and Nick were just fighting again, and it was hard to tune them out—

"This is your fault," Hamish said to Nick.

"My fault. *My* fault?"

"You just couldn't leave well enough alone, man. Matty went up those stairs and we didn't have to follow, but what do you do? Spend the next thirty years chasing his ghost, trying to find a way for us to join him in Hell. Stupid parents always asking, *If your friend jumped off a cliff, would you jump off a cliff, too?* but I guess it isn't that stupid of a question because your answer would be *yeah, shit yeah, and if I can't jump off that cliff just find me a new one to jump off of, and I'll trick my other friends into jumping right alongside of me.*"

Nick sneered as he brought his voice low, almost to a growl. "Weak. *Weak.* That's what you are, Hamish Moore. *W-E-A-K* weak. Weak like watered-down liquor, like decaf coffee. Everything you were is gone now, isn't it? You're in your *diet soda* era, a fading photograph of who you once were. I can't even see you in there. You changed that day. We all did. And *that* is what this was about. Fixing it. Finding not just Matty but..."

His voice died in his mouth.

Hamish leaned in, baring his teeth. "You didn't fix shit, *bro*. This doesn't feel fixed to me. This feels fucked. Extra fucked. And you—" Hamish seemed to notice Nick was barely listening. Instead, he was looking down. Toward the floor.

Toward Hamish's feet.

Lore looked over, still reading aloud from the diary. "She said she's gonna kill herself and even talked about how she's gonna do it, she's gonna end it all, and then—these brown spots, I think they're blood—" But as she was talking about blood, so were Nick and Hamish.

"What?" Hamish asked, sounding irritated.

"You're...bleeding," Nick said.

"What? I'm—"

Sure enough, she saw a pool of blood spreading out from between Ham's feet. The blinking Christmas lights danced in the red-black puddle, like fairies trapped in syrup.

"Wait, what the fuck?" Lore said.

Hamish, half panicking, said, "I—I don't think that's from me."

A hand shot out from under the bed, grabbing Hamish's ankle.

Hamish screamed as he yanked his leg free and nearly fell over as he pivoted hard in a clumsy leap off the bed.

The hand, messy with red, smacked at the carpet, leaving bloody handprints across the floor. The fingers grabbed at the fibers and were joined by a second hand that did the same. They gripped and *pulled*—

Nick was yelling now, too, screaming, "Jesus fucking fuck!" as he backpedaled off the bed. Owen jumped out of the chair, pressing himself into the corner of the room, watching transfixed as a young woman dragged herself out from under the bed. All parts of her slick with gore, the blood a fresh wet mask, a second skin, crimson in the lights but thick with strings of black clot. T-shirt and pajama pants soaked through, too. She rose to her feet, shaking. Blood dripping.

Lore felt sick. Scared. But also—in awe.

The girl looked around at them, head low, shoulders hunched. The look of a kennel-kept dog, starving and wary.

Still smiling. Eyes big.

Lore stepped forward. Owen hissed at her, tried to get her to stay back.

But she couldn't do that.

"Are you ... Marshie?" Lore asked.

The girl opened her mouth and choked out an incomprehensible reply. As she did, a vent in her throat opened like a steamed envelope, and fresh blood oozed. So did slashes up the length of the undersides of her arm. Owen failed to stifle a bleat. Black ichor splashed over the girl's teeth and lips as she tried—and failed—to speak.

But she's still smiling, Lore realized.

To the others, Lore said: "Maybe—maybe we can talk to her. Maybe she's trying to tell us something."

But the way the girl tilted her head this way and that—Lore wasn't so sure. Her eyes flashed with what Lore could only describe as *joyful hate.*

She loathed them.

Lore then remembered the message sliced into the wallpaper.

"Hey!" Nick barked at her. "*Hey*. We're looking for someone—"

But the girl fixed her gaze on Hamish, like a nail in drywall.

"*Youuuu*," she said, the word clearer after a fresh push of black blood from over the dam of teeth and lip.

"M-me," Hamish said.

"*Lllllllooook. Liiiiiikkkkke. Himmm.*" Her smile broadened. Eyes wider. A fat glob of coagulated blood danced on her tongue, like a breath mint juggled around her mouth.

"Him?" Nick repeated.

"Him . . . who?" Hamish asked her.

"*Gggggggraaaaaady,*" the girl said, with nearly a swoon.

"Grady," Lore said. "That's the boy she liked."

Hamish forced a smile. "Okay. Okay. So she liked him." To the bloody girl: "You liked Grady? That's good. You, you like me, then. Maybe—maybe you can help us. We're looking for—"

The girl said in a wheezing, whimpering, breathless croak: "*I loved him.*"

"That's—that's great. That's sweet. Our friend, Matty—"

The girl's smile sank. Her stare narrowed.

Darkly, she said:

"*But he . . . didn't love me.*"

"I'm—I'm so sorry—"

"*So I dddddddid this.*"

She held up her arms. The slices down the undersides looked like fish gills. Lore thought she could see bundles of artery and raw muscle in there.

Pulsating.

"I don't like this," Hamish said to the others. "What do I—"

The girl moaned a terrible sound, a despairing, hateful sound, and her fingers were sharp, now, sharp like broken bone, and she moved fast, *so fast*, the whole of her body summoned to Hamish as if she were not walking or running but rather *floating forward* on the bent curls of her toes—

Hamish ducked and lurched forward, the girl's sharp fingers cutting the air above him—he scrambled forward, first on the floor, then over the edge of the bed, toward the bedroom door. Lore wanted to stay, in a way. Wanted to talk to the girl. But she knew it was smarter to go. Nick was following Hamish through the doorway, and Lore trailed after even as the girl moaned and wept, blood spattering on the carpet, on the walls.

In the next room, Hamish crashed forward into the dining room table, the plates of cake sliding toward the edge. The words gabbled out of him: "*Closethedoorclosethedoor—*"

Lore turned to do just that.

But it was then she realized.

Owen hadn't come through with them.

32

Linger Longer

Owen could still feel it in his hand, the Old Timer penknife. It had two blades—one longer, pointier, with what he thought was a cool angle to it. A *clip point blade*, it was called. The second was smaller, a *pen blade*. Each opened at opposite ends. He always felt the smaller blade, the pen blade, was strange—too short, too stumpy, to be of much use anywhere.

(That's why it was the one he always used.)

He still remembered buying that knife. He'd gone to a flea market with his father that morning over across from Peddler's Village. Owen hoped to love something someday the way his father loved flea markets, and he went with him every week because it was one of the few times he might see his father be happy, one of the few times when he wasn't yelling at him, when he wasn't sad or angry or fed up with his son and his wife and the world around him. At the flea market, Edgar Zuikas would be generous, too, buying for his son most of whatever the boy wanted: old comic books, used paperbacks, some weird *Star Wars* toy.

At the market, every week, they passed by a table operated by a man with a big bushy black beard and long hair pulled back in a ponytail, and this table was a bounty of violent delights: ninja stars and nunchucks and M80 firecrackers, empty hand grenades and stun guns and Zippo lighters. (It's where Nick bought his Jack Kenny–branded lighter.) Plus, there was always a big Plexiglas case *full* of knives: Swiss Army knives, weird fucked-up fantasy daggers, hunting knives, kunai throwing daggers, and of course, switchblades and butterfly knives.

One day, when he was twelve years old, Owen got it in his head that he wanted a knife of his own.

So he asked his father, and Edgar said, to his shock, "Sure. Boy like you could use a good knife." And so they went to the bearded man's table.

Owen said that he wanted one of the butterfly knives.

And his father laughed, said no, that's not the knife for him. "Flipping that thing around, you'll cut your goddamn pinky finger off. No, I think something like this is more your speed—" And Edgar Zuikas pointed to the Schrade two-blade Old Timer penknife at the very bottom of the case, a knife that was hard to see given how it was obscured by the much larger, flashier blades in the case.

Owen knew not to fight his father on this.

And a knife was a knife was a knife.

So he said okay, and his father bought that Old Timer penknife for Owen. Upon conclusion of the sale, the bearded man said, and this is another thing Owen would never forget, "*'And the angel sent his blade into the earth, and the vine of the earth was cut.'* Book of Revelation, dontchaknow. Jesus is Lord and Jesus is among us, thank you for your purchase, friends." Owen's father, not a particularly religious man, just said "Okay, thanks, pal," and off they went.

That memory came back to him full-fledged, in Technicolor stereo sound, as he stood there in Marshie's room, staring at the blood-soaked suicide girl.

Even as the others fled—

Owen remained.

He eased toward the door, Lore having already fled through it—

But paused.

The girl was at the wall where Hamish stood, and she clawed at it, wailing and thrashing about. Then she froze, and slowly, her head craned toward him.

"*Do you love me?*" she asked in a small, raspy kitten's voice.

"The knife," he said quietly. "The knife you used. The photo, on the computer—" He gestured toward the screen, but found nothing on it. The glass had cracked in a spiderweb pattern. *But it had just been on . . .*

"*Knife*," she repeated. Then in her hand, there one appeared, suddenly—

Not his knife. Not the Schrade Old Timer. This was a boning knife, the thin blade curved like her returning smile.

"Why did you have a photo of that knife? The Old Timer. I . . . I had one just like it." *Just, juuuuust like it. With the red on the blade and everything.* "I don't understand. You have to help me understand."

She took a step toward him. Then another.

A trail of red, viscid footprints behind her.

"*Knife*," she said again, holding up the blade so that the metal caught the glow from the blinking string lights.

"I wanted to be loved, too. I wanted to be something to someone."

Her smile dropped again even as she stepped closer. The next words were like the grinding of a millstone. A grinding, crushing sound.

"*We can d-d-diiiiie together, ugly and alone.*"

He nodded in agreement.

He felt something shift inside his mind. Almost like the air around him when he stepped off that staircase into that hallway. Inside him, his mental furniture shifted. Rooms moved and doors opened.

Owen was about to step toward her—

When someone grabbed him and dragged him backward through the door.

33

The Rotten Cake Room

Wham. It was Hamish and Nick who closed the door and held it fast, Nick fumbling at the knob for a lock—a lock that ended up just being one of those little turny things. He engaged it just the same. *Click.*

Lore, meanwhile, was the one who pulled Owen through the doorway and into this dusty, musty dining room with the rotten cake smell and the cheap-ass wood paneling. She spun him toward her and found his gaze lost to a horizon that wasn't there. "Owen, what the *fuck*," she hissed at him, and then snapped her fingers in front of his eyes. "Ping? Hello? You there?"

"Yeah," he said, though he sounded unsure about that. "Hey."

"Are you okay?"

A small nod. "Yeah."

Bullshit. You're not okay.

"Owen. *Owen.* Why did you stay . . . ?"

Behind her, the other two were panicking. Lore looked over, saw blood spreading out underneath the closed door. Pooling between the feet of Nick and Hamish. The doorknob rattled. The girl's fingers squirmed under the door like searching worms, sliding through the thickening blood, twisting through the red muck.

And then, like that, they were gone. Sucked back under the door.

The blood vacuumed back into the room, too—reversing course, rewinding like a movie. No blood, no fingers, no rattling knob, nothing.

Silence, long and cold, waited for them.

"I think she's gone," Nick said finally, his ear pressed against the wood.

Hamish pulled him back, giving him a *WTF* look. "These doors are cheap, man. One of those... fucking fingers might punch through this shit like an icepick into your ear. So be careful, damn."

"She also had a knife," Owen said quietly, as if to himself.

Lore told Hamish to stay there at the door, just in case. Nick, too. Owen, though, looked fragile. Not that he didn't always look a little fragile, but something in there had really cracked his plaster. What was the deal about the knife? That was maybe a conversation for another time.

Instead, she ushered him into a chair. "You should sit."

"Yeah, okay."

Her mind felt calm. That, strangely, was how Lore knew things were really truly fucked—she wasn't so great navigating her regular life, but she was *aces* in a crisis. The worse things got, the sharper and colder she became in response. An earlier partner of hers, a Web3 guru named Trevor, lived in Austin, said of her: *You're like one of those extremophiles; you thrive in the worst possible conditions.* She told him, *That's right, I'm a tardigrade, bitch,* and they laughed at that. Though later, when they broke up, he called her an "emotionless love assassin," and it was like, dramatic much, Trevor? Fucking Trevor.

Still. He was right about her thriving in the worst conditions.

Like right now.

Since the moment she stepped onto the stairs and into this place, she was locked into crisis mode.

For her, crisis mode was *evaluation* and *action*. One without the other was no good. Act without evaluation and you were likely to run into traffic. Evaluate without acting and the problem was going to bury you.

So evaluate, Lore.

The room. *This* room. It was a dining room. The cake on it was rotten and old—looked like birthday cake, cheap cake from a grocery store. Half eaten, like whoever was here had just, what, gotten up and walked off? Disappeared? What was it Nick had said? *Raptured.* Or maybe they were killed by that thing in the other room, the thing that was, in theory, a teen girl who unalived herself in . . . the 1990s? Which meant she was a ghost, or a demon, or a living dead girl, and none of that mattered. What mattered was a way out. Like in *The Matrix.*

"First up," she said. "Phones. Let's make sure we don't have signal yet?" They all got out their devices, checking them. Nothing. No bars. No Wi-Fi. No anything. She didn't expect differently, and even still, her heart sank. She sighed. "Okay. So we need an exit."

"No shit," Nick said.

"Maybe the room will shift again," Owen said.

Good, he's back with us. Not just staring into the void. "You might be right. Only way to check is to open that door—"

"Which we are *not* doing," Hamish said. He was leaning back, bracing his hands against the door, and shaking like a leaf while doing it. "Nobody open this door. Okay?"

Lore went around to the other side of the table, to the louvered split-door closet. She opened it—

Inside sat a series of shelves, and on those shelves were clumsy, dusty arrangements of glassware, drinkware, plates, all of that. Every piece radiating with that seventies-era vibe: Everything was puke green, fading amber, Dreamsicle orange. She looked deeper into the closet for something, anything—she reached back and felt along the back wall of it, and instantly, she felt the seam.

There. A split down the middle. A split with hinges.

Another folding door.

"Found our exit," she said.

She reached over a stack of green glass plates, through a small galaxy of spiderwebs, and pushed hard in the center of the second door—

It moved, tenting outward a little.

Grunting, she pushed in farther, searching the back wall for an edge to the door—her fingers found purchase and, shoulder burning, she tugged on it, and inch by inch, the door folded up to the right side.

Thus revealing another room.

"Fuck is that?" Nick asked, standing right next to Lore, startling her. She nearly jumped out of her skin. He didn't apologize, and instead just pushed past her and looked through the space.

"Excuse you," she said.

"Whatever. Sorry." Nick leaned forward. "It's another room, holy shit."

"Yeah, I know. It looks like a—"

"Like a living room. But—more modern."

He was right. It was an expansive, expensive room. A sectional couch of white leather tucked into the corner on the right side of the room, and in the center of the room looked to be a stand with a flatscreen on it. And the color scheme—that gray-brown greige palette that made Lore want to throw up her soul.

"We go through," she said, a declarative statement.

Hamish, on the other side of the room, still holding up the door, objected: "Hey, whoa, what? Maybe we shouldn't . . . I dunno. Be hasty. Maybe we sit tight for a second. Maybe we grab a chair and talk this out—"

Nick scoffed.

"Sure, we all plant ourselves at this dinner table and enjoy a meal of half-eaten, just-moldy cake." He swiped at the air, scattering a few flies that had found him. "It'll be like our own little party."

"I'm just saying maybe we should take a beat."

"I'm just saying, the cake already smells bad."

"*I'm just saying,* maybe it's not a good idea—"

"There's a thumb on the cake," Owen said suddenly.

He was staring at something intently.

Lore looked, and sure enough, on the side opposite to Owen, the piece of cake had a severed thumb in it. Pressed into the icing, straight down—just before lopping it off.

The cut was clean, too.

The thumb was old. Not mummified old, but shriveled up. The blood dried to a rusty crinkle.

Hamish made a horrible sound in the back of his throat. A low, scared-animal whine. Owen just stared at the thumb, unblinking.

"It's like someone mashed their thumb down into a piece of cake," Nick said, "and then while it was there, they, or someone, sliced it clean off."

"Wonder what kind of knife was used," Owen asked idly.

Something tickled at the back of Lore's brain stem. *A knife, again.* For the first time since coming here, Lore returned her mind to the fight they'd had. About her game. *Their* game, if you were to ask him. How mad was he at her? Would Owen try to hurt her? Would he ever try to hurt himself?

That thought seemed to scurry around her head. Like rats through ductwork.

"Well," she said abruptly, "I think that's a pretty good sign we should get the fuck out of this room. Something bad happened here, and I don't want to be here anymore."

"Sold," Nick said. "Let's tear those shelves out."

"We don't have to. This middle one—if we move all the shit out of it—is big enough for us to just crawl through."

So the two of them got to work moving plates and glasses and a particularly ugly gravy boat onto the table, next to the slices of ruined cake. Owen sat staring numbly at the thumb, and Hamish remained at the door, standing a diligent vigil over it. Still shaking, still sweating.

Lore wanted to say, *A little help over here?* but decided against it. Those two were best where they were.

Finally, they got all the dinnerware off the middle shelf.

The gap between shelves was now a portal into the living room.

"Let's go," she said, casting one more look into that room to make sure it was, well, *still there*. It felt crazy. Of course it was still there. Marshie's bedroom was still on the other side of the door, too, right?

Could it be gone? Would it be different if they opened it? She *burned* to find out, to waltz over there, shove Hamish out of the way, and fling it open, defiant in her curiosity. But then she remembered that girl rising up out from under the bed—all that blood, those cuts down her arms and along her throat, her sharp fingers. Lore felt sad for her, so sad it felt as if those fingers were pushing into her own heart and tearing it out.

But that sadness didn't mean Lore wanted to meet her again, either.

Meanwhile—

Nick was already starting to wriggle through the gap.

"Hamish, Owen," Lore said, again snapping her fingers. "C'mon."

Owen stood, nodding silently as he lined up at the closet door.

"I can't leave the door," Hamish said. "If I do, she—*she* might come in."

"It's locked. We gotta move."

"Lore—I don't think I can. You all go ahead. I'll—I'll catch up."

Christ on a clamshell, she thought. If she had guessed anyone would be melting down right now, it would've been Owen. Hamish, once upon a time, was Mister Go-Along-to-Get-Along Guy; whatever you told him to do, he'd do it. *Hamish, drink this shot of hot sauce. Hamish, crush this can with your head. Hey, Ham, I dare you to press your asscheeks against Principal Schnur's office window.* God, there was one time they went to an old quarry that had long ago filled up with water, and someone had set up a rope swing, and they told Ham to swing on it and jump in. It was a *long* way down, and the water below was cold and black, and he didn't give a shit, didn't stop to ask any questions, didn't have *one iota* of concern over it. He just whipped off his shirt, bolted toward the rope, and swung his ass like Tarzan out over the void. Then: hands-free. He let go, dropped like a bunker buster bomb. *Splash.* They all went in then, except Owen, who stayed up top—he said he wasn't scared, but that "someone needs to watch our stuff." Later, they learned that years before, a kid had died in that quarry doing exactly what they did. Turned out, there was a whole bunch of strip-mining equipment down there. Rusty, jagged metal, hiding under the surface. Kid landed in the wrong spot, crushed the center of his face on the top of a bent crane or something. Died instantly. When they all heard that, it was like, *Whoa, what the fuck, we came really close to death.* Except Hamish. Hamish said, and she would never forget this, "Yeah, but we had fun, and we all gotta die sometime." Then he laughed and took another epic hit off his bong. *Gurgle, gurgle.*

What a difference then and now, she thought before marching over to Hamish and cupping his chin, turning it toward her.

"We gotta go. There's a thumb on the cake. This room smells awful. We have to find an exit, and the exit is not in here. We can leave the door. Leave the door, Hamish."

In a small voice, he said, "She looked like my Emma."

"Who?"

"The girl. The bloody girl."

Ah. So that's what this was. That dead girl looked like one of Hamish's daughters. Lore could not relate to that. She had no children. Had no pets. Didn't want them. People you chose to love, chose to fuck, they were doors you could walk through or not. But you get dependents? Spouse, kids, a dog? You owe them and they owe you. They aren't doorways. They're whole houses. They're a mortgage, and Lore, well, Lore was ever the renter.

"She's not your daughter, Ham. Do you want to see your daughter again? Your wife? Your other kids?"

He nodded like a little kid being asked if he wanted ice cream after getting shots at the doctor.

"Then we have to move. Okay?"

That seemed to do the trick.

"Yeah, yeah, yeah. Yeahyeah. Okay. Yeah."

Hamish let go of the door.

And then together they went to the closet and followed Owen through to the living room.

34

Gone, Matty, Gone

JUNE 6, 1998.

Just after midnight.

Matty Shiffman went up the stairs, jumped into nowhere, and was gone.

Just after *that*, there was a moment when none of them were looking directly at the staircase. Owen was bent over, throwing up. Lauren was looking at the trees in the darkness, watching the shadows shimmy and swim and sway, and she was sure that when they moved just such a way, she would see Matty out there playing hide-and-seek, all while she did her very best to try to remember *you're on drugs you're on drugs none of this is real Matty is still here you're just hallucinating really fucking badly*. Hamish ran around the back side of the staircase, yelling for Matty. And Nick? Well, all Nick had to do was blink one long blink.

And when they looked at the staircase again, it was gone.

One A.M.

Lauren screamed into the woods. The woods screamed back, taking her voice and turning it into an arrow and firing it into her ear, an ear that drizzled blood now. So she screamed louder. A fox screamed back. A fox with a human face but sharp, sharp fox teeth. Beyond the human-faced sharp-toothed fox, Lauren thought she saw a staircase rise up out of the dark, and beyond the fox's screams and the fox's cackles, she was *sure* she heard Matty calling her name, and she ran toward it, she ran top speed because she wanted to climb the staircase and be with him, and she was so, so, *so* sorry that she screwed things up for them, and her legs burned and she charged hard toward the stairs and toward the voice and then—

A dark shape, the fox with a human face, *no,* a wolf, a werewolf, a creature dark and hirsute, slammed into her, knocking her to the ground.

The beast's face resolved into Owen.

"You almost ran off the cliff," he said, breathless.

"Fuck you," she whimpered, because though she did not know it was a cliff, maybe that's where the staircase was. Maybe it was out there, over the edge. Maybe that's where Matty went. He went over the cliff. *I want to go over the cliff too. I want to fly like Matty did.* Fly, climb, fall, die. Absurd, that. She was sure he was dead but sure he was alive. What did that mean? What could that *possibly* mean? *It means you want to join him,* she thought. Wherever he was.

And at that moment and in all the moments for years to come she would always think, *I made him do it, I pushed him away, and if I hadn't acted like such a dick that night, he would not have gone up that staircase like a cocky angry show-off. He is dead and gone, and I should be dead and gone too.*

She struggled and tried to push Owen away. Her skin felt hot and crawling. He was a heavy shadow, a cruel presence. He told her it was fine. He said it would be over soon. Lauren wasn't sure what that meant, not exactly, but somehow in those words she found the deepest lake of darkest comfort and she stopped struggling, instead choosing to sink into the waters of his words.

Three A.M.

The flashlight beam cut a swath through the woods. Hamish held the light. Nick followed behind, his Zippo in hand, its flame starting to gutter.

"It has to be a prank," Nick said. That was his take on it, and over the last few hours, he assured everyone, *assured them 120 percent,* that

Matty was cleverer than all of them and that somehow he'd rigged a staircase to appear and disappear, and he went with it. Never mind that Matty had never shown any aptitude for magic. But he was a prankster sometimes, and so Nick was sold on this. He said, "You'll see. Morning comes, that clever prick will pop out of a tree stump like a Keebler elf, and we will shit our pants and we'll laugh and cry and punch that fucker in the shoulder for what he put us through." Hamish said he wasn't so sure. Nick told him he was a naïve fucking idiot. "You'll all see."

Five-thirty A.M.

The sun was just starting to burn the edge of the paper of the universe. In the growing light of day, the four of them stood in the spot in the woods where Matty Shiffman had climbed a mysterious staircase and jumped off into nothing.

"You can come out now!" Nick screamed into the woods. His voice was hoarse. All their voices were rough from yelling for Matty all night long, their vocal cords rubbed raw by the belt sander of fear and desperation.

Nick and Hamish did most of the searching.

Owen stayed with Lauren, who was coming down off her trip and now sat in the leaves, her cheeks and forehead streaked with dirt, staring at the space where once a staircase stood.

In the slanted morning light, the intersection of reality and unreality was dizzying. The truth of their situation felt more and more like a dream, as if Matty had never existed at all.

"We have to tell someone," Owen said.

"Tell them what, exactly?" Nick asked. "*We found a magical staircase and our friend went up it and fucked off to Fairyland. I'm sure he'll be back in school on Monday, don't sweat it?*"

"No one's going to believe us," Lauren said in a voice so quiet and so ragged, it sounded like a smoker's whisper. "I don't even believe us."

Hamish kicked a rock and started sobbing.

Owen got up and put his arm around him, had him sit down next to Lauren. It just made Hamish weep all the more. They all watched it and waited for the storm to pass before they spoke again.

Nick said, "We're going to need a plan."

"Why?" Owen asked.

"Jesus, Zuikas. Because—because Matty is missing. He's now a missing person, like, in a crime. Who do you think they're going to blame for that?"

At that, Hamish's head lifted off his chest, a look of hope brightening his face. "What if he's back home? Like, what if he just went home? We're up here in the woods and—what if he's at his house?"

"I mean, I guess he could be," Owen said.

Lauren shook her head. "He's not. He's gone. Just gone."

"She's right," Nick said. "Matty is gone. Okay? Let's say he is back home, then that's great, then we don't say shit and we just kick his ass for fucking with us. But if he's not there—and we don't have a story? Then they're going to say we murdered him. We're going to be in jail. Even if they never find him or find a body, then—"

"What if he fell off the cliff?" Owen asked, suddenly.

"That's the story you want to go with?"

"No, I mean—last night. Laur almost fell, what if he . . ."

Looks of horror crossed their faces. The thought that Matty somehow stumbled away into the woods and off the edge of the cliff—

That, then, was the next round of searching. Now in the light of day. Walking the perimeter of Highchair Rocks. Looking down over the edges for some sign of him. Some part of all of them thought they'd find him down there, a broken body, bent every which way atop the boulders. It took hours.

But still no Matty.

Ten A.M.

Nobody was eating. Or drinking. They were back at the camp now. The fire had gone to dead gray ash. Everything looked sad and empty and ruined.

"It's gotta be simple," Nick said, of the story they needed to tell.

"I don't see why we need a story," Owen said again.

"Because of the Satanic Panic. Because of the West Memphis Three. Because just last year, remember in Perkasie those three kids who went missing? Kids younger than us. They were killed on a turf farm up there by a couple of twenty-year-old pot dealers who lured them there and stabbed them, chucked them in a fucking *water tank*. They're gonna think we lured our very successful, most excellent friend up here and executed him. They'll look at Owen, with his black clothing, they'll look at me and see some skeevy scumlord, they'll see that Lauren was high on acid and Hamish was stoned and drunk and they'll say, *Those kids killed their good friend, Matthew Shiffman, who would never drink a drink or eat a drug. They sacrificed him to the devil up there at Highchair Rocks.* And god fucking forbid we say something about a mysterious staircase that came and went and took our best friend with it. That isn't *credible,* you understand? They'll hang us."

That sold it.

They needed a story.

It would be a simple one, they decided. Too complicated and that meant nobody would remember it, and it might strain credibility.

At some point that night, they just couldn't find Matty. He'd taken some of his stuff and gone. They'd throw some of his things off the edge of a cliff to make it look like maybe he fell.

"We can't do that," Owen said. "That is a crime. That means we're committing a crime. Right?"

Hamish agreed. He sniffed and said, "And if they think Matty is dead, they'll—they'll stop lookin' for him."

"Where do you think they're going to find him?" Lauren asked. "Up the staircase? There is no staircase. It's gone."

"Maybe there never was one," Hamish said, stammering. "Maybe we were all too drunk and high and we imagined it. Like, like, mass hysteria. A shared hallucination, you know? Weird shit happens like that. And maybe Matty really *is* out there somewhere. Lost and alone.

Maybe we should just tell them. His family. The police. Maybe we should tell them he just wandered off, and they can look for him, too. We can all look for him."

"Fuck that," Nick said. "The cops are shit. Cops don't wanna do that work. They'll want to pin it on us. We have to do this right."

Lauren agreed with him.

Owen and Hamish shot each other dubious looks.

But the train was moving. The ride was starting.

And they were all on it, like it or not.

And so, the Second Covenant was born.

35

How to Sell a Murder House

This, then, was the Greige Space Room:

It was a living room broad in the shoulders—nearly three hundred square feet, longer than it was wide (or wider than it was long, depending on your perspective), but it was big, roomy, with a high double tray ceiling and a big airplane-propeller-looking ceiling fan. The white leather couch was crisp and new. On the other side of the TV stand in the middle of the room was a sitting area with more leather chairs, these with the color and texture of faux rhino skin. The chairs, and a white marble table, were arranged around a black electric fireplace nestled in a façade of whitewashed brick. Built-in bookshelves lurked on either side, and those shelves were lined with books. On the adjoining wall, the wall they could not see when staring through the closet, was a massive aquarium. In it were a dozen fish of several varieties, all dead, so dead they were nearly disintegrating, wisps of *fish fiber* floating off of them. The life bled out of them, same as how the color was bled from the room.

The room had three doors:

One, the closet, which they had just come through. That door, now closed.

And off the sitting area, two more doors, one on each wall in the corner, both greige, both closed.

The room smelled like sweetly sour vanilla candles and new carpet. It was overwhelming, the smell. Like it crawled up your nose and laid eggs in your sinuses. Lore felt assaulted by it—by the smell, by the non-color color, by the fibrous wads of dead fish. She worked at the puzzle of this place. What was it? *Where* was it, *when* was it, *why* was it? It rotated in her mind, a Rubik's Cube of all gray-beige, the lines of cubes turning and turning and resolving into nothing.

That's when Hamish said: "Jesus. I know this room."

They all turned to give him a look.

He stared at it, mouth agape. In horror, he said, "I know this room, I know this house. I *sold* this house."

He told them a story. Said it was back when he worked in the "real estate trenches." This room was one room in a murder house—that's how everyone referred to it, and any house, where a murder had happened. Murder houses. Hard to sell because you couldn't hide it. Couldn't keep it secret. It was public record, and they had to tell buyers anyway. So you always knew you were going to take a hit—if you were smart, you rented it out for a few years at a cut price, kept it up and updated so it didn't get that *haunted house* vibe about it, and then, *then* you sold it, when the market was hungrier, when the stain of death had been forgotten, when the worst dip you'd take was ten, fifteen, percent.

This murder, though, he said it was a real bender. It was a family of three that lived here—the parents, upper middle-class, well-put-together people. Father was some kind of finance guy, wife was an art broker, and their son was a seventh grader at a local private school. But the parents, they hated each other. Hate so strong it trapped them together, like chains. Fought all the time, so loud the neighbors—an acre away—could hear. Then one day, Hamish said, "The father lost it. He took one of the mother's own art pieces—she didn't make art anymore, but she had this piece from college, this heavy blown-glass piece that looked like a, a, I dunno, a melted heart, like the heart from a playing card, not a human heart? And he beat her to death with it. In front of the son. The son tried to run, but he held the boy down in front of that fish tank, and choked him to death on the floor."

Hamish said the dad fled. Calm and cool, got in his BMW, went to the airport, headed to Europe. They found him dead years later, on a yacht in Italy.

"That art piece," Hamish said. "They kept it on the bookshelf."

They all turned to look.

The bookshelves, full of books, and only books, except for the second shelf from the top. A tall shelf, tall enough for coffee-table books and art books and—

And a blown-glass heart.

The glass red.

The blood flecks on it darker than the glass.

Bits of skin and hair matted to the side.

"So we're in a murder house?" Nick asked. "That's what you're saying?"

Owen said, "That girl, Marshie. She didn't kill anyone but herself."

"Suicide is a kind of murder, the murder of self," Lore said, and she realized it sounded haughty, pretentious, like she was trying to score points with an English teacher or a psych professor. Still. She wasn't wrong, was she?

"Last room had a thumb on a cake, so that's pretty murdery," Nick said.

"The other weird thing?" Hamish said. "Every living room I've ever been in—big, small, rich, middle-class, poor, TV, no TV, carpet, hardwood, whatever, they all had one thing in common. Always."

The room looked to him expectantly, so he gave them the answer:

"Windows. There's no window here. No window in that dining room either. Not in the bedroom. Not in the hallway where we came in. There should be windows here. Somewhere."

A chill settled over all of them.

Hamish spoke aloud what they were all just realizing—

"There may not be a way out of this place."

Lore felt her contrarian blood rising. "No. No. Bullshit. You don't know that, Ham. It's a house. There has to be a door. There's gotta be a way out."

Hamish fell backward into the couch, looking exhausted. His gaze, distant, the gaze of a man at war. "Matty didn't get out."

"We don't know that," Owen said, but Lore could hear his heart wasn't in it.

"Yeah, we do," Hamish said. "We didn't save him and now we're trapped here." He made a small, troubled grunt. "We deserve it."

Nick sat catty-corner to him on the couch, elbows on knees—a predatory, fox-like lean to him. "Sure, *now* you feel bad about leaving Matty behind."

"Fuck you, Nick. I always felt bad. We all *always* felt bad."

"Always," Owen agreed.

Lore shook her head. "Not me. I let it go. I had to."

"I call bullshit," Owen said.

Whoa, look who's got a little fire in his belly? Good. Lore wanted the fight. She longed for the fight. Fights got shit done.

"It's not bullshit. I choose to live a life without regrets."

"Then why'd you run up those stairs? We didn't even have a chance to talk it out. You just—you booked it right up the stairs, and we had to deal with that."

"Oh, please, stop. I made my choice, and it didn't have to be your choice, Owen. See? That's your problem. Always basing *your* decision off everybody fucking else's, always *waiting*—"

"No, *no*," Owen said, now raising his voice—he really *was* on the edge, wasn't he? Owen rarely, *rarely* raised his voice. Especially to Lore. "This isn't that. You took off like a fucking gazelle. We were there together. We're supposed to be friends, and your decision became *our* decision. But that's always been *your* problem, hasn't it? Lore does what Lore wants, fuck everybody else."

"See, now I think you're talking about more than just the staircase, Owen."

Nick turned his hand into a gun and pointed it at Owen. "I see you. I *see* you, Zuikas. Clear as glass, buddy. Lore goes up those steps and oh, little lost puppy has to follow after, go on, puppy, chase the girl. But Matty goes up there, *Matty,* our best friend, our fuckin' *leader,* and you're like *Nah, bro, we're fine."*

Hamish laughed an unhappy sound. "Oh fuck off, Nick—"

"We were kids!" Owen said.

"We were *kids,*" Hamish echoed. "We didn't know shit from shit. Matty went up there and then he was gone. You wanted us all to go, too?"

Nick stood up, arms out in an incredulous crucifix. "You *just fucking said* we deserve to be here—"

"I didn't say I didn't regret it!"

"You never looked for him! You never answered my emails! I tried to get us to look for him, for a new staircase, for years, *years,* you fucking dicks, you fucking cowardly shitty dicks, so where was that regret, then? Huh? Instead, Owen's too scared to live, Lore is off making precious *video games,* and Ham, you're off, what, getting fucking married and having fucking kids and selling toxic fucking mortgages to poor stupid idiots who don't know any better and living the kind of life *Matty never got the chance to live!"*

That last part, yelled so loud it filled the room, with the roar of blood, with a sharp tin-scrape noise. And then it erupted. A cacophony of noise—everyone standing now, their blood up, shouting and pointing and *seething.* It was like the room wanted them to fight. Like it trapped them here in this soul-killing place, a room of greige walls and cloying vanilla and spilled blood. Lore could feel something working its way through her, like a rabid animal looking to take a bite out of someone.

She barked then: "Everyone shut up!"

To her shock, they did.

"We are in a situation none of us understand, and we need to keep it *together.*"

"Doesn't feel like we're very *together,*" Nick said.

"*Nick.*"

"Fine. Whatever."

Lore held up the palms of her hands. "We are all very tired."

"And hungry," Hamish said, with a half shrug.

"That, too. We spent half a day marching through the woods and then we came here—and since then it's been, I don't know. I don't know how long it's been or what this place is, but it is not our imagination. It is a real place, and we are here in it, and we will need to find our way out of it."

"No, we need to find *Matty*," Nick said.

"We need to get *out*," Hamish mumbled.

"There he goes again, folks. We have a shot at finding our friend and you don't even want to take it, you just want to run for the hills *again*—"

"Yeah, I do! I want to find a fucking exit! A front door, a back door, a—a fucking *window* to jump through—"

Lore yelled at them again to *shut up*.

And again, they did.

"We need to stay here in this room for a bit. We're safe. We need to rest a little—"

"No way," Nick said. "We pick one of those doors, and we go find Matty."

"None of us are good right now. We need a minute. And we need to stay together. No arguments."

Nick groused, but he gave a pissy thumbs-up.

"Everybody, take a few beats. Just, um, just be quiet. I need to think. Maybe rest my eyes a little," Lore said. "Everyone go to your corners. Chill out. Take a nap or something. We will regroup in a bit."

And Lore wandered away from them. She had to. She needed some space alone just to let her brain work. Alone was always how Lore worked best—without distraction, without nonsense, without other people's *bullshit*. She needed that clarity to figure out how they were going to get out of this place—

This place without windows, without exits.

36

Examinations

Now, amid the sea of greige.

Nobody talked to one another. It wasn't hard for Owen to vibe the raw feelings in the room. It was like a telepathic frequency buzzing in the air, lines of black electricity linking them all, transmitted in dark looks.

Owen wanted to go look at the books on the bookshelf, but Lore was already over there, and . . . he didn't want to be near her now. He felt like shit for throwing her under the bus like that. But he felt like shit, too, for what she said to him, and how she'd been ignoring him for years, and how she'd used *their* idea without ever asking him, and, and, and . . .

He wanted so badly to chew his fingernails right now. Not just the nails—he wanted to bite into the tips of his fingers, eating the tops off like bits of carrot. The urge was intense, and he realized suddenly he did not have his trazodone—the one drug in a long litany of drugs he'd tried over the years to blunt those urges. So now it was, what, willpower he had to rely upon? *That's not going to go well!* he thought, madly.

Instead, he chewed his tongue. Bit into it like it was jerky—not hard enough to draw blood. But it might be swollen later.

He looked over at Nick, who sat there, also restless, his jaw working. Nick was intimidating. Like sharkskin, you rubbed him the wrong way, you bled. One drunken night, Nick had told Owen, "I'm just jealous of you, Nailbiter," but Owen figured that was bullshit because what was there to be jealous of? Nick had a great relationship with his father, even if his mother had passed on years before. Nick didn't seem to have cares or worries—he did what he wanted, without fear.

Over the last several years, Nick emailed the group again and again, talking about Matty, sending them links to some Reddit thread or another about staircases people found in forests, swamps, deserts—about doors in the middle of nowhere, or furniture that just showed up somewhere, or whole houses. Owen, he realized now, was the only one who actually *responded* to Nick, even if it was just head-patting, over-polite, placating condescension. And he also realized now that maybe he and Nick had more in common than he knew. Nick really had no reason to be jealous. Neither of them had their shit together. Neither of them had done anything at all with the time they'd been given.

Owen hazarded a look at Hamish, who sat there, head slumped back, mumbling something to himself. A prayer, maybe. God, he was a Christian now? That tracked, he guessed. Back when they were kids, Hamish was, in his words, "just spiritual, dude, no organized religion for this guy."

Do I want to be him instead of me? Owen wondered.

No, he did not.

Do I want to be like Lore?

Successful but cold, driven but alienated?

Owen didn't know.

All he knew was that right now, he wanted to be alone. Somewhere in a dark corner, chewing his fingers down to the literal bone.

But being alone right now . . .

Didn't seem smart. And certainly wasn't possible, anyway.

Instead, he went to look at dead fish.

Owen didn't know anything about fish, or aquariums. He had a hamster once; it escaped its glass-walled prison and got into their walls and died, creating a smell that made his father so mad, he swore up and down to Owen that they would never again get a pet of any kind, because the death of any pet would just be a grave inconvenience to the man. In college, at Sarah Lawrence, in the short time when Owen and Lore got an apartment off campus, they had a cat—a silky black shadow named Invader Zim who bit them all the time. And at no point did he ever have fish.

(Owen told himself he was simply not capable of sustaining another life.)

(He was, after all, barely capable of sustaining his own.)

The fish in the tank numbered thirteen, and they consisted of varieties he'd seen before, though only one he could identify by name: angelfish. Two of those floated at the top. Flakes of them falling away like fish food—fish eat the flaky food, fish die and become the flaky food. He wondered if the other fish—fish once golden, once black, once silverish-see-through, fat fish, skinny fish, tiny fish—would eat that mess if they were still alive. He suspected they would. That was the world they lived in.

The tank was long. Were Owen to stretch out his arms in cruciform, the tank would be roughly the distance of fingertip to fingertip.

The water, brackish.

A little astronaut—not a deep-sea diver, but weirdly, an astronaut—stood at the bottom, a tiny escape pod opening and closing, puking up a weak flurry of greasy yellow bubbles each time.

And next to it—

Was a penknife.

A Schrade Old Timer penknife.

Angled blade open and pointed down, stuck in the aquarium gravel.

A small trail of blood arose from it, diffusing as it drifted.

Owen's heart caught in his throat, and he blinked and took a step back—

And the knife was gone.

You're just seeing things, he told himself. *You're tired. You're hungry.*

And this place is—it's just messing with your head. It's messing with all our heads.

It took Lore a minute or two to realize—these books on this bookshelf, they were just curated bullshit. All the books were new, untouched, unopened, unread—few novels, no poetry, almost all of it was, like, books about architecture and books about pedestrian art and books about fashion, and all of them pale and few of them offering much color, and she was sure now that whoever put these books here did it because of the way they looked and because of what the books said about the owners of this—

House? Was this a house?

Was it just a room?

Were these rooms connected at all—physically, or thematically, or what?

Nick wandered over near to her. He shot her a bored look, and she shrugged at him. They didn't exchange words as he walked to the two doors in the corner, and her middle cinched up. *He's going to leave us*, she thought. He lied to get them here for one purpose: to find Matty Shiffman. *And why did you come here, Lore?* she asked herself, having no answer. Still. Nick seemed now like a bullet fired from a gun—it would not be turned away from its trajectory, not until it hit what it was aiming at. She admired it. She *understood* it, more to the point. Because though Nick hadn't been like that through much of his life, *she* had been. Lore always saw the target and went for it. Never distracted, never dissuaded.

Except, lately . . .

She killed that thought before it had babies.

Nick opened the first door.

Darkness awaited him.

No lit room. Just the dark.

Lore thought she could see something in there—the geometry of furniture. Not sure what kind, or where. A bedroom? She couldn't be sure.

Nick gave her another look.

She said nothing, just shook her head a little.

Don't go in there was the message.

He sighed and gave one long look into the dark before closing the door.

Then, the next door.

This one Lore couldn't see, so she idly walked behind Nick—not too close up on him; she didn't want to seem over interested (though why that was, she could not say), hovering behind him as he opened it.

This room: lit, but poorly. A small bathroom. Grimy subway tile shower behind a filmy curtain. A toilet in the corner. A white sink, above which hung a mirror that was shattered from the center out, as if it had been struck.

No other door in that one, and no window.

Nick grunted, closed the door, then wandered off without further commentary. Lore stood there for a moment, staring at the doors with a sharp twinge of fear and suspicion. Then something caught her eye. Something back at the bookshelves. One pop of color on a low shelf.

A *familiar* pop of color.

It was her book.

The one she'd written ten years ago.

It was *The Crazy Bitch's Guide to Game Design*, a title she loved then, hated now, and had almost gotten her canceled on Twitter about five years back when everyone was trapped in their homes during the pandemic and was bored and vengeful and looking for any taste of blood in the water to excite them. They said the title was ableist and misogynist and it probably was, but like Grandpa Simpson said, *It was the style at the time.* And all of it was based on how an early meeting with an Activision executive had him ranting at her that she was a "crazy bitch" and her ideas about gaming were "pretentious trash" and "full of avant-garde horseshit."

After that meeting, she vowed to do her thing without the help of some fucking megacorp, and she raised some capital and went on to make her own game—The Robot Relationship Simulator, which was less about robots and relationships and more about navigating trauma and how you infected others with your own bullshit, like a computer virus spread from person to person. It was really hot for an indie game, in part because (at least, this was her theory) she made it so you could romance and fuck different robots, and games where you could romance and fuck the other characters were always going to be a winner.

Soon as they announced it was on the ballot for best indie game at the Game Awards, who came swanning into her DMs but the same Activision exec, Kevin something-or-other. Or maybe it was Kenny? Whatever. He wanted to hire her and, by the sound of it, wanted to fuck her, too. She told him to eat nails. He sent her a photo of his cock as, what, revenge? Enticement? She posted the DMs to Twitter, and it caused a huge shitstorm—she outed him, a guy whose name she couldn't even remember, and not only did a lot of other women say he'd done similar to *them*, but then women started naming names of other rapey scumfucks in the industry. That snowball didn't just get bigger—it made a hundred other snowballs, all rolling downhill, all growing larger and larger, crushing anything in their paths.

Thing was, it didn't change shit, not really.

The men who got called out had to spend some time out of the industry, but they came back eventually, just at other companies. Like priests shuttled from church to church after they diddled a kid. And women didn't suddenly get hired in record numbers. Furthermore, all Lore got at the end of it was just more harassment from Gamergatey chodes who pretended to be serious "devil's advocates" who were "just asking questions" but who really just wanted to slut-shame women and keep them from getting their cooties all over their Important Men Games. You know, the ones with the guns and the bouncing-tit physics.

So Lore wrote a book. Because she was angry, and because yelling about stuff on social media didn't do anything except make her life worse.

That book was *The Crazy Bitch's Guide to Game Design*.

And here it was, on this shelf, in this place.

It felt like—

Like a message.

But what *was* that message, exactly?

Lore reached for her book.

"You okay?" Hamish asked Owen as he stared at the fish tank. *The knife. It was there. It was just fucking there.* Yet now it was gone.

"Oh. Yeah. Just—just peachy. You?"

Hamish laughed a little. "Oh yeah, man, fucking great, this has been a really killer vacation. Love this Airbnb Nick picked."

Owen chuckled—a small, dark laugh. But a real one.

"Yeah, this is pretty messed up."

"I . . . I shouldn't have come here, man, I shouldn't have left my family, and I should have never set foot on that staircase, and I did, and then—then you came after, and I wish I had stayed behind because maybe then you would've stayed and we, you and me, we'd still be okay—" He tried like hell to hold it back, but a single gulping sob came out of him like a gasp of agonal respiration.

Owen thought, *I would've gone anyway.*

Because Lore did.

"Ham, listen. It's not like that. You and I being left behind wouldn't have made it any better. That would've been its own kind of hell." *As it has been since Matty went away.* Owen shrugged. "Maybe this is the only way *out*. You don't have to be sorry."

"Nick does," Hamish said, in a low voice.

Owen's gaze flicked toward Nick, who wandered back to the closet door that they'd come through. He gave them each lifted eyebrows, then pulled the door open a few inches and peeked in. "It's just a wall now," Nick said. "The way we came is gone." He bared his teeth. "This fucking place."

Owen and Hamish said nothing.

Then Nick wandered off again, back toward Lore.

"I dunno," Owen said, once they were out of earshot again. "It seems like Nick has been trying to figure this out for a long time. All those emails? He's been trying to get us to look for Matty since forever. He's been trying to tell us something, and . . . we didn't listen. He just wants to find Matty."

"Yeah. Okay. Maybe." Hamish sniffled. "We good, though?"

"You and me, we're good. But this place—we're not good here. Something's wrong with this house. Something is rotten."

"If it even is a house."

"Yeah."

"Yeah."

"Shit."

Page after page of hate.

That's what Lore was looking at. It wasn't her book. Well, it *was*—on the cover, and some of the pages in the book, especially pages toward the front? Yeah, those were hers. But then—one page had a series of tweets about her. Another page was a Reddit thread, again, all about her. Forum posts supposedly about her game but really about her quote-unquote "mannish face." Gross memes using photos of her to make her seem crazy, ugly, insane. A naked porn-star body but with her face deepfaked onto it. Then, most hateful of all, awful reviews of her games, her books, her art. One stars, fuck her, commie leftist bitch, crazy whore, I heard she fucked this guy, fucked this girl, I heard she's Antifa, I heard she's a dude, she's bi, she's trans, she's a liar, a narcissist, a thief, she didn't even write these games, she stole them, *she stole them*—

The fucking nerve of these people, it made her want to vom a hot rage geyser all over the page—

"Yo," Nick said, hand on her shoulder.

She reflexively closed the book fast—it snapped shut like a crocodile's mouth. "Jesus. What?"

He shot a conspiratorial look over his shoulder.

"You and me, we get it," he said.

"Get what?"

"Why we're here."

"Nick, just spit it out. I don't want to play games."

"You ran up those stairs. Owen was right. You did not hesitate. I got us here and you were off like a shot, and I just wanted to say, I see you. Okay? I see you, and I appreciate you. I know we weren't always the closest in the group, but—"

"Nick."

"But I'm just saying, I admire you, and I admire that you went up those stairs and did the right thing. Those two over there, ehh, I don't know about them."

"*Nick*. Listen. Nick. You lied to us, and maybe it was for a good reason—"

"It was. You can see that! *It was.*"

"—but this is all pretty fucked up, and I'm not interested in this little whisper campaign thing you're doing right now. I'm kinda pissed at those two and maybe they're pissed at me, and honestly, I'm real pissed at you too right now because all of this is screwing with my head in a big, big way. And so like I said, I have no interest in playing—"

Games.

Games.

Lore looked at the book in her hand.

Quietly, she slid it back onto the shelf.

"You strokin' out?" Nick said.

But she ignored him and pushed past. Then she said to the other two, "This isn't a regular house. It's not a haunted house. It's a *game*."

37

Ludonarrative Dissonance

They all sat down again on the white leather couch as Lore stood there and told them again: "This whole place is a game."

That earned her confused looks.

Hamish said, "What?"

"This place. This . . . experience. It's a game."

"Yeah, we heard you, *Lauren*," Nick said, suddenly angry. "You can't call it that. You can't just . . . you can't just *say* that and make it true. It's not a fucking game. It's serious. You're a hammer, so everything you see is a nail, but—"

Owen interrupted:

"She's maybe not wrong."

It was his turn to get the looks. Even from Lore, who seemed shocked he was agreeing with her. Which was fair, because *Owen* was shocked he was agreeing with her. But again, she wasn't wrong.

At least, not entirely.

"It's not a game," he said, "but it's *like* one."

Lore snapped her fingers and pointed at him. "Yeah. That."

"Think about it. We come here from another place, through—not a portal precisely, but a staircase that functions as one. Kind of like the moongate in the ring of stones from *Ultima*. Then we get here and it's like—"

"It's like *Zork*. Or any of the old text adventures from Infocom. What's the opening? *West of House. You are standing in an open field west of a white house, with a boarded front door—*"

Owen joined in, said the rest with her:

"*There is a small mailbox here.*"

He remembered it well—he and Lore used to play games like this all the time. They'd play them sometimes together, in the same room. Or when on the phone with each other until two, three o'clock in the morning. *Zork, Ultima, Wasteland, Elder Scrolls, Bard's Tale, King's Quest, Space Quest, Maniac Mansion* 1 and 2, all the PC games that made them want to make games, too, or tell stories, or make *experiences* that other people could join. Of course, only Lore really got to do that part, didn't she? Owen found that dark core of bitterness inside him rise up like acid in the back of his throat. He choked it back down.

"It's like that," she said, "or like *Bard's Tale*. You have a room, you have things in the room, you have your exits—"

He continued on, staring darkly at her. "And if you go the wrong way, if you make the wrong choice, you're eaten by a grue. Game over." *Just like it was game over for me.* That thought turned in his head like a screw.

"I don't know what a 'grue' is," Hamish said, looking confused.

"Yeah," Nick said, "we weren't nerding out and jerking one another off with this dork shit, okay? Me, Ham, and Matty were getting stoned like proper kids."

Lore gave him a look like he'd just spit in her soda. "Nick, we used to play D&D every Sunday. You were there. We took turns being the Dungeon Master, you dick."

"Yeah, but we got *high* while doing it."

"No, but see—" Owen jumped in. "Even with D&D, it's like that, too. The grid paper, designing dungeons, choosing which door to go through, finding monsters, avoiding traps—"

"This isn't a fucking game, man!" Hamish bleated. "Okay? This is fucked." He stood up. "Nick's right. Let's pick one of those doors and just walk through, let's just keep moving, okay? I say we pick a direction and we hard-charge it until we find the way out. It's like going on a hike and getting lost. You pick a direction and you walk until you find a highway or some shit."

Lore barked a bitter laugh. "That's *not* what you do if you're lost in the woods, Ham! If you get lost in the woods, you pick a spot and you stay there. You shelter in place, same as you'd do in a storm or a zombie apocalypse. And this isn't the woods. Those doors? Don't go in a straight line. Right now, one seems to go to a bathroom full of broken mirror glass and the other to a—a dark bedroom. And we can't go back through the closet—"

"The way is shut," Nick said. "Where we came from is gone again, and there's no door. It's just a wall now."

Hamish buried his face in his hands. "Fuck, fuck, fuck."

Owen felt bad for his old friend. Somehow, Hamish was handling it worse than he was. And Owen wasn't handling it well at all. He felt he had to disassociate from this experience entirely unless he wanted to grab fistfuls of his own hair and rip them from his scalp like grass from a lawn.

Lore continued: "I'm just saying, there is no 'straight line path' to a highway. Maybe there's an easy way out, and if there is we will find it, but we're going to have to do this in a smart way. Like in a game, in a dungeon, we have to think about our choices here. And we have to do it together."

"One problem," Nick said.

"Which is?"

"We're going to need to eat food."

She nodded. "Yeah. Right! Of course. Here—" Lore still had her backpack, and from there, she pulled out a couple of protein bars. Some bougie brand called Elation. Lore tossed one to Hamish and kept one. "Ham, you and Nick split that. Me and Owen will have the other. I have more, but we should ration." Implicit in that last sentence: *just in case*. And implicit in *that*? Just in case they're stuck here. Really, seriously stuck here. Trapped in the maze. Owen pictured it in his head like a game map. *Staircase to Hallway to Marshie's Room to*

Thumb Cake Room to the Greige Room. Hallways between them. Shadows lurking.

"I'm not fucking hungry," Hamish said.

Nick was already unwrapping theirs, though—breaking it in half and shoving that piece into Hamish's hand. "Here. You need to eat. It's—" He checked the crumpled up label. "Hazelnut Crunch, with lion's mane, rishi, and cordyceps mushrooms. Jesus, Lore. Can't wait to chow down on the forest floor!" He popped the whole thing in his mouth and gamely chewed. Hamish mumbled something about "I like this brand" before biting into his half, nibbling at its edges.

As Lore ripped at the packaging of theirs with her teeth, she said, "Have a snack. Then let's try to, I dunno, rest a little. Lie down. Shut your eyes. Even if you don't sleep, I think we need it. Again, remember, we were all trudging through the woods a few hours ago. And since then it's just been adrenalin and cortisol dumps, and I know I feel like someone has run a serrated steak knife across my brain—and maybe if we give it some time, the rooms will shift again."

Owen looked to the doors at the far end of the living room.

One of them which apparently opened into darkness.

They all agreed. Hamish sat back, staring at the ceiling, eating his bar with the hesitation of a pukey fifth grader. Nick went to the other end of the couch and lay right down, shoes still on, his arms crossed across his chest like a mummy—it was the way he slept, always. Owen wondered if he was still so sound a sleeper. Nick would pass out *hard,* and the only way to wake him was essentially to waterboard him with a washcloth. That always got him up.

Owen pushed himself into the couch as Lore walked up to him and offered him his half of the protein bar. "It's peanut butter, quinoa, and collagen."

At that, he couldn't help but laugh a little. "God, Lore, why do you have these cursed protein bars?"

"Trying to, like, min-max hack my health."

"Is it working?"

Her turn to laugh. "Probably not. I still have a BP high enough that

I could probably squirt blood out of the corners of my eyes, like a lizard."

"Mine's so low, they're worried I'm dead."

"Shit. Getting old is stupid."

"Yeah."

"Yeah."

They ate their protein bars. It was somehow both good and gross. The peanut butter flavor was real, and not chemical-tasting, and the quinoa provided real crunch. But it also had a weird oily taste—and not edible oil, but almost as if it had been run through a dish of aloe vera lotion beforehand.

He finally said, around a mouthful of the weird food, "I'm . . . sorry I rolled up on you so hard earlier."

"Nah. No. You were right. I fucked it. I fucked us. I ran up those stairs without thinking. I could've been smarter. I *should*'ve been smarter. I just . . ." Her voice withered to a soft sigh. "Mistakes were made."

"You missed Matty."

"Yes. But no. I—" She shook her head and said stiffly, "I can't do this now. But I just wanted you to know, you were right. This is my fault, and I should've been better. I will be better. I'll get us out of this."

"You're not our leader, Lore. It's all right."

Her mouth formed a hard line. Her words were firm when she responded with, "I *said* I have to do better. And I will." She took the wrapper trash back from him and looked around for a trash can. Shrugging, she just stuffed it back in her pocket. "Whatever. Get a little rest. Then we figure out what's next."

"Lore, I think we need to talk—"

But she was already walking away from him, to the other side of the room, where she moved one chair across from the other and used them as a kind of clumsy, makeshift cot. Already he could see her eyes were closed.

Owen sighed.

And he shut his eyes, too. A valiant, if worthless, endeavor.

38

The Voices

The voices were soft at first, so soft they almost sounded like nothing at all. But as Owen pressed himself deeper into the couch, those voices pushed their way into his head like fingers through soft dough. They were everywhere. Worse when he pressed his ear to the couch; there, they seemed to vibrate louder, bullying their way through the atoms and molecules of the leather. They came from below. From the sides. And even from somewhere up above.

He assumed they were just a dream, some hallucination as he skidded across the surface of sleep like a flat stone skipping across a still pond. Sleep could be like that for him sometimes: He would lie there, and just as he started to dip into sleep, he'd pop that perfect bubble and tumble into some terrible dream space, plunging into nameless nightmare before waking suddenly, his heart hammering.

These voices, though, conjured in him a peculiar kind of nostalgia: when you're a child, and you're hearing adults talk in an adjacent room, but they're trying to keep quiet enough not to wake you. You cannot hear their words, only the soft murmur and mumble of the voices themselves. And in that sound, you can detect emotion, you can hear the rhythm and the rise and the fall, but you can't make out what they're actually *saying*. In his case, those moments usually, maybe always, ended with his father yelling at his mother. Then a door slam. Then her crying, still softly, because she tried to keep her sobs a secret. So as not to wake her one son.

Finally, Owen inhaled deeply and sat up, his eyes open.

He still heard the voices.

Hamish was in the crook of the sofa, where it bent, and he too was awake. Looking up and around. The look of someone hearing something.

"You hear it, too?" Hamish asked, quietly.

"The voices?"

"Yeah." Hamish sat upright, rubbing his eyes. "It's like when my parents had a fight. Man, they fought all the time. Night and day."

Owen nodded. "Mine didn't fight that often, but when they did..." It was mostly his father who yelled. Mom just... went along. He never hit her, never hit Owen. It was always just words, but that whole thing about sticks and stones was a lie. Words hurt as bad as a fist. Maybe worse. Because a fist, maybe you excuse that as oh, he couldn't help it, he's just an animal, a primate, his blood was up. But someone cuts you with words? Calls you names, tells you how little they think of you? That bypasses all your armor. A razor sliding across the meat of your heart.

One time, though, his mother came hurrying up the steps as he was going down, and she stopped him midway. Her face was streaked with the runoff of ruined makeup. Her nose rimmed with snot. Mom was usually quiet, usually sweet, didn't say much, didn't take up much room, rarely had a bad word to say. But that day, she said in the coldest, cruelest tone, "I hope he hangs himself. He's miserable enough to do it. You'll see."

And Owen remembered nodding along with that. Agreeing with her. And a little part of him felt like maybe, just *maybe*, things would turn around after that—maybe Mom could stoke that little fire in her belly into a proper bonfire. Maybe she would fight back. For herself and for Owen. But it didn't happen. After that day, the fire went out and she mostly melted into the background again. Then, when he was in college, came the car accident. A pickup truck T-boned her Chevy Malibu at an intersection—a car she hated but that Dad had bought for her—and she died at the hospital that night. And a few years after that, Dad died, too. Not of suicide, like his mother had hoped. Cancer. He remembered visiting him then and—

He flinched at the coming memory, and cut it off at the knees.

He felt along the ridges of his ears, found a hair there, plucked it. A tiny spike of pain felt clarifying. He wanted to pluck more. He wanted to dig a finger deep into his ear, scrape out the wax. Then stick a pencil even deeper, puncturing the drum. In the fullness of blood he wouldn't be able to hear the voices through the walls. Owen gritted his teeth; he needed to shake it off.

So he stood up and walked to the wall next to the closet where they'd come in. He pressed his ear to the drywall. The voices were louder this way, but he still couldn't make anything out. Two people? Three? A man, a woman, at least. A laugh. Then, agitation. Not a happy laugh. More babble and gush. More from the teachers and parents in *Peanuts. Womp womp womp womp.*

"I think it's coming from this direction," he hissed to Hamish, who was on the other side of the room, at the end of the couch near Nick's head.

But Hamish said, "No, I hear it here."

Owen went over and listened.

Sure enough, more voices there. Same voices? He couldn't tell.

"Fuck are you two doing?" Lore asked, plodding over, yawning.

"You don't hear it?" he asked her.

"Hear what?" she asked, but then she seemed to take a moment. Her head tilted and her face tightened in concern and confusion. "Are those voices?"

They said yeah. Voices.

Lore blinked. "There are people here. Other people." Hope bloomed on her face. "We have to find them. Where are they?"

"I think they're... everywhere," Owen said.

Murmur, mumble, hum, and babble. Muted susurrus of conversation.

Nick slept through it all, because of course he did.

In a whirl of motion, Lore stalked to the pair of doors at the far side of the room and threw both of them open. They remained what they were: one an entrance to a small bathroom with shattered mirror glass everywhere, the other a dark room, with just the barest of shapes outlined in the black.

The voices came from neither.

Hamish shuddered and moved around Lore to shut both the doors.

"Sorry," he said, defensively. "In here, open doors feel . . . weird."

Like a threat, Owen thought idly. *A cruel promise.*

Lore moved back to the other side of the room. Ear to the wall. Then she started pounding on the wall. "Hello?" she called. "*Hello!*"

But the voices continued, unabated, no response.

So she pounded louder, and yelled louder.

Nick, at this point, snorted awake. "Jesus fuck," he grumbled.

Lore dragged over a chair and started yelling at the wall, the ceiling, just saying, *Hello, can you hear us, are you there?* over and over again, and she hit the ceiling one last time and—

The voices paused.

Then:

Mumblemumble

Murmurmumble?

Mum

Mrrm

Womm wemm numm!

Suddenly, the voices erupted. A man yelling. A woman ending his tirade with a dire scream, the kind of scream that was one of fear and torment and pain—then, finally, a *thud.* It shook the room.

Silence in the aftermath.

They all looked to one another before Nick interrupted with: "What was that? Were there people? Are there other people?" He struggled to escape the trap of the couch but finally managed to stand. "We need to go. We need to go and find them, they could know Matty—"

"I . . . don't think so," Lore said.

"What?"

"We don't know what that is. Or *who* that was," Owen said.

Hamish pointed at Owen as if to say, *Yeah, exactly.* "Last voice we heard came out of a dead girl with her throat slit."

"And those voices we just heard? They didn't sound friendly."

"But one of them was a woman. And she could be hurt."

"She could be *dead*," Nick said, bluntly. "Or dying."

Hamish had an *of course* look on his face. "God. It's them. It's the people who owned this house. That sound, the thump . . ."

He didn't have to finish the thought. They all understood what that meant. The father of the house killing his wife. As one, they again turned to look at the bloody glass sculpture on the bookshelf.

"We should go. We have to go. I mean—" Lore shrugged. "Not like we're going to be going back to sleep. The rooms haven't changed. Still a bathroom. Still a dark place. We'll just—we have our phones, yeah? Power them up, we can use the flashlights to make it through."

Owen sighed. Fear prickled his skin. He didn't want to leave because—well, this room was safe. Safe enough, anyway. No dead girls, no thumbs on cakes. Just some dead fish and ugly greige. It would be easier to stay here. To remain here. *To wait and stop and be safe and shrivel up and deliquesce until you're just a comfortable, soft gelatin soaking into the gray-beige carpet.* That thought, sung to him like a song from outside himself. A lullaby of sorts. The comfort of doing nothing. The peace of waiting. The easy contentment of slow death.

That's what you've been doing your whole life, he realized.

Just watching and waiting and—

And dying.

He shuddered.

Lore was right. They had to go. They had to *move*.

"Good?" Lore asked, rhetorically, not waiting for an answer before she said, with some finality, "Good. Meanwhile—I can't believe I have to say this, but it's like we're going on a road trip. That means if you have to go to the bathroom, do it now, since we . . . have a bathroom. We'll go in one at a time, but *keep the door open*. No room for embarrassment here, cool? Door open."

They all nodded.

"Line up for potty breaks," she said. "Except I'm first, because I know you animals are going to soak the seat."

She headed off to the bathroom. Nick followed after.

Hamish took Owen aside. "Fuck, man. I don't know about this. I don't know if this is a good idea."

"I don't know either. But I don't think we can stay here."

"Tell me we're going to be all right."

"If you're looking to *me* for reassurance, we're pretty fucked."

Hamish shrugged. "I still need it. I still need to know we're going to be okay, that we're going to get out of this place, man."

It dug into him to see Hamish rattled. Hamish, who for so long lived what could best be described as an *unexamined life*, looking to Owen, who lived what could only be described as an *overexamined life*.

"We're going to be fine," Owen lied.

"Yeah?"

"Yeah."

"Covenant?"

"Covenant."

They hugged.

It was the last time they'd do so for a long while.

39

The Loneliest Number

The Broken Glass Bathroom.
    Before Lore went in, her mind felt occupied, her mental fingers sliding around the margins of the puzzle of this place. Because that's what it was to her: a puzzle, a game, a maze. Like Owen had said, a D&D dungeon, a *Zork* adventure game. Solve the puzzle. Choose the right path. It felt cold and clarifying.
    But then she went into the bathroom.
    She had to be careful—the whole room was full of broken mirror glass. Easy enough to step over, but it was a little slippery. Some of it was in the sink, too. The mirror itself was broken from the center out—as if someone had struck it with a fist or an object. Most of the glass was gone, though a few pieces still stuck to the backing. Slivers of Lore stared back at herself. But also: words. Someone had drawn words on the glass. Not on every shard, but on half of them, at least, drawn on with what looked like lipstick.

HELP
RUN
LOST
PAIN
SCARED
NO

    What the fuck. She tried to add that to the mystery. What was this? What were these messages? Were they written by someone else?

Someone like them, someone trapped in this place? Her heart froze in her chest—

Were they written by Matty?

Was he still here, or was he long gone?

Had they waited too long to follow him?

Her bladder reminded her of why she was in here, so Lore went and sat on the toilet and did her business, leaning forward as she peed. She wanted to keep thinking about the mystery, the puzzle, but something else pushed those thoughts out. As she stared at the mildewy tile and at the broken glass, anger bubbled up in her. Anger at herself for not following Matty up the staircase—she'd wanted him to take acid, and he didn't. She'd wanted to tell him how she was good with them being in a relationship, a proper real boyfriend-girlfriend thing, but she didn't. She got mad, pushed him away, and he acted out. Called out the Covenant and they blew him off—and not long after, up he went, and then he was gone. *You stupid bitch. You did this. This is your fault. Your fault for not chasing Matty then. Your fault for running up those stairs now.* There was no winning. Every move in this game was a net fucking loss. A *Choose Your Own Adventure* book where every page turn led to being eaten, drowned, incinerated, trapped forever.

And then the anger multiplied—a mirror broken, one image into many. She was angry at the others for following her here. For not going up the steps when it mattered most. None of them cared about the Covenant. They'd all broken it. Nick talked a good game but what had he ever done? He sent them emails about staircases and doorways he'd read about, but did he ever go up one? No.

Suddenly she was sure as anything that she should do this alone.

Get rid of the others.

They were dead weight.

Holding her back. Like they always did.

Especially Owen. Weak, pathetic, do-nothing, go-nowhere Owen.

He's the shadow on your X-ray. The cancer in you bringing you down.

Killing you.

If you want to find Matty—
If you want to escape—
You need to escape them first.
Then, a loud sound—

The door to the bathroom, thrown open. *Wham.* Lore startled as Owen (*shadow, cancer, pathetic*) barged into the room.

"What the fuck?" she asked, throwing up her hands. (Modesty was not one of her character traits, so she did nothing to hide anything.) "I'm pissing."

"What the fuck to you," he said, giving her his own *what the fuck* look. "You said to keep the door open when we went."

"Yeah, so?"

"You were starting to close the door."

"Closing the—what? I'm on the toilet. I wasn't closing anything."

Hamish's head popped in over Owen's shoulder. "It was drifting closed, I guess."

"Well I didn't close it."

"Fine," Owen said.

"Fine."

Now, Nick peeked in. "Can we hurry this up? Hearing you piss makes *me* gotta piss, so ándale, ándale, let's move."

Lore nodded. "Yeah. Yeah. Okay. Jeez."

It struck her then—them coming into the room seemed to chase away those dark thoughts. Like cockroaches when you turn on the light. Skitter, skitter.

And the door, drifting closed without her touching it . . .

This place wants us to be alone.

Lore hurried up, flushed—the toilet worked, and so did the sink. The water was clear, had no smell. She cupped some in her hand and took a sip, and it tasted minerally and metallic but not like poison. Lore cast one last look at the words across the broken mirror shards, then she hurried out of the bathroom, a chill chasing her back toward her friends.

40

You're Not Scared of the Dark, You're Scared of What's in It

"Everyone have their phones out and powered on?" Lore asked.

They did. They also each checked again to see if they had any service—

Still nothing.

No way out, and no way to reach out. Fine. *So we push through.* But pushing through had to be smart. They had to have strategy. Not like Nick, wanting to just bum-rush every room. If this was really like a game, like a dungeon, they needed to take it room by room, and do it *slowly*. Check the corners. Check for traps.

Lore always thought that in movies and games, the characters never did the right thing—more to the point, they never did the *smart* thing. It's why she loved tabletop role-playing way more than video games, even though she was more a video game designer by trade. (She would gladly have designed pen-and-paper RPGs instead, but the money there was lower than Lowly Worm. She could not afford cool cross-body bags and magic shrooms and bougie-ass sex toys on the pennies tossed at her feet by the RPG industry. Not their fault, of course. Mostly.) At the game table, you could bring strategy, you could make plans, you could try *crazy shit* to help solve a situation or just stay alive. So here, in this situation, she knew they had to do this the smart way.

It would not behoove them to go stumbling around blind, here more than anywhere. But moving ahead with lights in front of them wasn't enough. Not in a place where a dead girl crawled out from under a bed.

The plan, then, was this:

She wanted lights in every direction.

They'd walk forward in a diamond configuration.

Her at the front.

Hamish and Owen behind her to the left and to the right.

Nick at the back.

They'd point their lights in their respective directions: forward, left, right, and behind them.

Their last problem, and this was one she could do nothing about:

The light from their phones' flashlights was a weak, sad thing. They offered pale, wan light—thin like moonlight. But it was better than nothing. She asked Nick if he had his Zippo, and he flinched. "No," he said. "I, uhh, I lost it."

"Okay, no lighter," she said, taking a deep breath. "This is what we got. Let's do this."

She opened the door. It drifted open, the unoiled hinges whining.

The room ahead was pitch black.

Her heart pounded as she stood on the verge of darkness. It felt mad to be so scared of it—she'd long conquered her fear of the dark, like most adults, even though sometimes she still felt that little twinge of primeval fear, a *tweak* of certainty that something was hunting you in the shadows. That was the funny thing about a fear of the dark: you weren't really afraid of *it*, but rather what lurked *within it*. A perfect emblem of the fear of the unknown.

A smell scurried through the opening to meet her. An antiseptic smell, but something else, too. Something sour—the pickling brine of sweat, piss, and sickness. Like what you might smell in a hospital room. The cleaning chemical scent was strong, but not strong enough to beat back the perfume of death.

"Ready?" she asked.

They were.
And with that, she stepped into the room.

Lore went in. Then Hamish.

Owen was next.

He stepped forward—

Gazing into the dark, a darkness slowly lit by the thin blooming light from Lore's and Hamish's phones. He saw furniture, like a dresser. A bedpost. A bed.

Owen stood in the doorway. Not going through. Not yet.

Because the smell hit him then—

It was a grotesquely familiar scent. It hit him deep, like a hand thrust into water, stirring up mud. That bleach smell, the way it didn't cover up those ill odors, the rancid tang, but underneath it all, a smell of shitty dark instant coffee, the kind you might put on a bedside table and never drink, because you couldn't drink it, because you were too full of meds and your body puked up anything you put into it anyway. And as the lights of Hamish and Lore turned to converge on the bed, and the shape of the person lying within it—

No.

Owen panicked—

He took a step back and slammed the door.

"What the fuck?" Nick asked, pushing past him.

"I—I—" *I know that room. I know that person. Dad. That was Dad.* "It was just reflexive, I didn't mean to—"

Nick opened the door.

The dark room was gone. No bed, no smell.

The next room was now a playroom, by the looks of it. Sunny-yellow walls. An IKEA-looking low shelf on the one side, full of toys. Another shelf on the other side, full of picture books. In one corner, a cozy white recliner, like for a parent watching over a child, maybe even for a nursing mother. And in the corner next to it, a Christmas tree, ratty and dead, a carpet of dead brown needles littering both the floor and the unopened gifts tucked beneath its now brittle branches. No Lore. No Hamish.

"They're gone," Nick said.

No, no, no—no no no.

But Nick said it again: "They're fucking gone. Owen, what did you do?"

41

New Room, Who This

The lights from their phones swam through the dark. The room here felt humid, thick with that sour diaper smell, with the odor of human rot—and as their beams converged, Lore and Hamish found themselves looking at a broken twig of a man, buried under covers, the weak flashlights illuminating a gray face that seemed more like a mask of skin gently and awkwardly laid across a skull than a face. The eyes rotated in the skull. Breath wheezed.

Then they heard it—

The click of the door behind them.

Lore and Hamish spun as it closed.

Hamish didn't understand, but Lore instinctively did. The door closing meant something, she knew that now, same as it had when it closed in Marshie's room (though who had closed that one, she did not know)—

Lore moved fast, three long strides to the door—

She whipped it open, already saying Owen's name. "Owen, why the fuck did you—" But even as the words were falling out of her mouth, she knew in her gut what had happened. The door no longer opened on Owen and Nick. It did not find the Greige Room. It found a new room instead. A strange country kitchen. Garish. Tacky. Her guts churned. Her head spun. *Fuck. Fuck. Fuck.*

Hamish, now behind her. "Wait. What happened? Where are they?"

"They're gone," she said. And when she said the words, a little voice slithered into her mind, a voice that she feared was not her own but still sounded like her, and it said: *One step closer to doing it yourself, Lore. Like you always do. The only way anything ever gets done.*

42

The Tear-Drowned Playroom

Everything felt sluggish. Owen threw out a hand to brace himself against the doorjamb so he didn't fall forward into the room ahead of him—a playroom. A playroom that was not his father's bedroom. A playroom with a dead Christmas tree but not his two friends, Lore and Hamish.

He shut his eyes so hard it hurt. He thrust his free hand toward his mouth. He bit down hard on his pinky, yanking a crescent of fingernail free—like a vine pulled loose from under the dirt, it unzipped down the side of the nail, freeing fresh blood. He tasted that blood, dark and coppery. He suckled the finger and tried not to bite it clean off.

"The fuck did you do that for?" Nick growled at him.

"I—it was my father's bedroom."

"What? So what?"

"He—" Owen had to bite back bile. "He was in it. My dad. I saw him. I *smelled* him. He had cancer and . . ." His voice died on the vine.

"You really fucking did it now, Zuikas." Nick grunted. "You're bleeding, by the way."

Owen looked down at the pinky finger. Fresh blood oozed toward the crook of his fingers. Over his knuckles. "I know." *And it feels good. It feels right.*

"Lore! Hamish!" he called suddenly. A desperate plea.

No one answered. Because they were somewhere else now.

The rooms had shifted. He'd closed the door and that was that.

"Do we go through?" Owen asked Nick.

"What are you asking me for?" Nick said, sounding defensive. "I've never been here. I don't know shit from shit, Nailbiter."

"I think we go through. Maybe . . . maybe the door will reset then. Maybe the rooms will shift and, and, I dunno, and they'll be there. In the next room. This place can't be infinite. We're going to see them again, right?"

Nick didn't say anything.

"Nick. Right? We'll see them again?"

All Nick did then was shrug, then step through the door.

Owen cursed, and followed after.

He stepped into the playroom—

Then turned, closed the door behind him, and opened it again.

The Greige Room was gone.

In its place waited a crowded attic space full of boxes and bins and the detritus of domestic life: a rack of bagged clothes, a leaning stack of framed paintings, a crooked tower of *National Geographic* magazines, a beat-up-looking tricycle. And at the far end, under a gable vent and small wooden door, there was a disheveled futon mattress. On that mattress was something else, a body-shaped thing swaddled in filthy bedsheets, bedsheets the color of rust and old chocolate.

The body-shaped thing on the lumpy mattress sat straight up.

Owen let slip a small cry of alarm, then slammed the door.

What the fuck was that thing. What the fuck.

He fumbled with the doorknob as he turned the lock.

"What was that thing?" he asked Nick.

"I don't know, and I don't want to find out."

Owen backed away from the door. He nearly tripped on a toy—a stuffed plushie, a fuzzy blue dog with floppy ears. The stuffed dog started barking. A garbled sound, as if through a tinny speaker. It started off fast, too fast, *ruffruffruffruff,* but then began to slow and dissolve—*rufffff ruuuuuuffff gggkkkkrrrhhhhkffff*—before the sound died out. Owen, heart now hammering against his breastbone like it was a punching bag, kicked the dog and it thumped against the wall.

"Fuck. Fuck." Finally, he said, "So they're really gone. Lore and Hamish."

"Yeah," Nick said quietly. "They're gone. And we're gone."

"Yeah. *Yeah.*" Owen pushed the heels of his hands so hard into his eyes, he saw the universe exploding into greasy streaks of white light. He staggered over to the chair and sat in it, pulling his knees up to his chest and hugging them. "I don't know what we're going to do now. How are we going to find them again? There's only one door out of this room, and it . . . it doesn't go where we need it to go. This was your idea. Your idea to find those steps, to get us there, to go up them. So you tell me, Nick. What do we do now? Nick. *Nick.*"

But it was easy to see in the way that Nick searched the middle distance with his stare that he had no answers.

"I don't know, Zuikas. I honestly don't know."

43

The Sick Boy's Kitchen

They waited for a while in the Dying Man's Bedroom. Sometimes they stared out at the kitchen through the open door. Sometimes Lore closed that door and waited. *They might come through still,* she told Hamish. *We shelter in place. Like I said. We wait for them.* But time bled out. The clock was ticking. The smell of this place was starting to overpower her. Hamish said he couldn't take it either, said he was going to puke if they had to stay in here.

So through the door they went. Into the kitchen.

Lore closed the door after she stepped through, then opened it anew.

No more Dying Man's Bedroom. On the other end of the door now waited a different bedroom. This one, almost boudoir-like—Lore would've thought it Victorian if she hadn't spied an electronic alarm clock on a bedside table.

(The time read *00:00,* blinking red.)

"It shifted," she said. Trying to hide the confusion and despair in her voice.

She turned around to regard this new room.

This kitchen: a little dining nook area off to the right, just behind them. Proper kitchen off to the left, sink along the far wall (where there should have been a window, she could tell), fridge and range on the other side. It was a country-style kitchen, powder-blue cabinets and a cheap laminate countertop, and white shelves everywhere offering tons of random junk (little ceramic chicken tchotchkes and various kitschy egg timers, Precious Moments figurines, fake fruit, a jar full of rubber bands and twist ties). At the far side of the room, another door.

And in any other house, that door might have been anything from a pantry to a trash closet to a way into a garage, but here, there was no way to predict. It would go, most likely, to another room in this ever-shifting mismatched nightmare house.

It was a house, wasn't it? Had they seen any room that was not a room from someone's home somewhere? House, apartment, condo, whatever. All of it, places people lived. No cubicles, no factory floor, no museum displays, none of that. Everything was a bedroom, a kitchen, a bathroom, and so on.

So far, at least.

This place couldn't be infinite. It had to loop back around, right? Had to be some way to get back to Owen and Nick. Problem was, she couldn't communicate with them. The best move was for one of their groups to stay in place and the other to move in the hopes of finding them, but determining who would stay and who would search was impossible. They might both stay in place, or they might both roam this domestic labyrinth.

And what *was* this place, anyway? As in, why did it exist?

Where did it come from?

Was it even *real*?

It felt real. Looked real. *Smelled* real. Even now she could smell odd kitchen smells. The scent of burned cookies. The odor of a trash can gone off. The slick stink of too much cleaning spray to try to cover up something foul.

These rooms are all ruined somehow.

Dead fish, rancid cake with a thumb in it, dead girl, now this.

What waited for them here in this kitchen? In the next room? In the next after that? She could feel, even now, that *pressure* in her head, the one that told her to go out on her own—just leave Hamish here, she could tell him she'd be back, then forge on without him. It felt like a thought someone else had put there. But at the same time, it made sense. She did well on her own. Always.

Weariness wrapped itself around her bones, slowly crushing her. Lore went to the nook table and sat down, slumping forward.

Hamish paced the room.

"I hated having to sell a place like this back in my real estate days. Like, it's obviously well-loved and whatever, but it's ugly and it sucks. So the most painful thing was telling the seller, *You gotta get rid of all this stuff, paint it white, try to make it look a little less like the cottage of some middle-aged upstate farmer type.* Every house, you just wanted them to paint the personality out of it so that the next people could see a place to put their personality into."

"Yeah," Lore said, barely listening.

"Owen. Nick."

"I know," Lore said. "They're gone." *Or we are.*

"We need to—they can't—they're out there and—"

"*I know.*"

She scanned the room even as Hamish paced.

What stood out suddenly was the wheelchair. She almost didn't realize it was there, since it was at the far side of the breakfast nook table—what she thought was a chair with four legs was instead a chair with two wheels. And at that place was a plastic food tray mostly empty but for bits of dried food—like maybe baby food? Something blended. Chopped. Easy to chew or gum.

Lore stood up and rounded the table to get a closer look.

Pills. There were pills in that tray. Pills of indeterminate origin— two capsules, two little tablets, a big dry horse pill. The cleaning smell was really strong over here, too, and then it hit her—

She looked around again—

Oh, god.

She knew this kitchen.

She'd *seen* this kitchen before.

Never been in it, no, but she'd watched enough of the

documentary—which used a lot of footage from the family—to recognize it.

"This is Billy Dink's kitchen," she said.

Hamish froze and arched an eyebrow in confusion. "Who?"

She explained. Said that Billy Dink was a thirteen-year-old boy whose mother kept him sick on purpose, who told the world he had a number of rare conditions in order to elicit their sympathy, their money, and most of all, their *attention*. Because his mother, Brenda, was a narcissist monster in the throes of MSP: Munchausen syndrome by proxy. She fabricated his illnesses and kept him both sick by dosing him with various cleaning products and doped up via the pills she got from the doctor. Somehow, at some point, Billy had enough presence of mind to fight through the fog of poison and pills and realize what was happening to him—that he wasn't born sick, but rather was *made* that way by *his own monstrous mother*. He started to hide his pills instead of swallowing them, and in a moment of clarity, he stole a serrated steak knife from one of the kitchen drawers, and on a Tuesday morning in May, just before his mother was about to talk to local reporters about her son's condition, he stuck the knife in her neck and she died.

She died here *in this room*. In fact—

Lore walked into the kitchen, looking down.

The floor here was tile.

The tile was clean.

But the grout was not.

The grout had been . . . stained rust red in an erratic patch.

Where the blood had left her neck. Where it had pooled. Where it had used the space between tiles as canals in which to travel and spread.

"Okay," Hamish said, confused and uninterested. On a lark, he went poking around the kitchen. Lore's brain set to work. This was a kitchen she knew. That Greige Room was one that Hamish knew. And it had that book—*her* book in it.

She remembered then the message sliced into the wallpaper.

THIS PLACE HATES YOU.

She could feel that now. That was the pressure pushing itself against her—trying to push *into* her. Making room for itself. Making *rooms* for itself.

Hamish, opening a cabinet, said, "Holy shit, food—"

And she mumbled in acknowledgment as she tried to process what was happening. This room was part of a house of tragedy. Tragedy that culminated *in* this room, right here in the kitchen of the Dink household. Billy Dink killed his mother here. And because justice was blind in the worst way, Dink went to prison for ten years. Was still there, according to the documentary she'd watched (and the podcast she'd listened to, and the series of TikToks she'd scrolled).

Was every room they'd been in like this?

The staircase brought them here.

Then Marshie's Room: a girl who killed herself because she was depressed and because the boy she liked was mean to her.

The cake room: somebody's birthday that had gone really fucking wrong, ending up with a severed thumb on the cake.

The greige room: a parent, a child, killed by the father.

The bedroom: a cancer man, dying there, wheezing.

And now, this place.

The kitchen where Billy Dink was kept sick.

The kitchen where he killed his mother.

Hamish pulled out some kind of snack bag. Like potato chips, with the requisite bag crinkle. A crinkle sound that suddenly stopped. He mumbled something about them being stale.

But then . . .

". . . Lore?" Hamish asked.

"Yeah?" she asked, distracted.

"You need to see this."

She looked up, saw Hamish standing in front of an open cabinet. There were snacks in there. Potato chips, a bag of Hershey's Kisses, a little plastic bin full of sundae-making gear. Lore remembered something about this. The mother, Brenda, wouldn't she eat all the junk food in front of her son? And not share any of it except when she was using it to give him a little taste of poison?

What was so disturbing was how the mother filmed it all. Right there in the open. Not filming exactly what she was doing, no—she was filming life with Billy in order to get on the news and solicit more money, attention, love. But there were little signs in there, if you knew what to look and listen for. Like when she gave Billy a piece of chocolate and he said, "This tastes weird, Mama," and she told him, "The pills make everything taste weird, sweet baby." But it wasn't the pills making it taste bad. It was the Windex. Or the drain cleaner. Or the dust of metal shavings she sometimes put in things.

But that's not what Hamish was trying to show her.

He stood back and pulled the cabinet door wider.

Something had been etched on the inside of the door. Erratically, as if with a knife. Lore's blood went cold as she read it.

It said:

THE HEART IS WHERE THE HOME IS.

It was Matty's handwriting.

44

The Tale of Tank Thunderforge

1998.

A week after Matty's disappearance.

They all sat around in Nick's basement. Nobody was having much fun. Nick and Hamish were drinking Rolling Rock beer pilfered from the beer fridge in the garage upstairs. Nick's father wasn't home, but they all knew he wouldn't mind. He was fucking awesome, Nick's dad.

The rest of their parents, not so much.

"My parents know we didn't do shit, but my dad..." Owen started to say before shrugging. "He's still pissed anyway, like even though we didn't do it, it's still somehow our fault. Whatever. He fucking hates me anyway." Which was true. Not a guess. His father had told him once, while drinking schnapps: *I didn't want you. You're your mother's child. I take responsibility for you, because you're mine and I know it—but I don't love you, Owen. I regret having you. And some days, honestly, I hate you. I hate that you're here. I hate that you happened. You're like a boat anchor, dragging us all down.*

Lauren stared off into the corner. Her gaze trapped by lost space. "Same shit for me. Mom's gone most days, most nights. Few moments I get with her she's only half there. I think she's on pills now? Whatever. She tells me everything is fine, tells me not to worry. She doesn't know. She doesn't know shit."

"My mom pretends it's okay but she cries at night," Hamish said. "Dad fights with her about it, tells her we need to lawyer up. She says

God will fix it—did I mention she's been going to church now? Ugh. I dunno." Way he said it was *aye-unno*.

Nick just stood up and circled the room, the beer in his hand sloshing around the green bottle. He plugged it to his lips and drank some down, pulling it away with a *ploomp*. Nick sniffed. "Yeah. Well. My dad's cool and he knows I didn't do shit." He tapped a cigarette out of a soft pack and went in search of an ashtray. Finding it on a shelf next to his D&D books, he said, words half muffled around the cancer stick: "I talked to his lawyer."

"What?" Lauren asked. "Why?"

"Because I'm gonna do something stupid."

Oh, shit, Owen thought.

"Niiiiiick," Hamish said, setting his bottle down. "Whaddya mean, dude?"

"So, I've been thinking."

"Never a good sign," Lauren mumbled.

"Fuck you, Laur. This is real shit. Okay? We're kinda fucked. That detective lady, Doore, she isn't going to let this go. She's looking for some way, *any* way, to hang this on us. On all of us. And so I'm going full-on Tank Thunderforge."

In any other context, in any other group, that would've been an absurd, honestly nonsensical thing to say. But to this group, right now?

They understood it immediately.

Thunderforge was Nick's old Dwarf character from their D&D games—he was an ex-blacksmith, kicked out of his guild for too much, in Nick's own words on the character sheet, *killin' and whorin'*. He was a self-hating plug of pure dwarven rage (and because of this, Owen sort of loved the character, even if the others mostly found him annoying), and demanded that he be used as a meat shield and trap tester. Any time they entered a new room in a dungeon or crypt or forgotten temple, Tank was first through the door, drawing all the fire from whatever monsters awaited them. And failing that, should the room be quiet—someone, usually Matty's paladin (Erik the Fist of the Golden God) would pick up Tank and literally chuck him onto spots that might've been trapped in order to trigger whatever poison gas vent or fireball spewer was gonna get them.

So, if he was going full Tank Thunderforge—

It meant he was going to jump on the traps.

He was going to draw their fire.

Nick was going to be their meat shield.

"Nick," Owen said. "Whatever it is you're thinking, you don't need to do this, okay? We can figure something out—"

"Nah," he said, using his Jack Kenny whiskey Zippo to spark the cigarette. (He was allowed to smoke down here, as evidenced by the fact the basement smelled like a creosote cancer factory.) He spit out a nit of tobacco. "Listen. People are going to hate us. They already hate us. Looking at us like, you know, we did it. Or we did something. We're never going to live this down, so I'm gonna try to take a little of the heat. Doore is going to find some angle on us, maybe even make one up, I dunno. But I'm going to give her the drug angle."

The room erupted in protests, but Nick yelled for them to shut up.

"It's the easiest thing. I tell her, hey, I bought drugs, bad drugs, *weird* drugs, ooooh, ahhhh, and I gave them to Matty, and maybe Matty didn't even know what I'd given him, and he freaked the fuck out and disappeared on us. The lawyer says I'm gonna take a hit, obviously, and they're going to arrest my ass, but he's pretty confident he can get them to leave me out of juvie—I'm seventeen still, so. It'll be like, probably probation and rehab and counseling and random drug testing—" He took a deep hit off the Camel, then blew twin streams of smoke from his nose. "Blah blah bullshit blah. I'll be fine. I'll be the asshole. You'll all skate."

"*No*," Hamish said, standing up and marching over to Nick. "No fuckin' way, man. No way, dude. This is the Covenant. We all go down together."

Lauren nodded. "Yeah. Let 'em come for us. Fuck 'em. We have our story, we can stick to it. And we didn't do shit. We shouldn't have to hang."

"We got your back," Owen confirmed. And he meant it. Though the fear of *what* that meant, exactly, gnawed at his brain stem like a pack of rats. "You don't have to do it."

"I know you do, Zuikas," Nick said. "And thanks, everybody. But it's too late. I already did it. I already put a statement in with the lawyer, the lawyer's talking to the detective, and I'm expected to surrender myself—" He looked at his empty wrist, where a watch would be had he owned one. "By four P.M. today."

At that, the mood became funereal. A dark pall settled over all of them. What this meant, they didn't know. They'd find out, of course, soon enough: Nick would take the hit, and the lawyer wouldn't be able to keep him out of juvie—it'd be six months in detention, upstate Pennsylvania, near Scranton. And while it would save the rest of them any legal entanglements—Nick really did jump on that trap, Tank Thunderforge–style—what it would not save them would be the judgment, the isolation, the harassment. Matty was beloved. He was a fixture in school, in town, and everyone would always look at them as if they did it. As if they'd killed him. They'd find their lockers spray-painted. Their houses and cars vandalized. People would either look away, or mutter curses about them, or even spit at them. They were killers at worst, fuckups at best, and everyone knew—falsely—that it was the four of them who took Matty from this world.

But that was the truth of a later day.

On this day, the funereal feeling turned fast toward the vibe of an Irish wake: a lot of drinking and laughing and crying. Reminiscing. Cursing the world. Lamenting the loss of their friend Matty, and soon their friend Nick. And they sang for Nick a champion's song, a paean to his heroism like he was the hero, Tank Thunderforge, charging forth into the fray, into the fire, his hammer hot, his soul hearty with the love for—and the love *of*—his friends. "The Covenant," they said to him. And he said it back: "*The Covenant.*"

45

Shelter in Place

It was Nick who wanted to keep moving, Owen who wanted to stay where they were. "We gotta go, we're not gonna find them under that dead-ass Christmas tree," Nick said, incredulously, in the way that Nick often spoke—like he was angry, dismissive, like he thought you were fucking stupid.

"Listen, Lore was right. This place isn't a game, but it might be *like* one. Games have rules. This place might have rules, too. The rooms move, yeah?"

"Yeah. So?"

"So we can't just walk out there and expect to find them. It's a maze, but it moves. But maybe it moves in a *pattern*."

Nick rolled his eyes. "What?"

"Think about it. They shift. The doorway leads one place, until it doesn't. But maybe it cycles through. Maybe it eventually ticks back to the same room, forming the same pathway. Like on a clock, like a carousel going around and around. Maybe it goes through a set number of rooms until it returns."

"And how long does that take?"

"Well, I dunno. That's why we wait. We wait and see."

"You want to just sit on your hands. It's bad enough Matty might still be out there. But now we've lost two of our friends—"

"They lost us, too."

"—and you just wanna *sit here* like a dildo."

"Better than running off half-cocked. Like, say, I dunno, charging up a set of evil nightmare steps into a, a, into some evil nightmare dimension—"

Nick raised his head and laughed a tired, rancorous laugh. "Here we fucking go *again*. Just say it, Owen. Say it. You blame me. Fine. Blame me. I don't care. I did what I could do to do the right thing. The *loyal* thing. For the Covenant. For our friendship. For *Matty*. I always did! But you, you little prick, you were always too scared, scared like a little mouse, trapped in your stupid nowhere life, living in Lore's shadow, to ever come out and do something *brave*, to do something *right*. Well, not me. I got nothing, buddy. I got *no one*. Matty went away and I stayed on the search, but you all abandoned him, and when you abandoned him, you abandoned *me*." On that last word, he grabbed at his chest, his shirt, so vigorously that it looked like he was trying to pull out his own heart. And maybe he was.

Silence bled out between them.

"I'm sorry," Owen said. And he meant it. "I didn't . . . think about it that way. I didn't think about you being alone. I think we—I mean, I can't speak for the others, but I think we just wanted to get over it. Or get away from it."

Nick sniffed. "And how'd that work out for you guys?"

Owen's turn to laugh a hollow laugh. "Yeah. Good point."

Another stretch of silence yawning between them. Nick kicked at the stuffed dog at his feet.

"How much did you know?" Owen asked.

"About what?"

"The . . . staircase. I don't mean as a blame thing, I know you didn't know all of *this* was here. Or where Matty went. But obviously you've been looking for staircases." Nick emailed them enough with sightings of the things, like they were Sasquatches or lake monsters. "Did you have *any* idea?"

Nick hesitated. "What? No. I mean, not really. I knew staircases showed up sometimes in weird places. Not just the woods. One time, in a farmer's hayfield. Another one popped up out in the middle of these wetlands—a blue heron breeding ground. A lot more in forests, though. And some of them were just, y'know, regular staircases. Parts of houses built in the middle of nowhere and places that went to ruin. You put a staircase in a house, the house falls to ruin because the people die or get sick or can't afford to live in the forest like that, and then it falls down. But a staircase is stable. Has to be. It's a bedrock part of the house. And it's protected from the outside world by the walls—until they fall. So the staircase stays behind, for a while at least, even as the rest of the house goes away, gets eaten by the roots and the dirt and whatever. But other staircases, they show up only for a little while. They show up. Until someone goes missing. Then they go away again. Like . . . like they got what they wanted. Like it's a fuckin' *jaw trap* laid out in the woods, and once it snaps shut on the leg of a deer, the hunter doesn't really need the trap anymore, so he takes it back."

The hunter, Owen thought. It gave him a chill.

It gave a kind of agency to this situation he hadn't considered before.

So who is the hunter here?

Who, or what, is hunting us?

Again that warning: THIS PLACE HATES YOU.

Hate was active. Vigorous. Not a passive thing—but an emotion. Something had to feel that emotion. Maybe that warning was more than something theatrical, more than something metaphorical.

Maybe the house was alive. Or at least had a *mind.*

Nick tensed up, continued: "So no. I didn't know shit about shit."

"Okay. Yeah, okay. Again, I didn't mean—"

"I know what you meant. It's fine."

At that, Nick went to the door—the only door out of this room—and stood in front of it.

"Nick," Owen cautioned.

"I know, relax. I'm not walking through. But I want to see."

Owen stood and crept closer, as if the door might suddenly open all on its own. Because there was *something* on the other side—at least, in the attic. The thing that sat up in the bed. Like the dead girl.

Maybe the attic was gone.

"Fine, yeah, open it up," Owen said.

Nick opened it fast.

The attic remained.

At the other end, the sheet-swaddled body remained.

Nick held it open a few more seconds, sucking air through his teeth like he was thinking. *He's thinking of just running through,* Owen knew. He could tell. Nick was edgy. Upset. Owen understood. He was tired, too. Hungry, also. At a certain point, this was going to wear them down to nubs. Nick's instinct to keep moving—*just keep swimming,* like that Disney fish said—was one Owen understood, even if he thought it was the wrong one.

But then, sighing, Nick let the door drift closed.

"We wait a little while. See if it changes."

"Okay," Owen said.

"Maybe try to get a little more sleep. I dunno. I just dunno."

Nick went and sat in the corner of the room, leaving the chair for Owen.

Owen went back to it and sat down. Over time, he closed his eyes. And sleep slipped in, creeping like a shadow, and stole him away.

46

Messages from Matty

"That's Matty's handwriting," she said. Given that it was carved, not written, she couldn't be absolutely sure, but he used to write her these notes between classes, pass them to her in the hallway. It looked like his writing. Then Hamish said, his voice quiet but firm:

"I think you're right."

"Means he was here."

"Yeah."

"*The heart is where the home is.*" she said, repeating the phrase. What could that mean? She repeated it a few more times, and each time it felt more and more like gibberish. The words running together into mess. It felt like what they called *semantic satiation:* when you say a word or a phrase so many times it becomes just noise. Repetition until meaninglessness. *Like this house,* she thought, idly, though even that didn't make total sense to her. Not yet.

She opened the cabinet next to it.

Another message was carved there:

I FEEL IT INSIDE MY HEAD

A chill clawed its way up her arms.

She and Hamish looked to each other, then promptly began opening all the cabinets, and in several of them, Matty had carved other—other what? Messages? Warnings? Deranged ramblings?

IT WANTS TO LIVE INSIDE YOU

YOU CAN TELL BY THE EYES

HAVE TO FIND THE CENTER
I SAW MY PARENTS
YOU WILL BECOME THE HOUSE
DON'T LET IT IN
DON'T LET IT WIN
I WANT TO GO HOME

Each of them was carved into the wood of the cabinets. The lettering was crude and hasty. And it only took a moment to see the small paring knife in the sink, the tip surrounded by meager curls of wood, like bits of bitten fingernail.

"The fuck," Hamish said, mouth hanging open. "What does all of this mean, Lore? Jesus. It's crazy. These messages are fucking *crazy*. Matty came in here and he went . . . he went nuts."

She thought, but did not say: *He didn't go crazy.*

It made *him crazy.*

But then again—maybe he wasn't crazy. Maybe these *were* warnings. To them? To anyone? Was he just carving these thoughts into the doors like a message in a bottle thrown into the open ocean? Just in the hopes someone would see them?

Or did he know they were here?

"What does it all mean?" he asked her. "You're smarter than me. By like, a country mile. What is this place?"

She heard the fear and desperation in his voice. Hamish was on the edge. Every part of him on the verge of breaking. *But you're fine,* she told herself, even as she feared it was a lie. Well, sometimes a lie told often and with conviction became true, at least in a way. *You're fine, you're fine, you're fine.*

"I don't know. But I think if we can figure out what it is . . . maybe we can find Matty and maybe we can escape. These are his words. He came here. Maybe he's still in here."

"But we know he never came home, Lore. He wanted to come home and he never got to, and we'll never get home either—"

"Fuck that shit, Hamish. I don't believe it. Look. *Look.*" She tapped Matty's message, the one that read DON'T LET IT WIN. "This is our mission. Okay? We can't let it win. He's right. You can feel it, can't you? The house? It's *present*. Like a—a worm crawling around inside your head, like a spider trying to nest in your ear, like that parasitic isopod, the one that eats a fish's tongue and replaces it with itself. This place is a parasite. It's like what someone cut into the wall in that hallway: It hates us. I can feel it now. I didn't know that I could, but it's there, like the sound of a chainsaw or a leaf blower in the distance. Both a sound and a pressure. The hate. Can you feel it? It's not just me, is it?"

Hamish shook his head slowly. "I can feel it."

"Good. So that message is true. And we're going to do what Matty said. We're not going to let it win." She choked back despair, and tried very hard to believe her own words. "For now, there's food in these cabinets. Let's gather it up, find a way to carry it with us, and then we are going to keep moving. Somehow, we'll find the others. Okay?"

"Yeah. Yeah. Okay."

Hamish pulled the meager foodstuffs—their rations, now, all of it out of date, hopefully none of it moldy—from the cabinets. Meanwhile, Lore tried to block it out, the hatred from this place. Because she really could feel it. Like hands around her throat, a gun to her head. A voice already in there. Whispering, nattering, *Matty's dead, you left him alone, Hamish is holding you down, they all keep you down, if you want to get free, you have to do this all by yourself, same way you do everything, Lore, same way you survived, same way you succeeded, you have so much work to do, so much life yet to live. Matty's dead but you don't have to be. You don't have to be.* She hissed at the voice, told it to shut up. But it wouldn't. It just kept going, and going, and going.

Endless, like the house.

47

The Funeral

They weren't welcome at the funeral.

It wasn't said out loud. Nobody told them, *You're not welcome here.* But they each knew it. Matty's parents and siblings made no bones about giving them the evil eye whenever they saw them in passing—in town, at school, at the Wawa, wherever. And they weren't the only ones giving them that look. Or casting the accusations at them in mumble and whisper. *Druggies. Freaks. Killers. They killed Matty. They worshipped the Devil. Satanists. They took him up there and hid his body. I bet you can find it if you look hard enough—the cops don't know what they're doing. I heard it was jealousy—Matty was better than all of them. No, I heard he was sticking it to the girl in the group, and they didn't like that. No, I heard it was ritual sacrifice. They probably killed people's pets, too.*

Matty was never implicated in any of these stories. He was always the good guy, the best among them. It was never his fault. Always theirs.

So they knew they weren't welcome.

And yet, they went.

The family held the funeral a year after the incident. In the summer. It wasn't at a funeral home—there was no body, after all, because Matty was still formally listed as *missing*. No, they held it at Hansell Park, in the evening. A candelight vigil, they called it, and people would come and share memories and poems about Matty. In remembrance. Most of them believed in their hearts that he had died and could not return—to them he was not merely missing, but rather, a ghost. Only as present as the memories they could share about him.

Lauren, Owen, and Hamish went. Stayed in the back with their candles flickering. Saw Matty's parents and sisters get up there and break down crying, sharing all these stories about him—though Lauren whispered to the other two during it all, "Notice none of these things are about Matty. Not really. They're about his *accomplishments*." That's all Matty was to them, she said. He was like a gold medal they could hang around their necks—a shining example of the family, a human trophy.

Other kids from school showed up, read stupid fucking poems about him. Some of their teachers did, too. Teachers that the three of them were once close with, whom they loved a lot—and teachers who now wouldn't give them the time of day. They were lucky to get a few recommendation letters out of those teachers who still believed in them, who still held faith that they weren't the *mega-jealous super-Satanic thrill-kill cultists* others made them out to be.

(And even there, they had to solicit those letters on the down-low. As if the teachers did not want to be seen with them. Lauren joked darkly with their English teacher, Mr. Knetemann, that it was like they all wore the Scarlet Letter, but he didn't humor her, and did not seem to find it funny, or even ironic.)

Lauren had a poem she wanted to read during the funeral. The others didn't know that. They didn't bring anything, but she did— and when there was a lull, when they were asking if anyone else had anything more to share about Matthew Shiffman, Lauren stood up, handing her candle to Owen before walking to the front, fumbling with the little crinkly piece of paper in her hand, holding it reverently like it was a prayer—

But Matty's mother walked around the podium with a vigorous stride. Her hand was up, finger pointing. Already she was saying, "No, no, *no*," until it became a bellow: "No!" She stood in the way of

Lauren's path, and even as their friend kept going, Matty's mother grabbed her by the shoulders, seething. "You little whore. You little druggie whore. Corrupter. You corrupted my son! He was better than you. *Smarter* than you. He had a future, and you have *none*. None!" Already people were gathering behind Matty's mother to ease her away from the teen girl—Lauren, who was already shaking, already starting to weep. But those gathered didn't work *too* hard to pull her away, did they? It was a half-hearted effort because, really, they wanted this. They liked the taste of blood in the water.

They thought the three of them deserved whatever they got.

And the mother said as much in her final words—

"It should've been *you*. You should've disappeared. Not my son. *Not my son.*"

Then, finally, as they eased her away, back to the podium, Lauren turned tail and bolted away from the vigil, dropping her poem, which the wind caught and carried away.

Owen and Hamish followed after, of course.

It took them a while to find her, and when they did, she wasn't alone.

She sat there, at the base of a tree, sharing a cigarette with Nick.

Nick, whom they hadn't seen since he went away. His hair was short now—buzzed nearly to the scalp. He had a crustache of facial hair. He was thinner than usual—all parts of him looked *sharp,* from his cheekbones to his elbows to the edges of his shoulders. Owen and Hamish hugged him, and his hug back felt tense, tenuous, like he didn't want to be touched.

Already he launched into his pitch: He was back from juvie, no he didn't want to talk about it, yes he got his GED, and yes, it was time to find Matty. He said he heard from another kid in detention that there was another staircase out toward Pittsburgh, and so Nick said it was time for a road trip—

It was Lauren who told him no.

She sniffed, wiped the last of her tears away, and said coldly, "We're not doing that. It's over. They just held a funeral for him, for fuck's sake."

Nick scoffed. "He's not dead."

"He might as well be."

That's when Nick turned to Owen and Hamish. "You hear this bullshit?" he asked them. He told them, "I know you're both in. You're with me."

But they looked to each other, and then to Lauren—

And it was like a star collapsing. A year of bright heat and pain and terrible blinding energy crushing in on itself, a soft implosion. They sagged. They said no. No, they weren't with him. No, they would not be trying to find Matty. Like Lauren, for them this was over. They were going away soon, to college, and it had to—*had to*—be over.

Nick was mad as yellowjackets. He pushed Hamish. Threatened to punch Owen. Called them names. Screamed at them in a froth, told them he'd sacrificed so they could all go away to college—he'd gone to juvie, he'd given up so much, they didn't understand what he'd been through. And now, he said, it was time to pay up.

It was Lauren who dealt the killing blow.

She stood up slowly and said to him, "Why are you doing this, Nick? Matty didn't even like you that much."

It looked as though she'd just hit him without ever throwing a punch.

But Nick screwed up his resolve then and told them all: "Matty was a better friend to me than you know. Better than any of you ever were."

Hamish protested—the two were close, after all—but Nick told him to fuck off. Told Owen to kill himself. Told Lauren to go ruin someone else's life.

And then he was gone. Stormed off.

He didn't have to say it.

Didn't have to say what this meant for them, for the Covenant.

They all walked away and went away. Hamish went to Virginia Tech. Lauren—Lore, soon—and Owen went to Sarah Lawrence. Nick went nowhere, at least not for a long time. And Matty was, after all, already long gone.

The three of them, without Nick, saw one another at holidays at first, but already by their second year in college, Owen and Lore and Hamish stopped coming home. Why would they? What *was* home to them, anyway, except a place that reminded them constantly how much it didn't care about them?

And soon even Owen and Lore were done with each other.

So withered the Covenant.

Brittle, poisoned, broken.

Though, perhaps, not forgotten.

48

In the Mansion of Sleep

Owen slept, and in the darkness of sleep, he saw a house. He was above it. Outside of it. It floated in a crimson void, the house a mutant shape of jagged roofs and gabled peaks. Siding rippled. All of it strained and stretched and bulged. The house had no windows, and no doors. It turned in void space, rotating on every axis.

It was awake, and aware.

And it was growing.

When its siding swelled and buckled, a shape would burst out of it—like a swiftly growing tumor, a pillar of wet cement and raw flesh hardening with callus and chitin, wrapping itself in a skin of brick, of stucco, of crackling slate. Whole rooms grew this way, one next to the other, until its exterior was again flush and level before another growth burst forth.

Then, a single window—a shifting window that was first a bay window, then a circular porthole, then a casement, a transom—appeared in its center. But it was no window. Not really. It was an eye. It saw him. It knew him. He felt himself itch. Heard his father mumbling in the dark. Asking him to come inside. To come home. To a room whose floor was bitten fingernails, whose walls were lacerated skin.

Come inside, the voice said again.

Then the same voice, *Let me in.*

Knock-knock.

Suddenly, Owen found himself wandering the ever-shifting rooms of this place, but they were half formless, bubbling and melting even as he passed through them, like the sloppy hallucinations of so-called artificial intelligence. Eyes bursting in electrical sockets, heating vents like grinning mouths, torn wallpaper showing gleaming threads of muscle. Doorways danced away from him. Trapdoors opened beneath him.

A voice, again partly his father's, but also a hundred voices singing together with it, braiding together:

Look at the room in which you rest your head, Owen.

The voice faded and what was left was one sound: the soft sobs of a crying woman. The kind of weeping that was like a storm—the crashing rain and the howling wind and the lash of rising waters. He couldn't help but follow it forward and up and down. Stairs underneath his feet turned to wet, clayey mud. The floor buckled and turned to splinters, sinking deep into the soles of his feet. Streaks of blood trailed behind him in his wake. But still he went, moving forward, almost tumbling, like something had him by the throat—a noose dragging him through the house, because that's what this was, a house, one big endless nightmare house. And then it dragged him through a door, one last door, and as he bouldered into it, it burst open and—

The playroom again. The same room in which he slept. But he wasn't there. And the Christmas tree had not lost its needles. Lights danced up and down it.

A woman sat in the center of the floor, sobbing. And with each hitching sob Owen felt himself sliding backward and forward in time—she and her husband, both young, both ruddy-cheeked and with chestnut hair, almost looking as though they could be brother and sister, and they were playing in this room with a little girl, maybe two years old. Mutate, shift, warp—now they were building those big chunky LEGOs with her, the ones for kids, the DUPLO blocks. The floor fell out and Owen landed in the playroom again, and they were there putting up the Christmas tree and popping ornaments on it, and the child looked a little older now, maybe three years old, and in her hand was the blue doggy plushie, and she coughed, one good cough with blood in it, and it wet the floor, and then—somewhere behind it all, the crying rose again, and there came the sound of medical machines, a ventilator hissing breath, a heart monitor beeping, then all of them in alarm, a cacophony of sound. A single tone. A flatline sound. The crying rose, rose, and the tears came pouring out of the woman's eyes and then her nose and then her mouth, streaming forward, filling up the room, coming now not just from her but purging from outside the room, coming in—from around the light fixture, through the socket, out from the vents, tears and snot and spit and flecks of lung blood from a dying child, and Owen felt it all rising around him. Rising to his chest. Pushing toward his mouth. He could barely breathe, and then he plunged underneath it. Holding his breath for—how long? Not long at all. He couldn't do it. The woman's tears were drowning him. Trapping him at a crushing depth underneath. And as the darkness stained the edges of his vision—

The woman, the mother of a now dead child, swam toward him, her mouth open just enough so that he could see the pills on her tongue, gummy with spit—she closed her eyes, closed her mouth—

Gulp—

Then *gasp*—

Owen gasped awake in the chair, his body thrashing once in a hypnic jerk.

"Jesus," he said, coughing as if his lungs were still full of floodwater (tears, spit, snot, blood). He wiped at his mouth. All dry.

And there stood Nick. Right over him. Eyes like windows. Teeth like the flat bright boards of a freshly painted picket fence. Skin like popcorn ceiling.

"Rough sleep, huh," Nick said, and once more he looked . . . normal. Eyes, skin, teeth. *Just the dream lingering,* Owen thought. Or at least hoped.

"I . . . yes."

"It's really something, huh? You and me paired together. The two washouts. Lore got huge, did everything she wanted. Hamish—well, fuck him, but at least he made something of himself. But us? Not so much."

Owen grunted and sat up. Again he saw something flash in Nick's eyes: eyes like window glass. And like something moving behind that glass. *Your mind is playing tricks on you,* Owen thought. *No, the house is playing tricks.*

He didn't want to have this conversation with Nick. So instead he talked about his dream. About what he saw, there.

"I think this house is . . . alive."

"It's not alive, Owen. It's just a house."

"Sure, a house that's an endless labyrinth, with shifting rooms."

Nick scoffed. "Doesn't mean it's *alive.* Just means it's . . ." He shrugged.

"I think this room belonged to a family that lost their child."

"I saw some ornaments on the tree, one had a picture of a kid in it. Cute kid. Sucks they're dead." Way he spoke, he sounded lost, almost. His voice flat, his tone a straight line.

"But the house wanted to show it to me. To us. That something happened in this room. Why?"

Nick shrugged. "Who the fuck knows. This place is a mystery, Nailbiter."

"I saw my father's bedroom. And—" He was about to say, *I saw my knife, too. A few times, now. The Old Timer. The one I . . .* but he couldn't make his mouth form the words. "I just don't get it. What's the point of all this? This place? Trapping us here and showing us—what? Nightmare room after nightmare room? Some that have to do with us and a lot more that don't?" *Because you deserve it,* Owen thought. *Because you're weak and pathetic and Nick is right, you're both washed up and washed out and you deserve to be here, in this place, with him.* He shook his head to try to shake free the bad thoughts. He so desperately wanted to chew his nails, but he knew Nick would say something cruel. So he shoved his hands in his pockets and endured the vibrating *itch* that ran through him.

Chew, chew, chew.

Bite, bite, bite.

"I dunno what the fuck's up with this place," Nick said. "But one thing I do know? Your trick's not working."

Owen stood. His legs felt numb and wobbly. And still his chest burned from dreaming about drowning. He almost stepped on the blue dog toy—

And next to it was a small patch of darker carpet.

Smeared, as if someone had tried, and failed, to clean it.

Blood.

From that cough.

The sound of it looped in his head like sampled music.

Owen shook his head and walked to Nick. "Trick? What—what's not working, what trick?"

"The rooms changing. You've been asleep for a couple hours already—"

"Really? That long? Did you—"

"Sleep? No. Tried but didn't manage it. Fuck it. That's okay. I poked around and I checked the door, and, well."

He did a weary flourish toward the door.

The attic remained.

The boxes, the junk, the memories.

The mattress, the swaddled body.

"Same fucking thing," Nick said, an implicit *ta-da* added in his face.

"That thing move any more?" Owen asked, quietly, talking about the body.

"No."

"Good."

Nick sighed and eased the door shut.

"We need to go in there. It's like the staircase—we just have to do it."

"The staircase was the trap, the bait; once we went in, it was too late," Owen started to say, but then something clicked. Lore talking about games, about rules. About how things worked a certain way. "Maybe the doors are like the staircase."

"I don't follow you."

No, but we followed you, and what a mistake that was, Owen said to himself—a surprisingly acrimonious thought, intrusive on the face of it. He shook it off. "Um. So, okay. The staircase sits there, right? It sits there and waits. It waits till what—?"

"Until someone goes up the goddamn thing."

"And then—"

Nick grinned like a fox. "And then it goes *poof*."

"To us, it disappears. But really . . . it shifts. We don't know where it goes. Maybe it goes only to the inside of this place. But maybe it transposes itself somewhere else—some other forest, some other tract of wilderness."

"You think the doors work the same way."

"Maybe."

Nick's grin twisted into a fresh scowl. "Yeah, but how's that help us? Means I'm right, and we still have to walk through."

"What if we walk through, then walk back? Then close the door and . . ."

"And hope the roulette wheel spins and lands us on a new number."

"A new room."

"Wanna try it?"

"Better now than never."

Nick winked and grinned again, as if he knew this was gonna work. He practically attacked the door when opening it, like he had to sneak up on it—*gotcha*—and it swung open.

"All right," Nick said. "I'm gonna hop in, hop out—"

"Nick."

"What?"

"The body."

"The body?" Nick turned back toward the attic and looked. "Oh shit."

The body was gone.

The mattress sat there, filthy with stains, but bare of anybody or anything.

"Yeah. Shit."

"Maybe that's a good thing. It's gone. Right?"

"I . . ." Owen didn't have an answer. It seemed like that could be true. Though in this place, that didn't seem likely. "I don't know, Nick. But I think we should both step through. You go first, and I'll be right on your heels."

Nick batted his eyes. "We could hold hands, sweetie."

"Don't be homophobic."

"I'm not." He scoffed. "I'm actually kinda serious."

"Yeah. Yeah, okay."

Owen reached out, took Nick's hand. It was cold and clammy. But welcome just the same.

"Let's Thelma and Louise this shit."

Nick stepped through, Owen right behind him.

The air in the attic room was immediately different—it smelled like, well, an old attic. Like dust, mostly. It was still and stale. And behind it was something else, too: the pickled smell of death, like roadkill you passed in your car, its stink crawling up through the heating vents.

Owen scanned the room, looking for the strange sheet-swaddled body that had been on the mattress—that *sat up* before. But nothing.

Still, the skin on the back of his neck prickled.

"Let's go back," Owen said.

Nick nodded like he was vibing it, too.

Owen stepped backward through the door, and Nick came through with him, shutting the door as they did. Nick said, "All right, let's see if it—"

But as he spoke, he turned to look at Owen—

Owen, who was still facing Nick and the door.

Nick's eyes went wide as he stared past Owen.

Oh fuck.

Owen spun.

There, on the little microfiber loveseat—

Was the swaddled body.

It was in here with them now.

It lay there, still.

"Jesus fucking fuck," Nick said, swallowing hard. "You see it, too, right?"

"I see it, too."

Up close, it was easy to see that the bedsheet swaddling the body was once white, now stained with time, but also fluids. Blood, probably. Around the chest. Around the head and neck. The bedsheets themselves were cheap, nearly threadbare.

The dark brown stains began spreading. Shining wet.

From within, something whispered, a whisper barely escaping a clog of something thick and humid in its throat—

"*They kept me and they killed me.*"

"Who?" Owen asked. The word seemed to come out automatically, like it was part of a script and he had to read his line. *No*, he thought. *It's because I have to know. Maybe this person wants to talk. Maybe we need to listen.*

"Owen . . ." Nick cautioned, but Owen ignored him.

"Who kept you? Who killed you?"

A gurgled hiss. A slop of sound. Then: "*My next-door neighbors.*"

The stains continued to spread.

"Can you tell us more?"

"*They t-t-took me from my—*" The body shuddered with one racking cough. The sheet above the mouth went from a red-brown to black. "*Backyard. Right out from under my parents' noses. They searched and searched everywhere but I was next door. They used me. They used me and they used me and they used me, and then when I was all used up, they killed me and hid me in the attic. Do you know how they finally fffff-found me?*"

Owen couldn't say any more. He only could shake his head no.

Something under the bedsheets tumbled and swelled. A rise and fall, something pressing underneath and then sinking again. A tightening, then a relaxing. Little shapes, little textures, like—

Like macaroni noodles.

"Owen," Nick said, pulling on his elbow like a child hiding behind his mother, trying to get her to leave. "Owen!"

It was the maggots crawling out the attic vent.

The seams of the bedsheet ripped with a great tear—a bulge of raw, bruise-dark flesh bubbled up underneath it, the ribs gone gelatinous, the skin splitting as the sheet did, and even before the worms burst forth, it was easy to see their outlines under the dead flesh—

The young man's body howled a scream past the clot of worms in its throat, its mouth under the remaining sheet stretched wide, too wide, a tubular pillar of larvae pushing free of it, and Owen was frozen, struck in horror as Nick dragged him back through the door, the maggots rushing toward them in a tumbling, flopping river—

Wham.

The door closed.

The attic was gone.

This was somewhere new.

It shifted. We did it.

Deeper into the house they went.

49

What Hell Is

This, then, was Hamish:

As time passed in the nightmare house, bad, nasty thoughts chased Hamish from room to room, one after the other, day after day, night after night. If there were even days or nights anymore. No windows meant no sun, no moon, no daytime or nighttime. Only way to tell was the time, and the time on Lore's phone or his—did that even mean anything?—seemed to be from a different year, showing a different time from any clocks that might be present.

The rooms never repeated. They didn't blur, though. Hamish remembered them, each and every one. As if passing through them meant they lived with him, or that he was still living *in* them—every room a net, a web, a trap, capturing some part of him, some bit of his soul, and keeping it there like a stupid little knickknack on a dust-caked shelf. There was the Gas Leak Room, a wood-paneled den with two parents and an elementary school–age boy and a border collie, all dead, a stink in the air mixing their rot with the egg-shit stench of the gas—gas still hissing from somewhere. There was the Burned Nursery, a single untouched unharmed crib in the middle of a charred, cooked room—the wallpaper blistered and peeling, the carpet melted to grubby plasticky mess, everything blackened by fire and smoke. They went through the Moth-Eaten Closet, a walk-in full of clothes on hangers—as they passed through, their arms ruffled the fabric, and the outfits erupted with a thousand moths. The air filled with them, and they had them in their eyes and mouths and had to fight their way free, and long after, they were covered with dead moths and the powder from their ruined wings.

An attic was home to nothing except pinned photographs of underage schoolgirls, snapshots clearly taken in hiding, from behind hedges or between gaps in fences, none of them aware they were being stalked.

A sixties-era kitchen was waterlogged, the broken faucet still barfing sick-looking water, the floor and ceiling so weak, they thought they'd either fall through or have the whole room collapse upon them.

A bedroom had bondage straps fixed to the four iron posts, and a braless dead woman in an ouvert thong lay there with her wrists and ankles tied down—as they passed, she came to life, thrashing about, screaming around her ball gag.

Another bedroom, a boy's bedroom out of the fifties with faded teal walls and a bed made up with rocket ship sheets, had a Scouts uniform laid out on the floor, and on the ceiling above it, a swinging noose made from clothesline.

A room only for birds, birdcage after birdcage, some wrought iron, some fake gold, some ornate, others plain, each holding one dead bird—a canary, a parakeet, a cockatiel. In the center, a parrot—alive, not dead. Ratty-looking, its feathers rough and falling out, a fat featherless goiter bulging at its neck so that its head hung at a strange angle, and all the while it shrieked at them, just spitting madness: "IF GOD WERE REAL THE WORLD WOULD BE BETTER *RAAAAH* WE KILLED THE ANGELS AND THE DOORWAY IS OPEN *RAWWWWW* DON'T LOOK AT ME DON'T LOOK AT ME DON'T LOOK AT ME OR I'LL TAKE YOUR EYES LIKE I TOOK HERS THE LITTLE BITCH *SCRAAAAW*."

In some rooms, they were not alone. A dead kid reading comic books under a blanket, the flashlight on the book illuminating the rank puke slowly dripping from his mouth. A housewife from a bygone era, her hair in curlers, her face cakey with some kind of mask, chased them with a shotgun, blew a hole in the door as they ducked through and into another space. A man in a scrap-metal mask came at them with a hammer. A headless guinea pig ran around a playroom in circles, leaving a spiral of black blood in its wake.

(Somehow, it still squeaked and squealed.)

Other rooms were quiet, still, boring. They were what they were—kitchens, dining rooms, laundry rooms, though all of them had something in them, some aspect of rot and ruin: water stains, bloodstains, a puke smell, flickering lights, a fritzing television, mold, so much mold.

Other rooms were boring but *not* quiet. The sound of rats chewing in the walls, or the noises of arguing and crying and screaming coming from all directions, or fuck, the worst of all, the bedroom with the distant sound of a chirping smoke detector, letting all the cosmos know, *My battery is dead, my battery is dead, and now this sound lives in your head, my battery is dead, my battery is dead, I'll chirp forever wherever you tread!*

The terrible sounds were always worst when they tried to sleep.

Sleeping was hard. Not just because of the sounds. Even when it was quiet, closing his eyes was when Hamish's thoughts really reared up in full 4K nightmare video with spatial audio, baby—it was bad enough that when he walked through rooms, he'd sometimes see himself reflected in the glass of a cabinet looking all bloated and sick and fat, or he'd catch a glimpse of his family in a mirror, staring out at him, crying at him being gone, or laughing because he was never coming back, but ohh, when he slept? All that rushed upon Hamish like the bodies in a mosh pit, crashing into him with reminders of how awful he was, how stupid, how petty, how selfish, how hungry, how he was a fat fuck and a sick addict and a cheat and a liar and *just the worst*. And then when sleep finally took him . . .

He dreamed of the house they were in. Rooms they'd seen. He wandered the house when he was awake, and his dreaming mind did the same. These rooms? They never left him. It was like this awful nowhere house was opening up spaces inside him. Demoing everything to make room for itself. This place was building rooms inside him. As he walked through it, it walked through him. Tunneling through him. Laying pipe. Stringing wire. Digging out a foundation, a hollow space in his dirt, and building on top of that void.

New construction! Move-in ready!

It was in the home gym, the boring home gym that smelled like sweat and basement damp and sharp mineral water, that he decided that he wanted to die.

Then again, Hamish thought, *maybe we're already dead.*
That made the most sense, didn't it? They died, came to this place, and that was that. In fact, Hamish held no doubt now that this was Hell, literal Hell, capital H-E-double-hockey-sticks, you-fucked-around-and-here-comes-the-ultimate-finding-out *Hell*. He had made many mistakes in his life and they had brought him here, to this labyrinth of torment and tragedy, every room a story of pain and torture and death and terror. They were hunted sometimes. They had to run. They had to hide. They had to scramble for food and sleep. It was hellish. It was Hell.

Hell, a place always pictured as a land of fire, always burning you. Or maybe a place where demons trapped you down and tortured you for infinity—endless skin flaying or eyes being pulled out by greedy fingers or a tube shoved up your ass so you could have a centipede enema. Or, worse, torture that was emotional: *Here, watch videos of your loved ones dying; here, we're going to pump thoughts into your head of someone stepping on puppies till they pop; here, you're surrounded by your friends and your family and they're telling you how they never loved you and never even liked you, and they're spitting on you and kicking you, you fat piece of fucked-up shit, and did we mention you're fat again, and you've got a needle in your arm and a pill on your tongue and and and—*

It was about six months ago that he and his family had gone to church and Hamish heard something that stuck with him—or rather, stuck *in* him the way a splinter sticks in you. And that thought splinter was there now, for sure, throbbing to his heartbeat as he was reminded of what the pastor had said.

On that day, Hamish sat in the pews with his wife and daughters on one side, his son on the other. It was Deer Park Presbyterian, a small church, been there for decades, humble and unassuming. Hamish told himself he was a believer because he had to be a believer—after all, after everything he'd been through? He had a new life, truly. A brand-new chance, a brand-new everything! And in that new life, he was able to marry an amazing woman and have three great kids, and that was a miracle, wasn't it? God-given, literally. It was proof. His faith then was barely even that. Faith implied you had to force yourself to accept something for which you had no evidence, but to Hamish, God was in evidence because of all that he was allowed to have in this second life. So, to him, when the pastor spoke, that was just a man giving them the 4-1-1 from God. A conduit.

And the pastor that day—Pastor Greg—he was talking a little bit about Hell. He said he didn't like to make too big a thing about Hell because faith in God had to be about doing the right thing, the *righteous* thing, and Hell was about trying not to do the wrong thing. Sounded the same, but those were two different things, the man said. But Pastor Greg, he said, "Hell gets talked about like it's this bad place, a realm of agony and suffering put upon the sinner for having dared to sin. But that's not what Hell is. Hell is not a place, or a presence. Hell is an *absence*. Hell is the place where God will not see you. It's where you go when you're so sure you cannot believe in him that you place yourself out of his sight, where you hide from him in the darkness. It's about breaking that vital Covenant between God and man. It's about refusing to believe there ever *was* a Covenant in the first place. Hell is broken promises. Hell is wandering outside of God's sight, and away from his love. Hell is a *choice*."

On that day, Hamish of course focused on that one word, *Covenant,* because—well, because to him, *Covenant* was the word that just meant the friendship he had with the people he grew up with. And it only reminded him that their Covenant, their friendship, was a lost thing, not merely broken, but as with God and with Hell, a thing that Hamish had forgotten. In the years since Matty disappeared, Hamish had gone to a place where his friends would not see him, and he would not see them.

But then he told himself, so what? That's how it was sometimes. People grew apart. They weren't there for him when he died. They didn't even *know* that he'd died at that party. What kind of friends were they to him? Enough that he didn't feel the need to be a friend to them. Sometimes friendships didn't break in some big dramatic way. Sometimes they just dried out, curled up like a leaf on the ground, and turned to dirt. Like all things inevitably did.

Hamish had his wife, his kids. He had health. He had *God*.

And that was enough.

Though that was bullshit, wasn't it?

Jennifer, his wife? Well, he loved her and she loved him, but then why was he cheating on her? Why had he cheated on her with three other women in the past? He told himself it was fine, that the cheating was just *a thing men did,* that what he had with the other women was purely physical, not emotional or spiritual, and those types of cheating were the *real* types of cheating. Physical cheating was like, well, it was like cheating on your diet. You ate ice cream when you weren't supposed to. Oopsie-doodle. You'd get back to being good tomorrow. It wasn't like you were married to the ice cream. It wasn't like it was part of you. You didn't love it. Didn't give yourself to it. It was just a small pleasure resulting from a momentary lapse of judgment. It was like masturbating, but with a friend.

And his kids? If they were so great, why didn't he understand them? They seemed so selfish. He loved them, he was proud of them, but he didn't always *like* them, not really. He told himself that was fine, too—they were teenagers, and he had been a teenager once, and was *he* likable back then? No. Not at all. He was a dopey shit back then. High all the time. So he wanted to grant them mercy. But damn, it felt like the kids were just using him and Jennifer. Mostly her. He always made the joke to people, *LOL, it's like we're just an Uber for the kids,* though of course what he never said was, he never drove them somewhere unless he really, really had to. It was Jennifer. Always Jennifer. But he told himself, *That's what dads are for; we're not there for the administrative details, we're there for the big stuff, the life stuff.* But did he even know his kids well enough to know what their big life stuff even was? His children were mysteries to him. They were like those Russian nesting dolls except he never saw the smaller dolls inside, only the one on the outside. The one they showed to the world. He never bothered looking deeper.

And now, in this moment, in this place, it made him revisit that sermon from Pastor Greg, the one about Hell.

Hell being a place of absence.

He was absent from the life of his family. Not just because he was here. But in the bigger way. The worse way.

And they were absent, too. Gone from him as he was gone from them.

And he'd never see them again.

He loved them. He was awful to them.

These were the thoughts.

Around and around.

Like that bottles of beer on the wall song, except an endless reiteration of how much of a fucking epic piece of shit he was.

He wanted to die. Maybe he was already dead. Maybe he died in that bathroom and never really woke up in the hospital. Maybe Hell constructed for him a life, an imaginary one, that it would rob from him, and this was the manifestation of that. Maybe this wasn't where Matty went. Maybe the others were just hallucinations. Or demons. Or synaptic flares as his mind died.

It was in the Bottle Room that Hamish lost his shit.

The Bottle Room: a mid-century modern-style living room. Late seventies, maybe. A boxy square cathode-ray tube TV in a wooden console box sat next to a hi-fi stereo cabinet with the turntable and an eight-track player. In the center of the room was a sunken area of three chairs, a coffee table, and a burnt umber orange couch. An area they used to call a "conversation pit."

Bottles were everywhere.

Liquor bottles.

A hundred of them, easy. Some knocked over, a few on the floor, but most covering every flat surface available—the TV console, the top of the stereo, the armrests of the chairs. Lore went around sniffing them. "Booze, all booze," though then she sniffed one and made a rankled face. "Jesus, I think this one's piss."

Hamish nodded and mumbled wordless words at her, because he was only barely listening. Because his brain was preoccupied, the same way Owen would chew a hangnail or gnaw his lower lip—it kept all the bad thoughts orbiting. How he was a piece of shit, how his family was better without him, how this place was endless and they'd never get out, how this was a Hell he deserved, how he was dead and all of this was just part of his afterlife torment. He'd been sober now for years. And these bottles made him want to drink so bad. And not just drink, but worse—pills again. Coke, if he could find it. Anything. Stick it in a needle, cook it in a spoon, suddenly he wanted it. *I could go out the old-fashioned way. I could die easy. Maybe wake up again out of this place. A third chance at a new life.*

Then he passed by a mirror.

It was a sunburst mirror—the mirror itself a circle in the center, and radiating out were golden spokes, some shorter, some longer. A stylized sun.

In the mirror, he looked like a ghoul.

His flesh was gray-green and pocked with rot. His teeth, the yellow of flu mucus. And the face itself was bloated and jowly, patchy with tufts of red beard going gray. The eyes were purple like popped grapes.

This face, *his* face, grinned big and broad. Fat and greasy and wretched.

One of those burst-blood-vessel eyes winked.

And that did it.

Hamish drove a fist into the mirror. The glass shattered around him. Everything went white—a wave of rage bleached anything and everything. All he could see was the motion of his fist. All he could feel was the burn of his shoulder as he threw punch after punch, his knuckles crunching, skin tearing, the sting of blood. Then someone was on him, grabbing him, pulling him back—

He roared and drove an elbow backward.

His attacker's face racked back. An arc of blood in its wake.

Lore. It was Lore.

She staggered back, her hands already going to her face. Blood refusing to be dammed by her palm and fingers—sliding through her digits, dropping off the heels of each hand. Lore coughed and said, "Fuck, dude," except it came out, *Buck, dude,* instead. She pulled her hands away to look at them. Blood pooled in the cups of her palms, spilling over. And it kept pouring from her nose, which was already swelling up like a child's balloon.

"Fuck," Hamish said. "Fuck. Lore. Fuck. I'm sorry. I'm sorry. I'm so sorry."

He had hurt her.

He had hurt a friend.

He thought back to his wife, his kids. Now to Lore. The way he had talked to her in the car. The way he'd just busted her nose.

You stupid stupid piece of fucking shit.

You deserve this place.

You deserve pain.

He reached down and picked up a shard of mirror. For a moment, he saw himself in it once more. That dead, swollen face of his leering back at him. That grinning mug. So satisfied with itself.

He had to make it all go away.

Hamish turned the blade toward himself—

—toward his throat—

And *stabbed.*

50

Intervention

Lore wasn't ready.

Like, okay, she *knew* Hamish wasn't doing great. His mental state had begun to dissolve: a sandcastle under assault by the steady drumbeat of the sea. Except in this case, the sea was a nightmare tide, corrosive and foul. Whatever this place was, it was clear that it was marked indelibly by tragedy, and though it looked like a house, it was as tractless and wide as any wilderness.

But we're alive, she told herself. They had running water in some rooms. Food in others. Beds. Though there seemed to be something—what, ghosts? Illusions? Glitches in the Matrix?—afoot, they hadn't been harmed by them. Though some seemed inclined to chase after them, others were content to remain in one place, screaming or bleeding or sobbing. (In one bedroom, they found a man simply beating his head into the wall. Again and again. Over and over. *Whumpth. Whumpth. Whumpth.* By the time they arrived, his face was already swollen and burst like a ripe fruit. Strings of flesh and blood hung between his cratered visage and the jungle wallpaper, like a cheese pull from pizza, sticky with marinara. And he kept doing it. Mumbling muffled words from somewhere through the meat of his ruined mouth. Lore found it horrifying but also . . . coldly, weirdly fascinating. She could've stared at him longer if Hamish hadn't hurried her out of the room.)

Hamish always wanted to keep moving. Like something was chasing him—something other than the entities in these rooms.

In every room she'd see him twitch and flick his gaze around. Staring sometimes for long moments into mirrors or into a glass-top coffee table or into the dead screen of an old TV. He looked haunted by more than just ghosts. And her response to that was, *Yeah, well, who isn't?* It wasn't like Lore wasn't seeing things either. She heard Matty whispering underneath doors. She heard, nonsensically, video game sounds—from her own personal bank of audio files, the ones she'd been collecting to use in her new game, the game she hadn't even started yet. And sometimes just passing through a room, she blinked and behind her eyes, she saw a snapshot of something horrible that had happened in that place. Not something that *might've* happened. Something that *had* happened. She could *feel* it. She *knew* it. Intimately. Intrinsically.

Suicides and murders and abuse. But other, smaller, stranger things, too: Like in one absolute mess of a room, Lore saw in her mind's eye a hoarder trapped underneath a landslide of their own hoard, growing weaker and weaker, unable to even reach her pets to feed them—the dogs and cats wailed and howled and yowled. Until they didn't anymore. And the woman died there, like that, underneath the crush. Heart attack. In another room, a child in his pajamas found both of his parents dead—not from anything sinister, not from a murder-suicide, not from some serial killer, but just because one morning, the mother touched the faucet, a faucet which had been accidentally electrified due to some bad plumbing wiring mojo, and as she was being electrocuted, the father tried to pull her away, but was caught by the same current. Both died. A sad, stupid thing. A child, orphaned from a freak accident. Left alone, forever. (*Like me,* she thought, idly. *You're alone and you should be alone and you need to be alone.*)

And Lore had no idea if Hamish was seeing any of this or not. She told herself it didn't matter. Because she didn't need him. And if that was true, then the reverse was true as well. He didn't need her. Let him go through his own shit, she decided. Let him process it how he needed to process it. He had his God, he had his beautiful family and his sobriety and his smug fucking attitude. *Good luck, dude.*

But all that time, she realized, she had left him alone.

And he was flailing.

And a little part of her knew: *You're flailing, too, girl.*

It happened so fast.

His elbow in her nose. Pop. Him with the mirror glass. Plunging toward his own throat.

Lore rushed him. Caught his wrist. He was stronger than her, easily. She had slowed his attempt, but not stopped it. Three inches to an open windpipe. Two inches. *One.*

She did the only thing she knew to do.

Lore pumped her knee into his balls.

It did the trick. The air went out of him. The fight, too. He whimpered and staggered backward, and the mirror glass fell from his hand. After a while, Hamish calmed down. He sat down on the floor, his back against the base of the couch.

Lore sat next to him.

(She made sure the mirror shards were nowhere near them.)

(Just in case.)

Her nose had stopped bleeding. It throbbed, though, like it had its own heartbeat. *Bub-bub, bub-bub, bub-bub.*

"You hit me," she said.

"I know."

"The fuck, dude."

"I *know.*"

She let loose an angry, guttural, exasperated sigh. *Yuuuuggghhh.* Words tumbled out of her. "I think this place is fucking with you." *No, asshole.* She corrected herself: "With *us.* It's making me think that I can do this all alone, that I don't need you. But then—then!" She wagged her finger in the air as if she were manically lecturing an audience. "Then I realize, no, that's just me. That's just my fucking brain, wanting to shoulder all the burden and do all the things—reap the reward, but eat the pain. The house isn't putting that thought in my head. It just turned up the volume. And I bet it's doing that with you, too. Finding all those bad thoughts inside you and making them louder, and louder, and *louder* again. Am I right?"

Hamish, pale and sweaty, his hair a muss, gave her a weird look. "Maybe."

"Y'know, I've not . . ." Here she cleared her throat, because sometimes the truth wanted to get stuck there instead of working its way free. A bird trapped in a net. "I've not been particularly *good* at caring about other people. I mean—I care about them when I think about them. I guess I'm not good at the *thinking about them* part. I just hyperfocus on myself. Eyes on my own paper. I trust, falsely, foolishly, that everyone else has their shit together and just as I don't need their help, *they* don't need *my* help. And . . . they do sometimes need my help. And—" More truth that didn't want to come free, like she was holding in vomit and knew she'd feel better once she puked it up but still tried really hard not to puke it up. "*And sometimes*, I need their help, too. So I'm sorry I haven't been really here for you."

"You're fine. It's fine. I'm just . . . dealing with things."

Lore couldn't help but laugh. "Ham, we're *both* dealing with things. We're trapped in a fucking maze of horrible rooms. But I've been treating it like a puzzle, like it's something fascinating, and pretending that it's not absolutely goddamn fucking awful. And it is awful. It's so awful." Saying that out loud made her feel it all the more keenly. *This place is awful.* She felt it under her skin. And on it, too, like a thin layer of emotional, spiritual grease. Filthy with it. She'd heard stories about those poor bastards social media companies hired—first in America, later in other countries, because of course, fuck those people, right—whose sole job was to go through all the horrendous, heinous, awful shit that saturated social media. Not just the trolling and the doxxing and the death threats. But like, the real *dark* shit. Videos of beheadings. Child porn. Animal abuse. Nightmares from the deepest, most fucked X-chan mines. It broke those people. Broke down their walls. Shattered the foundations of their minds. That's what was happening to them in here. It's what the house wanted. The house was torturing them with the torment of others. *And sometimes, with our own torment, too.*

"Dude, I—I think this is Hell. I think it's my Hell. A real, actual Hell."

"Of course, a mediocre white man would think it's *his* Hell—maybe it's my Hell, you ever think that? Maybe *you're* in *my* Purgatory." She saw him flinch. Lore's words opened another wound. A little part of her knew that she wanted to hurt him—in part to get revenge for their conversation in the car, in part because she was always having to carry weak men, carry them and accommodate them and soothe their tender stupid hearts. (*Like Owen,* she thought, cruelly.) But in part it was something altogether worse. If she pushed him hard enough, maybe he would finish the job she'd just interrupted. Maybe he would kill himself. Then she could be rid of the baggage that was Hamish. That was a dark and terrible thought that sickened her, particularly because it came *from* her. She cautioned herself: *If you push too hard, you will break him. That's not what you want.*

A cold realization struck her: *It's what the house wants.*

She sighed. "It's not Hell, Hamish. I don't know what it is. Not exactly. But it's real. Not some afterworld. It's a real place and we are stuck the fuck in it."

"How do you know?" It was strange how much he sounded like a child asking that. Like he was lost and looking for reassurance.

"There's not a holy book around that says Hell is up a mysterious staircase in the woods. And besides, we're here together. Hell seems to be a lonely place."

He regarded her carefully. "You might not be real."

"I wish I weren't real, Ham. Then I wouldn't be here. But I'm real, and I'm really here, in this . . . this very real place." She gave him a hard stare. "You know, though, since we're doing *reckonings* right now . . . I am poly, pansexual, and despite the pronouns, I really do feel more at home in a body that isn't supposed to be explicitly male or female.

You were cool about stuff once. Easy-breezy, full of love, accepting of all things and all people, and now—now you're *this* guy. The guy who thinks this is Hell. It's not even the Creel thing, it's just—I thought you were better than that. I need you to be better than that."

His eyes shone with tears. "I know. I'm sorry. I just—things happen in life, you go through some shit and you start to get scared, you start looking for answers, and sometimes you find—" He wiped his eyes. "You find the wrong ones."

Lore gave him some side-eye. "We all went through some shit, Ham."

They were both quiet for a while.

"I died once," he said, abruptly.

"Uh." She gave him a look. "Say more, please."

He told her a story then. How after high school, he went to Virginia Tech, nearly flunked out, was an absolute party boy. Got hooked on half the drugs available to him. Ate poorly. Looked like hammered shit. And then one day, he was at a party and took too much of something and . . .

And he woke up in the hospital.

After having been clinically dead.

"And I just started to think . . . I died, I never came back to life, and this is our home now."

This is our home now.

That gave her the shivers.

But it also filled her with a special kind of rage. In her was an orchestral crescendo of anger, but also *motivation*. A swell of music like when you were about to kill the final boss. Matty's message came to her, again, the one he had carved into the door: DON'T LET IT IN. And then, DON'T LET IT WIN.

They'd let it in.

But they didn't have to let it win.

"We're going to get out of here, Ham. We found the entrance to this place, and if there's an entrance, there's an exit. I'm sure of it." She stood up with a grunt. Her knees cracked and popped. It only occurred to her now how sore her legs were. She shot out a hand. "Come on, let's do this."

Hamish nodded, and she helped him stand.

"Sorry again," he said.

"I'm sorry, too."

"Yeah, but—your nose."

"It's all right."

"Broken, maybe."

"Then it matches the rest of me." She turned and looked at the scattering of mirror shards and the busted mirror hanging broken on the wall.

"I'll try not to punch stuff," he said with a dark, dire chuckle.

"Yeah . . ." But she paused. A spark of destruction lit in the darkness of her wandering mind. "Well. Now, hold on. Let's not be hasty. Maybe it's time to *start* punching stuff. And breaking things."

"Huh?"

"Think about it. We've been meandering through this place, aimless. It's not getting us anywhere. It's like a ride we're buckled into and it's just . . . wearing us down." *Remember the warnings.* "This place hates us. We're supposed to remember that. It hates us, Hamish."

For the first time in—what, days? She saw Hamish's eyes brighten. That same spark in her was now in him. "We should break shit."

"Yes. Yes! We've been playing by its rules. Circling the drain. But this is like *Minecraft,* man. We can destroy this place. Start smashing it to pieces. What happens if we break the walls? What's behind them? Where does *that* take us? If this place hates us? Then maybe we need to *hate it back.*"

51

Agita

They were cycling rooms again. It was how they moved through this place, Owen and Nick. When at a doorway, they stepped through and back again, triggering the rooms to cycle. Then they waited till they found the right room—or, at least, the right kind of room. Place to eat. Place to piss. Place to rest their head. Safe places—as much as they could guess at, anyway.

But it was wearing on them. Grinding them down.

Owen could feel it. The endlessness of it. Rinse, repeat. Rinse, repeat. It felt like madness. Doorways and staircases and dead rooms. By now, he was chewing his nails in secret. They were ripped, jagged things. Hangnails and ruined cuticles. They hurt. Nick had seen it, but blessedly had said nothing.

Presently, the room they were in seemed safe. A laundry room from 1992—easy to know that, since there was a calendar on the wall, one with normal family things written in the calendar blocks. *Valentine's Day dance. Church bake sale. Barbecue at Bob's.* Only awful thing in this room was the bloody bedsheets in the washer. It gave the air a faint coppery stink competing with the oversaturation of hyper-clean chemical laundry smell. Otherwise? This room was quiet as they hopped in and out of the doorway, then closing the door and reopening it again to see what the randomizer gave them.

On the sixth time, it gave them a bedroom where a filthy-looking orange lump of a cat was eating a dead woman's face. She lay there on her back, and the cat ate from her head like it was Fancy Feast. Wet, smacking sounds. Gore clinging to its whiskers like morning dew on onion grass. It made little happy sounds, *mow mow mew mow*, as it gorged.

Owen wanted to throw up.

They stepped back, shut the door.

Nick backed away and sighed before hopping up on the washing machine, his legs dangling over the edge. He had a bag of stale cheese balls from a few rooms back, and he crunched on those and stared at the middle distance. Owen gave him a quizzical *what the fuck* look.

"I just need a minute," Nick said. "I'm tired. This is tiring."

"You're always the one who wants to keep moving."

"Well, now I'm the one who wants to cool his fucking heels. Relax."

"Okay. Yeah. Fine."

Owen stood there. Awkwardly. His stomach flirted with hunger, but then—the image of the cat, the woman, the red mess on the animal's face. Then the hunger was gone again, replaced with a sour pool of acid.

"You don't like me," Nick said. "You never liked me."

"Jesus, Nick, c'mon. We're friends."

"'Friends.'" This he said with one hand up doing the lazy bunny ears of air quotes. "Friends, but not like you are, or were, with the others."

He kept crunching cheese balls between his teeth, showing what he was chewing with an open, almost feral mouth.

"Nick, why are we doing this? Far as I can tell, I was the only one to ever answer any of your emails."

A shrug. "Yeah. Always so polite, too, overly, *obsequiously* polite, like you were responding to a weird neighbor asking you to sign up for their pyramid scheme or send around their chain email or some shit. But you never said yes. Never joined me in trying to find Matty."

"Well. I'm sorry for that, but—" Owen did a half-assed, weary gesture around him. "Look where it got us."

Owen knew he was goading Nick, poking that bear. And he instantly felt bad about it. Did they really need to do this? But Nick just shrugged.

"You were jealous of Matty."

"No, I—" Owen sighed. "Fine, whatever, I was jealous."

"Lore and him had a thing, and you wanted that thing to be with you, not Matty. So." Another shrug. More crunching.

"What are you getting at?"

Another shrug.

Owen persisted. "I'm half waiting for you to say I killed Matty."

"Not saying anything. Just saying, you didn't do much to find him."

"And you did?"

From Nick, a piercing gaze, like a pair of hot needles. "I tried."

"And we followed."

"Only because I lied to you all. I had to trick you into giving a shit. Ain't that a bitch."

He was about to say, *Yeah, about that, how's your pancreatic cancer, Nick?* But what was the point? "I don't want to fight."

"I know you don't. You never did. Not much of a fighter. Not for Matty. Not for your own life. Not even for Lore. That's the thing, Nailbiter. I didn't make much of myself, either, but at least I *tried* things. At least I fought."

"Didn't amount to much, did it?"

Nick laughed then. "There it is. A little fight in you. Come on, Zuikas. Let's do that. Show me them nails, them bloodied nails. Scratch and claw, you little bitch. Tell me how much you hate me. Or hated Matty. Come on. Lay it on. Talk about how Lore left you behind, you poor thing. She kept going and you laid there, belly up, pissing and moaning."

"Fucking hell, you are relentless."

"You ever finally get together with her, by the way? You two went off to college together, right? Or was it that you followed her there, like a lost puppy? Or chased her. Like a stalker."

"I did not fucking chase her there. Sarah Lawrence was a great school for people who wanted to be . . . creative. And yeah. Not that it's any of your business, but we got together a few times over our time there and . . . it didn't work out."

"Doesn't seem like anything really worked out for you, Owen."

And then another shrug. Dismissive. Prickish. Pouty.

Something broke inside Owen. A boot pressing down on a bone. *Snap.*

He felt himself lurch forward, finger in Nick's face, a finger curling inward toward the rest of the hand, forming a fist as he seethed: "I swear to god, Nick, you *shrug* at me one more time and I will bust your fucking teeth—"

—down your throat till you choke—

And in that moment, he cut his words short.

And he wanted to do it.

He really, really wanted to do it.

How easy it would be.

Not just easy.

Freeing.

How *freeing* it would be to let that fist slip its leash and force Nick's teeth down his throat, just like Owen wanted, and then, even better? *To keep hitting.* Oh because all the teeth wouldn't be gone. No, some would remain. He'd have to keep pistoning his fist into the other man's face. His *friend's* face—but a friend no more. A stranger. A *foe*. He could keep punching, keep knocking the rest of the teeth down into his throat like he was tossing a bowling ball to get the straggler pins, *no strike on the first go, only a spare,* and the blood would bubble up as he pushed his fist into Nick's mouth, Nick's lips splitting like torn lunch meat, Owen's knuckles bulging down into the esophagus, finding the teeth that were lodged there, and Nick would try to scream, but how do you scream around a fist, a wrist, a pushing arm, and Owen thought it would be funny—no, that it *was* funny, because this wasn't a vision, this wasn't a dream, it was really happening, *it had already happened,* oh god, oh god, *no, Nick, I'm sorry*—

His fist—slick with blood, some of it his own from when the teeth shredded his fingers and hand—throbbed.

He stepped back from his dead friend.

His dead friend, who was grinning now through his broken teeth and ripped plastic bag of a mouth.

"Maybe you are a fighter after all," Nick said, voice whistling through the thick blood in his mouth.

Owen blinked.

The blood was gone.

The teeth were there.

His fist didn't hurt at all.

Nick's fine.

"This place is messing with us," Owen said.

"If you say so."

Still alive, so still a prick.

"We weren't close because we weren't close," Owen said. "You and me, I mean. We just weren't. You were scary in a lot of ways. Intense. Kind of a dick, honestly. But I also respected you and looked up to you because you never seemed to give a damn what anybody thought. And all I did was care what people think. You were fearless and I was always afraid. I'm sorry we weren't closer, but we just weren't. If we get out of here alive, maybe we can do something about that. If we don't, then just know I admired you. And I love you."

There.

Nick looked like he had just been *actually* punched.

Like something had rocked him, knocking his head for a loop.

He said nothing, just offered a small, sad little nod, then stared down into the tube of cheese balls like he was an oracle reading the future in cheese pollen.

What the fuck was all that about, anyway?

Impatience suddenly nagged at Owen, so he said, "I'm gonna

open the door, see where we landed, at least, and then we should get back to it."

Nick, in a small voice: "Sure thing."

Owen went and opened the door and—

And his breath was nearly stolen from his chest.

Because he was staring into—

52

Reiteration

It was Marshie's room.

The teen girl's bedroom. Though presently, she was nowhere to be seen. Owen saw all of it was the same otherwise: the bed, the computer. Still bloody handprints on the floor. Still a glitching spray of pixels on the monitor.

"Holy shit," he said. "Nick, you need to see this."

He felt Nick behind him already. "Hey, isn't that—"

"It's her room. The girl, the dead girl. We're back to it."

"Okay. That's weird."

Owen almost laughed. "It's not weird, it's—it's a good thing. An amazing thing. It means this place isn't *infinite*."

"How d'ya figure?"

"The chances of cycling to the same room again are infinitesimal—if this place is endless and infinite. But we found her room again."

"And again, that's good how?"

"Nick, it means we might see our friends again. There's an actual chance we'll run into them. It also means—maybe there's a way out. That this isn't just some unspooling nightmare but a . . . a system, a design, a blueprint that makes sense somehow, to someone. Like Lore said: a game. Just a really fucked-up one." *In which we're the player characters. And if there are player characters, that means . . .*

Nick, still seeming to be uncomfortable after the end of their confrontation, muttered an "okay" and then added, "But let's cycle past this fuckin' room."

"No," Owen said.

"What?"

"I want to go in."

"The fuck? Why?"

Because I want to try something.

"Just trust me."

And then Owen stepped through into the dead girl's room.

53

Between

The Bottle Room was rent asunder, the wall busted wide, leaving behind a craggy mouth of dangling plaster, tufts of insulation, and broken framing studs. Bits of particulate matter hung around, floating here and there, glittering when they touched the light. The floor, too, had a few broken bottles shattered around, and the smell of spent whiskey, tequila, and gin perfumed the air.

Hamish panted. In his hand: a tall floor lamp. He took out the bulb, tossed the shade, and used the lamp and its faux brass base to bash the wall. Lore stood near him, her face still bloody, though the blood had now dried to an almost black mask on the lower half of her face—weirdly reminiscent of the face masks worn during COVID. She held a leg from the coffee table—wooden, easy for her to unscrew and use like a baton. It was powdered with wall dust.

He coughed and cleared his throat.

Inside, the wall was . . . well, what was expected, mostly. More framing studs. Also some pipe, some loops and bundles of wire, a few junction boxes. Hamish said he didn't do much work on his own home these days but knew what he was looking at. And there were a few things that didn't add up.

For one, the studs were erratic in their distance from one another. Usually studs were sixteen or twenty-four inches apart—the former for load-bearing walls, the latter a standard for every other wall. These were spaced differently. He didn't have a tape measure or anything, but could easily see the discrepancies. One gap was around twelve inches. The next, twice as much. The third? Six inches, maybe.

The other thing, the pipes and wires didn't make sense. The junction boxes seemed purposeless. Wires seemed to go to theoretical outlets where no outlets existed. They were designed to *look* okay, in passing, but nothing really seemed to connect to anything else. And yet, sometimes they could hear running water going through the pipes. And this whole place seemed to have power.

The final thing was the kicker, though: The space between the walls, from this room to the next, was way too wide. Usually walls were six inches apart, because, he said, most homes were trying to maximize space, not steal living space from their inhabitants. But here the space was easily two feet or more. In this case, the opposing wall was raw, red brick. Dusty, pocked with time, strung with wisps of cobweb. He explained all of this to Lore, who paused for a moment to finally wipe some of the blood crust from her face.

"You thinking what I'm thinking?" she asked.

"Crawlspace," he said.

"Crawlspace."

Together, they went over into the wall breach that they had made.

And sure enough, it was not only wide enough to fit through, it was wide enough to walk down—long as you squeezed past or ducked under the pipes and wires. Lore stepped into the half-dark. Stepping into this space, the air was cooler. Thinner—in a good way, like it wasn't thick, like it wasn't trying to smother them. Easier to breathe. And Lore's head felt . . . clearer, somehow. Like a bad hangover dissolved by a good cup of coffee and a little sunlight. That's what this place felt like. Sunlight.

That's when Lore saw it, and pointed. "Look."

There, on the ground, a can.

Hamish squinted.

A *soup* can. Campbell's, maybe.

"Whoa. Someone's been here," he said. "In the walls." He didn't say what they both hoped: *Matty*.

"In *between* the walls," Lore said. That felt important, somehow, in a way she didn't yet understand. "So we know that the rooms shift. But what about the crawlspace? What... happens here?"

"Guess we should check it out," Hamish said.

"Guess we should." She paused. "You think Hell has crawlspaces?"

Hamish took a deep breath. "I don't think so. You're right. This place is something different. I feel... different here."

"Me too. Clearer."

"Yeah. Clearer."

"All right. Team Crawlspace. You wanna go first, or should I?"

"Have at it," he said.

Lore nodded. She picked a direction—right, not left, because wasn't left the direction of evil?—and they descended into the darkness of the in-between.

54

It's Time for Some Game Theory

Owen stood in the room, with Nick just behind him, and he scanned the space, looking for—

Well, for what, he didn't know.

But his mind returned again and again to games.

Video games.

Growing up, it was nearly all he and Lore did.

They played them, talked about them, wrote fanfic of them, and eventually... wanted to design them. Those designs still lived inside him, somewhere.

And he was thinking about them now.

Lately, aside from stupid time-wasters on his phone, he was pretty into indie games. He'd really taken to playing ones that were, in essence, *spot the anomaly* games. A new subgenre, of sorts. Games like *I'm on Observation Duty, Exit 8, Peculiarity Room*, and *The Inverted Lighthouse*. They were more than just walking simulators, more than just interstitial backrooms shit. The goal of these was simple enough: spot the anomaly. The consequences for not? Death, usually. You did not survive the night if you did not see and identify what had changed. *Exit 8* made it creepier not by raising the stakes, but rather lowering them: You, the POV protagonist, walked down a well-lit, well-rendered subway tunnel, with one man walking past. As you went around the corner, the scene repeated, and you had to scrutinize *everything* to answer the question: Had something changed? If it had not, you could keep walking forward and it would take you to the next area. (Which, admittedly, was just the same area *again*, but this time, the number of the area went up by one, all the way to eight.) If you saw an anomaly, like a face reflected in the subway tile, or the man walking past now grinning instead of frowning, you had to turn back around and go back the way you came—in which case, the number of the area went up, and you were one step closer to being able to leave. If you missed an anomaly and went the wrong way? It would all reset. You were trapped in this shiny, bright liminal space.

It unsettled Owen to the core.

And it reminded him very much of where they were.

This was a house that shifted rooms, and there were clearly rules on how to cycle those rooms—and now, they'd finally found a repeat room.

It felt like a blessing.

More to the point, it felt like he had *done something right*, like he had made the correct move, spotted the right thing, gone the correct way, performed the proper sequence, up up down down left right left right A B select start, and now he was rewarded with the prize of revelation: They were *not* in an infinite prison. This house had finite rooms. It was not on a repeated loop, not exactly, but there were ways to *get* rooms to repeat.

Now Owen stood in their first repeated room. Marshie's Room.

Bloody handprints. Glitching computer. Spice Girls on the wall.

Plastic phone. Feather pens.

And maybe, just maybe, a dead girl under the bed.

"What are we doing here, Zuikas?" Nick asked.

"I'm just... looking around."

"For what?"

For anomalies, he thought, but didn't say, because it sounded insane and because it meant he'd have to explain the whole video game thing, *and* because Nick would have the patience to hear exactly none of it. To Owen, the question became, had something changed in here? Was there something to see that was different, and could that unlock... something else? Anything else?

An exit?

That might not be the case. He wasn't seeing anything, really.

But he still felt there was something to learn here.

And he wanted to take the time to learn it.

This might not be a game, he knew.

But it still could be a simulation, couldn't it?

That felt crazy to believe, but he'd long had the nagging suspicion that... everyone and everything around him wasn't real, that the reality of reality was too good, too perfect, that there always seemed to be a narrative that the world and its people neatly slotted into. And coincidences were strange—so-called glitches in the Matrix were a fun joke, but you looked for them, you found them, and once you found them? You had to wonder if it wasn't a fun joke anymore.

He never necessarily *believed* that all of life was a simulation—but it was a sort of comforting, modern, almost techno-spiritual view of the world, right? It provided a kind of faith-based structure. Instead of there being a Heaven or Hell or ghosts or demons, you instead believed that you were a part of a created, *manufactured* world, and that there had to be a real world, a *true* world, beyond it. A place both after and around this one. And now, *now,* he and his friends were in, what, a smaller version of that? A simulation inside the simulation? A smaller shard server? A game running a game, like someone designing and running *Doom* inside of *Minecraft*? Or was the real world real, but this was fake?

Owen wasn't sure.

He certainly wasn't sure that any of this was fake.

It felt real. Horribly, profoundly real.

But it also felt impossible, and that made him pause and really think for the first time since they got here, what, a week ago? Two? He didn't even know anymore.

What if none of this was really real—and the way to escape was to figure that out? What if he just needed to find proof?

Like in a game, that meant *trying things.*

So Owen walked over to the bed, and around to the side where

Hamish once sat. He stood next to the bloody handprints dried into the carpet.

"Zuikas," Nick cautioned.

"It's fine. I . . . got this."

He wasn't sure he did. Owen felt every part of him resisting, every *cell* in rebellion against the action he was about to take. *You're being foolish,* his brain screamed at him, which was a helluva thing, that your brain can basically scream at you, the you that is also your brain—your mind going to war against itself. (But that, he supposed, was what it meant to be human. To exist in constant opposition to yourself, you as your very best friend at the exact same time you were your own worst enemy. Oh, how stupid it was to be a person.) What he was doing was foolish because if he was wrong, what then? The stakes were either very high, or entirely imaginary. *Maybe I'll die,* he thought, which made him want to throw up. *Maybe I'll die and wake up from this place,* was the next thought, and that thought only terrified him further.

Owen took a deep breath—

And got down on his knees on the floor.

Then he slid his legs out and got down on his belly.

All so that he could be facing the shadows under the girl's bed.

"Hello, Marshie," he said in a trembling voice.

A white smile and eyes like moons opened in the darkness.

55

Clipping

If she was being honest with herself, Lore was happy for the mystery of the crawlspace. It allowed her—just like when writing, or designing a game, or throwing paint on a canvas—to simply *be present* and focus on what was in front of her rather than life's many grievances and inadequacies. It was comforting to put all the bullshit and the garbage outside the bubble of *making something*. And making something felt like progress.

It felt like moving forward.

And in designing games—hell, in playing them, too—the greatest joy was exactly that. Find a path, and go down it.

You had a progress bar. A percentage of the game complete. Parts of the map uncovered. Secrets revealed, items discovered.

So this was her focus. Progress. For now, that meant the task ahead was simple:

Examine the crawlspace.

Like a mission in a game. A task to complete with a checkbox right next to it, enticingly empty and desperate to be checked off.

The crawlspace was, as Hamish explained, wide—too wide, really. And it seemed to be one continuous space, unlike the rooms, which were defined by their doors. Not just doorways, but *doors* that could be opened and closed. But this went on and on, and formed junctures—crossroads, really—between rooms. Except it didn't necessarily seem to retain the same physical structure of the rooms, either. When the Bottle Room ended, there should've been a turn in the crawlspace. But there wasn't. It kept going straight and went left and right farther on.

"Clipping," she said, idly.

"Huh?" Hamish asked, just ahead of her.

"Like in graphics. In a game. Clipping."

"Lore, dude, I don't speak this language."

She explained: "In a game, you have your defined areas, right? The player areas, where they're going to travel, where they can interact with things. You define this as a clip region, and outside of that is where all the excess visual and programmatic garbage gets, well, clipped. Cut off. You don't want to expend computing power rendering things into infinity, you only need to render where the functional game space 'exists.' But sometimes a player breaks that accidentally or on purpose, like with a *noclip* cheat, and ends up ... essentially here. Beyond the borders of the game. In the walls."

"Games have crawlspaces?"

"Kinda?" She made a face. "It's not a one to one. A lot of times you can see excess programming artifacts there—though other times you might just fall through the universe and die, or worse, break the game." Which made her wonder: *Had they just broken the game?* Since she was behind him, she nudged him forward. "Let's keep going, see where we end up."

"It's darker ahead," he said. And it was. What light they got from the hole in the wall behind them did not travel far beyond this corner.

"All right. My phone's almost dead, but ... yours still good?"

He hesitated. "I ... shit, it's out." He sounded suddenly sad. Pathetic. "I was looking at pictures of my kids and my wife, Lore, I know, I know, I'm sorry—"

"Okay, *okay*, hey, it's—" Again, Lore doing the hard work of actually having to be calm and nice and not just laying into him. It was hard for her—but easier in the crawlspace, somehow. *Like the house can't reach us here.* Was that insane? It sounded insane. It also felt very true. "It's fine. You're fine."

"I am sorry. I just needed to see them—"

"Really, I get it." That was a lie. She didn't get it. Not remotely. Lore was an island. She did not feel the urge to look at photos of other people from her life for a host of reasons: because they were gone when she didn't look at them, in some cases, and in other cases, because it was too painful to remember them, an acknowledgment that they mattered to her and she didn't do enough to show them. "I still have a little juice." *I wish there was a charger I could find in this godforgotten house maze.* It was what it was. She got out her phone and powered it up.

Nine percent left on the battery.

Good enough for now. Flashlight on, they continued forward, turning right at the junction.

The boards creaked underneath them. The walls, too, seemed to groan a little on both sides—like the sounds of a creaky old ship at sea.

Ahead, something was there on the floor. Trapped by the meager light.

As they got closer, they saw it more clearly. It was more snack trash: this time, an empty bag of Lay's Hickory BBQ chips, with packaging old enough to drink. And next to that bag? A pair of sneakers. New Balances, ratty, torn on the sides, the soles worn so far down they were smooth.

They stank. Like dust and time and, well, *foot*.

"These aren't programming artifacts," Hamish said. "Matty..."

"Matty wore New Balances." *Gray, just like these.* They each had their signature footwear back then, didn't they? Nick wore janky work boots. Hamish had his Birkenstocks. Owen went through pair after pair of black Chucks. And she was an early adopter of Doc Martens, baby. Black leather, yellow thread.

"We don't know that they're his."

"No. But..."

"Lore, every room is filled with shit. Some of it's trash, or old food or ... a room full of booze bottles. I don't know who they belong to or if they belong to anybody. Except maybe the—the people we see."

"The ghosts, you mean."

"Ghosts."

"Ghosts, or illusions, or whatever they are. They're something. They're not people. Not people-people." She clicked off her phone light for a moment to conserve battery. "They're all dead or half dead or insane. They're as ruined as the rooms they inhabit. This is a haunted house." *A haunted house,* not like one that was really, actually haunted. But one that was put on, created, *staged* for Halloween. A haunted house attraction. Which was, in its way, a kind of game, wasn't it? Enter. Move forward through the rooms. Exit. That was a thread she wanted to pull on. But so were these shoes. "These sneakers are old. Like, late nineties old. What if Matty was in here, too? He could've found this place, same as we did." But now, hope that Matty was still alive dimmed. How could he be? All they were finding of him were remnants. And even if he *were* still alive in here ... he'd be older, like they were. And almost certainly broken, deranged, a mess of a man lost in this labyrinth. But then, an enticing thought—

What if he got out?

What if he found an exit?

If he had, why wouldn't he have found them?

None of it made any sense. Lore, frustrated, felt like it was all there in front of her, but she couldn't put it together.

"Hey." In the darkness, she saw Hamish shift suddenly. Like he was *differently alert,* if that made sense. *He's looking at something.* "Yo, what the hell's that?" he asked.

She turned to look back down the crawlspace channel.

Farther down, a little prickle of light. Shining in a small, faded beam from the wall. About twenty feet or so. Lore lowered her voice, not that it mattered much now. "Let's go check it out."

"Lore, what if we can't get back to where we came in?"

"Then we bust our way out same as we got in."

"Yeah. All right."

She pressed on. Hamish close behind her. The walls of the crawlspace feeling like they were closing in. But here, Lore noted something: While it felt like the walls were closing in, that was just regular old claustrophobia. What she *didn't* feel was that oppressive, crushing feeling. The one that felt like she was in a vice grip of pure hatred. Squeezing the air from her. Pushing the blood to her head. Draining the hope out of her heart.

We really are outside the game, she thought.

They closed in on the source of the light.

It was thin, weak light. As if it were blocked.

Closer, closer now.

The light revealed itself to be thin cuticles—little crescent moons of light. Two of them, one next to the other. Right at face height.

Lore went to turn on her phone flashlight, but Hamish figured it out before she did.

"They're eyeholes," he said.

56

Conversations with a Dead Girl

A bloody hand shot out from underneath the bed, grabbing a tuft of carpet. That hand *hauled* the girl's body forward. Another hand shot out, this one holding the same knife as she held before: the thin, curved blade of the boning knife. The stainless steel dark with dried blood. As the girl began to emerge from the dark space, grinning broadly, Owen scuttled backward, barely managing to stand without falling over. He braced himself against the wall to keep himself upright, his hand planted in the midst of the gathered Spice Girls.

"*Owen,*" Nick hissed in warning.

But Owen stood his ground. Even though he was shaking so hard he thought his molecules might vibrate apart. But there existed a clarity to the moment; Owen felt sharp as that knife in the dead girl's hand.

"Marshie," he said, quiet at first, then again, more firmly: "*Marshie.*"

She rose before him, almost as though she was a bundle of rags and bones reconstituted into a girl. Her pale face regarded him carefully. A whisper of air hissed wetly from the vent in her throat.

"*Graaaaady,*" she said.

"I'm not Grady."

"*I lllll—*" She choked, and tried again, the voice sounding so sad this time, like the peal of a funeral bell. "*I lllloved you. And you were s-s-ssssso cruel.*"

"Why did you have a photo of that knife on your computer?" It hit him then: Did she? Did she really have a photo of his old penknife?

Or did his brain just make it up? Did this *place* just make it up? Lore hadn't seen it. Only he had. He raced to another question: "Tell me something about yourself. From when you were alive. Anything. What were your parents' names? What was your favorite food, your favorite color, your—" He still had his hand on the wall, on the poster. "Your favorite Spice Girls song—"

"*You were so mmmean to me. You cut me with your w-words. So I ccccccut myself to match.*" Her voice was sad. Her words a lamentation—and it hurt him just to hear them. She held up both arms, showing him the deep slash down the inside of each. From wrist to elbow. The movement squeezed thin, brown fluid from the openings. It dribbled to the floor.

"That wasn't me, Marsha."

"*You hurt me. I hurt me. Now—*" Her voice turned angry. "*I hurt you.*"

"No—!"

She raised the knife—

—Owen cried out—

And buried the blade in his chest.

57

Jeepers Creepers,
Where'd You Get Those Peepers

They were not only eyeholes—the light coming through them was meager because they were blocked by little slips of cardboard thumbtacked into the drywall. Lore shone the light over them, and pulled one aside—as it seemed it was meant to be—but even then, it remained blocked on the other side, too. She shone the phone light in there, and saw—

Pages. Bound pages. Like from a book.

In both of the eyeholes.

Lore poked at one of the books. It moved, sliding forward. She looked to Hamish and said, "Your fingers are big, can you push on one?"

"I'm not fat anymore."

"Jesus, Ham, it wasn't a fat joke—and god, you were never fat. You always looked good. Girls wanted to get with you, man. *Guys* wanted to get with you. You were comfortable and confident in your body, and that's hot."

She shone the light toward him.

His eyes gleamed. He was about to cry.

"You mean it?"

Sigh.

"Ham, I do mean it, and I want to give you this moment right now, I do, but therapy time has to be over, and we need to solve the mystery of this awful place. Can you please push past this and just poke the fucking book?"

"Yeah. Okay. I got this."

But then, before poking the book, he hugged her.

Hard.

And admittedly, Lore was not one for uninvited touching. It generally squicked her the fuck out. She liked to be in control of those things. She liked the way things felt when she wanted to feel them, hated the way they felt every other time. Textures were hard for her. Clothing was weird. Sometimes the air felt like it was solid, enrobing her, making it hard for her to catch a breath. So a surprise hug was, for her, often very bad, and totally deserving of a knee to the crotch of whoever dared to foist such a thing upon her.

But right now, in this house, in this crawlspace, with this person—

It felt pretty all right.

She hugged him back.

The "pretty all right" feeling did not last, and she patted him on the back and said, "I need to be done with this, and you need to push the book."

"Right." Hamish let go (*whew*) and he reached forward and stabbed with a finger. The book popped free, and on the other side of the wall, she heard a *fwump*. Hamish did the same thing with the other one—it took two finger pokes, and it sounded like the one book fell atop the other. *Fwathump.*

Light shined in.

Gray light. Beige light.

Greige light.

Lore pressed her eyes to the holes—

"It's the Greige Room," she said.

The living room with the white couch, the TV, the dead fish, the greige everything. From her angle, it meant she was staring out from the bookshelf—the eyeholes cut out behind it. She could almost feel the presence of the bloodied murder weapon on the shelf just past the wall.

"Really?" Hamish asked, and she let him look. His jaw fell open.

"Whoa. Holy shit, this is the first time we're seeing a room repeat. That's a good thing, right?"

"It is. Means this place isn't as boundless as I thought."

Could mean there's an exit.

She didn't want to get ahead of herself there, though.

After all, hope was what killed you.

Maybe Matty got out...

Maybe Matty died in here...

Maybe he's been in here the whole time, watching us.

She backed away from the eyehole and looked around some more. There, a little farther down, the ground rose up a little into a pile of mess, and it took her a moment to realize what she was looking at: a filthy twin mattress crammed into the space, and heaped with a pile of blankets and clothes. Plus some more snack bags and soup cans. Like something from a homeless encampment.

"Lore, over here."

Hamish gestured with his foot toward the wall at the bottom. The space he was gesturing toward was below the eyeholes. Lore knelt down and saw that someone had crudely cut through the drywall here, as if with a steak knife or some other totally inappropriate implement. She gently pressed on it. It moved.

"It's a door. A hatch," she said. "From the crawlspace into the Greige Room."

Hamish was right. It was right underneath their noses the whole time. A way in and out of the crawlspace. And a way to watch them.

Suddenly, she hoped like hell it was Matty who had made those eyeholes and this door. Because otherwise, it meant others had come through here. Others who could still be here, even now. Watching them, like one of those freaky motels where the proprietor watched you through the walls.

Maybe it's whoever built this place.

But even there, she flinched. Because this place didn't feel built.

It felt... born.

But for what purpose? Was this some kind of deranged horror house panopticon? Were they players in this game? Or its designers? Were they victims, or architects? Or somehow, both?

Just then, her light went out.

She clicked it back on—but nope, nothing. Lore growled out a frustrated sound. "My phone's fucked. *Shit.*"

"Lasted longer than I figured it would."

"Yeah. All right. We can't stay in here. It's too dark."

"Right. But—I don't really wanna go back out there, dude."

"It'll be fine. And at least we have a way back in." She pushed on the drywall cutout and found some resistance. *The books,* she realized. The eyeholes looked out through the shelf, which meant this door was concealed by the books, too. It's why they couldn't see it when they passed through the Greige Room. She winced and pushed harder, and all the books ahead of the makeshift "hatch" slid out and tumbled into a clumsy pile. The light of the Greige Room brightened the crawlspace. "Ready?" she asked Hamish.

He nodded.

Back into the house they went.

58

A Map, Drawn by a Knife

The boning knife slid effortlessly into Owen's chest. The pain that bloomed there was numb and cold, as if she'd stuck him with an icicle. The blade through the rib. Into—what? His heart? His lungs? He swallowed hard. Gasped for air. Tasted blood. Heard Nick calling his name. But standing there. Just standing there. Watching.

And to think, this is what I wanted once, he thought, idly, madly, almost hilariously. All those times of him hiding in his closet or walking out into the woods across from his house, the Schrade Old Timer penknife in his hand, and he'd go out there and peel up the sleeves of his black tee, exposing a biceps. He'd suck in air, holding it tight, his heart thudding anxiously in his chest as he pressed the blade of the knife against his too-pale skin—his technique was always a quick tug, never slow, always fast. Making a thin slash, like a thorn scratch or a paper cut, but just a *bit* deeper every time. The skin of his arms showed older scars, like a crisscrossing of lace just under the skin. Whenever he cut, he thought, One day I'll do the real thing, one day I'll show them, and that last part was the thing, wasn't it? *I'll show them.*

But it wasn't even them, not really. It was him. His dad. *I'll show him. He'll see that I'm dead and he'll feel bad for all the things he said about me.* One day, Owen would stop cutting the biceps and he'd do the right thing the right way. Not across the wrist, ohhh no, that was the loser way. And Owen was smart. He knew he'd put the knife starting at the middle of the wrist and then pull it to the elbow. Like he was opening a box. *Vvvviiiiip*. And the blood would pour. And the life would leave. And they (*his father, okay, maybe Lore, too, maybe Matty, maybe anybody who wasn't ever appreciative of him*) would all regret the way they'd treated him. But he never did it. Never managed. *Never had the courage*, he knew. Because that was Owen. Too scared to get it done, to see it through. Always easier to fail, and even better not to ever try in the first place.

Here he was, finally having succeeded at the thing he'd failed to do every day—he put himself in the way of death, and death was happy to continue in its path, throwing him beneath the hooves of its horse, the wheels of its carriage. Like Emily Dickinson had written: *Because I could not stop for Death, He kindly stopped for me.* Yet in this moment, it felt all wrong. A surge of something surprising arose in him: *regret*. Then, on its heels: *despair* that he was going to die, and the *desire* to undo it, to change it, to *continue*.

Owen didn't merely *not* want to die.

Owen wanted to live.

I still need time.

But here he was. Out of it. The last sand sliding through the glass.

The dead girl, her hands still on the knife, did not meet his eyes. It was like she was staring at a point near his eyes, but not in them, not at them. "*Now you're like me*," she said in a small, sad voice, the anger all gone, finally. In that way, they were like each other. Owen saw only now that he'd had anger in him—anger at himself, at Lore, at Matty, at the entire world—and it dissolved in that moment, like cotton candy on the tongue. He wondered if Marshie felt regret, too.

If she'd wanted to live in the moment she pulled the knife across her arms, then brought it to her throat and swiftly drew it left to right.

Slice, slice, slit.

Owen stepped back, and the knife slipped free from his heart. It made no sound as it did. It felt like nothing at all.

He looked down, waiting for the blood to soak his shirt.

It did no such thing.

Marshie continued to stare through him.

He pawed at his chest.

Still no blood.

The pain that he felt receded quickly. Like it was the ghost of pain, not the fresh pain of a new injury. A memory of it, referred from the past, given a moment to live in the present before fading anew. Owen gulped air and lifted his shirt—

There was no wound.

The knife hadn't cut him at all.

Nick stood toward the door, frozen in place, staring in horror and, now, confusion.

"She's not real," Owen said, softly. Then, to Marshie: "You're not real."

She froze, then. Froze in place like a busted animatronic.

Owen laughed. "She's not real. They're not real. The—the people, they're..." *NPCs.* Non-player characters. Just bits of program written into the story, unplayable, interactive only to a point. *If we're the player characters, they're the non-players.* Like fragments of artificial intelligence.

"No," Nick said. "This is all real. It's *real*. You don't get it—"

But the entire thing unspooled in Owen's mind. It *wasn't* real. Seeing the knife that cut him on that screen, and later, at the bottom of the fish tank? All the dead people, the half-dead people, the ones who tried to chase them, or the ones who just sat there screaming? All the sounds behind the walls? It was all just part of a grand, horrid illusion. Like a haunted house in the most mundane sense: a place of trickery meant to scare the rubes who walked through it.

"It's just fucking with us," Owen said, spreading his arms wide, feeling more alive than he'd felt in—well, forever. *This place hates you.* That thought, it felt like a warning, a curse—but in a way, it was also the key. "This whole place is here just to break us down and fuck with us. I don't know why. But I know I'm done with that." He bellowed to the walls around him, to the ceiling, the floor, all the rooms around them: "You hear that? I'm *done* with this. I know your tricks, and I'm not falling for it anymore."

Then, a pause.

Admittedly, he hoped it would all just . . . what? Collapse? The house of cards falling around him, the trick exposed, the secret mechanics revealed? A door would magically appear? A staircase back out? A glowing exit sign? Or maybe applause from a secret audience, or text messages from the crowd watching this event being streamed live to the dark web? Lore and Hamish and Matty, emerging from that door, smiling warmly, telling him that he had indeed beaten the game?

None of that happened.

Okay. Fine. Okay. It would've been too easy anyway, right?

To Nick, he said: "We need to find the others and get out of here."

"Zuikas. Owen. Listen to me—"

Marshie twitched.

Her eyes snapped to focus on Owen. It was the first time he felt she was truly *seeing* him—and his heart nearly stopped in its chest.

"*Owen*," she said, her voice buzzing with not just her voice, but dozens of voices. Deep voices, high voices. An erratic, buzzing chorus. Humming together like summer cicadas.

"You're not real," he said again. But suddenly, he wasn't so sure.

"*Your father's in here, Owen. He's real, isn't he?*"

Owen could barely find his voice when he said, "My father's dead."

"*And yet, he's waiting for you. So is the knife, Owen. So are your bitten fingernails. So is Lauren. Your mind is a house of pain, Owen. Let me add its rooms to mine. And let me add my rooms to yours.*" And then the chorus of voices pared away until there was only one voice left—not Marshie's voice, no, even though it came out of her. "*I wish you were never born,*" said his father.

His words. Her mouth.

He hadn't heard his father's words since that day in his bedroom. And those words—*I wish you were never born*—were the last things Owen heard before—

No, don't think it, don't go there, you think about it it'll never stop, that thought will never leave—like a vampire, once you invited it in, it could always come in, would never ever leave.

Instead, he pushed past Nick and opened the door—pulling his friend through and slamming the door shut behind them.

59

Checks and Cross-Checks

Soon as they came back out into the house, Lore felt it. Like getting into cold, slick pond water—sinking into oily foulness, drowning in toxic runoff. Hamish didn't need to say anything—it was clear he felt it, too. He looked sallow-cheeked. Almost like he was getting sick, like a fever was on its way. A hint of jaundice to his pallor. A sheen of sweat.

Lore sniffed and looked at the bookshelves in front of them.

"There was a book here," Lore said to him, as she stood by those shelves, scanning them first with her eyes, then with a finger running across their spines.

Hamish didn't hear her at first—he was instead on his hands and knees, looking back into the opening leading to the crawlspace. "What?"

"A book. By me." *Sort of.*

"Wait, there was a book by . . . you? Here? In this room?" He grunted as he stood. "That seems fuckin' goofy."

"Yeaaaaah. Yeah." She chewed on her lower lip. "I wrote a book once about game design. *The Crazy Bitch's Guide to . . .* whatever. And it was here, and I flipped through it, but it wasn't entirely my book. It had other things in it. Hateful things. About me, mostly. Stuff I'd seen online or gotten over email. Gross sexist shit. Death threats. Doxxing. I dunno why it was here. And you're right. I can't find it now, but . . . it's insane it was here in the first place." She used the toe of one of her boots to move the books on the floor to see if one of those was hers. Didn't look like it.

"Maybe it was real, now it's gone. Maybe it wasn't real in the first place."

"What do you mean? Say more."

"Uhh. I dunno. I just figure—so, like, this is a room, and it feels like a real room that exists. Or . . . existed."

"Like the ghost of a room. Or a copy of one."

"Maybe a ghost *is* just a copy."

Lore felt a little rocked by that comment. "God. Maybe. That's pretty smart thinking, Hamish. So these rooms are or were real, but maybe they're not the actual rooms. They're ghosts of rooms, copies of rooms, programs of rooms. So why would my book not be here anymore?"

"Like, maybe it was just put here to fuck with you."

She nodded. That felt right, didn't it?

"This place hates you. Gets inside you. Like Matty—or whoever—wrote on those cabinets. If this place wanted to get inside me? Well, it would probably show me a book full of people who hate me. It would deliver that hate in a form I would not easily be able to deny. I'd definitely reach for a book I wrote, because, let's be honest, I'm a raging narcissist." Hamish looked like he was about to protest, but she shook her head. "It's okay, I already know it. This place served my anxiety to me on a silver platter of my own making."

"It's . . . been fucking with me, too. The first bathroom we found—the one off this very room?" He walked over to that door, not yet opening it. "That was the bathroom I died in. At the party. Just some dude's bathroom. I . . . I didn't even realize it at first but then it hit me, that's where I died. The mirror was broken because I broke it that day. With my head, when I passed out."

"Jesus, Ham."

"Yeah."

He winced, and then threw the door open. The door that once led to that bathroom of which he spoke.

She walked up behind him to see what room it had become.

Now it was a garage. No garage door—just a cinder block wall. An early nineties minivan sat there, running. The smell of exhaust was thick, choking, and they had just enough time to see the shadow of a body slumped over the wheel before Hamish slammed the door shut.

Another body.

A suicide.

Torment and tragedy.

A show put on for us. But why?

What was it Matty had carved into the cabinets?

It wants to get inside them.

It wants to move in.

Hamish said, "We saw that home gym, earlier, too. Remember?"

"Yeah, I remember."

"That was from our first house. Before we had our first kid, Tyler."

"Okay. Why . . . would it show you that? What happened there, Ham?"

He hesitated. "That's the thing. Nothing. Not really. It's where I really started working out. Where I changed my body from that fat kid to . . . this. Except . . . that room, it's where I learned to really hate myself, Lore. Where I learned to hate the way I looked, where I punished the fucking *shit* out of my body. I would stay down there for hours. Guzzling energy drinks and pushing and pushing and pushing. I put up all these mirrors in that room too so I could look at myself and—and I told myself it was because I wanted to see how much I was improving, but every time I looked, it was never enough. Never. I'd stare in those mirrors and I'd say the worst things to myself. Things you'd never say to your worst enemy, man. I hated myself in that room. That's when I figured . . . you know, this house was Hell, literal Hell. And that maybe I died way back when. I dunno." This was hard for him. Lore could see that.

"Let's refocus. Let's talk about what we know. The place hates us. Wants to get inside us. *You'll become the house,* whatever that means."

"Yeah. And that thing about the eyes."

"*You can tell by the eyes.*"

"Tell what, then?"

"I dunno. Maybe . . . the eyes of the ghosts here? The copies? Maybe you can see something in there. Something that tells you . . . it's not real? They're not real?" *Just NPCs,* she thought.

"Or maybe it's about the eyes of people the house . . . infects."

At that, she shuddered. A new fate for Matty revealed itself to her: *It got in him, filled all his rooms up.* Just like it might do to them. She could feel it even now. Like furniture moving inside her head. Like footsteps. Hands rattling the knobs of her many doors. She wanted to go back into the crawlspace, and said as much.

"Me too," Hamish said. "The crawlspace—has it changed?"

They each got down and checked, peering into it. There was enough light from the Greige Room to show that it hadn't.

"The rooms shift. But the crawlspace doesn't," she said.

Hamish said, "You know anything about mortgages?"

"Delightfully little."

"Well." He dusted off his pants. "So, like, with mortgage rates, there are two primary kinds: fixed rate versus variable. Fixed rate means you know what you're charged every month. Variable goes up or down on you, though truthfully, it pretty much always goes *up.* Swells like a balloon. So. Fixed rate is what you want. And it's kinda true here, too. You want a fixed place, a constant doorway. Like the crawlspace." He hesitated. "I dunno. It's dumb. Listen, at work I'm just a monkey, I punch people's info into the computer and it calculates if they get a mortgage—"

"It's not dumb," she said. And it wasn't. "You step through a door, it's like pulling a slot machine lever. It's a random draw. But the crawlspace doesn't change. It stays, like you said, fixed. Or in my world: a constant. In math, science, or fuck, in programming especially—a constant is a thing that stays the same, and cannot be changed by internal forces. It's a thing that *remains true.* Sometimes even against external forces, if it's final." She *hmm*ed. "I don't know how it all adds up yet. But I know we need to get back to the crawlspace. That place is safe. And out here . . . I can feel how this place hates us. It's like something worse than white noise. *Black noise. Empty noise.* But in there I felt free of it. I felt more clear. Did you?"

"Yeah. We're gonna need lights in there, though."

"Right. Right. Okay. We go through some more rooms. Cycle them, see if we can't find some gear. Flashlights, phone chargers, extension cords."

Hamish nodded.

Lore stared him up and down. "All your life, you just thought you were some dumb, fat kid, didn't you?"

He sighed. "Mostly. Not when I was with you guys, though. You know. Back when. I felt pretty good about myself then. But later . . . I dunno. With Matty gone and everything. I just felt worse."

"Same here," she said. It wasn't a lie, not entirely. She'd found a better life. But had she ever felt as good as she did when she had her friends? When they were bound by the Covenant? She didn't think so. "All right. We'll keep looking for Matty. And more importantly, for Nick and Owen. Good?"

"Good."

As they headed to the door to cycle the shifting rooms—

A stray thought pinged her. A phrase from the original *Legend of Zelda* game. Right at the start, a cryptic old man hands Link, the protagonist, a sword. It's just a wooden sword, but it's enough. And when he hands it over, he says:

It's dangerous to go alone. Take this.

And that's the thought that hit her.

It was dangerous to go alone. If Hamish were alone in here, he would've killed himself. If she were alone, who knows what would happen. The house would have its way, she feared. Climbing a ladder made of her worst thoughts. Crawling around in her mental attic like rabid rats.

She nodded to Hamish, and reached for the door.

60

The Light Reveals What We Don't (Want to) See

Owen didn't want to talk, and Nick didn't seem inclined to push. Instead, they walked into the next room—a child's bedroom with many empty beds, all of them spattered with blood—and he pressed the heels of his hands against his temples, trying to sort through what had just happened. Marsha wasn't real. Her knife wasn't real. But then she spoke. With not just her voice but—

The house's voice.

It's talking to me.

Why now?

Because he saw through the illusion. Saw through to something else—some truth he hadn't yet grasped. To Nick, he started to say, "That was my father's voice there. At the end. I don't know how—"

But Nick barely seemed to be listening to him. He seemed off, like the experience with the dead girl, Marsha, had done something to him. Nick was not one for being quiet.

"I'm hungry," Nick said. His voice cold and flat.

"What?"

"I'm hungry, Nailbiter. I need food. Let's find food."

"Yeah. Yeah, okay."

Owen realized that *he* was hungry, too. How long had it been since they'd eaten? Did that matter? They didn't have any more food on them, but cycling rooms seemed to work well enough in getting them to find food. "We'll find some food, then figure out . . . what comes next."

It took them four cycles (first three rooms: a long hallway with something moving behind the fleur-de-lis wallpaper; a dusty old study with walls of books, one of which Owen just *knew* was bound in human skin, and he had no idea how he knew this; and a basement room where the water heater was hissing and clanking, something dripping from the corroded underneath, something red and rusty, and once more Owen knew something, and that something was *there's a body in the water heater*)—and then they had it. A walk-in pantry.

At least, that's what Owen thought it was. Hard to tell—the bare bulb at the top was dim, slick with what might've been grease, and flickering.

Still. Had to give it a shot.

So, in they went. The shelves that lined each wall on both sides were metal, but covered in what looked to be a white enamel. And those white wire shelves were lined with boxes, cans, bags. Owen pulled them out one by one, squinting through the half dark to try to make them out.

One box was the size for cereal, and rattled accordingly.

He said as much to Nick, who grunted.

"What's up with you?" Owen asked him.

"Nothing."

"Bullshit."

"Leave it, Zuikas."

"I don't wanna leave it. Here—maybe it's like those stupid candy bar commercials. The Snickers ones. You need something to eat."

He popped the top of the cereal box, ripping it open, finding the bag inside closed. Tearing that, he reached his hand in and ate a fistful of stale cereal. He handed another box to Nick, who held it, but didn't open it.

So Owen kept looking, even as he downed another mouthful of what tasted like store-brand Cap'n Crunch. It tore at the roof of his mouth. It felt weirdly good, that pain. Like it helped to break the circuit of his looping thoughts, the ones that kept replaying his father's voice in his head, *wish you were never born, wish you were never born, wishyouwereneverborn, neverborn, neverborn,* and flashing up images of his father deliquescing there in his bed, the cancer pulping him like a juiced fruit, next to the bed that little blue suede bag...

That's when his foot hit something. A dull crunch that gave way. Like a pillow or couch stuffed with driveway gravel. *Kkkrrrch.* He squinted in the dim, erratic light. It was a bag of something. Dog food, by the look of it. Two bags, actually. "I don't think you want to eat—"

Dog food, he was about to say.

But something between the two bags—there, on the floor—glinted.

Something metal. Squarish.

Owen stooped to pick it up and—

It was a lighter. A metal lighter.

He picked it up. It felt cold in his hand, and a chill grappled up his arm, all the way to his neck, where the hairs rose like the restless dead.

Idly, his heart in his throat, he flicked the lighter open and sparked it.

Fire danced in the dark. Owen tilted the lighter just so—and the flame illuminated the side of the lighter, where it showed the Jack Kenny whiskey logo. He ran his thumb along the underside of the lighter, praying he didn't feel what he was about to feel: four letters etched into the metal there.

NICK.

It's like the penknife, he knew. Just another trick. An illusion. It was never here. *This isn't really in my hand, and the fire isn't even burning.*

But he could see Nick staring at it. Transfixed.

"Nick," Owen said, cautiously. "I found something."

"Yeah. Yeah you did."

Nick's eyes were wide, unblinking.

And in them, Owen thought he saw something. No—not just one something, but many somethings, little flashes, pulses, images in the dark of his pupil.

Paisley wallpaper in one eye.

A doorknob in the other, tarnished brass.

The horizontal slats of a heating vent.

The black hole of a garbage disposal.

And then they were both, for a moment, the same image:

Each pupil a hole, and in each hole a set of steps. Staircases in the deep dark of his gaze. *Starecases,* Owen thought, madly.

Owen said the thing he didn't want to say out loud:

"You've been here before."

Nick sniffed, coughed a little to clear his throat, as if the truth was stuffed down in there deep, had to be jostled free. "Just let it in, Nailbiter. Open the door and let the house in. The house always wins, Zuikas. The house always wins."

Owen's head spun with questions. None of them good. None of them with answers he wanted to hear. *Still. You have to say the words.*

"You knew what this place was."

"I did."

"And yet—"

"And yet."

Deep breath. "Did you . . . find Matty?"

"You don't care."

"I care, Nick. I care, don't say that. Did you find Matty?"

"Fuck off, fuck you."

"*Did you find Matty?*"

A sharp, cold laugh from Nick, one ruined by the sound of the threat of tears.

Nick was right up on him now. The light from the Zippo casting his face in a hellish glow. "I found the truth, is what I found. I found the body. Matty's dead, kid. I wish this place would've killed me, too, but it won't let me die. It emptied me out. Filled me up. Painted me the black of fire-char, the red of blood. This is home for me, now. I'm home. I'm home."

"Nick, I—I don't understand—"

"You will," Nick said, his voice now the same throaty, buzzing chorus as Marshie's. "You will, when you're all alone. Which is what you deserve, as you well know, Nailbiter."

"Nick—"

"I'm going to leave now. You're on your own."

Nick backed toward the door.

"Wait," Owen said, reaching out and grabbing at Nick's elbow—

Nick shoved him backward.

And that's when Owen hit him. At the end of his fist rode a world of resentment, weariness, and above all else, anger. Anger at himself, at this place, at Matty for climbing those stairs, at Lore for abandoning him, at Hamish for changing, and at Nick for leading them to this house.

Nick's head rocked back, the nose popping—

Owen opened his mouth to speak—just one phrase, only part of which he got out: "The Coven—"

But Nick was fast to counter. He launched himself at Owen, slamming his forehead again and again into Owen's skull—it felt like taking a hit from a sledgehammer. Stars went supernova behind Owen's eyes as the lighter went out, falling from his other hand. He staggered backward, his feet slipping on loose cereal. Pain fired up his spine like a signal flare as he fell hard on his tailbone. Blood slicked his tongue. The half darkness returned as the lighter bounced away—he cried out, tried to call to Nick, but it was too late. Nick went through the door, closing it behind him.

61

Triage and Sojourn

Owen woke up when a cockroach was trying to get into his ear. It got halfway in, its front legs scrambling against his eardrum. It hurt—a sharp ache. With it, a sound like crumpling aluminum foil deep in the well of his skull. He gasped, his lips tacky with his own blood, and panicked as he reached for the bug and couldn't get a grip on it. He realized, *I'm pushing it in farther, I'm mashing it up and smashing it deeper into my ear, oh god, oh fuck, oh god*—but then he managed to finally grip its hind end and unmoor it from his ear canal.

He threw it as far as he could. He heard it *tick-a-tack* against the wall somewhere before scurrying away.

Owen sat up. Panting.

Everything hurt, and he was alone.

Hasty, probably incomplete damage report: Owen knew his lip was split. It felt fat and numb for the most part, like a microwaved slug. But in the middle of it he could feel the cleft, the crusted blood, and it hurt like battery acid. He had all his teeth. His jaw ached. He couldn't breathe through his nose—it felt like his nostrils were stuffed up with cotton, which meant they were probably stoppered up with plugs of blood instead. His one eye felt swollen and he could neither open nor close it and wasn't really sure which was which anyway because it was dark in here. Totally dark now, and as he stood, he realized that Nick must've broken the bulb. Glass crunched like little bones. Owen wanted to cry but didn't really have it in him. Among the shards, he found no lighter. Nick must've taken that, too. Shit.

He ate. Idly and without joy. He brushed aside cockroaches and found some of the cereal, so that's where he started. More of the Cap'n Crunch. No crunch berries, just the shitty yellow mouth-scouring bricks of stale sweetness.

Slowly he pulled himself up and found some other food.

Some of it, much of it, filled with more roaches. Where had they come from? Were they another trick of the house?

He ate potato chips. Cheese puffs. Wheat bread. Peanut butter. None of it good. All of it well past its time—none of it tasted moldy, but it didn't matter. He found plastic bottles of water, too, and drank a bunch of those. His stomach hurt. But not as bad as his face and head, so whatever.

Anger laced through him, cinching his heart tighter and tighter.

He wasn't ready to think about it. Not all the way, not yet. All he knew was that Nick had fucked them all over. And Owen wanted to kill him.

It felt eerily clarifying. Like his brain wasn't on an anxiety loop. He didn't feel that crushing tightness in his chest, didn't feel the need to chew his fingers down to the bone. He just wanted to find Nick and beat him to death.

Half dizzy, he opened the door and cycled rooms till he got to a bathroom.

Big bathroom. Opulent and gaudy. Walk-in glass shower and lots of gold, fake gold, whatever. In the corner sat a jetted tub, and an infant floated dead there, face down in soapy water, bloated like a wet loaf of bread. Skin gray like a plastic bag from a grocery store.

It's not real, it's not real, it's not real, Owen thought, but again, something there nagged at him, *needled* at him, something pulling on the fabric of his brain like a dog pulling the stuffing from a dog toy.

Because it *was* real, wasn't it?

These things in these rooms, they happened.

The dead baby in this room was not a dead baby now, but it was, once—someone, somewhere, killed their infant in this room, or got high in an adjacent room while their kid drowned, or had their babysitter kill the kid while they were out running errands, or, or, or.

It was true, once. These rooms were real to someone.

Just because it was a show didn't mean it was *fiction*.

This was not a game. It was a true crime documentary. These were more than just ghosts—they were memories. Rooms of tragedy and terror built into this living house. Stolen and conjured anew for whatever dark purpose it served.

Just like how his father was dead, but he saw his father.

The house stole that room from him, and built it here.

They were all wandering through the ghosts of bad houses, weren't they? Through the rooms papered with awful memories, carpeted by tears and by blood.

All of it pushed on him, pushing at the center of his forehead first like a pressing thumb, then like a power drill. Vibrating his skull, opening up a tender, red-rimmed hole. *Let me in. Let all the awfulness in, Nailbiter.*

Home was supposed to be a place of safety and comfort. But it wasn't for him. Leaving school every day made his guts tighten, his legs cramp as if they didn't want to carry him home. Owen knew the sound of his father's Chevy Blazer the way a faithful dog did—it lived in him, that sound, and whenever he heard it in the driveway, he always ran to his room and locked the door. Not because his father would come in and beat him, no. But he'd find Owen eventually. He'd berate him. Make him feel small and worthless. *Because you were small and worthless,* he thought. *Are small and worthless even still.* Was that his own thought? Or an intrusion by the house? Or worst of all, was it his father's thought? Played from a speaker mounted on the inside of his own skull?

It doesn't matter.

He tried putting it out of mind.

Still woozy, he washed his face. *Might have a concussion,* he thought. His mouth tasted like blood and cheese puffs.

Nick had come here. Knew what this place was. And led them all to it. He was poisoned by it and wanted to poison them in turn.

I hate him. I hate him. I hate him.

These thoughts chewed at Owen like rats. Pushing into him, like roaches into his ears. Behind him, the dead infant struggled in the tub water. A flurry of bubbles burping up. *Ignore it. Don't look.* He wanted to find Nick. Wanted to kill Nick. Beat his head into a red mess the same as he tried to do to Owen.

Owen eased both of the blood plugs free from his nose. They looked like caterpillars of dried meat. Fresh blood flowed. *Fuck.*

He stuffed toilet paper up there to stop it up.

The dead infant twitched, one hand splashing.

Shut up, shut up, shut up.

He looked at himself in the mirror.

His face was wrecked. Swollen and misshapen like an old Halloween pumpkin. *Ugly as you deserve,* he thought. *Nick should've killed you. You deserve it. But you're still here and you'll find him and kill him first.* He felt something crawling around inside his head. Settling in. Putting up shelves. Hanging photos of its family. Magnets on the fucking fridge and everything.

Still woozy, he leaned on a doorjamb and cycled rooms, dancing unsteadily in and out of each doorway, dizzier and dizzier with each turn of the ever-changing maze:

—The Too Many Guns Room—

—The Broken Wall and Broken Bottles Room—

—The Hanging Man in His Home Office Room, his toes tickling the keys of his laptop—

—The Dead Rabbits Room—

—The Flashback Home Theater Room, screen showing a penknife filleting flaps of skin off pale, exposed biceps—

—The Garage with No Garage Door Room—

—The Stuffed Animals with Real Eyes Room—

—The Deafening Arcade Room—

—The Neat-and-Nifty Storage Room, everything in its place, neatly arranged, 1990s vacuum, Tupperware, plastic bins, various wicker baskets, a glass pickle jar with a severed hand floating in the brine—

—The Blood Spatter Music Room, teenager playing an electric guitar, fingers ruined and bloody, the blood spraying with every power chord, rock on, kid—

—The Black Mold Bedroom—

—and then, finally, Owen stepped through one door, sweat slicking his brow, his heart thundering in his chest. His mind felt as though it were swimming outside of him, alongside his body as it moved. It was a long hallway clad in art nouveau wallpaper, green-and-gold leaves layered upon leaves layered upon leaves and as he looked up, he saw two others at the other end of the hall, walking away from him. At first he thought, *What ghosts are you—*

But they were no ghosts.

Lore. Hamish.

I found you.

Lore was already at the door at the far end of the hall.

Owen called out to her—

But his voice was a strangled croak, the weak bleat of a frog under a crushing foot. Darkness bled inward from the edges of his vision as he staggered forward, calling out again—"*Lore. Hamish.*"—but once again the voice was weak, too weak, run across a rasp until it was just sawdust. He reached for them. Willed his arm to stretch out like Mister Fantastic, shrinking the hallway with his mind as if they were on one of those moving walkways at the airport. He fell to his knees. Owen imagined them getting closer to him but still they opened the door at the other end of the hall. They went through it. *They escaped me.* They weren't getting closer to him at all. *Just a hallucination,* he thought. *They're not even here. They're not even real.* The door at the far end began to close. He launched himself to his feet once more, crying out as he hard-charged down the hallway, the green-and-gold leaves to his left and right peeling off the wall toward him, like the scales of a great beast rippling, and he reached the door and threw it open—

Beyond that door waited a finished basement. Wood paneling and a beat-up couch, and Lore and Hamish were nowhere to be found.

Owen stepped through it, still alone.

62

...And Yet So Far

"Did you hear something?" Hamish asked.

They'd just left an eerily long hallway—no doors along the side, only one door at each end. And just as they'd come through this door...

He turned, the door already closing behind them.

"No," Lore said, her voice distant even in her own ears.

Ahead of her waited a room so messy it verged on a hoarder's labyrinth: dead plants and open, half-eaten boxes of butter round crackers and shit bought from cheap Chinese internet companies (spatula, blouse, spice grinder, Hummel knock-offs, Bluetooth headphones) still in their packaging. Most of it mounted on tables and on the wrap-around couch. The room, dim at the edges. At its center, the glow. A flatscreen sat on a cheap Walmart-bought TV stand, and it pulsed and flickered with images: scenes of war, of White House insurrection, of rallies and red hats, of the man with the face like a melting citronella candle, of transgender women made to look demonic, of a border wall going up, of starving migrants in a sun-fucked desert, of a big red X flashing cartoonishly over a vaccine needle, of red-cheeked froth-mouthed white men thrusting tiki torches forward into the dark night as if to burn away anything that wasn't white and bright like them, all of these images and more, flashing faster and faster, melting into one another as if turned into AI-generated soup, and there—*there!*—Lore saw herself in those images, didn't she? A static pulse of her own face, cartoonishly edited, an image she'd seen of herself online, manipulated by mouth-breathing chodes who made her look like a blue-haired bug-eyed Karen.

In front of the TV, a woman sat watching. A sludgy woman, melting into her recliner, a blanket over her lap, a scraggly white cat in her lap.

Hamish stepped in and said, "I thought I heard—"

"Shh," the woman barked at them.

"I hate these ghosts," Hamish said.

"She's not a ghost," Lore answered.

"What?"

"*Laurie,*" the woman said, her voice raspy. "Is that you? Tell your friend to be quiet. I'm watching something."

Watching something. Fox. OANN. Newsmax. Their logos juddered on the screen, before spraying into broken glitch pixels.

"Laurie?" Hamish said, his voice cautious. "Wait. Lore. Is that—"

"It's my mom." *Finally,* she thought with grim irony. *A room for me.* She was, in a weird way, starting to feel left out—like, wow, don't I get a room, house? Where's my torment? Just one book on a shelf? She'd started to come around to the idea that the whole *house* was her torment, because she'd been left alone so long and so often—practically the prototype for the Gen X latchkey kid—that to be wandering through an empty loveless house was a perfect reminder of how dead and undesirable her home life had been growing up. But now, *now,* here was a room just for her. No dead bodies, no torture porn, no blood, no horror but for what flashed on that TV screen. All of it beamed into her mother's glassy, unblinking eyes.

"We can go—"

"No," she said, stiffly. "I can take it."

"*Laurie,*" her mother barked. "I said, be quiet. Just take a seat. Or make me something, will you? One of them little pizzas."

Hamish watched Lore carefully.

"It's not her," Lore said. "I know that. But it's not a ghost, either. My mother's alive. If you can call *this*—" She held out her hands as if to demonstrate the pathetic realm in front of her. "Alive. What fucking irony, Ham. All my life, my mother stayed out of this house, leaving me alone. Off with some guy, off on some trip, off at work, and me at home, just having to figure shit out. Toilet broke, I figured it out. Needed food, I figured it out. Raccoon got trapped in our screened-in porch, I figured it the fuck out. But then, finally, late in life, Mom comes home, and what does she do? Plants herself in a chair, and downloads this shit into her brain day in and day out. Brainworms feeding on brainrot. Fuck. She came home, but then went away again. She's here, but she's still not here for me."

"Lore, I'm sorry."

A pulse on the TV—Trump's face again, frozen like a halted Zoom call, half his face in a dissolving glitchy mess.

"And she *still* has shit taste in men," Lore said. *Get it together, Laurie.* Her mother's name for her. She had to shake it free from her head. *Not Laurie. Not Lauren. Lore.* "Whatever. Look. She bought a bunch of dumb stuff from the internet. Temu or Alibaba or some other garbage. Let's go through it. I bet we'll find a charging cable, maybe a flashlight, in there."

"Lore, we don't have to do this—I don't know what's going on here, but your mom, we can just try another door—"

"I'm cool. It's not real. It's just the house fucking with me." *Right? That's what this is, isn't it? It can't be real. Just a game. Just a simulation.* "Hey. You said you heard something? Before we came in?"

"Nothing, I guess," Ham said. "I thought maybe it was Owen, but..."

"We'll find them, Ham. I promise. Now let's go through this shit so we can get out of this room and get back to the crawlspace before our brains turn to treacle."

Treacle, she thought. That word again. It made her think of Owen. And it made her realize that she missed him very much. She hoped wherever he was out there in the house, he and Nick were doing okay.

63

Full Circle

It took Owen a moment to realize where he was.

For a while, he just stood there, bracing himself against the wood paneling. Owen had to stoop over, chin to his chest, drool easing out over his lower lip before dangling there in a gooey drip. His head spun like he'd been drinking all night.

It was the simple touch from his finger that pinged his memory radar.

The pad of his index finger found a hole in the wood paneling—a hole that had been filled with something not quite flush against the surface. Something pushed in a little too far.

The memory was full-fledged, then—

Nick, fourteen years old, a bow and arrow in his hand, stoned. He let fly with the arrow—one topped with the barebones target tip, just a pointy metal bit straight off the shaft. It flew right into the wall, *thud-d-d-d,* and stuck there, waggling. All of them were there, and their jaws dropped because, well, none of them could just *shoot a fucking arrow into the fucking wall* and expect to get away with it. But Nick had been mad, pouty, shouldering his way through every conversation with brute contempt—nobody knew why he was so salty, but he was, and that's when he, out of nowhere, got the bow and the arrow and shot his own basement wall.

Thing was, Nick probably could've gotten away with it, or so they figured. Nick's dad was famously cool—he waved everything off and was Good Times Guy. He had a high-profile money job somewhere—

banking or investments or something. But after hours, he let that all go and was A Cool Dude. Lore joked that he was *Wall Street in the streets, Jimmy Buffett in the sheets,* but Nick told her that joke sucked because *street in the streets* sounded dumb. Lore didn't like to be criticized, though, so she sack-tapped Nick hard with the back of her hand. That, though, was another day—on *this* day, the day of the arrow-into-the-wall, Nick did it and seemed *immediately* freaked out that he'd done it.

They all told him, relax, your dad won't care, but he didn't want to hear boo about it. Said he had to fix it. Like he was in a panic. So, like always, they set to figuring out how to fix his fuckup, and it was Owen who had the idea:

Take a number two pencil.

Stick it into the hole.

Then get a saw and cut it flush against the wall.

The faux-wood grain on the paneling was pretty light. The pencil, he theorized, might just disappear from view. It would look like a "knot" in the "wood." So that's what they did. It wasn't perfect— when they cut through it, it wasn't pushed forward all the way, so it still sank a little deeper. But even still, for the most part? It worked. Owen felt weirdly like a champion for once, as if he'd had the good idea, not Matty, not Lore. And he remembered that Nick was nicer to him that day. How special that felt. And how stupid he felt remembering it.

That divot was what his finger was finding right now.

Which meant—

This was Nick's basement.

He lifted his head up, spit slicking his chin.

The shitty couch. The stairs up. The card table mounded high with all kinds of shit: D&D books, fantasy books (*The Eye of the World* in easy view), ashtrays, an Altoids tin full of stems and seeds, a BB gun, a bunch of arcade tokens, a purple Crown Royal bag once for whiskey but now for dice.

Why was Nick's basement here?

From the corner, off to his left—

A stifled sob.

In that corner, there sat a mushy, cushy recliner—faux-leather Naugahyde; they called it the Slumbering Beast.

There sat Nick.

"Nick," Owen said, his voice small.

But this wasn't Current Era Nick.

This was Nick from Back When.

He looked... young, but how old? It was the hair that gave it away. For a year, when he was fifteen, Nick had the faux-hawk thing going on. (A year later, he shaved it all off, though everyone said he looked like a skinhead, which made him immediately grow it back out, because "fuck that neo-Nazi shit.") It was the faux-hawk Owen was looking at now.

Nick, at fifteen.

He was sitting in the chair. Hands in his lap, staring at his knees.

Softly crying. A bubble of snot in the one side of his nose.

His belt was undone.

From the other side of the room, a rattle-and-clink of bottles. There was a low wooden cabinet there. The fridge was upstairs, but down here, that IKEA-level cabinet had in it a bunch of bottles of liquor. Mostly cheap, nasty stuff: Goldschläger and Yukon Jack and Jäger, maybe some schnapps, stuff Nick loved and that all of the rest of them hated but drank anyway—and usually ended up throwing up. (Even now the memory of the taste of them was so visceral, Owen could taste the sour-sweet bile at the back of his throat.)

Owen turned his head—which took what honestly felt like a Herculean effort, like the whole room *smeared* as he looked that way— and expected to see Hamish, or Lore, or Matty there. Maybe even himself. (And there, a new question: *Am I in here somewhere? Some teenage version of me, an Old Timer penknife in his hand, his arms bleeding from the cuts, his feelings hurt from his father's vigorous disdain?*) But it wasn't any of them.

It was Nick's father.

The man stood there, shoulders sagged, a troubled look on his face. He had a polo shirt on, with a tropical print. No pants, just underwear, and he was tugging on the elastic of them, pulling them up tighter as he stood, fetching a bottle of what looked like peach schnapps. Jacquin's brand, with the squared-off bottle.

He looked to his son, asked, "You want some, kiddo?" Pause. "You know, if it hurts, this helps."

Nick just stayed in that chair, staring at his knees. *Through* them. Through his body, through the floor, to some great emptiness beyond them all.

He shook his head in a small, barely perceptible way.

"If you're sure," Nick's father said, then spun the cap off with his thumb and took a swig of it. He headed toward the staircase, then shot a look at Owen—

Right at Owen.

He winked.

Then headed upstairs and was gone.

Owen turned to look back toward Nick—

And Nick from Back When was here. Directly in front of him. Damn near nose to nose. Still had that snot oozing. Still had tears brimming at the bottom lids of his eyes. "You never noticed," he said, his voice a raw, chewed-up sound. *Like night bugs. Like cicadas.* "And it kept happening. The things he did to me. But it didn't break me, Zuikas. Not till I came here."

And then Nick was gone. But the imprint of him remained, like a feeling in the air, a strange pocket of disturbed space. It shimmered like a cloud of flies.

Again, his gorge rose. Owen wanted to vomit. The taste of that peach schnapps crawled up the back of his tongue like a wet slug.

He pivoted back to the door from whence he came, shoving it open and stumbling into a filthy guest room piled with rags and mess, smelling of a gas leak—he gagged, not even making it to the bed before he threw up what he had eaten from the pantry. Everything swam around him.

Sweat streamed off his skull as his consciousness bled out—veins of shadow closing in like the black mold from the Black Mold Bedroom.

He cried out in the agony of both pain and the revelation of how much pain was here in this place and in the world beyond. And in all that, he thought of Nick. Poor Nick. Nick in that basement. Nick with his father.

64

Nailbiter Neverborn

Owen staggered through the house, room to room, barely looking, moving forward, always forward, even as his mind looped and looped—

Thoughts like carousel horses, round and round, the calliope playing.

Nick was in pain and you missed it. Nick was in pain and you missed it. Nick was in pain and you missed it.

Always up your own ass, Owen. Always about you you you YOU YOU, never about them. Selfish selfish, preening little ghost-boy narcissist, pale skin like a grub, sad body like a beach-dead jellyfish, selfish selfish, a lamprey leech eating eating eating. Parasite. Tick. Jealous of Matty. Hungry for Lore.

Doing nothing to earn their friendship.

Doing nothing for their love.

Wanting but not giving, weak little fucking shit, wish you were never born, wish you were never born, never born, NEVERBORN.

Can't do shit can't make shit won't accomplish shit too cowardly to even kill yourself, instead you do it bit by bit, chewing this nail, biting that lip, grinding your teeth down to powder, picking a scab, plucking a hair, and the cuts, the little cuts, the Old Timer cuts, gentle cuts so that none can see, can't even be smart enough so you cut yourself to get some fucking attention for once, I mean, wow, what the fuck, Owen. You could've killed yourself, but you didn't. You could've shown others your little injuries, but you didn't. Just more Owen, classic Owen, basic bitch Owen, doing the minimum and getting nothing out of it. Coward. Fool. Fuck up.

Nick was in pain and you missed it.

The others had their pain, too, but did you see it, did you help it, no no no, you didn't, but now the staircase is here, the house is here.

Neverborn
Ghost boy
Parasite
Nailbiter.

Were these his thoughts?

Were they his father's words? Had they buried themselves in his dirt so long ago that the plants that grew there felt like they were part of his garden instead of invasive root and choking vine?

Were they the thoughts of the house? Pushing into his soft stupid skull like fingers breaking apart warm bread?

Did it matter, if all the thoughts were right on the money?

The house hated him, he told himself. When the thoughts looped, he tried to put that thought in between them—

Neverborn
The house hates you
You missed Nick's pain
The house hates you
You're a parasite
The house hates you

Like a call and response inside his own mind, the spiraling thoughts like a buzzsaw, chewing into his sanity. Even as he stumbled through the house, back through rooms he remembered and more he did not, he *felt* its attentiveness to him. The house. It watched him. It saw him. It *knew* him. And like his own father, it hated him for reasons that, he realized, had nothing to do with him.

He was present, and so he was hated. He was Owen, and so he was hated. He was *human,* and so he was hated.

Every room, every wall, every floor, and every lamp—every water stain, every bloodstain, every shadow sliding through the wallpaper, every cabinet, every corner, every dead girl and drowned infant and hanged man, every tormenter and abuser and killer, every cat and parrot and pup, every cry in the dark, every face in the mirror, all of it part of the same pulsing throbbing *raging* hate. Tendrils and pseudopods of the greater beast: the endless house with its nightmare rooms.

It was angry, but that anger had purpose. It had direction.
It wanted something.
It wanted Owen.

It didn't just want him. It *needed* him. He didn't know why this was the case, but it was—he could feel its urgency. A new thought interjected itself into the loop: *You can still make something of yourself yet,* the voice, maybe his own voice, said. *You can still do good work, Owen. If you're strong. If you are brave. And most of all, if you are willing.*

He passed by a hallway mirror. The wallpaper all around it swam and crawled. Ants from flowers. Spiders along vines. In the mirror, he could see the ghost of that wallpaper on his cheeks. He could see the glass in his eyes—the pupils crossed with windowpanes. His lips were dry stucco. His teeth were the columns of an old iron radiator, painted bone white.

The house wanted to fill him up.
His voice—or the house's voice—told him:
If you let me all the way in, then I'll let you out.
In for out.
It's a bargain! What a steal!
He clenched his teeth, squeezed his eyes, and hurried away from the mirror.

The house doesn't hate me, he realized. He'd been wrong. They'd all been wrong. Whoever carved the message in the very first room they found had been wrong, wrong, wrong. The house did not hate them. Not at all.

No, the house *loved* them.

Then, one more door, one more room. Even as he reached for it, he thought, *I know what this is going to be*. A little bit of prophecy foretold.

The room he'd been avoiding—
The room he'd been so afraid to find—
It found him.

65

Peeling Wallpaper

His father's skin was the color of the pages of a paperback book soaked in piss—a gray-yellow jaundice. That, the work of the cancer, a cancer that had crawled its way through all parts of him, and was now perhaps the only thing holding him together.

Owen knelt by the bed even as Owen stepped into the room.

Two Owens—both, he supposed, belonging to the house.

The first by the bed, just the memory of Owen. Younger by ten years, that Owen. An Owen that was a little bit healthier, a little bit happier—he had a stable job at a library, he smiled once in a while, he was *just* starting to do a little writing on the side, just short stories and stuff posted online, but it felt like the seed of something. Like a little spark of promise that might, in the right wind, catch fire.

And then, through the hospice nurse, his father summoned him.

He was dying. Metastatic cancer. Owen didn't even know where it started but it didn't matter now. His father was in palliative care for the end of his life.

And here, Owen thought, this is it. The last chance to make it all right. There would be no fixing what had been broken so early on in their relationship—you couldn't mend a bridge that had never been built. But there might be some hope of understanding each other. His father, who hadn't wanted him to be born at all, hadn't seen him since Owen went away to college—and now had called upon his son one last time. Owen wanted to believe it wasn't too little too late, that this was something they both needed. They would find each other at the end, before it was too late, and maybe, just maybe, his father would give him—what? If not love, then a little acknowledgment. If not acknowledgment, then just a moment of conversation, however deep or small or shallow it needed to be.

But that wasn't what his father wanted.

His father wanted one last thing—a final opportunity to stick in the knife. Because when Owen showed up, his father summoned his strength enough to sit up, focus his gaze upon his son, and destroy him one last time.

The words weren't new. They weren't even particularly cutting. It was the same-old, same-old. He babbled about how Owen was weak. Worthless. Made his mother weak. Spent too much of their money. Ruined his father's life just by being born. Check the box marked "all of the above" for: stupid, lazy, a retard, a faggot, ungrateful, an embarrassment, a disappointment, a turd that wouldn't flush, and all of it kind of just *washed* over Owen, and it didn't take anything from him, the way a wave would take sand from a beach. No, he was stone against this current—it splashed against him, cold, and he let it come and let it go. And that felt good, too, in its own horrible way. And as his father purged his poison, his cheeks grew redder and redder, his lips more spit-flecked, his eyes bulgier like fruits about to burst—

But then he found the breach in Owen's armor.

A place to really get the knife in and twist.

"I know you wanted to kill yourself," his father said, slow, sluggish, wormy. "You should've, but you didn't even have the courage to get that right. Still got a chance, though. Still got a chance." That last bit, said all mushy. *Shtill godda shansh.* And that was when Owen—that Owen, the Owen from ten years ago, an Owen on the Verge of Feeling Good, instead went the other way. He stood up. He found the little suede bag by the nightstand, the one the hospice nurse said contained the essential hospice drugs—the Haldol, the atropine, the morphine, the lorazepam, the Dulcolax, the fentanyl patches. Owen took them all out, and one by one he emptied them into his father's mouth. The old man couldn't fight it—all his energy had been summoned to hate his son. He couldn't even cry out. One by one, the meds went in. Owen clamped the mouth shut to make the old man swallow. And then, when the cocktail was applied, Owen watched his father die. As his dad slid from the mortal coil like a coat poorly hung on its hook, he said the words he'd wanted to say his whole life, but never did:

"I hate you, too."

And then that Owen left, and as he did, he looked up at *this* Owen, and he said, "He's all yours."

Now, this Owen was all alone. After having watched himself murder his father. *It was mercy,* he told himself. *It was mercy. Mercy. Mercy. Neverborn. Nailbiter. Parasite. Mercy. Mercy. Mercy.* And as his mind repeated these phrases, as his father mumbled and echoed some of those same words—even beyond death—"Mercy, mercy, never born, parasite"—he slid his hands along the lengths of his forearms, feeling rigid, fabric tags there in the flesh. Like the curl of a book cover or the stiff corner plastic from a piece of packaged food.

And even without looking, he started to *peel* those corners, those tabs, and they ripped free and fresh from his arms with slippery wet tears—which gave Owen great gulps of cathartic pleasure. He looked down, saw that he was peeling wallpaper from his arms. His skin was the wallpaper and beneath it were beautiful walls of stone and wood. He realized he'd always been this, always been a strong foundation covered up with cheap décor. *Hardwood under the carpets. Beautiful colors under the primer coat. Timeless antique fixtures left to molder in a box in a garage.* He thrust his fingernails into his mouth, found old nails and drywall anchors there, and he used his teeth to pull them out one by one, spitting them onto the floor. Red paint splashed underneath him. Red paint and bright wood stain. *I'm a fixer-upper. Just need some TLC. A spot of color and some new furniture. Then I'll be as good as new. Or better than I've ever been.*

His father gurgled.

Owen laughed around his painted, gooey fingers.

The room spun and drifted. He felt dizzy and alive. Inside him, rooms built onto rooms onto rooms. He felt the new occupant moving in. He was the house and the house was him. A house of hate, a house of love. He laughed and thought about which part he could renovate next. Get rid of that old radiator (teeth) or hammer down those stuck-up nails in the floorboards (toenails) or rip down those nasty old curtains (ears). He fell toward a door, a door that wasn't there before, a door in the wall, and he wondered, *Did I make that, did I make that door, is it a doorway into me?* But then hands reached out from the darkness, the arms stretching, the fingers long and probing. He fought against them, struggled to get away, but they were too fast and too many. They gripped his arms. He thrashed. He tried to bite. But the arms, they were strong, and he was weak—and before long, they dragged him into the wall even as Owen screamed and screamed and screamed.

66

The Art of Self-Destruction

Time passed after they pulled Owen from that room and into the crawlspace. He was soaked in red—his own blood. Oozing from his chewed fingertips, but worse, from the sores and scratches in his arm. In one spot, he'd literally pulled a Band Aid–sized strip of skin clean off; the muscle lay exposed, glistening crimson. It took everything she and Hamish had to get him into the wall.

They didn't have much by way of first aid—just a bit of gauze, a bunch of painkillers, a tube of off-brand Neosporin. Stuff they'd gathered over the last few days since seeing the copy (because that's how she thinks of them, as copies, not as ghosts, copypasta, creepypasta) of her mother in that room.

They did what they could with his injuries. Thankfully, all the screaming and thrashing about stopped as soon as he came into the crawlspace. Like one of those videos where a tornado appears, rips shit up, and thirty seconds later is gone again, replaced by the serenity of clear skies. He hit the crawlspace and his body sighed and sagged; he moaned and fell into an unconsciousness so deep Hamish said, "I think he's dead." But a pulse still fluttered fast in his neck.

Hamish offered to go out and look for more medical supplies, but that was a fraught mission. Already Lore knew you couldn't go alone out there—and worse, though you could always make it back into the crawlspace, the passages between rooms were themselves a labyrinth, and so Hamish might have a hell of a time finding her and

Owen again. And they couldn't leave Owen alone, could they? Maybe they could've. But she didn't want to.

So, time passed. They waited. Slept when they could on the pillows and blankets they'd pulled in here. At one point, they found a string of Christmas lights on an old dead Christmas tree in a nursery, and Lore pulled them in here, and plugged in using an outlet on the other side of the wall—the inside of the house.

The lights twinkled.

Owen stirred, moaning, but not waking up.

Hamish said, "Where do you think Nick is?"

"I dunno."

"You think he's okay?"

"I dunno, Ham. I really hope so."

While Hamish slept, Lore stayed up. She was a natural night owl, a habit born from years of insomnia—her brain would not quiet itself and so she often used it to work. It was trained to stay awake, to remain ever vigilant, especially when there was some kind of game design issue or story question she was working on. Her mental teeth worked every problem like gristle, at the cost of rest.

I'll sleep when I'm dead, she always said.

Blatantly, vibrantly awake, she talked to Owen. Not because she wanted to work out the house's puzzles or win this game—rather, it was just because she needed to *say some shit*. Needed to talk it out. And okay, fine, it was easier for her when he was unconscious. And she was awake anyway, right? So she sat down, plopped his head in her lap like she used to do sometimes, and babbled.

"So, I saw my mom. Not my real mom. She's still alive outside this fucking place somewhere. But the mom I saw here was . . . just like her, the real her. For so long she left me alone and it fucked me *all* up. And now she's alone because she pushes me away, hates what I am because the TV tells her to, and . . . it's bad for her, dude. Being alone like that. And it was bad for you in the house. And I bet it was bad for

Matty. Fuck. Alone. Alone, alone, alone. Always thought that was my superpower. Latchkey kid. Didn't need anyone or anything. Didn't need Matty, didn't need you, didn't need the Covenant.

"But the Covenant, it was everything. We were interlocking pieces and it made the whole of us stronger, I think, but then . . . I pissed off Matty, or Matty pissed off me, or whatever, and he went up those stairs and then, that was it. He was gone. The Covenant . . ." Her voice gave out. The words, dissolving.

"Friendship is like a house," Lore finally managed to say, Owen's head cradled in her lap. "You move into this place together. You find your own room there, and they find theirs, but there's all this common space, all these shared places. And you each put into it all the things you love, all the things you are. Your air becomes their air. You put your hearts on the coffee table, next to the remote control, vulnerable and beautiful and bloody. And this friendship, this house, it's a place of laughter and fun and togetherness, too. But there's frustration sometimes. Agitation. Sometimes that gets big, too big, all the awful feelings, all that resentment, building up like carbon monoxide. Friendship, like a house, can go bad, too. That air you share? Goes sour. Dry rot here, black mold there, and if you don't remediate, it just grows and grows. Gets bad enough, one or all of you have to move out. And then the place just fucking sits there, abandoned. Empty and gutted. Another ruin left to that force in the world that wants everything to fall apart. You can move back into a place like that, sometimes. But only if you tear it all down and start again."

"We were just kids," came a groaning croak from Owen.

"Owen." She pushed her forehead against his. He felt hot, like he was fighting off a fever. "You're awake."

"I guess."

And he's been listening the whole time.

"Sorry to have woken you."

"It's okay."

"I'm . . ." This was hard for her. She had to willfully unclench her jaw to get the next bit out. "I'm fucking up the new game. The one I was working on before we came in here. *Our* game. The one we came up with. I'm fucking it all up. I can barely get anywhere on it and they paid me money and I will have nothing to show for it. And part of the reason why is that I know deep down it isn't just mine, it's ours, and it needs you. And I *hate* that it needs you." She sighed. "But it does. It really, really does."

He grunted and pushed back against her a little, getting more comfortable but also allowing his head up, more. She gave him some water, then, from a plastic water bottle. He sipped weakly at it, then said: "We get out of here, we work on it together. Like we always said we would. That'd be nice. For me, anyway."

"It'd be nice for me, too. We were hot shit together, man. Somewhere I lost that. I thought I had to do it all myself. That I was *better* doing it that way."

"You were better than me. I couldn't get my shit together on my own. I always needed a crutch. Someone to lean on. Someone to carry me."

"It wasn't like that," she said, even though it was. It wasn't that Owen was a burden. But he needed her more than she needed him most times and that started to sour how she felt about him. It felt imbalanced. Unequal. But she could've been less shitty about it. "I shouldn't have just discarded you. Like trash. I'm good at that. Good at just moving past things. Moving past ... people. Like Matty."

"Like I said, Lore, we were just kids. Losing Matty and then having everyone think we killed him—the way people *looked* at us. Jesus. That would've fucked anybody up. We gave up on each other because it was easier than staying together and being reminded of what we lost."

"We should've gone after him. Like Nick wanted." She paused then. Asked the question she didn't want to ask. "Owen. Where's Nick?"

At that, Owen's eyes pressed shut. In pain, but a different kind of pain. Something deeper. Something sadder. "He led us all here, Lore. The house had him. He was alone, and it took him." He seemed in agony thinking about it. Owen's eyes shined with tears. "Maybe that's how we didn't lose ourselves," Owen said to her in a low whisper. "We weren't alone in here like Nick would've been the first time. He asked us to help him find Matty and we never did. We all abandoned one another. And he came in here by himself and the house got him. But when we came in together, it was different. We weren't alone. I know when it was just me, when he left me . . . the house had its chance. I could feel it, Lore. It wasn't just creeping around. It was *confident*. It opened me up and walked right in. But Nick, though? How long was he in here? By himself? What did that do to him?"

Lore tried to imagine it but couldn't. It was too awful to think about. Especially because though he led them here—they'd let him come in alone the first time. They just hadn't realized it.

Shit, she thought.

This really is all our fault.

"We broke the Covenant," she said.

"Yeah. We did." Owen sighed. "Nick said Matty was dead. He found him. He died in here. I think that was what did Nick in, at the end."

"We couldn't save Matty."

It pained her, saying that out loud. Admitting something was too late, that there was something you fucked up that you could not fix.

"We couldn't save Matty, but you saved me. And we might still be able to save Nick. If he's still here. If we can find him."

"Then that's the plan," she said. "We find Nick. We free him from this place, somehow, some way."

"The Covenant," Owen said.

"Motherfucking Covenant."

And with that, Owen passed out in her lap.

67

An Extended Stay

They told Hamish the plan. To find Nick. To *save* Nick, or try, at least. *The Covenant*, they said to him, each intoned like an oath, like a prayer.

"Fuck that," Hamish said, shaking his head. "No, no, no. No. He did this to us. He lied about his cancer, he lied about this place. He *led* us here. I mean, fuck. How can I let that go? My wife. My *kids*. I wanna see them again and because of *him*, because of that little prick—"

His voice broke under the assault of both grief and anger. Both born of the betrayal he felt. Owen understood it. Hamish had been close to Nick. The two of them shared parts of friendship that Owen and Ham couldn't—and a lot of the time, Owen hated that. He didn't understand that friendship wasn't a one-to-one deal, that you didn't have to be *all in* every second of every relationship like that. People got to share different parts of themselves with different people. Hamish had Nick for some of that. And now Nick had done this to them.

So Hamish said, "I'm not here to save him. I'm here to get out."

"He didn't know," Owen said. "The house . . . it's alive. Some kind of mind. Some kind of entity. I wasn't myself anymore. It started to take ownership. So when he did what he did to us, who knows how much of it was Nick and how much of it was the house? We lost Matty and Nick went after him, and that's how he got this way. So we can't lose Nick the same way. We gotta fix it."

Hamish scowled. "Okay. Okay, yeah. Fine. In the meantime, we just ... what? We wait?"

"We survive," Lore said.

They went over the rules.

The crawlspace was safe. The house couldn't get you here.

You could get to the crawlspace through many of the rooms in the house, but not all of them. Yes, the crawlspace existed behind every wall, but that didn't mean every wall was something you could get through. Cinder block? No way. Drywall? Absolutely.

Excursions were necessary, though. Food, water, a shower now and again. Excursions, then, couldn't be deep into the house. They were from the crawlspace only—open the crawlspace, go into one room, never deeper. Then back into the crawlspace.

And you never did it *alone*. Horror movie rules applied: You were alone, the monster could get you. And the monster was all around them.

Out there, the food replenished over time. (*Like in a game,* Lore noted, and Owen thought again how this place was like a simulation—maybe not one of bits and bytes, but one that ran on a program of hate, designed on the human-made locally sourced artisanal blueprint of horror. Lore also worried that maybe they shouldn't eat the food. Same as you shouldn't in all the myths of other lands, fairy places, and strange realms. *Too late,* Hamish said, eating Spam out of a can.)

Time passed in the nightmare house.

Days turned to another week, to two, to three. A month, now gone.

Excursions outside the crawlspace made it clear how different the crawlspace was. In the crawlspace, you might feel the house's presence at a distance—especially while you slept. Like wolves waiting in the dark past the firelight. But in the house? That meant leaving the firelight. That means the wolves could start to hunt you.

And oh, could they ever feel the house hunting them. It was a presence. Sometimes it was far away, creeping up on them like a stalker. But eventually it surrounded them. Pressed in on them at every side. Not a physical thing you could see or touch but still, it *felt* physical. Like the way certain noises made your heart race, like the way heat could feel oppressive and smothering.

Then, of course, it had its tricks. Whispers in the vents. Laughter behind the walls. Ghosts of victims, ghosts of murderers, those who'd killed themselves, those who'd died from grief, those who'd perished under the weight of a difficult and unloved life, those who'd killed for the same reason, those who'd tortured because they were themselves tortured, on and on. A dead boy whose scalp had been peeled back. A woman bruised from head to toe, reaching for them, calling for help. A father straight out of the 1950s with the Ronald Reagan hair and the pipe in his mouth, his salmon pants and trim cardigan spattered in the blood of his family.

None of it real. All a show.

And they're not even ghosts, Owen told them. *The house is the ghost. The people are just the house's memories. What it saw. What it felt. People being monsters to one another inside the walls of their home. A place that was supposed to be safe but wasn't. So the houses went bad and joined this place. This is like Hell, but not for you, not for me. This is the hell of bad houses. Where broken, hate-poisoned places go after they die.*

(Hamish said, "See, I told you this was Hell.")

They watched for Nick. They used the eyeholes that had been cut out—and they cut their own when they could. They listened at the walls. They left messages for him in the rooms around their crawlspace. Messages that they loved him, and were looking for him, and to let them find him. Please, please, please.

And yet, there was no sign of him.

Which made them worry: Had he already gone again? Owen told them that the house said it would let him go if he let it in. Before they pulled him into the wall, he'd seen a door. Was that his exit? Clearly

Nick had already been allowed to leave once. Had he escaped the house once more? And to what end? "To bring more people like us back into the house," Hamish said.

Lore added: "Maybe worse than that. Maybe to go out there and make more bad houses. More tragedy, more terror. Spread the pain like cancer. Like metastasis."

68

That Mortal Wound

They had hope. But even in the crawlspace, a place safe from the house's intrusions upon their sanity, they could feel time scraping it away, like meat off a bone. More days, more weeks passing. The food, odd and inconsistent. Their sleep, stitched together with fraying thread. Hamish said he'd never see his family again, and at night he wandered the crawlspace, crying out in sadness, and yelling in anger—at Nick, at the house, and most of all, at himself. Lore feared she'd never make another game. But she didn't cry or scream, she just grew empty and cold, and Owen could feel her pulling away. Taking notes and marching the crawlspace like a sentry. Hoarding items. Watching and waiting. Owen, for his part, just felt lost. Sometimes he tried to talk to Hamish about better days, but Hamish didn't want to reminisce, said it hurt too damn bad. He tried to talk to Lore about their new game they'd make when they got out, but she blew him off, said she had things to do. So Owen, for the most part, fell silent. The house was not in their heads here, but it had still done its job. It was emptying them out. First of hope. Then everything else could go, too, drained out like blood from a butchered deer.

69

The House Always Wins

Soon, they would come to hate one another.

It wasn't there, yet. *Hate* was a strong word, Owen knew.

But the road was straight, and the destination was clear.

They spent so much time together in the tight space of the crawlspace, Hamish said he felt like a "trapped rat." They had to wander that between-space, finding ways into the house from time to time, looking for food or items or just a space to breathe. Necessary, even though it meant the house could whisper its hate in their ear and show them yet another tableau of human pain. And they had to do it together—it was, after all, one of the rules. But spending that time together was increasingly an act of agitation and irritation. They didn't have much freedom from one another. They were bound together, a chain gang of friends.

Being together so much in such a terrible place made them not want to be around one another anymore, not at all. It may not have been hate, no, but it was certainly not friendship, not anymore. They sniped at one another. Argued. Insulted. Wandered the spaces as if they too were ghosts of the house. Lore even hissed like an animal sometimes, as if she'd gone feral. Whatever warmth they started to again feel toward one another had gone cold—summer into a hard winter. Owen felt the resentment in his belly building, and even sensing it, he couldn't quite do anything about it. His forgiveness for Lore was short-lived, and he wanted to punish her for what she'd done to him—treating him like he was expendable, a resource to be used and not a friend to have or a person to love. He was angry again toward Hamish, too, for the way his friend had changed—Lore told him one night about how Hamish had literally died from an overdose, and at the moment, he felt such immense sadness about that. Sadness that was now a kind of disdain, for how weak it was that his friend had done that. How pathetic. How much he'd *changed*. And coming out of those addictions just gave him new ones: addictions to a church, to his family, to working out, to his self-image.

Sometimes Hamish prayed out loud. Lore told him to shut the fuck up.

Owen would tell Hamish it was all right.

Hamish would tell *him* to shut up.

And all the while, the house pushed on them. Owen felt it most keenly, because he knew what it was to become a domicile for the entity. Now, he could feel it creeping around them, a shadow slinking around their margins. And in them, too. Cockroaches in their walls, scuttling about. Even in the crawlspace, its whispers were distant, but ever present.

They alternated between long periods of simmering silence that erupted in bouts of yelling at one another. Hamish called Owen weak. Owen said Lore was a thief. Lore said Hamish was a fool. Around and around they went like that.

Then one day—or one night, did it even matter anymore?— Owen remembered thinking, *I want to kill them,* and the thought was crystalline in his head, like a fork tapping against a drinking glass. It was not the thought of, say, one sibling to another, fed up with their nonsense, *I'm going to kill you, Becca. No, I'm going to kill you, Jeremy!* It was a clear directive. He wanted to kill them. Same as he'd wanted to kill Nick.

And that's when he knew, the house had them. This time, it was not so dramatic as it had been when he was alone—there, it felt big, bold, like he was an empty house on a buyer's market, move-in ready, and one day, there it was, this entity, this *demon*, and it came in right through the front door. But this time, they'd left the crawlspace often enough, and the house had slipped in when it could. Like a squatter sleeping in the attic. All the while working on them, in them, at them. One beam or brace at a time. A scrape of putty, a splash of paint. Bits of décor, design, architecture. Slowly building a panic room inside each of them.

He realized this when they were back in the same pantry where he'd found the lighter—and where Nick had beaten him and left. By now they each had flashlights, and were grabbing whatever they could find off shelves. Lore grabbed a box of crackers, and Hamish groused at her, snatching it out of her hand and shouldering her aside. She barked at him, called him a "Republican piece of shit thief," and Owen felt himself want to say back to her, *Lot of nerve calling someone else a thief,* but he bit back those words and instead started to say:

"The house always wins."

And then, as if on cue—

The door opened—

And in walked Nick Lobell.

70

Pupillary Light Response

It erupted. Happened so fast, Owen barely knew what was going on.

Lore was the one who saw Nick first. She let slip a shriek of rage, a Valkyrie's cry, and grabbed him bodily and hauled him into the pantry—dragging him through to the far side, slamming him against the wall. Hamish pushed in, a fist up, ready to fall, but Nick was fast, got under Lore, pistoned a fist into her ribs. Hamish clubbed him. An elbow—from who, he didn't know—popped upward, into Owen's temple, and it rang him like a bell. He saw supernovas swallowed by black holes, and he staggered into the wire shelves. One bit into the meat of his skull, and he felt warm blood going down his neck.

Flashlight beams went akimbo, and for a moment, all was in darkness.

Owen struggled to bring his back up to level—

And when the beam clicked back on, he saw that Nick was behind Lore.

She, facing out.

He, a knife to her throat.

Kitchen cutlery. Serrated steak knife. Ready to drag across the flesh of her windpipe, opening it up.

"Back the fuck off," Nick hissed.

"Kill him," Lore seethed. "*Kill him.*"

Hamish raised a fist. Every inch of Owen's brain lit up like fireworks—*he's going to do it, he's going to go for Nick, and Nick is going to kill Lore.*

What have we become?

What has this place done to us?

Owen reached out, caught Hamish's fist—

Hamish spun on him, roaring, shoving him backward.

Nick, cackling mad. The knife in his hand gleaming as the flashlight beam caught it and then spun away, throwing them into darkness again.

One pull, Lore is dead.

Hamish, too, probably.

Then me.

Dead in this place—

Just like Matty—

Except.

No.

The words gushed forth, same as the violence in this room, fast and without warning—

"Matty isn't dead!"

And like that, the fight stopped for a moment. Just small sounds now—Lore breathing heavily. Hamish, a low growl in the back of his throat. And from Nick, a small, low whine. The whine of an animal in a trap.

As Owen reached for the flashlight that had fallen—

Ta-ting-ting.

The sound of something hitting the ground.

Something like a knife.

Hand around flashlight. Beam up.

Nick stood there, his back pressed against the far wall of the pantry. The look on his face was struck in a chokehold of panic. Lore pulled away, rubbing at her throat—*was she cut, had he cut her throat?* No, Owen didn't see any blood. The beam fell to Nick's face, washing him out, a moon of white, and his eyes flicked toward Owen—staring right into the bright beam, the pupils dilating down to pinpricks. "You can't know that," he said, breathless.

"I think I do," Owen said, slowly pulling himself to standing.

For a moment, nothing. Then Nick opened his mouth to speak—

But Hamish's fist pushed any words back down. Nick's head rocked against the wall, and then it was *click-click,* lights out for Nick Lobell.

71

Not Dead Yet

The hit was hard. Nick was out. But he was still alive, at least.
If they had killed him...
If *he* had killed *them*...
Lore couldn't bear to think about it.
They dragged Nick into the crawlspace.

And it was like, *whoof,* the air of their anger was sucked out of the room. Melted away, a sandcastle under a single wave. They all cooled their heels now in the crawlspace, and Hamish shook his head and said he was sorry. "I just got so mad. I was so mad at everything and everyone. I want to say, you know, that it was strategic, that I was hitting him because I thought he'd go for the knife or because I thought he was tricking us, but that wasn't it, man, that wasn't it at all. I hit him because I wanted to hurt him. For the way he hurt us. *Shit.*"

Owen told them he had wanted to kill them both, too.
Lore just nodded, staring at the wall.
Above their heads, Christmas lights, red and green, twinkled.
At their feet, Nick lay, his body in a tangle. Still breathing. Moaning.
What they'd find when he awoke, Lore did not know. But first, she had something she had to ask Owen, didn't she?

"Why did you say that?" Lore asked Owen after having pulled him off to the side, leaving Hamish to watch over a slumped-over Nick, his hands and ankles bound with electrical tape.

"What?"

"To Nick. You said Matty wasn't dead."

"Yeah. I did."

"You know that? You're sure of it?" She wanted to grab him and shake the answer out of him. But suddenly everything felt so precarious, so *delicate,* that she instead just stood there, quietly quaking.

"No. I'm not sure. I just—" He hesitated. "The house got in me. It's been getting into us all lately but before? When I hurt myself, it . . . it *really* got in me, Lore. I don't even know where I ended and its walls and hallways began. And there was this moment when I understood the house. Where I knew what the door I was about to open would show me. Almost like I could feel it, or like I could control what came next. And somewhere in there I just felt like . . . Matty wasn't here. That it hadn't killed him. It showed Nick what it wanted to show Nick to break him. I think . . . Matty got out."

Hope, cruel hope, hope so bright it blinded her, burst forth in her chest. It felt dizzying. She felt buoyant and sick. "If he got out—"

"It doesn't mean he got out the right way, Lore. This place will let you out if you serve it. We saw that with Nick. It . . . could be that way with Matty, too."

That hope went supernova. Bursting so bright it burned the universe, flaming out into a dark, dead lump. Of course. Of *course* it meant Matty might not be Matty anymore. He might just be . . . like Nick. Like the house. A monster carrying its pain into the world and using it to make more pain.

"Maybe we can find him. And save him."

"First we have to help Nick."

The cooling lump of hope in her heart forced her to ask the question: "Can we? Help him, I mean. You were out there on the edge, Owen. So close to falling over it. We got you here in time but Nick—it's been in him for, shit, we don't even know how long. Months? *Years?* When did he find a staircase? When did he go up it, take the place into his head and bring it back out? He's *with the house,*" she said, gesturing to Nick. "He is in the house and the house is in him.

He is its *agent*. Poisoned by it for so long it's hard to know where the poison ends and where Nick begins." She crossed her arms. "How do we fix that?"

"I think you're going to have to table your discussion," Hamish called to them. "Because somebody's waking up."

72

The Possession of Nicholas Lobell

The awakening did not arrive well, or easily, for Nick. At first, his stirring was slow and restive—little hypnic jerks coupled with moans and mumbles that grew louder and louder with each utterance. But then, his eyes wrenched open, as if by invisible fingers, and he screamed an unholy sound. His head ratcheted back on his neck and through his upturned mouth, the words poured out of him in a raging river:

"*WhyamIherewhatwhatwhereizzitpleaseputmebacktherewhyWHYWHY. IneeditneeditneedityouliarliesMattyMattyIsawMattyfuckyouFUCKYOU.*"

Slurs erupted from him. Slurs punctuated by screams. Hideous profanities as his head whipped back and forth—screaming about how he wanted to fuck Lore in the ass, how he'd shove his cock in Owen's mouth, how he'd slit open the bellies of Hamish's children and piss and shit and ejaculate inside their chests.

Then his body seized up for a moment before unlocking itself in a thrashing wave of movement—his bound hands swinging left and right like a loose pulley, his heels kicking down on the ground, *wham, wham, wham,* his head hammering back into the wall then knocking into the drywall studs, back and left and right, back and left and right, his entire body caught in this earthquake of rage and panic.

They had to pounce on him and hold him still. His head spun on his neck far, too far, *impossibly* far, and he opened his mouth and sunk his teeth into the meat of Owen's shoulder. Owen cried out, stumbling backward, blood already sliding down to his elbow, clinging to the underside of his forearm. Then Nick drove the top of his forehead forward into Hamish's eye, and it rocked Hamish, though still he held on, using his shoulder to press into the side of Nick's face, bolstering it against the wall so it couldn't move. Lore, meanwhile, fumbled for the electrical tape, and clumsily, desperately managed to unwind some and start to get it around Nick's mouth. Owen got back in there, and helped her hold his head up as she wound it around and around. It didn't manage to cover his mouth—the tape was too thin for that. Nick bit at it, but that did little good—the tape was, for now, too thick, unyielding to his teeth. At the end of it, it wound around enough times, pressing into his mouth like a gag.

He hissed like a lizard and stared at them. Hate effulgent in his eyes. His nostrils flared. His cheeks puffed out with rapid, shallow breaths.

But he stopped thrashing.

Carefully, they each backed off. The crawlspace did not afford them much room, so they flanked him to the left and to the right. Lore and Owen on one side. Hamish on the other. They knew it would be easier to go out there, in the house—but the house was the house, and it's where it got into Nick.

He needed to be here, they believed.

Was it possible to free him from the house? To evict it? None of them knew, but if it was going to happen anywhere, it was going to happen in here.

Something had crawled its way into Nick—the entity. The demon. The *house*. It was easy to see when you knew to look for it. His eyes, open and glassy, sometimes showed flashes of strange wallpaper, or cracked window glass, or tarnished spigots. In Lore's peripheral vision, she could see his skin rippling like living wallpaper. His tongue, a staircase. She couldn't see them when she looked head on. But looking just away . . . he was a human-shaped structure, crackling and crunching as it thrashed in its bonds.

They had only the loosest plan. They told him they loved him very much. They missed him. They begged him to push the house out. To remember who he was, who he really was. They reminded him of the Covenant.

Nick bellowed—a banshee's wail that was both mournful and fed by rage, and he reached for Hamish with choking hands. But his hands were bound together and he could only lurch forward so far, even as he started to bite through the tape, spit springing from his mouth and hanging in strings from his lips, even as the whites of his eyes burst red from the fury of his effort. Lore and Hamish held him back, shushing him, trying not to hurt him *or* be hurt in the process—

And Owen, standing back, felt the pain coming off of him—bleeding like waves of heat. That pain came from something. From somewhere. The house had seized upon it, and it was the key that opened the lock that was Nick Lobell.

Pain that had been locked away, festering.

And never once reckoned with.

The house wouldn't have reckoned with it, either. It didn't heal that wound. It didn't push the pain away. It just took it and used it against Nick.

As Owen watched Nick spasming violently, teeth snapping at the faces of Lore and Hamish, he felt the words coming up out of him—

A mistake, perhaps.

A reckoning, definitely.

A risk, 100 percent.

He said: "We know what your father did to you, Nick. And it wasn't your fault."

There. Nick froze in his attack. Frozen still, except for the trembling of his body, the gentle clacking of his teeth.

Lore and Hamish looked at him, half angry, half confused. Because they didn't know. Owen knelt down in front of Nick and took his hands. Blinking back tears, Owen said, "It wasn't your fault. It was his fault. We love you, and we're sorry we didn't see it. But we see it now. We see you now." Owen hugged his friend and said in his ear: "We're so fucking sorry, Nick."

The fight went out of Nick. But so did everything else. He slumped forward, and then when the hug was done, backward. Instantly, he fell into a catatonic state. Rarely blinking. Just barely breathing. They tried talking to him some more but it didn't even seem to register. Owen wondered if the house was gone from him. And further, he had to wonder:

Was the house the only thing propping him up?

If it was gone, did it take too much of Nick with it?

What was even left of their friend?

73

Midnight Interruption

Owen told them, of course. He had to, now. Though it was not his secret to share, the house had shared it with him. And they needed to know. So he told them what he saw. How Nick's father was abusing his son.

They, of course, were horrified. Nick loved his dad. His dad was the Cool Dad. They *all* loved him, loved hanging out there.

How had they missed it?

"I still loved him, was the worst part."

That sentence, spoken in the darkness of the crawlspace.

They startled awake to find Nick standing there. He'd freed himself from his bonds. Chewed his way free of the tape. He was a shadow above them.

Owen saw: *He has something in his hand.*

"Nick," Lore said, calmly.

Nick kept on talking, his words weak and weepy, strung together with sniffles and small ill-stifled sobs: "Like, he was my dad, and he was . . . *doing stuff* to me. And I wanted to hate him, but I couldn't. Because he was my dad. And how fucked is that? How fucked is it that I didn't even like myself enough to hate him for what he did to me? Was *doing* to me. Christ. I didn't like myself enough to stop him. Fuck. I didn't tell any of you. Covenant this, Covenant that, blah blah blah, all bullshit because I kept that to myself. Because—fuck, I dunno." His voice trembled and shook. "I dunno why."

"It's okay, dude," Hamish said in the darkness. Slowly standing.

"I let him do . . . stuff to me. And then I let the house get inside me, too. Sometimes it talked to me in his voice, you know that? Jesus. Jesus! And then I bring you all here and now we're all fucked, we're all just empty houses waiting for this *monster* to move in and take us over . . ." His voice rose to a sad pitch, a whine like a buzzsaw cutting. His arm—the one holding something—slashed out at open air. "But I'm not—I'm *not* letting it get in here again, I don't deserve to be here. I'm sorry. I'm so sorry—"

Owen knew:

He was going to hurt himself.

Maybe *kill* himself.

As his eyes adjusted, he could see the shape of what was in his hand. A knife, but not a knife. Long and tapered to a sticking point. Like a huge splinter.

That's what it is. A long splintered piece of wood.

From the wall, from one of the stud beams.

Nick turned the point toward himself.

Time seemed to go slow in the darkness—

Hamish and Lore moved toward him—

Nick tucked the weapon toward his chest, pointing it upward—

Toward his chin.

He's going to stab it upward.

Through jaw, neck, maybe into his brain.

"I used to cut myself," Owen said, abruptly.

Silence and stillness ensued as the shock of what he said stayed everyone's hand. He had not planned on saying this, not ever, but here he was. He had to say it. Felt the poison of it purging out of his mouth as the words kept coming:

"I had a knife. A little penknife I bought from the flea market we used to go to and—and I'd cut myself, but not in places you could see. Like, on my biceps. Outside, inside. Sometimes on my inner thighs or even—even around my hip bones. It was stupid, so stupid like—a cry for help that I hid from everyone else, a cry for help I wouldn't let anyone hear. How fucking insane is that? It's why I never wanted to go swimming—never wanted to take my shirt off because the scars on my arms were still there. *Are* still there."

Lore, quietly: "I wondered what those were."

"I hated myself, too, in a lot of ways because, I dunno, same stupid shit as the rest of us. Daddy issues. How common. How *dull*. Oh my father was shitty to me and mean and so I cut myself to feel something or ... or to make his words true and right, so that he wasn't just *mean* to me, he was *telling the truth,* and that made it better somehow, or so I told myself. But I never said anything either, Nick. I could've and I should've, but I didn't. So please put the sharp thing down. We're all really fucked up and just trying to get through life, and it's better when we do it together instead of alone. That's how we'll survive this house. That's how we'll get out of this place. Together, and not alone. But that can't happen if you do what you're about to do. Okay? I know that now. Don't hurt yourself anymore. That's what this place wants. So go the other way. Okay? Please."

"Please, Nick," Lore said.

"Please, dude," Hamish begged.

Nick let slip another gulping sob.

The weapon he'd been holding—the sharp wooden shaft—clattered to the ground at his feet and he toppled over, sobbing. But they caught him as he fell.

74

Of Fantasies and Fingerprints

Somehow, they found rest. Nick in the middle. The others around him. Lore's head resting against a cold pipe, listening to the sometimes running of water. The sleep was not good, not complete, but it felt nice, just the same. It was the next morning, them drinking shitty cold instant coffee from some bygone decade, that Nick finally spoke to them like Nick.

"Fuck you guys for making me cry," he said, smirking. He sipped at the coffee and made a face like he'd just licked a booger off a wall.

"Fuck *you* for making us *make* you cry," Lore said.

Hamish reached out and put a hand on Nick's shoulder, giving it a squeeze. "Dude, I'm just glad you're all right. This is all fucked, but I'm glad you're okay, and we're all okay, and—shit. I'm just sorry, man." He put his head on Nick's shoulder, pressing his forehead there and sighing.

For a while, all was quiet. Then Nick said: "I'm not okay, though."

They all palpably stiffened.

"It's still in my head. The *thing*. The monster. It's . . . retreated. Like it went into my mental vents, or into some dark corner of the basement you never look at. But I feel it in there. Biding its time. Waiting for me to be alone out there again. The only way out is to let it in. And even if you don't let it . . . it'll get us all eventually. You can feel it, can't you?"

Lore wondered, could they stay here? In this crawlspace? Forever?

A small, strange fantasy played out of them hiding here, just the four of them—pillaging snacks and water, playing little games, mapping the crawlspaces for any who would come here after them. Maybe they could live here. The adventuring group, colonizing the dungeon in which they were trapped.

It was a lie, she knew. A comforting one.

But Nick was right. Eventually, it would get them in here. She did feel it—that ambient *hatred* of them, pulsing against the walls like the beat of a diseased heart.

Vwommm, vwommm, vwommm.

She sipped her coffee.

Felt the anxiety crawling through her like ants.

This isn't you.

You're better than this.

Focus, Lore. Fucking focus.

This is a game.

Not a real game, no. Not a simulation, not exactly. But it helped her to continue to think of it that way—to categorize, to compartmentalize.

(To control.)

But what kind of game?

All this time, she'd been thinking about it like it was purely a puzzle to solve. An adventure game that needed all the clues, needed you to make all the right choices for you to get to the end of the story.

But that wasn't right.

It was PvE—player versus enemy. This was survival horror. This was *Final Fucking Fantasy*. It was *Zelda, Skyrim, Bioshock*. Somewhere here, the enemy lived. The final boss—the Ender Dragon, Sephiroth, Hades, Ganon. It guarded the portal home. They had to find it. They had to kill it. But where? Where was it? *What* was it? She stood up suddenly, her coffee splashing over onto her knuckles.

"You know things," she said to both Owen and Nick.

They looked to each other quizzically.

"Owen, you knew Matty was alive. Somehow, the house . . . it left that impression upon you. And that was just for the short time it was in you. But *you*—" She pointed to Nick. "You were in there a lot longer. It's still in there now, according to you. You must know something."

"Lore, I don't—"

"It won't want you to know that you know it. But you do. You *must*. It's got fingerprints all over your appliances, man. I need you to dig deep. Please, Nick. You're right, we can't stay here, and it'll win eventually. Like Owen said, the house always fucking wins. Unless we figure out how to burn it all down."

Hamish clapped Nick on the shoulder. "I believe in you, man."

"Thanks," Nick said, but he said it in a wry way, as if he wasn't sure. He settled into himself, easing back, setting the coffee down. He took a deep breath and looked like he was trying to relax. He blinked—

And Lore nearly gasped when she saw it. His eyes: drywall marked with striations of black mold. Another blink: siding stained with ill-colored algae. A third blink, and his eyes became gleaming doorknobs, promising ingress—doorknobs so shiny she could see herself reflected back in them.

Nick stiffened suddenly, sucking in a sharp intake of breath—

And then he told them a story.

Interlude

THE HOUSE WAKES UP

A house, at first, is not a home.

At the start, a house is just a house: It is a structure designed for the purpose of someone to live in it. Perhaps you! You move in. You bring your things—all your most precious *stuff*. You pack into this place your whole life—and that effect is multiplicative. Life makes life, a fungal efflorescence of existence begetting existence. You bring in a spouse, you have more children, you get one pet, another pet, a dog and a cat and now a bearded dragon; it's where you learn to cook and fill the house with wonderful smells; it's where you rest your head and give birth to dreams that are ambitious and strange. And it is in all this that a house becomes a home: You imprint yourself upon it, and it imprints itself upon you in return. It becomes a part of your very identity—your house, your *home*, is part of the tapestry that is you. You carry it with you, in your heart, to the end of things.

That, of course, is where the saying comes from:

Home is where the heart is.

The other thing about a house—a *home*—is that it is a private place. It has walls. You can draw curtains over the windows. You can lock the door.

And in that place, you can be you and do whatever it is you want to do.

You pig out on ice cream. You masturbate. You fuck. You sing in the shower. You take a shit *multiple* times a day. You watch the very worst of reality TV. You plunder the liquor cabinet. You talk absolute *trash* about people you know, people you work with, people you love, and others you hate. You get your hands tied behind your back, you get bent over a desk, you take a gag in your mouth and a cock—real or artificial!—wherever you so choose, done consensually, with a loving partner, or two, or three.

This, too, is part of a house's purview: a home away from prying eyes where you can finally drop the mask, lose the pretense, and be who you need to be.

It is necessary and it is good.

Until, of course, it's not.

That privacy also keeps hidden the fights you have. The cruel words, sharp as a tack, stuck in those you purportedly love. Your house is where you rage and punch drywall. Where families fight. Where relationships start to rot like fruit left long on the ground. It's where kids learn to hate their parents. Where wives learn to hate the men they married and wish instead they'd fucked off to the woods and taken their chance with a bear. It's where bad habits take root: too much drinking, too much eating, too many trips to the medicine cabinet, too much hoarding, too much sitting in the dark drunk-texting someone or trolling people on social media or flicking through the pics of an ex. Little seeds of neglect and pain, thumbed into your fertile dirt—seeds that grow best not in the light, but in the dark.

And if allowed to grow, to flourish, these invasive vines tangle—a braiding mat of suffering begins to form. A man hits his wife. A mother speaks the cruelest words to her child. A teenager pops all the pills in his parents' bathroom and dies in the tub. An angry loner drinks beer, beats his dog, doxxes someone on the internet whose identity he hates. A whipping belt. A gun under the bed. A knife in the knife block. A computer archiving grotesque images of children. In the deepest dark of a house, of a *home,* hate and pain and suffering can fester. All that effervescent *rage*. All that crushing *despair*. Flourishing. Festering.

Dreams curdling fast into nightmares.

It's where home stops being where the heart is.

Home is where the *hurt* is.

Where the *horror* lives.

Home becomes another name for that place where monsters go to hide and do their terrible work.

In the secret dark of such a place, sometimes, something awakens.

Something new.

Something terrible, with eyes open wide and a powerful hunger.

Enter: Dan Harrow, the man behind the Harrowstown planned communities of Pennsylvania, New Jersey, and New York.

It was 1945, and Dan was in his favorite drinking hole in Philadelphia, sitting at the bar, sipping an Irish whiskey, doodling pictures of houses. Dan loved houses, having grown up in a cramped West Philly apartment in a crowded apartment building. He loved that single-family homes felt like *islands*—a private oasis, a retreat from the world. He sketched Craftsman style and single-floor Spanish Colonials and funky little Art Deco bungalows (though these were a bit too extreme for Dan, who really liked the confidence of clean, straight lines). That's when a man sat down next to him, a fella who introduced himself as Eddie Naberius, and Eddie, well, he clocked right away that Dan was down on his luck. (Perhaps not too hard to clock, Dan figured, since he was drinking whiskey at an Irish bar at half past two on a workday.) Dan had in fact been fired from his architectural job for wanting to do more than work the damn mail room—he'd been there for five years, and he had ideas, why wouldn't anyone listen?

But this fella, Eddie, he says after hearing Dan's story, "You know, Dan, the G.I. Bill passed last year, it's gonna change things. War's over—not formally, but it's all over but the crying." Dan made a face at that and then Eddie said the most curious thing: "Right, that one's not out yet, is it? Ink Spots, keep your ears out. Anyway. Point is, Dan, gonna be a lot of soldiers coming back from the war with money stuffed in their pockets from Uncle Sam. And they're not going to want to live in the cities, no sir, not with all that racket, all the smoke and those people. They're going to want some peace and quiet. I think you could be the man to give it to them with your—" Here, Eddie tapped the doodles. "Nice little houses here. Houses for good men with nice wives and lovely children. Soldiers. Upstanding fellas. The kind of people who upheld the dignity of this country. Who *restored* dignity to the world. People who are American as an apple pie. And I think we can repay them. Don't you, Dan?"

(It was only later that Dan realized: He never told Eddie his name.)

Dan designed four houses: the In-Towner, the King's Castle, the Ranchhand, and the Dreamboat. Each equal to the others in its category, and each category offering something a little bit different for different buyers. A garage on this one, three bedrooms on that one instead of two, different paint colors on the wood slat siding. Each house was some form of what they were calling ranch style, or ranchers—just one floor, but with an expandable attic and a basement. Each had a small parcel of manicured lawn, a paved and sealed driveway, and a white picket fence separating you from your lovely neighbor.

Eddie had money and he had contacts for government land contracts, and he helped Dan start a building firm using builders who learned to mass-produce things fast and efficient for the Navy during the war.

And by 1947, they had their first neighborhood—

Not just a neighborhood, but in fact a whole Pennsylvania municipality:

Harrowstown, PA, in the south of Bucks County, not far from the city.

A suburb. Clean and beautiful.

Each house was under ten thousand dollars. Most advertised at just sixty-five dollars a month. And best of all:

No money down for American heroes!

(Dan initially had it say "for veterans," but Eddie wanted that punched up a bit. "Marketing," he said, with a sly wink.)

Three months in, every house was bought.

(By white people, of course. Eddie said this was a neighborhood for a certain kind of person, and didn't the Blacks like the city better anyway?)

Enter: Alfred—Alfie—Shawcatch.

Shawcatch, a veteran of the 82nd Airborne, Army. There on the ground to liberate Wöbbelin, a sub-camp of Neuengamme just outside Ludwigslust. This camp was not one of gas chambers and experimental surgery suites, but rather had been used as overflow when Germans moved captive *Juden* and other inmates out of camps that were on the verge of liberation. At Wöbbelin, the inmates were forced to live like animals, thousands wrangled together, left to suffer thirst, starvation, disease—

And ultimately, cannibalism.

Alfie Shawcatch came home to his wife, Judy, and sought peace away from the nightmares of war. When it came time to settle down, thanks to the G.I. Bill, he was able to choose one of the inaugural homes in Harrowstown—

He chose the most handsome model of them all.

The Dreamboat.

And just like that, a house became a home.

Judy, pregnant, gave birth to the first of their three children— Marie was the first, then the next two were boys named Oliver and

Francis—Ollie, and Little Frankie, respectively. They bought a dog: a red hound they called Lou.

Alfie himself took a job in the city as a trolley conductor for the PTC, the Philadelphia Transit Company.

Judy grew roses and loved to bake.

Marie was a little firecracker—a whip-smart kid with dreams beyond her expected station.

Ollie was a church mouse, and Little Frankie was a clown.

Lou didn't understand how to play fetch. He'd fetch whatever you threw for him, but he did not return it and instead liked to be chased around.

Things were good.

Except inside Alfie's head.

Every night, a little bit less sleep. Eroded, chewed in sharp-toothed nibbles. Alfie dreamed so often of war, not just of the gunfire and the explosions and the eggy hell-stink in the air. Not just of the injuries he saw on his fellow soldiers—injuries that wouldn't close, that seemed to birth clots of maggots, that started to smell like old meat. Not just of who he had to kill—and Alfie did have to kill, because that was war, you became death or you got dead. Most of his dreams were of the camp. Of the starving and the sickened and the dead. Of people pushed so far they had to eat one another just to survive.

What kind of world is this? he wondered, never out loud.

As his sleep frittered away, so did his mental state.

Soon he stopped sleeping altogether.

And on one dark summer night, Alfie did something terrible. He got up out of bed, dazed, weary, seventy-two hours straight without sleep. He took out the paratrooper knife from under his pillow—not even sure when he'd put it there—and stuck it in his wife's throat. No logic to it. No thinking she was an enemy soldier, no hallucinating her as some kind of foul thing. Best that can be surmised, he had all that pain, all that bad stuff inside him, and it built up like an infection. Swelling and swelling until it popped. Until the rage needed somewhere to go.

Judy didn't get to scream.

Then he went after his children. Frankie and Ollie slept in one room, Marie in another, because the Dreamboat was one of those blessed three-bedroom models, wasn't it? A real beaut, that house. Powder-blue walls in the boys' room, suddenly sprayed red with what was kept inside them. *They* screamed. *They* fought. Like good boys, Alfie knew. Good boys knew to fight. Even when the fight was a losing one. And then, finally, Marie.

He went to find her in her bed, but she was gone.

She'd seen him, he realized. Seen him and crawled into the small attic of the house, and then slipped down into the crawlspace—like a little rat. He promised her if she came out, he would do okay by her. He would keep her safe and even bring her mother and her brothers back to life again. But Marie refused. Because Marie was smart. And that's when Alfie knew, only one way to get out a rat like that. He'd smoke her out. So he set a fire in the attic and waited for her to show herself, and ohh, that fire spread mighty quick. But Alfie wasn't about to leave and miss her sneaking out, so he stayed there in the house as it burned down around him, as it blocked the doors and choked him with smoke. Soon, it had him, too, the fire crawling up his legs and setting his hair ablaze. That's how Alfie met his end.

(Marie escaped via a panel in the back meant to access the basement.)

(She lived, though her family did not.)

The house watched it all.

It may seem strange to think of a house watching anything, but when a house becomes a home, it becomes *imbued* with life. Alive in an almost literal way—and certainly aware. If a house becomes haunted, it is not haunted by the ghosts of its inhabitants but rather by the *memories* of those inhabitants—it is the house that remembers, and the house that records and replays the lives lived there.

Houses, in this way, are like vessels. Waiting to be filled up. And what fills them can spill out—be it love, be it pain, be it hate.

And Alfred Shawcatch filled that house, his Dreamboat, with the blood of his family, the screams of his children, and the nightmares of war.

When the house burned, it was gone. Cooked to the earth—naught but a few black-char splinters sticking up from the ground like the teeth of a beast.

But gone is not always *gone*.

And in the great void where dead things go, the house was reborn.

It was reborn a cursed thing. It went to its death splashed with blood and burned with fire. It came alive in the dark, the prefab structure redrawn first as a mere sketch, but soon with walls and slab and glass. It became fully aware—with only hatred as its guide. Hatred for Alfie Shawcatch and what he had done to his family.

It was hateful, yes.

But it was also alone. And houses—*homes*—crave company. To be empty is the worst fate, and so the house, whether consciously or not, called out.

It sang a hammer-and-saw song to other homes like it.

A song of blood and fire.

The wages of civilization and the vagaries of the twentieth century saw more and more people, meaning more and more houses, more and more *homes,* and in the uncaring churn of industry and the ever-steady march of war, trauma and pain radiated out—the glassy, brassy pealing of a bell. More homes were filled with nightmares instead of dreams, and when some of those homes died—be they burned, demolished, abandoned—they sometimes could come back. They rose together in the void, sometimes one room, sometimes many, drifting toward the original house—Dan Harrow's Dreamboat model—called by its grim gravity. It reached for them, and they for it. They joined with it, room by room.

And as they did, its power grew.

Its hunger, too, in equal measure.

It had all this hatred, and nothing to do with it.

It needed people.

People to hurt.

So it put out staircases. Doorways. Windows. All in places where only a few might find them. Distant places where the portals would be safe. In forests, on beaches, in meadows. Bait for the ever curious. And when a person went in, the house had them. It could mine them for their own pain, making more rooms just for them. Torment, though, was not enough. The house learned that once it hollowed them out, it could fill them back up—with itself. And then it could set them free again, put back into the world. There they would return, sharing their hurt, sharing the horror, and making more of it for everyone. The more that went around, the greater the house became—

And the larger, too.

This, then, is where hate lives.

This is its home.

75

Matty's Clue

The story Nick told, he told as if he were possessed. It fell out of him—this tale of a house born when its owner killed his family, then himself, then the house. And how from it was born a cursed entity, a demon in the dark void. One that put out traps—like the staircase. An anglerfish dangling its glowing bait. Someone curious comes along and, *poof,* away they go.

And then it disappeared. It didn't *want* more than one person to come in. It was better if they were alone. Like Matty. Like Nick.

This time, when they all came in together—

It had a harder time getting hold of them.

Nick, now relieved of the story, looked dizzy and sick. As if he had touched some foul source. He was pale, sweaty. His eyes, furtive and darting. He muttered, "I had to get close to it. It wants us to know it'll get us eventually. It's close. So close."

Fuck that.

Lore snapped her fingers. "We—we know more about it now. Right? It was born—or reborn or whatever—in the late forties, on the heels of World War II, and it was forged in that pain. And it's why we don't see any rooms in here from before that point, right?"

"Or rooms that aren't American," Owen added.

"Right! Yeah." More finger snapping. "What else?"

Hamish shook his head. "I dunno how this is helping us, Lore. Nick looks sick now..."

"I'm *fine*," Nick said bleakly. It was a lie, plainly. His lips looked gray and wormish. He shivered. Owen put an arm around him, and to Lore's surprise, Nick leaned into it. Those two were not often close. It was nice to see.

Lore knew they needed to find a solution soon. Or what Nick told them—the warning from the house—would be spot-on. It would win. It would get in them eventually. Like erosion—all it took was time. It would, hit by hit, work them like a speed bag. Soon as there was one little rip in their fabric, it would climb inside.

She kept on babbling. "We know it's worse when you're alone. We know the rooms shift only when you go through them a certain way. The crawlspace is a constant; the rest of the house is variable." She realized now that the little girl in that story kept herself safe by climbing into the crawlspace. Some sort of fail-safe put in place by the house? Here she was thinking like a programmer again. But all things, in their way, were programmed, weren't they? Programmed by nature, programmed by nurture?

"We know it hates us," Hamish said.

"That it wants to take us over," Owen said, all too knowingly.

"That the people here aren't ghosts, exactly," Lore said. "They're like copies. Memories. Some from houses that perished. Others from . . ." At this, she shuddered, thinking of her mother. "Our own heads."

"The house wants power," Hamish said.

"Power," Owen said. "That's another thing. It has power—electricity, I mean. And running water." He pointed to the pipes and junction boxes here in the crawlspace. "Though where it comes from, I dunno. Or if it's even real."

There.

That was it.

A spark, struck in the darkness of Lore's head.

She repeated the thing Matty had carved into that cabinet door: "*The heart is where the home is*. Not the reverse. Not 'the home is where the heart is.' Why would he write it that way? Because he knew something. We're looking for the house. For the *home*. The original one. And if you follow that literally—"

Hamish made a gasp face. "It's an actual place. Here in the bigger house is . . . the original house. Somewhere at the heart of it."

"At the center of the labyrinth," Owen said.

By now, Nick's eyes were half lidded. His breathing was shallow.

We fucked him up by making him get close to the house. Shit shit shit.

Only thing to do was to keep going. Keep talking. *Keep figuring it out.*

"We gotta find the center of the maze," Hamish said.

"No," Lore said. "Not exactly. Look at the pipes. The wires. They don't go up into the ceiling. They all go—"

"Down," both Hamish and Owen said at the same time.

"Right. And if you were to think of where your heart was, where would you think of it being? In relation to, say, your mind. Your head, your brain."

Again, together: "Down."

"Yeah. Down. Down deep in your chest. Protected by all this bone and meat. Fuck." She looked down at the floor. "We busted through the walls and we came here. But . . . we never thought to fucking *dig*."

76

As Above, So Below

As Lore and Hamish took the lead ripping apart the floor, Nick sat there, shivering, sweating, as though he was retreating from himself further and further—like watching someone drift all the way out to sea. And Owen sat next to him, trying to ignore the pain throbbing through his fingers and his arms. The very pain that ensured he wouldn't be of much value here, digging through the floor.

At one point, Nick seemed to jostle awake—even though his eyes had been open the whole time, unblinking, suddenly it was like, boom, he was there again. He looked to Owen and said, "Sorry I left you alone. And dragged you here in the first place. You're all right, Zuikas."

"Sorry we didn't listen to you all those years."

A weak shrug as Nick stared out through nothingness. "Not sure I'd've listened to me either. Fuck. What a mess." His voice cracked, then, like a tree in a hard wind. "I'm scared, Owen. I don't like this thing being in my head and—and I don't think I'm going to make it—" At that, he gulped a hard sob. Owen pulled Nick close and let him put his head on Owen's shoulder.

"We're gonna get you out of here," Owen promised him.

"Gotta get this thing outta my head first," Nick said.

"We're working on it. We got you."

But Owen wasn't so sure. Whispers of doubt crept in through the floorboards of his mind like creeping vines. *You can't do this. You're too late. You can't do this. You're too late.* Over and over again. He gritted his teeth and winced, shutting them out as best as he could. But he could still hear them. Neverborn. Nailbiter.

An hour later, Lore and Hamish used all the tools they had at their disposal—a hammer, a brass lamp base, a loose cinder block, even the heels of their feet—to bash open a raggedy hole in the floor of the crawlspace.

Click.

Lore shone a flashlight down in the dark.

"It's a fucking pit," she said.

"A bottomless pit," Owen added.

They could see the bending pipes and the drape of wires descending into the darkness. Eventually, they were swallowed by shadow.

"Welp," Hamish said, taking the hammer and dropping it into the hole. He held a finger to his lips. Mouthed the word: "Listen."

The hammer clanged against a couple pipes.

Then: *thump, thump, thump,* a sound receding, its volume shrinking, until it was gone somewhere down in the dark.

Lore felt a shiver skitter over her, like dancing spider legs. The pit felt less like a pit now and more like a mouth. She eased back from the edge, in case the boards bent and dropped her in. "I—I don't like it." She was an early player of *Minecraft* when it was in alpha, and then beta, and this reminded her of the earliest days of that, when you'd come upon a hole in the crust of that blocky world. You'd hear things down there: the hiss and moans of *Minecraft*'s monstrous inhabitants. Creepers, zombies, spiders. You could easily fall to your death down in those places. Just like you could here.

To its credit, she heard no such monstrousness down below.

Instead, the pit seemed *to breathe* on her, a stale wind of strange smells: wet wood, rancid potpourri, bleach, lawn clippings. And a hint of coppery blood.

"It could be the way out," Owen said.

"It could be a way to die," she answered.

Nick stiffened. "It doesn't want us to go down there. Can you feel that? I can feel it. It *resists*. Wants us to be afraid of it."

"It's doing its job," Hamish said, "because I am afraid of that hole. It's a hole. Like, a fucking nowhere hole. There's no argument here, it just goes into nothing. If we go down there, *we* are nothing."

Owen looked around. "Maybe we can use a rope. Make a . . . a ladder."

"Nobody here knows how to make a ladder," Lore said.

"This isn't actually *Minecraft*, Owen. Besides, whatever rope you find? It's going to have to be a lot longer than any of us can even imagine. And then what? What if it's still not enough? We just go down into the dark? Hanging there? Dangling?" *Waiting for something to rush up out of nothing and close its jaws upon us?* An insane thought. A monster gobbling them up. *Maybe the house really doesn't want us to go there.*

"We don't need a rope or a ladder," Nick said, grunting as he stood up. He wobbled, but managed with Owen's help to remain on his feet. "God, for a bunch of smart people you're pretty fucking stupid." Lore felt a weird spike of hope. *He can still sound like Nick.* That was a good sign, right? Nick went on to say: "The pipes? The wires? Ladder and rope, right there. Look—the pipes bend. Up and down, back and forth. And the wires go straight down. It'll be like climbing the rope in gym class."

"You know they don't do that anymore?" Hamish asked.

"I always fell," Owen said.

"I'm going," Nick said.

Lore objected. "The fuck you are. We just got you back. We do this together or we don't do it at all. The Covenant, buddy. The Covenant."

To her, that was it. Game, set, match.

Nick did not seem to agree.

He leaned in, his face serious. His voice was hoarse when he said, "You want to talk the Covenant? The Covenant is about no bullshit.

And the no-bullshit thing here is, we're going to die or succumb to the house if we don't go down there. It doesn't want us to go down there. So that means we have to go down there. And if we die? Then we die together instead of up here, poisoned by this place so badly we bash one another's heads in with—" He gestured all around him. "Cinder blocks, table lamps, or the same pipes we should've used to climb down into the dark." He sniffed. "*I'm going.*"

"Nick—can we just talk about this—"

"Step aside."

"I think he's right," Owen said.

Lore shot him a look. "What the fuck, Owen? You, of all people, want to do the stupidest, scariest thing?"

"Respect, Zuikas," Nick said, offering him a fist to bump.

Owen bumped that fist, looking a little chuffed.

"I do," he answered. "Nick gets it. This place will wear us down. I don't want to wait for that. Maybe there's a reason we didn't think about digging, about the pipes and the wires. And even now you can feel the house outside these walls, whispering its hatred at us. What if—what if we go down there and it's the way out? The exit? This way to the great egress and instead of taking it we just stand here, too afraid to go that direction?"

"Owen, we could *die*—"

"That's true doing anything. I'd rather die trying to get out than die stuck."

"Yeah, hell yeah," Hamish said.

Fuck, you too, Hamish?

"Ham, you died once already—"

"So I'm already living on borrowed time. I'm going, too."

Every part of Lore resisted this.

Every molecule of her screamed, *This is a bad idea.*

Then again, that was how she'd lived her life this whole time. All the while she knew there was the safe way to do things, the quote-unquote "smart" path to take, and she always did the opposite. Took every risk she could. Any time there was a door, she didn't go through it knowing that's where everyone else was going—instead, she'd break a window, or punch her way through a wall, or—

Or bust a hole in the floor and jump down into darkness.

Parachuting into Hell itself.

"Fine," she said. "I'm in."

Down, down, down we go.

Nick was right. They could use the pipes almost as ladders, affording them footholds and handholds. The pipes were bent, inexplicably, in ways that betrayed sane design. (Once more, Lore's mind went not to a game, but to the old screen saver on her ancient Windows machine: the one that had colorful neon pipes ever growing and expanding, like a bundle of breeding snakes.) Sometimes, they heard water rushing through the metal—a wet susurrus as it traveled past. She could even feel it on her hands—it cooled her palms and she welcomed the sensation. Bundles of wires dangled next to them, with individual wires joining from random points in the darkness above, like threads pulled from faraway skeins. Sometimes they could use those to brace themselves when the pipe bends got tricky to navigate.

One of the things that tripped Lore out the most was . . . looking down? Darkness. Looking up? She saw meager light shining through the jagged, bitten shape of the hole they had busted in the floor. But everywhere else?

More darkness.

All around them: nothing but the black-teethed void.

It chilled her.

It was Nick who demanded to go first, so Lore went second. Owen after her, then Hamish last.

They did periodic check-ins up and down. *Everyone okay? Anyone struggling?* Owen was having a hard time with it. Nick wanted to push on but Lore asked him to wait—and to her shock, he did. She told Owen to hug the pipe close, rest against it. Everyone could take a rest then.

"I'm okay," he said, after a bit. "I'm good. Let's keep going."

And so they did.

Down, down, down . . .

Minutes gave way to more minutes, time unspooling before them. How long had it been now? No way to know. Lore's arms ached. Her calves were cramping. She worked out sometimes. Hamish definitely did. But the others? She didn't think so. Everyone was still okay, but they were grunting more, panting more. How long could they hold on and hold out?

Fuck.

This was a mistake.

She saw it now.

"We have to go back," she said.

"I . . ." Owen started. "I don't know that I can. I can keep going down. I'm not sure I can do up."

Fuck!

"I think we gotta try," she said, suddenly desperate. She looked down. The pipes continued to descend. The wires, now in a fat bundle thick as both her thighs, also snaked down into shadow. "We turn around."

"No fucking way," Nick said.

"Nick. *Please.*"

The pipes hissed and gushed as water ran through them. Louder than usual this time, so loud it drowned out Nick's response to her— though she could tell it was more of the same contrarian denial. He wanted to keep going, she wanted to turn around. At first, the water traveling through the pipes was cool—

Then it grew warmer.

No, no, no—

And warmer.

No!

And warmer still, until it was starting to get *hot*.

Her mind raced, a scattering of panic impulses. She started to yell out over the hissing pipes, "Okay! Okay, try to—*try* to use your sleeves, you don't want it to burn you and—"

Two words rose up from beneath her.

Nick's two words.

"Fuck this," he said.

Then he let go.

Lore screamed.

His body fell, feet pointed down, through the darkness. She looked up and still saw Owen and Hamish up there, both quickly changing hands on the pipes as the metal grew hotter and hotter—soon it'd be hot enough to blister their palms.

"I'm letting go," Owen said.

"No, Owen, wait, hold on to *me,* don't—"

Down beneath them, a voice calling up: "I'm okay," Nick said. His voice echoing. "Let go. Just let go."

Fear caromed through her. What if it was a trick? The house fucking with them some more? Mimicking Nick's voice? Or worse, having taken him over once more, puppeting him to say those things?

But the pipes were getting hot, now.

Owen told her to trust, then he let go. Hamish, too.

Why am I the scared one—

What is happening—

She kept her palms free, the pipes in the crook of her arm, but the heat was burning through her clothes, and she could feel it radiating out, hot on her face, hot against her legs and her hip and—what else was there to do?

Lore cried out as she, too, fell.

She fell a hundred feet.

Or ten.

Or only one.

She had no sense of it. She only knew the bottom of the world fell out, and she plunged through darkness—

Until, soon after, *wham,* her feet landed—

Right on a fucking staircase.

77

The Third Staircase

Together, they stood at the top of a long, *long* set of stairs. Here, the ground of it was made of bent pipe and braided wire, but as it descended, they could see it become a staircase of wood, its risers lined with scuffed red carpet, the steps framed with an oiled dark balustrade on each side. It seemed to loom and sway.

It looked as if it went on forever.

Down, down through the void.

Behind them, it did not seem to go anywhere.

And Lore wondered if it was a trick. If they stepped off the back edge of the staircase, and into darkness, could they be free? Or would it kill them? Would it be like in a broken, buggy game, where to leave the map meant not being able to get back into it? Could they be trapped forever off the literal grid? That was somehow worse than just letting the house in, wasn't it? Lore for so long had craved being alone, but that level of pure empty loneliness gave her a crushing sensation in her chest just thinking about it.

So, that meant the staircase.

That meant *descent*.

She looked over at Nick. His eyes were dim, half lidded. Parts of him twitched in myoclonic spasms. He swayed. The corners of his lips looked like inlets of froth, even bile. *We have to move quickly.*

"We have to go down," she said.

Hamish and Owen nodded, even as Nick stared at nothing. Because what other choice did they have but another leap into the void?

78

House in a House

The stairs changed as they went. From oiled wood to iron grate to old stone. Handrails of mahogany, cherry, brass. Some steps had leaves on them and other forest detritus, and when Owen saw that, he thought, *We're almost there, we're almost home, this is it—*

But then the stairs kept going, kept changing. It became a spiral staircase for a while, dizzying in its tightening coils down, down, down, the whole thing swaying and groaning, their heads spinning with vertigo.

He didn't know how long they descended. The burning in his calves and thighs was almost loud enough to drown out the pain in his fingers and arms.

And then—

It wasn't there, and then—it was.

Owen stepped forward, expecting another step in the staircase.

But instead, his foot landed dully in a patch of fresh grass. The smell of it—cut lawn, crushed onion grass—hit him fully, and again rose in him the sudden hope that they had done it, they had escaped, they had tricked the house and gotten away.

But reality soon refuted the certainty of their freedom.

Ahead of him waited a house. A small house. Siding the color of a cloudless summer sky. Like something out of the early 1950s—an overhanging carport to the side, a poured concrete walkway to the daffodil-yellow front door, high-silled bedroom windows, a partial second floor, which was more than you'd get with just a Cape Cod. An expanse of perfectly cut lawn was all around it, and around *that* a perimeter of white picket fence. And past the fence—

Well, was nothing.

No other houses, no other lawns, no streets, no daylight.

Only darkness, like what he'd just fallen through.

And above the house? A byzantine tangle of bent pipes and draped wires, all descending from the darkness and plunging into the newly shingled roof of this starter home. The wires sparked. The pipes hissed and steamed and shook.

Behind him, the others stepped forward. And behind *them,* the staircase was gone. It had returned to the void from whence it came. In its place sat an asphalt driveway, and beyond that a shiny metal mailbox. Glinting like it was in the sun, even though all around was only the thickest pitch black.

"Everybody okay?" he asked.

Hamish gave a half-hearted nod, but then darted his eyes to Nick, whose eyes had lost all focus. His skin had turned the color of Sheetrock. When he blinked, Owen thought he saw in his eyes a flashing of window glass. And something moving behind that glass.

Lore said nothing. She just stared at the house, a panic buzzing around her like a cloud of flies.

"You okay?" he asked her directly.

"I hoped we were getting out."

"It's not over yet." He lowered his voice. "Nick isn't doing well, Lore. We need to . . . I don't know what we need to do, but we need to do it soon."

"Is this it?" Hamish asked, rubbing his neck and staring at the house. "The house inside the house? The Dreamboat model from Harrowstown?"

"Home is where the heart is," Owen said, without even really meaning to. "The heart is where the home is. That's what this is. This is the heart of it."

"The center of the labyrinth," Lore said. "Heart of the beast."

Hamish walked to the mailbox, and sure enough, painted purposefully on the side, in nice writing, was a name:

Shawcatch.

"It's Shawcatch's name on the mailbox," Hamish said. "So what do we do now?"

Just then, down the walkway, the front door gently and silently opened.

Owen took a deep breath. "I think we go inside."

79

The Host

What they were to expect, Owen could not have said—this house, the heart of the larger house, the center of the labyrinth, seemed as though it should've been a place of great and grave horror. But stepping through the front door, across the threshold, gave no such impression, at least not at first.

The house that awaited them offered one larger room, bisected by half of a brick wall, into which was built a small fireplace at the fore, and a set of shelves at the back. To the left of the brick sat a broad-shouldered galley kitchen, nearly all white, pristine in its cleanliness, with a small cutout two-chair breakfast nook. Right of the brick was the living room, where a round coffee table sat on a simple tan rug over speckled black linoleum. And orbiting them a long squared-off diamond sofa, a pair of smooth wooden chairs and, in the far corner, a chunky teal sitting chair with requisite ottoman. The back wall on the right was nearly all windows—though all that showed through them was darkness.

It was in the corner chair that someone sat.

He was slumped over so Owen almost didn't notice him at first.

But as they stepped inside the house—

His head snapped up, to attention.

"Ah, guests," the man said. He leaned forward, reaching up to the tall reading lamp that teetered next to the chair—and when he turned it on, the man was revealed to be someone in his mid-thirties. Square-jawed, with chestnut hair in a cresting rise over his head, slicked back. "Welcome to my home."

But when he spoke these last four words—

Owen saw that he was not entirely . . . a person. Not *made* of person things, like skin, or hair, or teeth. Some of him was.

But not *enough* of him.

When he talked, his jaw moved like a puppet's mouth—as if the jaw were just a square block set in his long head, juggling up and down. The lips looked real. They glistened as they remained stretched out in what looked to be a permanent smile. His teeth were too white, too plastic-looking. The eyes looked real, too, but they were set back in skin that looked less like skin and more like wood and leather.

"Come in," he said. "Come on in, and have a seat."

They all looked to one another. Nobody moved.

"Alfie Shawcatch," Hamish said, spoken like an invocation.

"Sure thing," he said, lifting an arm with a loose, rolling wrist—the hand at that arm, half-human fingers and half wood, gestured at them with an unlit pipe. "None of you are sooties, are you? This is a white neighborhood, after all." Then he laughed—his teeth snapped together as he did so, *tick-a-clack*. "Oh I'm just joshing you. Come on in, come on in. No need to be chicken. You're not a bunch of cluckers, are you? I should think not. You made it this far, after all. Tells me you've got a heapin' helping of *moxie*."

Still, they didn't move.

His fixed smile suddenly twitched and cracked like a breaking branch—then it was a frown.

"Well, maybe you *are* cluckers."

Shawcatch stood suddenly. His body rattled and clattered like a bunch of bowling pins knocking together as he stood—and the *way* he stood was like a marionette pulled to its feet. A herky-jerky motion, led by the shoulders.

He took an erratic step toward them. Then another. Each time his hips twitching, his legs plucked up in the air and thrust forward.

"I see you," he said, his voice suddenly tinny, like it was playing out of a cheap speaker somewhere deep in his chest. "Been watching you all this time. Been sneakin' around your rooms sure as you've been sneakin' around mine."

"You're not Shawcatch," Lore said.

And Owen realized she was right.

"You're the house," Owen said.

The Shawcatch automaton winked—his eyelids clicking together as he did—and then went slack. The life out of him, like a robot unplugged.

Then a voice from the other side of the room—a child's voice.

"Right on the nose, cookie," said a little tousle-haired boy in his teddy bear pajamas. He, like Alfie Shawcatch, seemed to be half human, half automaton. Cabinet knob eyes and stucco cheeks. A vent in the real flesh of his throat from which hung red curtain fabric. Next to him, another child, a little smaller, with darker hair. His face looked painted on, with shiny semi-gloss house paint. The two of them judder-stepped forward, toward their father's limp, lifeless form.

"We just wanna leave," Hamish said, a bleat of desperation.

"Door's right behind you," the dark-haired boy said.

They turned to look—

But the front door was gone.

And when they turned to look back at them—

The door was behind Shawcatch. Impossibly placed at a cockeyed angle in the set of windows—as if someone had hacked a game of *The Sims* and simply plunked it into a place it shouldn't have been allowed to go.

The father's head jerked upright again, the jaw clacking. "Oh, gosh, me oh my, the door's *here* now, forgive my wool-headed nature."

"Get out of our way and let us through," Lore said.

Now, from the hallway off to the side, another shape: a woman. The wife, Judy. The blood coming out of the stab wounds that peppered her body hung in gleaming plastic beads, like cheap fake costume rubies. She brushed back her dish-towel hair. "Can't let you pass, doll."

"Fuck you, bitch," Lore hissed.

Then Nick stepped up. Hamish tried to pull him back, but Nick pulled away and staggered forward. He shuffled toward Shawcatch, and they all looked to one another, unsure what to do next. Nick walked right up to Shawcatch, whose rickety, loose-socket head turned right toward him, eye to eye.

Alfie Shawcatch, Judy Shawcatch, and the two little boys all said the same thing, in unison. In the voice of the house, they sang:

"Welcome back, my boy."

Then they went slack, and Nick turned toward them all, grinning.

80

The Trap

Lore thought, *No, no, no, please, no,* and she prayed to all the gods she did not believe in that Nick had done something to turn off the Shawcatch automatons, to rebuke the house, to pave the way forward—that the grin on his face was because somehow, inexplicably, they had won.

"Nick," Hamish said, cautious. "You okay, man?"

"You brought him back to me," Nick said, but in that voice Lore couldn't help but hear other voices, too, behind his: Alfie, Judy, the kids, and more, too. A chorus of stolen voices. Nick chuckled. "Thank you for that."

"Nick," Hamish said, louder, agitated. "Come on, Nick. Please. Don't fuckin' do this. Come back to us, Nick."

"*Please,* Nick," Owen said.

But Lore feared it was too late. They'd brought their friend here—right to the heart of the house, to the center of the labyrinth, only to be gored to death by the Minotaur. They'd wanted to save him, and they'd damned him instead.

"You want to leave?" Nick asked. His eyes flashed in the hollow wells of their sockets, showing off mirrors, lightbulbs, gleaming brass. He grinned bigger now, his mouth large, too large, and for a moment, his teeth were piano keys, then a metal ice cube tray, then cheap plastic Christmas lights, twinkling. "Go ahead. I'll let you. But I keep Nick. And I get the sweet little candy taste of knowing that you abandoned yet another friend to me."

They shared looks.

Lore, in her gut, wanted to leave.

It made sense, didn't it? Nick was too far gone. If they had a chance at freedom, shouldn't they take it? Her brain went through the logic of it: *You can go, you can leave, you can go live your life, fix your game with Owen like you promised, you can make good with the friends you have, Lore—but even then, even if you can't, do you even need those people? You only ever needed yourself.*

Owen looked at her, and she saw him there—her best friend for so long. A creative partner. He put her on a pedestal for so many years, and all she did was piss on his head from that lofty height. Then she looked at Hamish, a man lost because they'd pushed him away, someone who thought he was fat and stupid and who literally gave himself to the drink and the drugs and now to God and to fitness and to . . . who knew what else. And Nick. Nick, who had been loyal all this time. Loyal to the Covenant. Loyal to Matty.

You do need these people, she thought.

And they need you.

They all shared looks.

They all nodded to one another.

"We're here for Nick," she said.

Nick laughed. "Then no exit for you. I guess you're staying for the show."

He clapped his hands and the lights went out.

81

The Floor Show

The lights went out, and Owen's heart leapt in fear. The darkness felt palpable. Like it covered him—*smothered* him. Like suddenly he was alone with himself and in that moment all the bad thoughts came roaring up and roaring back, how weak he was, how he should've never been born, how Lore rejected him, how Matty was always so much better than him, and in that sensation his arms started to itch, and so did his fingertips, and he felt the greatest urge to dig into himself with tooth and claw, tearing himself down to the struts, ripping skin from meat and meat from bone, rendering himself raw and skeletal—

Then the lights came back on, and he felt blinded by them.

Nick remained in the center.

But Alfie and his automaton family were gone.

Now, three other automatons appeared.

Automatons that were *them*.

Lore, Hamish, and Owen.

The room had changed at the corners of the Dreamboat house, too. In the far left corner, the Hamish automaton—gray cinder block cheeks and carpet tufts of hair—stared at himself in a broken mirror. Vomit slicked his chin as his arm shot up suddenly in a robotic slot machine motion, dumping pills into his open mouth.

In the far right corner, Owen saw himself. A sad coatrack of a boy, skin painted with bone-white primer, eyes just dark holes in the cold ceramic face. All the while taking that Old Timer penknife and pulling the blade in short, sharp tugs across his upper arms, then his upper thighs. The sound of it was nearly deafening, the little *thkkk, thkkk, thkkk* of the cuts being made. The blood that spilled was not plastic beads, nor was it red curtain, but rather blood, fresh blood, real blood pooling around his feet and seeping into the carpet.

And then Lore. Lore off to the side. No. Not Lore. Lauren. Little Lauren. Young—here, maybe what, thirteen, fourteen? Porcelain doll skin. Hair of some old stuffy. Teeth of an old gray computer keyboard, and her eyes the spinning disks of a disk drive, whirring, whirring. She was the only one who spoke: "Hello?" she asked, her voice garbled, computerized, like something recorded on MIDI and played back through a Casio. "Is anybody home?"

Lore, the real Lore, not the Lauren Thing, stifled a sob as she shrank.

It bled through Owen's heart. Somehow, hers seemed the saddest to him, suddenly. Her pain was so simple, so clear, and they'd missed it this whole time: Lore was alone. Always alone. They barely ever saw her mother because *she* barely ever saw her mother. Owen felt crushed by that revelation. He'd always joked it was cool she didn't really *have* parents because his sucked so bad and none would be better than what he had, but was it? Lore went to bed every night wondering when her mother would come home. And sometimes she didn't, he guessed. He understood Lore there better than he had in a long time.

Maybe ever.

Defiant now, Owen said, "You can't shock us with this ... shallow, derivative theater. We know who we are. Give us our friend back. Now."

Lore nodded. "Fuck off, house."

"Yeah," Hamish said. "Nick, if you're in there? Fight back, buddy. We know you can do it. We're here, man. We're here."

Not-Nick chuckled again, and shrugged halfheartedly. "I didn't think that would work. But that's okay. I have one more thing to show you—and this, *this,* will be the thing that breaks your pretty minds like a baseball through a window."

82

Matty Shiffman

Lights out again. Then on, once more. And Lore's heart leapt into her throat as she saw Matty there, kneeling in front of Nick, facing them.

His arms were outspread, cruciform. Wire and lamp cord bundled together, wrapping around his wrists, anchoring against the walls of the Dreamboat house—for that house had returned fully, and their own automatons were gone.

Matty was only barely artificial—his teeth looked like keys, his eyes like little clocks. When he opened his mouth to moan in pain, Lore saw a staircase there, descending into the deep of his throat.

"He made it here, you know," Not-Nick said.

"What?" Hamish asked.

"He made it all the way to this part of the house—to the heart of it. He fought me every step of the way. And I didn't crack him. *Couldn't* crack him. I thought I could show him all the pressure his parents put on him, how they saw him as just an emblem of their own success—narcissists, they were. But he didn't care. I thought I could show him how his sisters conspired against him, and that didn't do it. Then I realized how good he was, how kind, and how he had a way of looking at the world thinking it should be fair, it should be kind—"

Always the paladin, Lore thought.

"And so I thought showing him how much misery went on in these rooms would break him. Murders and suicides, a tableau of pain and suffering, and still it did not crack him. He found the crawlspace. He kept away from me. And he figured it out, same as you did. Break through. Find the final staircase. Come to the ol' Dreamboat. And then, goodbye, Matthew Shiffman, enjoy your freedom. But I saw in his mind why he was doing it. Why he fought so hard. It was for all of you. He wanted to see you again. And there, his greatest strength—I realized then was also the thing I was going to use to hang him. And all I had to show him was how he fought for you—but you never fought for him. You all went your separate ways. You abandoned him. Left him alone here. *With me.*"

The Matty kneeling in front of them cried out in pain, his muscles spasming and contracting as his skull split open, side to side—

And from within his broken head, the model of monstrosity of a house rose. Victorian and Art Deco and Craftsman style crammed together at odd, impossible angles. It emerged and sat there, like something *hatching,* and his head slackened, drool oozing from his open mouth, blood rimming the edges of his fragmented face, shining and wet.

In horror, Lore realized that the toy house that popped free of his head had windows, and in one of those windows—

She saw Matty. Waving. A cruel little piece of puppet theater.

Part of her railed against this—this couldn't be true, that it was *them* and their abandonment of him that let the house gain access to Matty. But in her heart, she knew it to be true. They had abandoned him. Hell, *she* had abandoned him that night they found the staircase. Why? Because she felt stung that he hadn't taken acid with her? That his commitment to her wasn't, what, strong enough? She felt judged, she felt hurt, so she hurt him in turn, and then he ran up that fucking staircase to show her how he didn't need her—even as she was wolfing down the acid, pretending that *she* didn't need *him,* didn't need *any of them,* and that was when it all started.

Right there, in the woods, that night.

There was this moment of reckoning, where she stood still, shell-shocked by it all—

And that's when Hamish roared in anger, and rushed at Nick.

Hamish! Not-Nick's hand shot out, closing hard on Hamish's windpipe, lifting him handily up in the air. Ham's legs kicked fruitlessly as his hands struggled to free himself from Nick's grip. But Owen was already moving, following Hamish's rush with one of his own—Lore screamed for him to stop, even as she was quietly proud of her old friend for running headlong into danger, even as Nick's eyes fixed on him like a doom gaze. Not-Nick's free hand lashed out—

Something was in that hand now.

A knife. Small. Its blade rusted and chipped.

It slashed across Owen's face—

Lore screamed, running to him, even as he fell backward.

Not-Nick seethed, partly in his voice, partly in the voice of Alfred Shawcatch: "There, *boy,* a proper scar all can see, not the ones you hide. Be a man, Owen! Be a man and show the world your pain!" Then, as it shook Hamish like a rag doll, the man choking, his lips darkening, his face reddening: "Dying again, Hamish? Too bad, so sad. *Show us all your pain, you soft, sad things.*"

"Is that what this is?" Lore screamed at the Shawcatch Thing, as she dragged Owen backward, blood masking his face. "You showing your pain to the world? Another weak man inflicting his pain on everyone?"

"*Man?*" the Not-Nick thing bellowed, its voice no longer tinny but now warped, distorted, a boiler room rumble to it. "*I am no man, you slip of meat. I am the house, and I hate you all. I was a place of promise. Not merely a house, but a home. A place of love, a place of family. The smells of cooking, the sounds of lovemaking, a child's laughter, but that man brought back all the pain of war. Men's heads turned to mince in their helmets. French children crushed into the mud under German tank treads. Drawers of gold teeth in a liberated camp. The starving and the sick and the dead. The pain in us was electric and alive, it flowed through us like a boiling river. It became a part of us, and we grew to love the pain the same as Nick did—the same as you will.*"

The Nick Thing flung Hamish against the wall next to them. Hamish cried out, gasping, clawing at his throat. Lore looked down at Owen, the cut from the knife garish across the expanse of his forehead. He mumbled to her, "I'm okay, I'm okay, I'm okay." Hamish garbled his own answer: "Me too."

Not-Nick grinned and leered.

"Little pigs, little pigs, let me in."

83

Exorcism and Eviction

Nick, the bloody penknife in his hand, stalked toward her and Owen.

"You broke the Covenant, and now the Covenant will break you," he said, his voice singsongy.

The Covenant.

The words came out of her without thinking. There was no strategy to this, no great plan, just the desire to reforge something that had in fact been shattered. And the great hope that somehow they could free Nick from the monster that had him—that was *in* him. They needed an exorcism, but they had no holy book, they had no scripture. But they had, once upon a time, the Covenant.

Lore said, "Holy shit, remember junior prom, Nick, when you swore up and down you had a date?" Right there, Nick stopped in his tracks. The knife in his hand dripping against his shoe, *pat pat pat*. He flinched and scowled, so she kept going. "You said it was this girl you supposedly met at the Jersey Shore, and you two made out on the boardwalk and now she was coming to the dance, and ohh man, we were excited to meet her, but we also were like, she's not fucking real, right? He's just fucking with us. And what do you do? You bring her to prom except, guess what, she's a *fucking mannequin* that you dressed up like a *fucking mermaid* and you said her name was Ariel, and all night long you pretended she was real? Dancing with her and shit?"

With every word, Nick flinched, twitched, bit down on his teeth.

Owen wiped blood from his face and sat up and added: "Yeah and he glued shells to her face like barnacles and also put those plastic six-pack rings around her wrists because they sometimes trap and kill turtles, and he thought that was funny and fucked up. Which, in a nutshell, is pretty much Nick."

"*Shut up,*" Not-Nick hissed at them through his radiator teeth.

Hamish coughed and said, with a forced laugh, "Remember the time we snuck into that development being built next to your house, and we stole a shitload of PVC pipe and turned it into potato guns? Fired one potato so far, it went through the window at the Quaker meetinghouse on the corner."

Nick's head rocked back like he'd been slapped. His eyelids fluttered.

It's working. It's fucking working.

Lore jumped in again:

"Dude, dude, remember that time you stole my neighbor's golf cart, and you went up and down the street with a baseball bat, knocking off mailboxes—but you wore a fake beard the whole time? And so when the cops came, the neighbors all said it was some guy in a beard, and that stupid idiotic disguise actually worked and nobody ever caught you?"

Owen now:

"Junior year. I'm going to say a name right now, and when I do, I'm not even going to need to tell the story, because we're all going to remember it immediately. First name: Gary. Second name: Dunderbaum." Still, he told the story about Gary Dunderbaum, this stoner slacker burnout—a nice enough guy, but probably ate lead paint chips when he was a kid. They were in bioscience the one day and there was a test, and Gary was very, very unprepared for it, and poised to flunk the test and maybe the whole class. So Nick told him, "You know what you do, Gar? Test starts, just shit your pants. Just shit 'em up. Take yourself down to Browntown, buddy. Then you say, 'Sorry, Mr. Carboni, I shit myself, I can't take the test today, I need to go to

the nurse and get the set of pants the nurse keeps for times like this.'"
They all thought that was really funny except, well, Gary Dunderbaum *actually did it*. Five minutes in, he's over there sweating, red-faced, grunting as he squeezed one out—noisily. The kicker? He did it again *senior year* during a pop quiz.

They cried laughing, retelling that story.

And it went on like that. They told increasingly funny, insane stories about Nick, because that was Nick. A wild card, an agent of chaos, a trickster spirit. But it was also about how he was always there for them. There to pick them up if they got stuck somewhere. There to be a sober copilot if one of them wanted to get drunk or get high or trip balls. Always ready to bust balls, but if anyone outside the group ever said boo about a single one of them, he'd lay into that person so hard they'd piss themselves like a nervous chihuahua and develop a forever case of CPTSD from it. Nick was really the carrier of the Covenant. Each and every time.

And with each story—and soon, each sentence, each *word*—Nick looked rocked on his heels, pushed back farther and farther. A line of blood crawled from his nose. His eyes turned bloodshot. But they looked like *eyes* now. And his teeth were *teeth*, and suddenly, he screamed out and Lore worried, *Oh my god, this was the wrong thing to do, we're hurting him, we're killing him—*

But then Nick was on the floor, on his hands and knees, puking.

As the automaton of Alfie Shawcatch stood behind him, raging.

The house shook. They heard shattering glass. The floor began to split.

They'd hurt it. They'd actually hurt it.

And behind him, the door awaited, rattling in its frame. *We can do it. We can run for it.* Escape was in their grasp. But the house, through Shawcatch, was not done with them. The monstrous puppet bent down, reaching for Nick, pulling him up off the ground—

But something gleamed in Nick's hand.

A lighter.

A Jack Kenny whiskey–branded lighter.

"Burn again, bitch," Nick said, then struck a flame and pressed it to Shawcatch's face.

Fire crawled down the thing's body like a dozen burning spiders. Shawcatch screeched, a garbled, tinny shriek, dancing backward with a wobbly step—Nick fell to the floor, released from the thing's grip, a keening gasp howling from the monster's mouth as it pawed at its neck. Everything then seemed to go slow and fast at the same time: the Shawcatch Thing, spinning around, flames dancing upon it. Lore helping up Owen. Hamish helping Nick. Nick juggled past the Shawcatch Thing, and as he did, he gave it a swift kick toward the other side of the room—it screamed and crashed into a couch, where the fire handily leapt to the fabric, then to the wall. Flames bloomed inside this house, great heaving flowers of it searing the air, catching the carpet on fire, the drapes, the walls, everything.

All as they pushed open the door stuck in the far wall and tumbled through it, into—

84

The Great Egress

Into a forest.

It was day. It had rained. The air was humid and stuck to them like wallpaper. Somewhere, a songbird babbled. A squirrel scurried away.

The door behind them, a door hanging in the middle of the air at a cockeyed angle, snapped shut—

And disappeared.

Their luggage sat around them.

This was where they had entered the staircase. But now that staircase was gone, as was the doorway.

They had escaped the house.

Though it, perhaps, had not escaped them.

85

The Covenant

Six months later, they met again.

This time not in Pennsylvania, not in New Hampshire, but rather, just outside of Madison, Wisconsin.

The first stop: a little coffeehouse café called the Oasis.

They made small talk, catching up. Owen and Lore had been meeting every couple weeks, working on their game—they pulled out of their stall, got development moving together. (Nick asked if they were fucking, and they refused to answer, which told everyone all they needed to know.) Hamish had The Talk with his wife, told her that he'd been cheating on her. He spent a couple weeks in a motel, then they decided they were going to try a marriage counselor on the way to what at the time seemed the inevitable divorce lawyers—but during the counseling, it came out that Hamish had once died. A fact his wife never knew. And she hadn't known about his childhood, either—losing his friend Matty. It was enough, it seemed, to engender in her a specific kind of sympathy. She was angry at him still, but he was back in the house. And talk of divorce was off the table. For now.

Nick, for his part, did not, in his words, "have shit going on." Said he'd taken a new job at a local garden center—"none of that Home Depot shit"—and liked it. Also was seeing, to their absolute shock, a *therapist*. "I'm on drugs, now," he said, almost chipper, shaking a bottle of lorazepam at them like a baby rattle.

They got to the end without talking about their nightmares, but eventually, it came up. It was Owen who brought it up. He asked them if they were all having them, and they were. Nightmares about being in the house, wandering it endlessly, aimlessly. All that horror, all that pain. Owen asked them if it still felt like they were there, sometimes, in the house. Lore said sometimes when she was falling asleep, it was like her legs were walking her way through it, and then she took a wrong step down a strange staircase, and it always woke her up. Hamish said that for him it was just the bathroom, the one with the broken mirror. He dreamed of it constantly. Nick, for his part, just shrugged, said, "I just dream of you fuckin' weirdos. And it's nice. But then I dream of Matty, too, and . . ." He sniffed. "And that's why we're here, so I think we should get down to business. So, where's this house?"

The house was about five miles south of where they had coffee, in a town called Fitchburg. It was a farmhouse off of a back road called Oak Hall Hill, a road lined in spots with old bent oaks—though no hill to be seen.

The house was red, and looked like a sister to the black barn next to it. A pair of bent, corroded silos sat behind, and all around were fields—corn, mostly, or just scrub. The driveway was stone, but had long gone without renewal, and so pockets of weeds were sticking up. An old beater-ass Ford pickup sat parked. The sunlight flickered through the turning blades of an old tin windmill.

They let the engine of Hamish's rental car idle for a bit.

All four of them sat. Nick up front with Hamish. Lore and Owen in the back.

"This is it?" Hamish asked.

"It's what the investigator gave us," Lore said, looking at the map on her phone and the printouts in front of her—they'd hired a private investigator to look for Matty. He had, after all, supposedly made it out of the house—with the house still in him. Doing its work. Carrying its, what, message? The investigator found someone going by Matthew Shiffman living here. Took some photos, and the evidence was pretty convincing that it was their old friend. Amazing that he'd... been here the whole time. That felt extra cruel somehow. That he'd made it out and hadn't ever thought to find them. Then again, if what the house had said was true, then why would he? He thought they'd abandoned him. So he abandoned them.

Or worse, the house had so taken him over, there was no Matty left. No memories of his friends to speak of.

"We ready for this?" Owen asked them.

"I'm not," Hamish said. "What if..."

He didn't finish the question. He didn't have to. They all knew what the private investigator had told them. That there were women who had gone missing in the area. College girls, mostly. Six of them over the last ten years. None of their bodies ever found. Could it be Matty? Was it possible that he was carrying the pain of the house forward, hurting people on its whim? He didn't have a family. He lived alone, kept to himself here. Had ample space to hide the women, living or dead. Not that anyone had ever even looked at him as a perpetrator of these crimes. He was a nobody around these parts.

Maybe, they told themselves, it wasn't him. Maybe the pain he waged against the world was smaller, simpler; maybe he hurt himself. Maybe he just sat all day, stewing in hatred. Maybe he was fine. Maybe he had forgotten it all. Maybe Matty was too good for the house, and he had escaped it in his own way.

Hell, maybe the house had been lying to them all along.

They knew there was only one way to find out.

And then, the front door opened. A man stepped out. Lore knew him immediately. They all did. He was older, unquestionably. Gray in the hair at the sides of his temples. Maybe a little more weight in the front. But same build. Same posture. Same Matty, all these years later. But was it? Was it, really?

He came out, dumped a glass of water into a potted plant on the porch, then looked up, saw the car parked. Their car.

"It's him," Owen said, no uncertainty in his voice. No fear, either.

"He sees us," Nick said, a kind of warning.

Hamish finally asked the question:

"What if the house is still in him?"

"Then we get it out of him," Owen answered.

"And what if he's... done things? Things we can't fix?"

Lore said, "Then we deal with that however we have to."

She didn't tell them about the handgun she had in her bag.

Just in case.

Just in case.

She knew it was possible they'd find the house still in his eyes. They might see those rotten slats of siding. Irises like black windows with crying faces behind them. Brass knobs turning, ready to open into the maze of rooms his mind had become. Rooms upon rooms upon rooms of pain, filling up and spilling out. Maybe he was a real fixer-upper. Maybe they could save him. But maybe the only thing they could do was burn it all down. Sometimes that's how it was.

"The Covenant," she said, finally.

"The Covenant," the others answered, in unison. Meaning it in all the ways it could be meant.

They got out of the car, unsure what they would find, or what was to come—but ready to stand together, just the same.

ACKNOWLEDGMENTS AND FINAL WORD

On the Necessity of Being Lost

The question then is how to get lost. Never to get lost is not to live, not to know how to get lost brings you to destruction, and somewhere in the terra incognita in between lies a life of discovery.
—REBECCA SOLNIT, A Field Guide to Getting Lost

What I'm trying to say is, you need to learn to get lost. Getting lost is good. Going deep is good. Leaving the path? *Is good.*

I'm getting ahead of myself.

Let's start here: I was at a book event in Concord, New Hampshire, at the truly excellent bookstore Gibson's—a necessary shout-out to Ryan, who rules—and this was a book event for both my book *Black River Orchard* and the brilliantly upsetting *What Kind of Mother* by Clay McLeod Chapman, right? While there, Clay and I were asked what we were working on next, and my answer was, "Oh, I'm plotting a book about a staircase in the woods," and one of the attendees—I am sorry I do not know your name, in case you're reading this, but you're amazing, high-five—said, "There's a staircase in the woods not far from here." They thought maybe it was in the wrong direction from where I was going next on my tour, but as it turned out, it required only a minor deviation from my journey to go and see this staircase.

(For those who don't realize it, the Staircase in the Woods phenomenon is a very real one. I'm not even talking about any of the fictional creepypasta spawned from it. I mean, there are staircases out there in the woods. Go google it. Even though it has a perfectly rational explanation, it just *feels* freaky, a glimpse into some interstitial, intermediary dimension.)

The staircase in question is the ruins of Madame Sherri's Castle—long story short is that a costume designer from New York named Madame Antoinette Sherri thought to build an extravagant party castle tucked into the southwest corner of New Hampshire, except then the money ran out, and she noped it the fuck out of there. The castle fell to ruin. A fire eventually claimed it. The staircase remains.

(Also, I am now rapt by the phrase "extravagant party castle." My next novel must contain one, or I've really fucked up.)

I decided I needed to see this staircase for myself. Just to get the vibe of it, you know? Getting there looked easy on the map, as many things do, but in practice, the journey was far stranger. It took me off the highway and down a meandering circuit of back roads, and at one point, I was driving on something that was barely a road—my rental car bouncing along a dirt and gravel path, tires dipping in and out of ruts, and at that point, my signal was poor enough it wasn't tracking me consistently. I knew then I was not *lost,* not precisely, but I was definitely Off the Path, and there might've been wisdom in turning around and going back. After all, I was on a book tour, and I still had to drive through Vermont and part of New York to get to my hotel. I had work to do! Places to be!

Still. *The staircase enticed me*. It was out there. I needed to see it.

So—I committed. I texted my wife about how I was in the middle of Oh No, New Hampshire. (I'd just seen a sign not long before about how vaccines change your DNA, and RFK, Jr., signs talking about "Event 201," a pandemic exercise that he and others like him believe provided cover for some kind of New World Order government takeover scenario? I dunno. I was in Cuckoo Bananapantstown. Don't stop here, this is bat country.) But my text to her did not go through. It dangled, hesitant, over the void.

Onward I went, and just as I was saying to myself, "I have made a terrible error, I am sure now to be abducted by anti-vax Lovecraftian hillfolk," there it appeared: the small parking lot for Madame Sherri's Castle. I was alone but for one other family there, and the path took me into a humid, dark forest—the ground muddy and home to a number of hurriedly waddling salamanders—where, sure enough, there stood the ruins of a staircase. These stairs were unlike the ones in the book—they were stone, like, well, out of a castle. (You can't climb the stairs. Part of them collapsed a few years ago. Besides, who knows where they'd take you? Ahem, ahem, ahem.) They felt otherworldly—haunting, more than haunted, if that makes sense. As if the forest was not haunted by Madame Sherri but rather by the staircase, by its missing home.

I had seen the staircase, got its vibe. I thought, well, I guess it's time to leave, right? But I didn't leave. Compelled, I kept walking. I stayed for hours, wandering the woods, only partially sure I even knew where I was. I took photos of little salamanders. I listened to birds. I still felt the presence of that staircase somewhere out there, in the trees. Like a beacon of some beyonding thing that I could follow back, when I needed it.

It was a small detour, but an impactful one, and that day much of the story you just read tumbled forth and unrolled itself, a carpet of pill bugs showing more than their armor, revealing all their little squirmy grabby bits. What you read here is, in part, due to that little side detour—

But that's just plot, just flavor. The character stuff, the *story* stuff, that comes from a different kind of excavation—a deeper, gnarlier act of getting lost. I think just as we sometimes need to wander the world a little bit without a firm plan or clear directions, I also think there's value in getting lost *within* as well as *without*. We are creatures of extraordinary depth, a deep cavern with infinite strata, and we have seen things and felt things and experienced things—we're reckoning with a wealth of love and trauma and pain and wonder, and storytelling, at its best, represents that reckoning on the page. This is a book very much about fear, and very much about friendship—both friendships of the past and adult friendships and the difficulty of keeping them and the pain of losing them and the joy of reclaiming them. It's not a book for me about any one person or any one situation (outside the fact that every part of a book is both not at all about the author and also always very much about the author), but what appears in this book only gets to exist on the page because I was willing to wander the inward paths as well as the ones outside.

And I think those things work together. I think clearing your head and wandering the maze inside your skull happens more easily when you're wandering unfamiliar places in reality, too. There exists a meditative *detangling* that happens when you get lost. You get lost there, and you get lost in here, too.

Then, further, those meanderings, those wanderings, they culminate in the actual writing. Writing is perhaps best when it is exactly that: the act of getting lost. We lose ourselves in the first draft, and maybe, just maybe, find ourselves in the second and subsequent drafts. We amble about at first, sometimes with a direction that betrays us, sometimes directionless in a way that finds its North Star. So in that roving and roaming, a story is found, and when a story is found, it's told. The story found is the record of being lost. Writers at their best and their most honest are, I think, engaging in an endless loop of lost and found, found and lost.

Don't be afraid of being lost. It is at the heart of what we do and who we are, I think. Get lost. Be lost. Use that chance to find things you didn't expect to find.

Anyway, one more quote before I get to the infinite thank-yous—

Sometimes an old photograph, an old friend, an old letter will remind you that you are not who you once were, for the person who dwelt among them, valued this, chose that, wrote thus, no longer exists. Without noticing it you have traversed a great distance; the strange has become familiar and the familiar if not strange at least awkward or uncomfortable, an outgrown garment. And some people travel far more than others.... Some people inherit values and practices as a house they inhabit; some of us have to burn down that

house, find our own ground, build from scratch, even as a psychological metamorphosis.
>   —Rebecca Solnit, *A Field Guide to Getting Lost*

And now, the proper gratitude. First and always goes to Michelle and Ben, who are my own North Star in truly lost times—they're supportive and they're cheerleaders and their love and care of a dopey weirdo-beardo writer like me means everything. Second and vitally, my editor, Tricia Narwani, who helped me through an edit on this thing that was fiddly and esoteric and epic, a true Ship of Theseus rebuild of the book where the book fundamentally remained the same while also having so much of itself paradoxically changed? The whole Del Rey team is an amazing machine. Third and crucially, my agent Stacia Decker, without whom my books and career would not exist as they do.

Plus, a heapin' helping of thanks has to go toward a lot of the writers in the past year who—well, who have helped me in ways they maybe didn't even realize, whether it's from just doing bantery bits on social media or because they came out to hang with me on the *Black River Orchard* tour or just because their books were there for me when I needed them to be. Folks like (but not limited to, and forgive my porous brain for forgetting anyone) Matt Wallace, Premee Mohamed, Kevin Hearne, Delilah Dawson, Gabino Iglesias, Christopher Golden, Eric LaRocca, Pete Clines, Greg van Eekhout, Owen King, Lora Senf, Tananarive Due, Paul Tremblay, CJ Leede, Hailey Piper, Erin Morgenstern, Brian White, Keith Rosson, Cina Pelayo, Brian Keene, Sarah Langan, Nat Cassidy, Clay McLeod Chapman, John Scalzi, Stephen Graham Jones, Aaron Mahnke, and more. (Read all these authors, immediately.) And I got to visit some bookstores that live in my heart even now: Montana Book Company, you're the bee's knees; Gibson's is just the best; Oblong Books, you know how to throw a great book event; my two locals, Doylestown Bookshop and The End in Allentown; plus all the other great stores like Powell's in Portland, Porter Square, Books on the Square, Northshire, and so many others.

I'm a lucky ducky that I get to keep doing this.

And really, at the end of the day, I get to keep doing this because you keep reading these books, so the final and biggest thanks goes to readers and fans.

OKAY LOVE YOU BYE

runs up the staircase, leaps into the void, is gone

ABOUT THE AUTHOR

CHUCK WENDIG is the *New York Times* bestselling author of *Wanderers, Wayward, The Book of Accidents, Black River Orchard* and more than two dozen other books for adults and young adults. A finalist for the Astounding Award and an alumnus of the Sundance Screenwriters Lab, he has also written for comics, games, film and television. He's known for his popular blog, *terribleminds*, and books about writing such as *Damn Fine Story*. He lives in Bucks County, Pennsylvania, with his family.

terribleminds.com
Instagram: @chuck_wendig

ABOUT THE TYPE

This book was set in Arno, an expansive neohumanist typeface family designed by Robert Slimbach and released by Adobe in 2007. Arno's letterforms are based on fifteenth- and sixteenth-century Italian typefaces, including those of the Venetian calligrapher and printer Ludovico degli Arrighi.